FIND A WAY HOME

Hope you enjoy the reading

Sincerely

Lou Johnson

FIND A WAY HOME

W. Louis Johnson

RTP
Research Triangle Publishing, Inc.

This novel is a fiction. Any reference to historical events; to real people, living or dead; or to real locales are intended only to give the fiction a sense of reality and authenticity. Names, characters, places, and incidents either are the product of the author's imagination or are used fictitiously, and their resemblance, if any, to real-life counterparts is entirely coincidental.

Published by
Research Triangle Publishing, Inc.
PO Box 1130
Fuquay-Varina, NC 27526

ISBN   1-884570-75-5

Cover Design by Cameron Thorp

Library of Congress Catalog Card Number: 97-76541

∞ The paper used in this publication meets the minimum requirements of the American National Standard for Information Sciences—Permanence of Paper for Printed Library Materials, ANSI Z39,48-1984.

Printed in the United States of America
10 9 8 7 6 5 4 3 2 1

Introduction

THE ANCIENT WORLD WAS alive with activity, trade, and exploration. More than a thousand years before Columbus landed in the New World in A.D. 1492, advanced races of Greeks and Phoenicians spread their culture along the shores of the Mediterranean, around the Atlantic coast of Europe and Africa, and far beyond. Evidence exists that Nordic Vikings had outposts along the Canadian and New England coasts and even into Minnesota. South American findings tell of voyages from ancient Egypt in seagoing vessels constructed from reeds. Roman coins were found during the nineteenth century on the Elk River in Tennessee, issued in A.D. 140, as Rome invaded Wales. References in ancient Welsh ballads tell of a Prince Madoc ap Owen Guyenth who sailed west from Wales and discovered an unknown land around A.D. 1190.

Portuguese, their blood flowing with traditions of exploration and shipbuilding inherited from the ancient Carthaginians and Phoenicians, were constantly testing their skills westward. Conceivably, ships could have landed on the present-day North or South Carolina coast and migrated inward to the mountainous regions of Tennessee or Virginia. An old tradition reports white-skinned people already residing in East Tennessee when the Cherokee came to the region hundreds of years ago. But the white skin was relative to the Indian skin tone, and darker than the Anglo-Saxons who came later. Called Melungeons by outsiders, they lived at higher elevations and stayed to themselves. British, French, and Indian wars passed them by, as did Colonial politics that was to govern the New World forevermore.

By 1788, Congress drafted a Constitution following months of labor. None of the fifty-five state delegates was entirely satisfied. Patrick Henry said in the Convention of Virginia, "Who authorized them to speak the language of 'We, the people,' instead of 'We, the states'? States are the soul of the confederation." On it went; the states rights debate continued for decades.

At the time of the formation of the Constitution, all the states but two admitted Negro slavery. In addition to the commonly accepted Southern practice of owning slaves, there were even free Negroes who owned slaves as well as Northern whites, including those from New England. But, this institution was regarded by many as an exotic, inherited evil, to be borne as well as possible until it should pass away with time.

The nation rocked along until inevitable growth provoked the slavery question anew. Missouri was admitted to the Union with its slave-bearing Constitution: the proviso that forever after there should be neither slavery nor involuntary servitude in any territory of the United States north of the southern boundary of Missouri, but that south of that line, states might be admitted with slavery or without it. For the time being, everyone seemed content; it was believed that the firebrand of disunion was extinguished. But, alas, it smoldered.

When Chief Justice Roger B. Taney of the Supreme Court wrote to strike down the Dred Scott case, the Northern press and the abolitionists whipped their constituents into a rabid furor.

But slavery wasn't a factor that caused thousands of young men, most of whom were not affected one way or the other about the slavery question, to go to war.

The South had always carried more of the burden and furnished more soldiers than the North—in all wars. Moreover, many felt there were more influential Southern men in Congress than Northern. Still, the financial and industrial markets of the North were strangling their neighbors to the South. Enmity grew on both sides. This hatred was evidenced by Preston Brooks of South Carolina, who sneaked up on Senator Sumner, a Northerner, while Sumner bent over his desk in a deserted senate chamber. Brooks beat him senseless with a cane.

Then John Brown, an anti-slavery fanatic of the blindest and most furious sort, led an ill-fated raid on the arsenal at Harper's Ferry, Virginia (now West Virginia), and when caught was hanged by the state of Virginia. This set the stage for the strange presidential election of 1860. Few on either side of the Mason-Dixon line doubted the Union was far from being dissolved.

East Tennessee was unique through all this squabbling. It was a mountainous region of small valley farms in contrast to the humid plantation flatlands farther south. Once a crossroads for pioneers moving westward over the Appalachians, the region was later bypassed for better routes. In the early 1800s, East Tennessee had given public life a type of man with distinctive physical, intellectual, and moral qualities. Tall, angular, rawboned, these men were alert, positive, and sometimes narrow-minded; they were honest and patriotic, but vindictive and unrelenting—the truest of friends, the most aggressive and dangerous of foes. Scotch-Irish by birth, they hated the plan-

tation aristocracy of the lowlands, had little intercourse with
their Indian neighbors, and were indifferent to Negro slaves.

No wonder that when Tennessee Governor, Isham Harris,
called for a February 9, 1861, convention to secede, East Tennesseans led the remainder of the state to handily defeat the
secession motion. There was even a movement afloat to form
East Tennessee into a separate state.

But when President Lincoln called for volunteers from all
states, including Southern states, to thwart the growing Confederacy, popular sentiment changed in Tennessee. Another
convention was held in May 1861. The state went overwhelmingly with the Confederacy this time. Still, East Tennesseans
cast most of the minority votes and later sent 30,000 of its young
men into Kentucky to fight for the Union.

There were enough Southern sympathizers in East Tennessee to cause divided loyalties within families, animosities between neighbors, and overall violent and ruthless behavior. But
on a mountain in Hancock County, Tennessee, near the Virginia border, the Melungeon people went about their ancient
business of living and farming, oblivious to the clamoring in
the valleys below.

An old Melungeon grandmother had just given a beautiful
green stone with gold backing to Lochsley Collins, her eighteen-year-old granddaughter. The old lady said the stone and
her ancestors came across the waters long ago. She said her
people were known as "Portergee."

Prologue

City Of Carthage During Seige
Coast of North Africa
149 B.C.

She held her mother's hand as they bounded down the steps of the Court of a Hundred Magistrates. Her mother was there to alert her father that the escape was good for tonight, that the bribes had worked and by tomorrow they would be at sea long before roll call at the magistrates meeting. They felt the setting sun, warm on their faces.

"Mama, what is that man doing in that box?"

"You don't want to know, my sweet. Hurry along."

"But Mama, tell me. There was one like him last week before the Festival of the Full Moon. When I went to buy rice for you the next day, the man was gone."

The prisoner was being executed in "the boats," Carthaginian's favorite execution technique. The convicted prisoner was placed in a rectangular box with holes for the head, hands, and feet. He was forced to drink a honey and milk mixture, after which the remainder was smeared over his face. The sun would bring flies to attack the skin and eyes and

enter the nostrils. The excrement invited entry of other vermin. Death took two weeks or more.

"Little girl," the Nubian prisoner said, his voice rasped from
pain. "Look over there in the vase. Don't let anyone see you
get it. Keep it forever and pass it on. The stone you will find
holds the secret to the rhythms of the universe, the secret of
life and behavior, the key to the price of goods and why nations rise and fall."

The little girl stared, then turned and ran to a clay rain cistern. She put her hand into the water, explored the bottom,
and found a hard object. In her dripping hand was a large
oval-cut green stone. The sun's rays danced and darted within
the cut prisms. Quickly she stuffed it into the pocket of her
tunic and went home with her mother.

THE TWO MEN walked onto the portico from the double doors of
the council building. The sun had set and the activity in the
dusty courtyard had slowed.

"What will the historians call this one? The Third Punic
War? Day and night we prepare for the invasion and those
damnable mercenaries we must pay are emptying the treasury."

The other man grunted a faint agreement.

"Since Phoenicia founded us—to think we conquered this
whole coast, Crete, Greece—we filled our coffers with tin and silver from Spain and now look at us. We face extinction. May the
gods help us all. I'm going home. We'll work on it tomorrow."
He walked down the steps and disappeared into the shadows.

Yeah, there's always tomorrow, but not here, the other man
thought. He gazed across the way at the marble temple, its
door framed with massive columns above a concave cornice.
His eyes flitted to the frieze above, bearing a sun disc and a
hooded cobra. He knew he would never see it again. He
thought of the 600 acres of vineyards outside the city in the

fertile Megara. Those poor vintners will be the first to die when the Romans attack. He entered the door of his home.

"Daddy, where are we going?"

"Shhh! On a long boat ride. What is that in your hand?"

"Just a green rock, Daddy. The man in the box gave it to me." She handed it to him reluctantly.

In the faint light of the lamp, he could see lines etched on the underside. Maybe he could sell it when they docked in Spain.

He blew out the lamp and nudged the door open. The three grabbed their bags and entered the moist night air.

They stayed in the shadows along the path behind the boat-houses and quays. Sounds of drinking and laughter from thousands of soldiers preparing for sleep wafted over the water of the round lagoon. They stopped to rest on the portico of the harbor. The lantern lights reflected the ninety Ionic columns that lined the Tophet of Baal.

THE GNARLED OLD man nodded and beckoned the three to follow him down to the galley. He was thinking how crazy they were to believe they could survive the trip to Spain, and how he hated them for having the money to try it in the first place. "But Eeiie! With my payoff, who cares?" he said aloud.

He accepted Greek drachmas for the boat, but insisted on twenty gold, Roman libra for arrangements. Then maybe he could buy his freedom later from the Centurion slimes.

Nothing was said as he unlocked the chain guarding the mouth of the harbor. As the oars pulled the boat away, he noticed the little girl playing with a green stone on the floor of the boat.

The old man locked back the iron chain and went inside the guardhouse; he put a wine flask to his shoulder and gulped. It's done. "May the gods of the sea be with you all the way to the Pillars of Hercules," he said.

❖ ❖ ❖

CAPE SAINT VINCENT, Portugal
A.D. 1090

"I beg of you, please reconsider. Stay here in Portugal," the priest said, as he observed the frown on the face of the woman before him. "We've been over this a hundred times. You and your band of lunatics don't stand a chance of reaching land in those small boats."

"No Padre, you're wrong. We'll make it. We've selected only the strongest—the ones most willing to make the sacrifice. We all know el-Konez will murder us if he finds us. He's mad," said the woman.

"Ah yes, of course, but give Henry time. You're too impatient. He'll drive the Moors across the straits where they belong."

"Time Padre? The Moors have been on this soil 400 years, so I'm not waiting on Henry of Burgundy."

The priest stood on a large rock as he viewed a dull green sea. Storm clouds hovered. He stared at some fifty people in the two galleons. He knew his arguments were useless. This voyage was going to occur no matter what he said. Stupid fools. They have let this powerful woman talk them into enduring this nonsense, and they'll die with Neptune because of it.

"It's time to go, Padre. If it's God's will, we'll make it to the Azores and beyond. There's a whole new world out there."

"Don't even think about that. Consider the others—"

"Padre, generations ago, my ancestors in Carthage escaped the Romans the same way I'm escaping the Moors. It's destiny."

"Do you have the stone?"

"I have it. Safe and hidden. I pray it will carry us to a new life. Good-bye, Padre."

"Good-bye, my child." He made a sign of the Cross and bowed his head. "Go with God."

An hour later, the priest was still standing in the same spot. He watched two tiny specks disappear into the horizon.

Chapter One

JULY 1858, EASTERN TENNESSEE

He slapped at his sweaty neck to wave away the mosquitoes. The storm front had brought sapping humidity and torrential rains to the valley. His overalls were soiled and his shirt soaked.

"Damn bugs."

The scream of men and the thunder of horses' hoofs pierced the afternoon stillness. Spencer McAlpin slid off his horse and hid in the tall grass and cattails beside the creek. He crawled forward to get a better look, then froze.

Three men were in the clearing on steamy, frothy horses. The thin one handed a bottle to one of the others, then yelled and kicked the flanks of his horse.

"Gander grabbing," Spence whispered. He saw a poor greased goose hanging from a sycamore tree tied by its feet.

The older and thinner man was Virgil. His horse headed toward the target at full gallop while the two other brothers, J.D. and Moody, took a swig apiece from the bottle. They yelled in jubilation as Virgil's hand slid off as he rode under the goose.

"By God, I had the thing. I had it." Virgil pulled to a halt. He cantered back to get the bottle for another drink.

The other two took their turn at the goose with the same results, except Moody got a firmer grip. Before his hand slipped off, he yanked the goose hard enough to dislocate vertebra. Blood covered its body. The state was set.

Virgil raised the bottle. "Victory. I can smell it." He took the final drink from the whiskey bottle and threw it into the woods. He eyed the target, screamed, kicked his horse, and charged. His hand was held high as the stallion sprinted under the desperate bird. This time his grip was sure as the bird's neck parted from its writhing body and blood poured out. Virgil pulled to a stop and displayed his limp prize high above his head.

Spence wiped the rain from his face and peered through the tall grass at the scene before him. His Appaloosa neighed ten yards behind him.

The trio turned at the sound and rode their horses toward Spence until they were hovering over him.

"Well, what do we have here?" Virgil demanded. "What's your name, fellow?"

"Spence."

"I mean your whole goddamned name. Now!"

"Spencer Jay McAlpin," he answered.

"Well now. He must be old Harry McAlpin's grandson," J.D. said.

"That true?" Virgil asked.

"Yeah, that's true. Who are you?" Spence asked as the eighteen-year-old scrambled to his feet to meet them. The rain-soaked drunken men reeked of alcohol and sweat and were covered with mud and blood from their gander game. Their approach made Spence anxious, for he was hardly a match for these three rough characters.

"Makes no difference. What're you doing here? Answer up," Virgil said.

"I was just watching some good sport," Spence lied to try to ease the tense moment.

Virgil slid off his horse and grabbed Spence's shirt, while J.D. pulled Spence's arms together from behind.

Spence kneed Virgil in the groin. Virgil retaliated with his whole body and slammed Spence in the gut.

"We're going to teach you not to spy on us while we're having fun. Ain't that right, boys?" Virgil reached for his pistol.

"Your first lesson today is to do away with that horse of yours. Looks like a fine one, too." He raised the gun toward Spence's pride and joy.

"No. Please! Don't kill my horse!"

Spence wrestled away from J.D.'s grip and lunged for the gun.

The shot came anyway. Spence watched his horse fall to the muddy ground with its legs quivering and its nostrils flaring. Spence felt sick. He screamed in anguish when J.D. jerked his head back by the hair. J.D. spit the words in his face, "Your horse is dead and it's time for your second lesson, today."

J.D. spun Spence around and kicked him, sending him reeling in Virgil's direction. A stifling blow to his midsection doubled him. Virgil landed the blow to Spence's face that knocked him unconscious. "Speak when spoken to," Virgil said to the man on the ground.

Moody, the youngest, pleaded with his brothers, "Let's go, I'm cold and wet. He's had enough. If Pa hears about this, we'll be in big trouble."

❖ ❖ ❖

DUSK HAD SETTLED on Tuckaleechee Cove. The rain had given way to fog that fell into the draws and hillsides. Two riders first spotted the still body.

"Aye, Fletcher, I think we've found him," Harry said.

Without answering, Fletcher dismounted and walked toward his unconscious son.

"Spence, are you all right?" Fletcher knelt and gently rolled him on his back and stared into the bloody, swollen face. He checked Spence's wrist for a pulse and, when convinced that he was alive, began to gently slap his face.

"Spence, wake up. What happened?"

"Looks like someone was gander grabbing over there." Harry pointed to the headless remains of a bird hanging from the tree.

"Pa, I think he's coming around. Who do you reckon did this?"

"We'll find out soon enough. Get him off that ground and to your house. We'll get some broth in him and get to the bottom of this. Look over yonder at that horse, shot dead. Somebody is going to pay, I tell you. My gift to my grandson . . . destroyed."

❖ ❖ ❖

THE MEN WERE in sight of their homeplace, Aberdour. Spence clung to his daddy's waist as they rode double on the mare.

"I'll bet you'll be glad to get some of Ma's home cooking in you and a good night's sleep," Fletcher said. Spence grunted in agreement.

They passed Harry's mansion and headed down the hill to a log house, where Harry's only son, Fletcher, his daughter-in-law, Mary Clay, and his grandson, Spence, lived.

Harry said, "Take those horses to the barn, Fletcher, and I'll help Spence into your house."

Fletcher unsaddled the horses. Fletcher cursed under his breath as he watched his father swagger behind Spence. Good old King Harry. I'm nothing but a serf. So what if I limp and don't care about worldly things like Dad does. And so what if

I can't hold my liquor very well. But how I love it, even though it rules me. Just like Daddy rules me. But I let him do it. Fletcher slung the saddle over a hook in the barn wall. Shoot! I'm nothing but a God-cursed chicken. And what if Dad can stare down a mountain lion? I'm nothing but weak. He spit into the silent darkness of the barnyard and trudged toward home.

Fletcher threw open the door and stomped the dirt off his boots. Harry was already telling Mary Clay what his grandson had gone through.

"You men want some bourbon?"

"Don't mind if I do, Mary Clay," Harry said. He rolled his hips in the chair to fetch his pipe, stood to get a match from the spill box beside the mantelpiece, and lit the meerschaum.

Mary Clay opened the doors of the yellow pine corner cupboard and got the bottle and two glasses. She looked down at her husband after she handed him the glass.

"Fletcher, go get Spencer some laudanum to help him sleep and dull his paining, you hear? And not a speck more than a half-grain."

"Yes, right away, ma'am," Fletcher said. "I was going to go get it in a minute. Don't you think I have that much sense?"

"No," Harry muttered softly, just loud enough for Fletcher to hear it.

Fletcher shook his head and stomped off to the bedroom. Inside the wardrobe, a little shelf in the innermost part held the medicine. While he was at it he reached in to where he hid his flask and quickly took a swig.

"Here's to Princess Mary and King Harry." He could hear their conversation through the walls.

"He's so touchy, Big Pa. We both know he'd have sat right there until the fire gave out before poor Spence got any relief."

"Aye."

Fletcher took another swig. When he returned Spence was in a nightshirt sitting before the fire draped in a large patchwork quilt.

"You hurt much, son?"

"Yeah, but at least I'm dry and warm."

Fletcher spooned out Spence's laudanum dose.

"I'm going out back to heat some broth and cornbread before we hear what happened," Mary Clay said. "Willamae's already gone home, so I'll have to fix it, but it won't take but a minute."

She disappeared toward the kitchen building, thirty feet from the back door. The room fell silent except for the crackling of the fire and Harry's occasional puffing on his pipe. Fletcher got up to add another log to the fire.

"Don't add the big one," Harry said. "You'll smother it."

Fletcher ignored him and tossed it on the pile. The flames dimmed.

"See?"

"It'll catch in a minute." He poked at it to give it more air. "I'll go see if I can help out back." Fletcher went out the back door, but stopped under the eve of the kitchen where he could hear his wife talking to herself.

"Curses on all domestics. Why can't I have somebody here all the time? Why can't I have slaves like they do in Virginia and Georgia? Life would be so much better with more help." She stoked the fire and hung the soup kettle.

"It's a rotten day. My son's hurt. His expensive horse is dead. Fletcher is a pain and I don't have any help now with Willamae gone home. I think I'll have some laudanum myself."

She sat on the kitchen hearth and stroked the cat. "Oh my goodness, that soup will be so hot it'll burn 'em alive." She gently lifted the kettle off the fire, and began looking for the cornbread. Fletcher hurried back in the house.

"Sure took a long time for that soup," Fletcher said when Mary Clay returned.

"Couldn't find where Willamae left it. Now Spencer, let me hear your story." She pulled up her chair.

Both men got up and poured themselves another glass of whiskey. Between mouthfuls of soup and cornbread Spence related the events of the rainy afternoon.

Supper ended and so did the talk. Harry rose and tapped the last remnants of his pipe tobacco into the fireplace. Harry pondered the differences of the two families that lived eight miles apart and the secrets that bound them together.

"Old Heinreich Storch—they're his boys—nice to know he taught them manners." Harry spat on the burnt logs.

"Well, sir, what are we going to do about it?" Spence asked.

Harry straightened up and tapped the back side of his pipe into his palm. "Lad, of all the things that motivates men, revenge can be the most harmful and destructive. Don't worry, they'll pay in one way or another, and I'll not rest until they do. I never, ever forget things that are done to me or mine—good or bad. In the morning at first light, Blue John and I will pay a visit to the German's place and then we'll see what happens."

"But what about the horse and—"

"Shhh, quiet down, Spence," his mother whispered. "Get on upstairs into bed. It's been a tiring day for you and you need your sleep. Now get on with you."

"I best be going as well," Harry said. He paused in front of the door. "Fletcher, you work the fields tomorrow and start making those hired hands load the wagons for the next trip."

Fletcher slammed down his whiskey glass. "I'm going with you."

"No you're not. You work the fields like I told you. Thank you for supper." He tromped off the porch into the night.

❖ ❖ ❖

LAST NIGHT'S RAINDROPS silently dripped off the leaves of the trees as Harry and his Negro steward, Blue John, mounted their Morgan-bred horses. Harry was big and red-faced with white hair and beard. He loved his stable of horses, which to him represented the money and success he had acquired. Because he never had any as a youth, the sight of it made it all the sweeter.

He pushed his new Le Mat nine-shot revolver into the holster and looked over at Blue John. Light was barely breaking the summer darkness as the pair began their eight-mile journey to Heinreich Storch's house. As they passed under the Aberdour Farm sign, Harry was noticeably agitated.

He thought of Aberdour, named for his village in Scotland, twenty-five miles due north of Edinburgh, but separated by the Firth of Forth protruding inward from the North Sea. He remembered how his father had discovered his musical talent at an early age and had moved the family to the city so he could study at the conservatory. Oh, those hours of harmony, counterpoint, and solfeggio.

His dad had taken a position on the granary docks so Harry learned from him to appreciate weather, seasons, supply and demand, and the growth factors of wheat, millet, milo, and corn from America. He was diligent playing his French horn after school and the harpsichord after supper.

Yes, he thought, life is strange—those circumstances from whence I came and how they unfolded to shape the level of life that I have attained. Yes, I want justice for Spence's sake, but not at the expense of upsetting the delicate thread that holds Storch's and my empires together.

Harry and Blue John crossed the Maryville Pike and paused for the horses to rest. They crossed the swinging bridge that spanned the Little River, and were now on Storch's land. By eight in the morning, they were in sight of Storch's house.

Smoke lazily curled from the chimney. They figured that breakfast was over and Storch would be heading to the fields later than usual since this was Saturday. The ethereal early morning haze partly obscured the violet hues of the Smoky Mountains. The pink rays of the sun's ascension spoke beauty and comfort to Harry. Blue John slapped his horse in the flanks. Harry lit a fresh cigar as the two men rode down the hill toward the house. They tied their horses to the post and knocked on the door.

"Gentlemen. Come in. I've been expecting you."

Harry opened the door and ambled into the room, followed by Blue John.

"Morning, Storch," Harry mumbled.

"Wie gatus Ihnen, Harry, and a good morning to you, Blue John."

The house was plain but cozy. A stuffed Russian wild boar was mounted above a large sandstone fireplace. There was a miasma of smells, mostly sausage and beer. A red-and-white checkerboard tablecloth was turned sideways on the mahogany table.

Storch weighed over 200 pounds with black but thinning hair combed straight back to the crown of his head. A deep scar ran from the corner of his left eye and ended below the cheekbone. His stomach was paunchy from too many late-night beers and too much early morning schnapps.

"Have a seat please," Storch said, as he beckoned toward two straight-back chairs.

"No, thank you," McAlpin retorted. "Listen, Storch, I've come to go over a little matter with you concerning my only grandson. He seems to have had the hell beat out of him by your children and they shot his horse that I had just given to him and—"

"Would either of you like some schnapps?"

"No, damn it, I don't want anything except'n you to tell me if you know anything about what happened yesterday, and I want you to know it was a lowdown thing to do and I'm plenty irate about the whole thing. It goes against everything in Forbes' contract, and, by God, you should have seen that boy after your thugs got through with him. That horse cost me good money, and . . ." Harry was leaning toward Storch with his hand touching a chair to steady himself. He began to tremble like the leaves of a quaking aspen in autumn.

"Harry, please, please. Control yourself." Storch rolled sideways in his chair and slid his hand into his pocket.

Blue John took no chances as he stepped forward and reached for his pistol. McAlpin realized Storch was unarmed and held out a hand to let Blue John know it was all right. Neither of them took their eyes off the scurrilous German. He was unpredictable, and they had to be ready for anything.

"Listen you two. Your show of force is unnecessary. I knew about the whole episode last night. You see, Moody, my youngest, got out of bed after his brothers had passed out and came and spilled the whole story. He has a little softer heart than those other two and must have felt a kindred spirit with your grandson. Anyway, I can't tell you how sorry I am about the whole thing, and I'm prepared to offer you twenty dollars for the horse. In fact, how about thirty dollars for the horse, your troubles, and maybe a visit from Doc Hughes to patch him up."

"Money, Storch? All you have to say is 'give them a little money?'" Harry bellowed.

Harry saw Blue John's eyes shift from one man to the other in this spirited chess match.

"Nein, Harry. This morning I snatched them out of bed by their long johns and belted them both and kicked them. You should have heard me cussin' at 'em. They couldn't believe I'd be so mad at what they thought was such trivia. They reeked of bourbon and I was only happy to greet them with my cheerful good morning. Anyway, I kicked them again, sent them to the mines without breakfast, and docked them four days of pay."

Storch held up the cash and Harry reached out and jerked it out of Storch's hand. Harry couldn't believe it had been so easy. "Storch, once again you're such a riddle."

"Gerta, get these men something to drink to cheer them up. And a little breakfast too."

Harry relaxed, but not enough to forget the words of Proverbs 23, in the King James Bible: "When thou sit to eat with a man, consider what is before thee: And put a knife to thy throat. . . . Be not desirous of his dainties, for they are deceitful meat."

As the German housewife waddled into the room with a bottle of clear liquid and two shot glasses, Harry released his grip on the chair and said, "Nein, danka." He motioned to Blue John to head for the door. I love to imitate Storch's accent, he thought, especially after this *coup dé théâtre*. He and Blue John opened the door, stomped out, and mounted the horses.

Storch was at the door shouting, "I tried, I really tried to make it fair and to even things up, you hear? You won't tell Forbes, will you? Wish you would stay and have some break . . ."

Harry turned to look back. He saw the dust blow into Storch's face. He saw the wife put down the bottle and glasses as she took her dust rag from her apron and began to wipe the furniture.

As HARRY AND Blue John reached the pinnacle of the knoll above Storch's house, they slowed the geldings to a walk. The high grass on each side had lost its dew and was getting warm in the morning heat. Without looking back at Storch's large domain, Blue John broke the silence.

"Sir, you pulled it off real good back there. We done all right considering sparks could have flown, and somebody could have been hurt."

"Yeah, John, it could have been a real donnybrook. I guess we came away with what we were after. Storch is so crazy, you never know exactly what he'll do or what he's thinking." There was a pause in the conversation as the horses crossed a creek. "I'm hungry, aren't you, John? Let's get on over to Aberdour and work on lunch before we think about the new horse."

Blue John Nelson came from the island of Antigua in the Leeward group. His daddy was a slave and had labored to build the dockyard in 1784 as a young boy serving under the great English Admiral, Lord Horatio Nelson. In 1820 his daddy thought it good to name his son after the admiral. The boy grew tall and strong.

While Blue John rode, his thoughts went back to a day in 1848 when the sun was beating down on his lithe, sweating physique. He remembered how he concluded that working in the sugar fields was a never-ending job that would keep him sore and penniless. He thought about how he had despised the Protestant ethic of hard work and long hours. He remembered slipping onto one of the clipper ships bound for Boston—a ship owned by Mr. Robert Forbes. Once in Boston, he worked his way from dock loader to chief steward for Forbes. When the opportunity presented itself, he volunteered to accompany Harry McAlpin to Tennessee. He had grown tired of Boston harbor with the incessant cries of the seagulls and the stench of offal.

Blue John stretched in his saddle and breathed deeply. He loved the clean air, the mystery of the mountains, hunting and fishing, and overseeing the millet farming operations at Aberdour. He also loved Harry McAlpin. He was freer than any man of color he knew, and Harry made sure he was not confronted by any known or implied prejudice.

Blue John exercised and paid attention to his health and diet. He poured the cream off the milk and drank only the remainder. Mountain people called this type of milk "blue John," so they tacked on this nickname.

"I overheard some people in a store in Maryville whispering as to just how Aberdour could prosper so much by growing millet. Same old thing we've heard before. 'Course, they didn't know I was standing in the next row out of sight."

"Like I've told you before, John, never you mind that kind of talk. Being away from Maryville and Knoxville does have its advantages. I don't give a damn about their thoughts. What we sell in Memphis and Cincinnati is nobody else's sodden business."

As they rode on to Aberdour in silence, both thought about the coming harvest and the payoff in Cincinnati.

"John, I've been thinking about making a run up to Hancock County to see Collins before the Ohio trip. Might take Spence."

"Well sir, Collins is one of our best customers—trip would do you good. Mr. Collins loves to get his medicines and I love to make that money."

"Yeah, me too. Right now, I'm starving. Let's pick up the pace a little."

They crossed the swinging bridge over the Little River and entered Aberdour land.

THE SOUNDS OF hired hands swinging machetes at corn stalks were growing monotonous in Spence's ears. He had been in the fields since six that morning when the air was dark and chilly, but after four hours of labor, he had sweat and grime covering his face and arms. Still, there was another hour before mealtime.

They were cutting the stalks for bunching to feed cattle, and were gathering the last of the ears for loading in wagons to take to Cincinnati. This was the last corn patch to clear; to-morrow the crew would move to the last few acres of millet fields and then harvest would be over for another year. Spence was getting mad at the corn, and this made him chop faster and harder.

"Boring work ain't it?" Orvil Lee said, his voice squeaked.

"Orvil—I didn't see you come up behind me," Spence said.

"Bet you're starting to get tired. Why don't you rest a minute. I'm getting a bit wore down myself," Orvil said, cutting his eyes back and forth through squinty eyelids that looked like slivered almonds.

"Naw! Better not. Don't want anybody to think I'm loafing," said Spence.

"Hell, boy, I'm your field foreman. If I say you can rest, then you can rest," the dumpy man said.

Orvil reached into his baggy pants and brought forth a tin of Rooster Brand snuff; opened the lid, took out a pinch of brown powder and put it in his mouth, showing an uneven array of mottled teeth.

"Why don't you quit using that nasty stuff?" Spence said.

"Want some?" He spat across two rows of corn.

"I'll let you and the other men do that . . . never had any."

"Here—try a little. You're chicken if'n you don't." Orvil opened the can and held it forward.

"Nope, can't do it."

"Come on. You might like it." Orvil waved the can again.

"Well, maybe a little bit this once. Show me how."

"Look here. You just take a pinch and stick it in your cheek," Orvil instructed.

Spence did as told and put the bitter powder in his mouth.

"Do you just spit it out?"

"Yeah. Just take a spit."

"That's not so bad. Is that all there is to it?"

"Not quite," Orvil said. "If you want to get a little high feeling, let a little bit trickle down your throat."

"Aw, Orvil. You want to get me sick?"

"Now son, you ain't got a hair on your arse if you can't let a little go down your throat. Otherwise, it don't count."

Spence grimaced and swallowed and blinked his eyes in disgust.

With that, Orvil resumed his thrashing of the stalks. "There you go. Now you're one of us. I'm proud of you, son."

Spence took his machete and began cutting again on the corn, alternating a spit here and a swallow there. The sick feeling didn't take long to hit him. The rows and furrows began spinning and sweat beaded on his forehead like dew. He sank to his knees, all he knew to do. All he could do was to crawl somewhere, anywhere. He made it to the weeds at the edge of the field where he threw up breakfast. He could hear Orvil laughing first, then one of the other workers; a cacophony of laughter came from the remainder of field hands joining in as they realized what happened.

Slowly, he got to his feet and trudged out of the field. The hill he had to conquer was mocking him—not giving in to his youth—its gullies tripping him.

"Lord God," he mumbled, "if you'll get me back right again, I promise I'll be good forever—maybe go off and be a missionary."

It seemed like an eternity, but he finally rounded the corner of the barn and headed down the hill to his log house. His mother and Willamae were washing clothes over an iron pot in the yard.

"Spen—cer!" Mary Clay ran to him with outstretched arms. Willamae was right behind her.

"Got sick in the field. I'll be fine shortly, soon as I stretch out."

"What made you get this way, son? None of the rest of us got sick from breakfast."

"His face is whiter'n a ghost, Miss Mary. Lawd, we'd better get him in there to the house and put him in bed; give him medicine."

He walked up the steps to the loft and his bed.

"What were you all doing in the fields?" his mother asked.

"Chopping the last of the corn."

Willamae came up the stairs and gave him a dose of laudanum. She stood with her hands on her hips, staring down at him.

"He don't look so sick to me, Miss Mary. What's that on your collar, boy?" She leaned over and grabbed his shirt collar and held it to her nose. "Smells like tobacco—looks like snuff. That's it! You've been dippin'—no wonder you got sick."

"That true, son?"

"I didn't want to. Aw, we were just fooling around. Learned my lesson."

I could kill Willamae right now, he thought. She went and messed up everything—bad enough puking my guts out, but I could always get sympathy, and here this Willamae upped and ruined even that.

"Ha! If you asked me, I think he ought to be marched right back out there and made to work all afternoon without no din-ner, and see how he likes that. Bet he won't be getting no more tobacco any time soon. Who was it that made you do it?" asked Willamae.

"Do I have to answer her?" He paused . . . then breathed hard.

"Mr. Lee—Orvil, the field foreman."

"Who?" asked Mary Clay.

"That's the new man that Mr. Harry and Blue John hired from Kentucky," Willamae volunteered. "Never did like his looks. Said he came from some big farm up there and that he was on his way to Georgia. Said he ran out of money and needed work. Bah! Mr. Harry never wrote no letter to anybody up there to see if it was true."

Mary Clay and Spence glanced at each other.

"I tell you, there's a lot of meanness in people. Ought not hire somebody if'n you ain't got no information about them. Especially this day and age, what with hostilities heating up twixt North and South," Willamae stated.

"That will be all for now, Willamae," Mary Clay said. "Go on down there to the washing and I'll be there shortly."

The plump lady stared at Mary Clay, ran her hands over her apron as if to flatten out the creases, and then marched downstairs and out the door in a huff.

"Spence, dear, I know you're at an age that you want the world. It's a time of confusion, but don't be led around by the wishes of other people. Certainly not somebody you hardly know, and especially not a common field hand.

"Now, if it is somebody you or your family knows, respects, and admires, then you can seek their advice. But deceitful men, and women too, will tempt you all of your life with their deals and schemes, usually wanting your money or time. You need to develop your own set of standards, your own limits. Learn to say no. You won't be able to please everybody, so stand up and please yourself and your own interests—like your future family. You understand?"

He stood up. "Yes, ma'am, I think so."

"Spence, you should learn to read people. Learn to recognize their motives and learn how to protect your own. Nobody does anything without a motive. They'll butter you up and tell you how fine you are only to get a piece of you."

"When Sam Houston lived in this county forty years ago, his mother engraved a word on the inside of his gold ring, 'Honor.' I can't think of a better word to give you as a motto. Mr. Houston's mother only wanted him to give his best—not let people have his blood. He wound up being the governor of two states."

"I'll remember that. All right, back to work."

"Are you sure you feel like it?"

"Those field hands expect me to lay around the rest of the day and not go back out there. I'm tougher than they are— just can't handle tobacco. Nothing wrong with that."

"Stop by the table and get a piece of hot-buttered cornbread as you leave. And don't worry about what Willamae says. She's not family. Blood is important, Spence. Remember, 'Honor.'"

He headed down the steps and out through the kitchen, getting the biggest piece of cornbread he could break off. As he walked the hill, he felt strength returning. He felt good about what his mother had said and yet ashamed— ashamed he had been caught doing such a stupid, disgusting thing. Orvil, you little cockroach!

Chapter Two

Spence ran up the knoll leading to the big house, leaped on the porch and through the door. Harry and Blue John were eating on the dining room table when Spence entered.

"What happened . . . the Storch's . . . they did do it?"

"Their pa and I had a talk about it," Harry said. "We agreed to a settlement that was fair and equitable—plus Mr. Storch sternly disciplined his boys this morning."

"That's all? I was outnumbered and left for dead."

"Son, I told you last night about quick revenge. There is a time and a place for everything. Mr. Storch was cooperative and generous in the way things were handled. Isn't that right, John?"

Blue John nodded. "Yes, it'll be all right, I promise you that. Work hard with me on the farm. You'll heal."

"Your talking doesn't make me feel any better. That's the way Preacher Mayhew would do it—talking. Preachers think God's lightning bolt will teach them. Well, it won't. I want action because I was humiliated."

"Spence, now calm down. I've never heard you talk—"

"I don't care." Spence shouted with clinched fists. He left in a huff, untied a horse, and galloped off down the road lead ing to the Maryville Pike. After two miles he turned onto a path that ran along a rushing mountain stream. The brush gave way to a cane break, and fronds slapped his face and arms. The more the horse slowed, the more Spence urged him to regain speed. His rage was quenched when the animal tripped on a rotten log, and they were both flung to the ground.

When he opened his eyes and realized he wasn't dead, he checked the horse for broken bones. There were none and the horse was alert. As he got up, he saw an opening in the cane leading to a grassy clearing with graceful swamp willows on one side, and a canopy of beech trees on the others.

Fifty yards ahead, a man turned around from a bent-over position. A beautiful Morgan quarter horse grazed lazily nearby.

"You all right?" the little man yelled.

"I think so, sir." Spence walked toward the man.

"Where could you possible be going in such a hurry? Aren't many folks around here with that much get-up-and-go."

"I was going to visit my lady friend over the hill."

"Don't give me that," the man said with shaded contempt. "That path goes nowhere. Could me lad have been running from something? . . . Now, that's none of my business, is it? I'm glad you weren't hurt. My name is McGlothen. Professor Clint McGlothen."

"Spence McAlpin, sir."

"I'm filthy dirty, but then, so are you." He wiped his hands on his trousers and offered a handshake. "Good to meet you."

"Glad to meet you too. Guess I'll be sore tomorrow." He stared at the man's round, cherub-like face and gray beard. On his nose were oval spectacles with silver wire frames. In his mouth was a half-smoked cigar.

"Would you like to stay awhile and see what I'm doing? And if you have nothing better to do, I'm camping here tonight— we can share supper. I brought along beef and hardtack and peach brandy."

"I think I would like that."

"Good," he scowled out of the corner of his mouth. He turned his back to Spence and held out his arm with a sweeping motion. "Ginseng, my boy. That's what I'm about today. Panex quinquefolium."

"What?"

"Panax, from the Greek meaning 'all-healing', and quinquefolium from the Chinese for 'five-fingered root.' Flourishes only in woods like these; protected by the forest roof, from wind, rain, and sun. It's found among hardwood like basswood, paulownia, poplar, oaks, and of course, these majestic Fagus grandifolia, or to you, beech."

McGlothen was indifferent to how Spence was receiving his lecture. He bent over and pulled a plant from the leaf-mold soil. "See, young man, it has a root form that closely resembles the lower body of a man with legs spread apart. Have you heard of the 'doctrine of signatures?'"

"I haven't."

"Well, back in primitive days, many believed that ginseng acted as an aphrodisiac."

"Really?"

"This doctrine says nature places signs on certain plants to indicate their medicinal value. For example, lungwort resembles the spongy surface of a lung, so it was used to treat tuberculosis and pneumonia in ancient Greece. Get the idea? The Chinese use ginseng for everything from diabetes to colic to consumption."

"How do they take it?" asked Spence.

"Oh, they chew it, boil it and drink it as a tonic, or they grind it into powder.

"But I tell you, this plant is scarce, and it will not be tamed. Like a good woman. Takes years to get it ready for market. A hundred years ago, America had a thriving ginseng trade with China, second only to our fur trade, but those liver-bellied

French in Quebec ruined it for us down here. They sent roots collected too early, improperly dried, and cured in haste. They would even insert lead into the middle of the root so they would weigh more, thinking that would fool the buyers. Those Chinese caught that in a minute.

"Anyway, trade is improving. I'm augmenting my income from the college where I teach. I take it over to Louisville village and sell it to the paddleboat dealers."

"Where is Louisville?" asked Spence.

"You don't know about Louisville?" McGlothen said. "Little trading outpost at the other end of Blount County, on the Tennessee River. From there, it goes to New Orleans or Boston, and then on to the Orient. I get four dollars a pound; that brought me $400 last year. Not bad for an old math and botany teacher. Don't have any wife to fritter it away, so I get by. Sometimes I think I should be smart enough to make more."

McGlothen taught Spence how to gather ginseng roots. They talked and harvested until McGlothen said it was time to wash up in the creek and get supper. They made a fire, cooked the meat, and made coffee. Together they sipped on the brandy.

"You from around here?" Spence asked.

"No. I grew up in New Hampshire. My daddy was Scottish and made a lot of money making plows and hayracks."

"But, how did you get down this way?"

"My father's dream was for me to go to Dartmouth," said McGlothen, "and study the classics, and then return to the family business in Nashua where I could learn something worthwhile and run the company. Daddy and Mother could then retire to their house over the Merrimack River and watch my farm machinery float down the river on the way to Boston to be sold.

"Unfortunately, Papa lost his money from whiskey, cards, and cockfighting. I did make it through Dartmouth, but I was poor; had to work at odd jobs to pay tuition, but then my parents sent some money.

"I watched my wealthy classmates use college as a residence-in-waiting, marking time until they joined their daddies in business. The exception were the divinity students whose heads were up their arses anyway—going thither and yon in their pomp and piousness."

Spence stared at the glowing embers of the dying campfire. "Bet you haven't told that story in awhile."

"I'll say this, my studies captivated me and kept me going when times were hardest. I adored math, but later, I discovered botany. It was a perfect blending of the abstract and the living. Wanted to teach it to others. I didn't have a head for business, so I taught school in Concord and paid off my debts while I supported myself."

"Now I'm going to ask you again . . ." Spence drank the last of the brandy.

"I know, I know. The Department of Education in Tennessee contracted Dartmouth to inquire if there were teachers they knew of who would be willing to come to the South. I was reached in Concord and accepted the summons; thought it would be an adventure. Tennessee sent me to Van Buren County. Stayed there five years. No ginseng, few people, no eligible ladies, and no thirst for education, so I moved to Maryville and taught at the college."

After a pause, the professor lifted his chin and squared his shoulders. "You go to school, don't you?"

"I go three months a year to Coker Hill, a few miles from home."

"Is that all? You must go more than that. Is your family hard up for money? How much could a term cost?"

"No sir, it's not the money. I'm just needed on the farm. I think a term at school cost fifteen dollars."

"What possible chores require that much from you?"

"Oh, we kill hogs; make lard and table cracklings in the fall. Then we make lye soap from the pork scraps; after that, molasses, and then comes Christmas. I go to school for a while and when spring comes, I help set tobacco. Of course, there's always the millet," said Spence.

"The millet?"

"That's our main crop."

"I know of no one in this county growing millet." McGlothen paused to light a cigar. "Tell me more. Tell me all about your family."

Smoke from the fire curled upward into the night. For the next thirty minutes they talked. Spence admitted his tirade and why he fled Aberdour, but he dozed off to sleep sitting on the log, only to be awakened by a wildcat screaming in the distance. The professor lent Spence a blanket, so they settled down for the night.

AT DAWN, SPENCE helped his new friend load his ginseng and the two rode twenty miles westward into Maryville. After unloading the valuable roots onto the drying racks behind his house, McGlothen showed Spence around the college. Spence invited the professor to come to dinner at Aberdour Sunday. They parted.

DARKNESS HOVERED AS Spence slowed the horse to ford a creek. The sweet smell of new-mown hay lingered from the field he had passed. Meadowlarks were perched for the night on Chamon's telegraph wire above him. He smiled as he recaptured the events of the last twenty-four hours. As he turned off the pike, he glanced toward Rose's Tavern due east. The violet haze of the mountains was rapidly approaching the taupe color of the valley, but he thought he saw his grandfather's horse standing beside the tavern. Spence figured Blue John had already fed Big Pa, and he was looking for some company.

Spence quickened the pace toward home. He wanted to get his stomach filled and crawl into his own feather bed.

Chapter Three

ROSE AND F. L. CHAMONS kept Rose's Tavern neat and tidy, considering the riffraff who often frequented the place. Every so often respectable folks would spend the night, and Sunday dinners were popular with the more civilized mountain people, but it was the drinking room behind the dining room that held the appeal—at least for the men, and especially toward the end of the week.

The tavern was a colorless two-story building. Six posts rose from a shallow front porch to support a second-story balcony. There was one large chimney at the apex of the roof in the center of the building and four smaller ones to heat the four upstairs bedrooms for travelers.

Rose Chamons kept lily-of-the-valley plants under a crepe myrtle tree beside the hitching post. To the right of the tavern was an herb bed of dill, horehound, thyme, and chamomile.

F. L. Chamons was a chemist, or druggist, by trade, who migrated here from Scotland. Now in his sixties, he was proud of his family, his survival instincts, and most certainly his cached wealth.

Tonight was to be special. No one else was in the tavern but Chamons and Harry McAlpin, partners in their concealed venture.

A chill came in off the night air, and the two men alleviated the problem with a roaring fire, sheepskin covers on the chairs, and some mountain liquor that Chamons bought from his agent over in Cades Cove.

"How was your trip to Boston, F.L.?" Harry asked.

"Starting to get cold up there already. About as cold as Forbes' heart. It was a good trip. Drank some whiskey, did some business. But glad to get back down here. Forbes never stops thinking about ways to make money—that is, until this trip—maybe age is making him looser. He actually took me to the races and then to a cockfight the next day."

"Yeah, that's hard to believe," drawled Harry.

"He asked about you more than once, like when you would next be going to Cincinnati."

"God, F.L., I thought you said he was loosening up?"

"He is. I'll get to the fun part in a minute. But, Harry, Forbes and I want to know when you're going?"

"Two weeks I think," came Harry's reply. "Soon as I get the crops dried, milled, and loaded."

Chamons took a stick from the spill box and lit his cigar, then bent over to light McAlpin's.

"Well, like I told you, Thick Neck needs it soon, so he can get it to his distributors. The sooner you off-load that grain, the sooner he can load our opium. I've had three letters from our agents within the past week requesting more powder and I hate to keep them waiting."

Chamons enjoyed prodding Harry at times just to let him know the order of things in their business hierarchy.

"I know about the time element, F.L. You know I like to make money as well as anybody, probably more. The end of next week, I'm going to give Fletcher the responsibility of getting the crops milled this year. While he's doing that, I'm going to run up to Hancock County to deliver a shipment of powder to Collins. Don't you worry about a thing, F.L., this fall is going to be a good one, providing the nation stays in one piece," said Harry.

Harry took another sip of liquor. There was a pause as the two men gazed into the fire. "You know, I think it's time I took that grandson on the trip with me."

"That's fine," Chamons said, relaxed by this time. He knew to be careful around McAlpin. He was well aware Harry could fight like a bear and would do so at a minute's notice. "Just be careful and hide your bounty around Spencer. Wouldn't do for him to get wind of anything."

"I know. I'll hide everything like I always do. You're right—wouldn't do for him to know."

"Chamons. You said Forbes asked about me. What else was on his mind?"

"Oh, yeah," Chamons said, raising his voice, laughing and slapping his thigh. "We were about half-looped at this cockfight, and he said you would always be beholding to him for something that happened a long time ago. He wouldn't divulge what, but I gather it was about what made him send you down here. But he did say I ought to get you to tell me about it. I mean, what you did in Scotland. Why you left. Forbes said it was a great story and that I should pry it out of you, especially since it's been years ago and doesn't matter to anyone now."

"Forbes said that?" Harry asked.

"Sure did. He was feeling no pain that day—jovial, in fact. Now is a good time, Harry. Tell old Chamons. I've never asked before."

"Ah, I guess I don't mind. But tell no one. Promise it won't leave these walls."

"I promise," said Chamons.

"The family moved from Aberdour to Edinburgh so I could study at the conservatory. Daddy worked on the grain docks at Leith, two miles from the center of town. He speculated in forward contracts on the counting floor, and he taught me all he knew while I was still in my early twenties.

"After university, my career with the Edinburgh Symphony flourished, but it was still musician's pay, so I kept trading those contracts.

"After Kate and I were married in 1831, we became well known around the city. We went to plays, parties, benefits to raise money for the castle, Saint Margaret's, Order of the Thistle's Canongate Abbey, and other structures of medieval importance.

"One week, the men in the weaver's guild in Cramond were short-selling contracts on West Indian sugar. My group went after them and bought up all the contracts we could find. The weavers group had to scramble to cover their positions, at a huge loss.

"They learned I was behind the strategy, so two of the drunk blokes came to our apartment swinging pistols. There was a fight. I shot one dead and the other broke his leg after I kicked him down some steps onto a landing. Kate and I hid the body and decided we must leave the country.

"We gathered our valuables and made bank withdrawals the next day. The symphony was playing that night at Saint Giles and I needed to be there. The feature was Haydn's G major Symphony, but I knew that after the Allegretto, my part on the harpsichord wasn't needed for the finale. I slipped through the curtains and left.

"We used a two-passenger post-chaise vehicle and fit in our new baby, Fletcher, as best we could. The driver took us south into England through the Cheviot Hills along the Great North

Road the Romans built. At Biggleswade, we turned left to avoid London, and went onward to Ramsgate where we booked passage for Boston."

Harry stood up to walk to the table where the whiskey bottle stood. The bullet shattered the glass window and ripped through the muscle of Harry's left arm. He spun around against the hearth in a flurry of pain, surprise, and blood. He screamed incoherently as Chamons hit the floor amid broken glass and spilled liquor.

"God, get him. God, I'm dead. Oh, oh, Jesus, it hurts," Harry wailed. He writhed on the floor grasping his sopping biceps.

They heard distant sounds of hoofbeats fading into the night.

Chamons screamed, "Oh shit, my glass, my windows."

"A pox on your windows, you bilious son of a . . . ," Harry screamed before fainting. Then he came to. "Oh my, it hurts. Oh, God," his voice trembled, as he began to breathe shallow and fast. Everything went dark again.

Chamons crawled over and checked Harry's pulse. When he realized Harry was going to live, and that the danger was past, he jumped to his feet and yelled to his wife. Rose was already out the door running toward the tavern.

"Rose, get us clean rags, lambs ear, bourbon, and laudanum," Chamons yelled. "Some cockroach shot up our windows—the ones I had made in Savannah."

"Oh, not those windows!" Rose yelled. "Give me a minute."

Rose quickly brought the fixings. The puncture was soused with bourbon, lambs ear herb was stretched over the wound, and McAlpin's arm was wrapped firmly with rags. A sling was made and laudanum was copiously administered.

McAlpin began to rest easier as Chamons squatted beside the soft chair in which Harry sat.

"Whomever would want to kill you, Harry?"

"Chamons, do you know what shoots cartridges like this?" the Maryville sheriff asked.

The two men studied the casings they had picked up from the ground.

"Hell, sheriff, those came from one of those Maynard carbines. Bunch of 'em around, but who knows—someone with extra money to spend. They don't come cheap. Most of the mountaineers still use flintlocks."

"Yeah, guess you're right. Could have been anybody. We'll all need to start keeping an eye on carbines for the next little while," the sheriff said.

Puzzled, he began looking at the ground again. He walked around for a few more seconds and bent over.

"Looks like whoever shot McAlpin lost a pheasant feather."

Chapter Four

"WHERE ARE MY BLESSED boots?" Fletcher muttered. He groped on his hands and knees under his bed in the predawn darkness. The sounds from the kitchen called attention to his throbbing head, but the smell of ham and grits offered promise. Once dressed, he stumbled into the kitchen.

"Morning, Mr. Fletcher," said Willamae. "Want some coffee? The red-eye gravy is ready and the biscuits are hot."

"Coffee would be good. Is the boy up?"

"Yes sir. He's out to the privy. Here's butter and molasses."

"Thanks."

"Breakfast is ready. Breakfast is ready," Willamae yelled.

"Coming," Mary Clay called. "Spence, get in here."

"Sit down before it gets cold, hear?" Willamae scolded. "If I can ride over here in the dark and get it ready, then the least you can do is eat it while it's hot. My poor invalid husband sitting over there at my house would love me cooking for him like this. Poxy Mexican War. But I work here, now sit down."

The family sat down and awaited the usual choppy prayer that Fletcher invoked. It was the same words each time, but today was more dreary than usual. Fletcher's eyes were puffy and his mind was still affected from yesterday's fieldwork and last night's liquor. He envisioned not going on the trip and being relegated to another ten hours in the fields.

Fletcher said, "Now help Granddad all you can. Keep the wheels greased and help unload the millet when you get to Collins' house. He'll need you to bed down the team for the night. Big Pa hopes to get to Rutledge by sundown and then you'll go to Newman's Ridge the next day," Fletcher lectured.

"All right. All right. I know to do all that."

"Don't forget, he's taking you to help rather than Blue John. If Big Pa gets tired, he'll want you to drive the team. He's getting on up there in age and can't do as much as he used to do, especially with that gimp arm of his."

"Daddy, we'll be fine."

"Don't forget your manners," Mary Clay admonished. "No, ma'am and yes, ma'am and all that." Remember to say please when they offer things to you at the table, and thank you when food is passed to you. You weren't brought up out there in the barn, after all."

Fletcher rested his fork and pushed away his plate. He put his elbows on the table and stared at his wife of twenty years. She was evenly proportioned; not an ounce of fat on her, brown eyes and shiny hair parted in the middle. Her skin was fair with only a hint of creases at the corners of her eyes.

She was the granddaughter, on her mother's side, of the very Reverend Isaac Anderson, who in 1819 was founder and first president of the Southern and Western Theological Seminary, which later became Maryville College.

Fletcher remembered Mary Clay when she was seventeen years old with plenty of handsome men already vying for her hand. She was often escorted to the most important parties of the season in Knoxville; even to the Blount Mansion whose owner was the first governor. Maryville had even been named after William Blount's wife.

He remembered how he won Mary Clay from the others. They met at a barn dance on the outskirts of town one summer night. She was there with two girlfriends and he was with a friend.

He even remembered the string band that night. The finest five-string banjo picker he ever heard was there, a dulcimer player, a fiddler, a guitar picker, and a mandolin player. Blue John had given Fletcher one of Dad's liquor flasks from Scotland. He hid it behind a bale of hay at the far end of the barn. I was twenty-five, he thought, and with a little bourbon, I could dance 'till late in the night. We were married on Thanksgiving Day.

I wish I felt the same toward her as I did back then—wish I were as bold, as brave, he thought. Maybe I could stand up to them all better. Oh, Mary Clay has her acerbic side, but she's a good woman and wife.

"Fletcher! Fletcher," Mary Clay repeated. "Where are you? You're off daydreaming again. Get up here and see them off."

IN THE MISTY grayness of the morning, Mary Clay watched her son and his granddad disappear out of sight. She walked around her house and out into the orchard. The waft of ripening fruit filled her senses. She stepped on an overripe pear lying on the ground surrounded by a coterie of little fruit flies. Life is like that fallen pear—it buds, it blooms, it produces fruit, it ripens, and then it falls, only to be consumed by scavengers before it turns back to the soil.

She looked heavenward, closed her eyes and lifted her arms. "Behold that which I have seen: it is good and comely for one to eat and to drink, and to enjoy the good of his labor . . . this is the gift of God. . . ."

Oh Lord. Solomon had it right. I'm not about to let life's burdens, large or small, get me down, she thought.

She turned and glanced up the hill to the manor house of Aberdour, her father-in-law's house with the six Doric columns across the front porch.

"Harry, you pompous twit!"

❖   ❖   ❖

"HEY, MCALPIN, IT sure is good to see you," Claude Collins yelled. He bounded down the hill to the wagons and the two men shook hands.

"Where did you spend the night, Harry?"

"At the Holston Stand. Had the best boar meat, fritters, collards, and mulberry cobbler I ever tasted. Slept like a log."

"Eliza!" Collins yelled, "they're here. Go ahead with lunch."

"Claude, this is my grandson, Spencer. This is Mr. Collins."

"Nice to meet you, sir—heard a lot about you."

"Well, it's good to meet you, Spencer," Collins replied. "You all come on up here and meet the rest of the family."

The three climbed the hill and stepped onto the front porch.

"Eliza, you remember Mr. McAlpin, but you've never met his grandson, Spencer."

"Hello. Lunch will be ready in a minute." She gave Spence a quick glance, wiped her hands on her apron, and turned to go back into the kitchen.

"Let's see, where is the rest of 'em?" Collins took a few paces along the porch toward the end of the house.

From out of nowhere came two boys and a girl who gathered beside the well ten feet from the southwest corner of the log house.

"This is Jep, he's eight; this is Sam, ten; and this is our daughter, Lochsley."

Spence nodded and Harry smiled. The boys broke into a run toward the back of the house. The girl nervously stood there with her hand on the flat rock that capped off the well. She gazed at Spence. He froze a few seconds. Look at that! he thought. About my age too.

Lochsley was barefoot and had dainty feet; she had small ankles that arched into perfectly shaped calves before being interrupted by the ragged hem of her dress. A string of leather was tied at her midriff around a tiny waistline. *Why aren't I breathing normally?* Spence thought. *And why are my palms sweating?* He swallowed three times in a row.

Collins put his hand on Spence's shoulder. "Come on in, fellows. I think Eliza has dinner ready."

"I'm starving," Harry said.

"How about you, Spencer? I'll bet you're hungry after the trip." They turned to go in.

"Yes, sir." His voice broke. He cleared his throat.

Mrs. Collins pointed out the seating arrangements.

"Oh, Lord, make us thankful for that which we're about to receive and make it go to the nourishment of our bodies. Amen." Collins looked up after his prayer and began passing a plate of squirrel meat and hominy.

Spence would sneak a look over at Lochsley. Twice, they made eye contact and each quickly returned to their eating. Her skin was golden; her eyes were large, brown, and almond shaped; her hair dark and straight, and fell below her shoulders. Pristine nose, smooth lips, and perfect teeth. Natural, raw beauty.

"Eliza, that was mighty good blackberry cobbler."

Collins slapped his thighs with both hands. "Harry and I have business to conduct down at the woodshed. We'll be back in a little while." They got up and left the house.

"Lochsley, dear, go draw up some well water so I can wash these plates. Maybe Spence can help," Eliza said.

"Sure, ma'am, I'd be glad to help. Is there a bucket?"

"I'll show you where it is," Lochsley whispered.

Spence followed her outside. He wiped his palms on his pants.

"Weather's a little hot, isn't it?" Spence stammered.

"Hot? I've had chill bumps all morning? You feel all right?"

"Yeah, I'm fine. Where's that bucket?" He watched her grace-fully glide around the corner of the house.

She took a bucket and attached the hook at the end of the rope. Then she looked at Spence. He took the oak bucket from her hands.

"I'll do it." He released the bucket and watched the weight of it pull the rope off the spindle until he heard the splash below.

Spence cranked the heavy load upward. Lochsley bent forward and braced her hands on the side of the well.

It was at that moment that he saw the green stone, sus-pended forward of the cleavage in her breasts, hanging from a thinly cut leather string tied behind her neck. The sun's rays danced in and out of the cut facets around the edge of the gem. It was encased in a gold metal backing nestled against her soft skin as she stood up straight.

"I think I have it now," Spence grunted while he swung the load to the edge of the stones. "Where do I take it?"

"Around back." Lochsley motioned toward the rear. He hoisted the water onto another shelf—on which was a glob of lye soap.

Mrs. Collins came out the back door. "Thank you, son. I'll take it from here. You all can go get me some eggs in the henhouse and after that, I don't need you."

"Come on," Lochsley said, "over there is the chicken pen." She walked down an embankment. Spence followed closely.

"Sure is pretty country up here," he said.

"Yeah, it is. But I've been here since I was born. Another place might be good for a change."

"Oh, like where?"

"Oh, maybe to a city like Knoxville or Roanoke. No one up on this ridge goes anywhere much. The grownups talk of faraway places, but if they ever went, it was years ago."

"Well, you have time."

"Yeah, but still—I guess I'll be here forever until I die."

"But Lochsley, you must keep dreaming."

The two quietly entered the henhouse. Lochsley put her finger to her lips. She gently pushed the first hen aside and took two eggs. She handed them to Spence to put into his pockets. The air exploded in a flurry . . . clawing spurs . . . as a Rhode Island Red rooster landed on Spence's neck. He could feel his flesh torn by the angry bird. Confused and shocked at the attack, he flailed at the bird.

He heard a thump; the cock hit the ground and ran out the door into the sunlight. Lochsley held a broom.

"Spence. Oh my! Are you all right?" She put her hand on his neck to inspect the damage. Blood ran down his back, soaking his shirt.

"I don't know." He dropped his hands to his sides. Do I ever hurt? But she used my name—and I think I'm going to get some of her attention. "How bad is it?"

"Don't know yet. Let's get to the house and wash up. I'll put on some medicine. Mama?" Lochsley called. They ran to the porch.

Mrs. Collins came out. "Lord, Lord, what on earth? Let me get something and wash your neck, boy. Was it that mean rooster?"

"Yes, ma'am," Lochsley said and related the incident.

"Well, first thing you must do is get off that shirt. Do you have another?"

"Yes'um—in my duffel." He pulled the shirt over his head. Eliza squeezed a wet cloth and dabbed it into lye soap.

"Here, Mother, I'll do it. You can soak his shirt."

"Did you all get any eggs?" Eliza asked.

"Yes, ma'am, we got two." Spence plunged his hands into pockets of sticky slime and fragments of eggshells. "Never mind, I'll get some later."

"So now, any more breeches?" asked Eliza.

"They're in my duffel too."

"Well, these have to be washed as well. You can go into the girl's room to change after she gets you washed."

Lochsley's hands rubbed gently on his aching wounds. The soap stung a little. She went into the kitchen and returned with lambs ear and a tin of ointment. She applied them.

"That feels better," Spence said.

He trotted down to the wagon and returned to Lochsley's room with his duffel. There was a small bed with a straw mattress covered with three brightly colored quilts. Beside the bed was a wooden table with a water bowl, half full. Sitting beside the bowl was a pomander within which were sliced apples, cloves, and cinnamon for fragrance. Two dresses hung on pegs in the wall.

As he changed pants, he felt chills over his body. Just imagine, this is where she sleeps. This is where she undresses. When he tucked in his shirt, the sensuousness of the moment was overwhelming. Once outside, he realized he had more of life to experience.

"Could we take a walk?" Spence asked.

"I suppose so," she replied. She glanced over at her mother scrubbing away at the shirt. "Where do you want to go? I mean, would you like to walk up to the cemetery at the top of the mountain? I haven't been up there in awhile, but . . ."

"That'll be fine."

The two walked to a gate fifty yards from the house. Once by the gate, they were in a steeply sloping pasture with milk cows grazing. They became winded as they climbed along a fence row that ended at the edge of dense woods. He followed her as she turned along the edge of the woods until a warren of tombstones came into sight. A stone fence about two feet high surrounded the plot. Beyond, an area of grass looked cool and inviting. The afternoon wind blew over the stems in an undulating motion.

"Let's rest here," she suggested.

Spence said nothing as he fell to his knees, rolled on his side, and put his hand under his head for support.

"Tell me about these hills, Lochsley?"

"Well, we're almost at the crest of Newman's Ridge. Down below is the Clinch River. That stream joining the Clinch is Panther Creek. To the right is High Knob and then there is Powell's Mountain.

"On a clear day you can see all the way into Claiborne County. See that white patch of sand? Look right over the top of that sycamore tree. That's Buffalo Lick in Claiborne County." She was sitting beside him now and pointing out the landmarks. She turned to him to see if he was listening—and then . . .

Spence was looking into her dark eyes. They were mysterious, beckoning. They were transfixed on each other. Their lips met as their arms left the grass to tenderly embrace each other. Their bodies slowly reclined into the warm grass. Spence thought he could hear the drums of a hundred ancient battles, the commands of their victorious generals, and the shouts of a thousand charging soldiers as the trumpets blew, the swords clashed, and the muskets roared. The turgid excitement wouldn't leave him alone. Joyful torment. His heart pounded. He felt Lochsley's heart beating as strongly. Spence opened his eyes and noticed the swelling in her breasts had changed the angle of the gemstone against her skin.

They gently pulled apart and rested their heads on the grass. After a few moments, they kissed again.

"You keep looking at my necklace. Do you like it?"

With boldness, he reached over and held the beautiful gold-encased stone.

"Where did it come from?"

"It was willed to me by my grandmother Gibson on my mother's side. Her daddy had given it to her, and heavens! I don't know who had it before that. It's been in the family for hundreds of years. Maybe more. Why do you ask?"

"Just curious. Hundreds of years?"

"That's what the will said. Of course, I've never seen the papers, but don't you think it is unusual?"

"Unusual? Lochsley, nobody has been in America for hundreds of years, unless it came from the Indians. You all aren't Indian, are you?"

"Now, Spencer McAlpin." She straightened and leaned back on her hands. "Does it matter? I mean, we're not Indians. We're Collins." She paused. "And we're Baptist. And we're Tennesseans and Americans and I'm getting irritated."

"Forget it, Lochsley. I didn't mean any harm."

"Spence." She waited until he turned to look at her. "Spence, are you wondering about my olive skin? Don't you think it's pretty?"

"Oh yeah, Lochsley, I think it's beautiful. Just forget I even asked . . ."

"Didn't your granddad tell you?"

"Tell me what?"

"No, I guess he didn't. And, you've never been up here before. Have you ever heard the name Melungeons?"

"No."

"Other people around the county call us Melungeons, I mean, most of us who live on Newman's Ridge. We don't like it and Daddy gets mad if he hears somebody use the word, but it must mean pertaining to color. Mama says nobody even knows where the term came from, much less where we came from."

"Hey, all I was wondering about was the stone," said Spence. "You don't even know where you came from? Not England, Ireland, Scotland, or Germany?"

"No, I don't think so. One night before he died, my granddaddy Collins and I were talking at his cabin about half a mile from here. Now, mind you, nobody ever talks about this out in the open. I mean nobody. But Granddaddy was telling me about a fellow from Nashville who had come up to this place twenty years ago taking notes and all. Said he was writing a book.

"Seems some smart people had figured all these possible ways our people had come to this country." She paused and shifted her weight on the grass. "One thought was that we came from Sir Walter Raleigh's Lost Colony of Roanoke, wherever that was . . . and that the survivors intermarried with the Indians and settled here in the Clinch Mountains. Some said we're the lost tribe of Israel. Others said we're deserters from De Soto's Spanish expedition of 1540."

"You're mighty smart. Where did you learn those dates?" asked Spence.

"I go to school just like you do," she snapped. "Another thought was that our people were shipwrecked Portuguese who moved inland and mixed with the Indians."

"What do you think?"

"Wait a minute, I'm not through yet. Many people said we came from the Phoenicians through ancient Carthage. They were shipbuilders and had extensive knowledge of the seas, so it was possible they could have made it across the ocean to America. If you stayed up here on the ridge long enough, you would eventually hear somebody use the word 'Portergee.'"

"So? . . ."

"You want my opinion? I believe we really did come from Portugal, or through Portugal."

"What does that mean?"

"Well, it means we were an ancient race of people who came to live in Portugal, and then somehow came over here. Really, Spence, I haven't thought about it all that much, but since you asked, it just makes sense. If my ancestors were the Phoenicians, and they knew the sea and ships? . . ." She stopped to consider more details. "Do you know where the Phoenicians came from?"

"Never heard of them." This is interesting, he thought, but the mood has changed. I liked it the other way.

"They're mentioned in the Old Testament, book of Joshua. Do you know where Portugal is?"

"No."

"Near Spain. Someone could have given this stone to their daughter two or three thousand years ago, then they could have given it to their son who passed it on to his son. Who knows, those Phoenicians could have lived in Portugal hundreds of years before they came here with the stone in someone's possession all the while. Ohh! That's exciting. I wonder how long I would have worn this before I put these thoughts together? It's because you came today. Do you know how good that makes me feel?"

He wasn't that impressed.

"Thank you," she whispered. She bent over and kissed him.

"Let me show you the graveyard quickly, and then we'd best be getting back to the house." She got up and took his hand.

They stood and looked at the array of gray-brown headstones with primitive carvings scratched into their surfaces. Most had been chelated for decades with armies of lichens, wind, rain, and snow. Many of the inscriptions were illegible.

Each grave was covered with two crudely cut sandstone slabs pieced together in an apex resembling the roof of a house. The stones had long since turned a copper-brown in color. There were names like Mullins, Gibson, Brogan, Collins, Fields, Minor, and Goins.

Spence scratched his head, "Those names sound English to me." A hawk soared overhead. "What do you think, red tail?"

"It's a mystery, isn't it? How could this family of people have kept an ancient bloodline in these beautiful hills? But we can't solve it today. Come on."

The couple walked downhill through the pasture and along the fence row. The cows moved to a small pond to drink, to eat their hay and wait for nightfall.

They walked quickly and held hands until they reached the gate.

CLAUDE AND HARRY had been talking for two hours. They discussed their families, tensions between North and South, and the extensive distribution of remedy medicine and related products. Both knew the wisdom of planning their efforts in the event of hostilities.

They considered the logistics of getting opium to their merchants when the war began. They knew their agents well. Most were mature, successful merchants who would remain to continue the work and not go flying off to fight as younger men would do. With luck, they would grumble a lot about the injustices and hell of war, but stay neutral. Fortunes could be made either way. They could even arrange to get government contracts from the medical departments of either side. They reckoned that war might even be good for business.

They finally got down to the transfer of three tons of grain and several "items of medicines."

"All right, Claude, let's see." Harry took an old envelope and pencil out of his shirt pocket. "Three wagons of grain, each has twenty sacks of 100 pound apiece. Three tons. Each sack measures twelve by ten by thirty-six and that's 8,640 cubic inches. This divided by 2,219.36 cubic inches in a bushel comes to 3.89 bushels per sack. You with me?"

"I hear you," said Collins.

"Now I need to get $2.50 per bushel, so that's—"

"Harry, now you know I get the New York market reports—it may come two weeks late, but I know millet is going for $1.95. Believe me, I'm not that isolated up here."

"I know, Claude, but that's spot price at the granary—doesn't include my bringing it up here to your door. We go through this every time—"

"Two dollars."

"Two-twenty-five, not a penny less."

"Two-twenty." Collins knew prices were down at harvest season, and he also remembered the summer drought that occurred in the Midwest and upper-South. He knew he could win at that price.

"I don't know . . . that's pretty low." Harry shook his head and stared at the piece of paper.

"Then, two-twenty it is?"

"Collins, you drive a hard bargain, but we'll go at $2.20 per bushel."

"Harry, when we get back to the house, I'm going to get down my old violin and play a sad melody to commemorate your financially fallen state. My word!"

Harry began to scribble again. "OK! Two-twenty a bushel, times 3.89 bushels per bag . . . that's $171.16 per wagon times three wagons comes to $513.45. Agreed?"

"Agreed."

"Now Claude, it's dark, so come on to the wagon and we'll bring in the stuff."

The two walked up the hill to the wagon train. Harry's lead wagon was his favorite. It was a Conestoga he had bought in Philadelphia on the way to Tennessee years ago. The German settlers in the Conestoga Valley in Pennsylvania had made the wagon sturdy and maneuverable. It had grace and beauty that belied the swamp oak, ash, and gum and it was made with hand-forged iron straps, rails, bolts, corner plates, and pins.

They weren't made like this anymore; Harry had held on to it through the years. His sentimentality had a reason: the false floor about six inches above the base. With the removal of two well-hidden pins, he could swing open two horizontal iron plates and have access to the whole secret compartment. His other two wagons were Studebakers that Thick-Neck had bought for him in Indiana.

"Can you see to open the thing, Harry?"

"Shoot! Claude, I can do it with my eyes closed. Let's get the little bags down to the woodshed first, and then we'll come back and get the medicines."

Harry reached into the compartment and groped until he found twenty-two gray calico bags weighing one and one-third pounds each. The two men carried them downhill to the woodshed and lit the kerosene lamps for inspection. Each bag was a catty and contained 600 grams. One hundred bags would be a picul that weighed 133.33 pounds. This was the unit for shipping.

"Now, isn't that pretty?" Harry asked. "Now let's get back up there and finish."

Back up the hill they went for the remainder of the load. Their work took another fifteen minutes before they could rest.

"We have five boxes of laudanum from Allen & Hanbury's London. Uh, three boxes of Battley's Sedative from William Armitage, Doncaster, and four boxes of Dover's Gout powder from the Apothecaries Company, London. I've totaled those; forty-seven dollars for the lot."

"As for the opium, Claude, the Peking Emperor has taxed the powder at $44 per picul and has legalized trade. They're serious this time. And too, the demurrage fee has doubled, and the bloody cumshaw fee has gone up to $5 per chest in Canton Bay."

"That much?" asked Collins.

"Oh yes. The 'smug boats', 'centipedes', and 'fast crabs' are unloading as fast as they can to smuggle into the mainland, but as soon as the first friggin' coolie sailor gets shot, war will break out again like it did in '40 and that'll be the end of the trade. Yes sir, consignment of white powder on American ships is dead.

"You know what this means, Claude? Our big shipping houses will no longer be able to make a profit trading with China. Prices will soar. Forbes got our batch on open market auctions at Garraway's Coffee House. He said rumor has it that next May's Turkish crop has to be higher."

"So, Harry, what kind of a good deal am I getting this time?"

"Twenty-two catties at \$30.48 comes to \$670.56."

"No argument," Collins said. He already knew about all of this, and also knew his agents could get what they pleased for their products. "Total it up, Harry, I'm getting hungry and tired."

McAlpin scratched some figures—\$1,230.91.

Collins reached into the bulging pocket of his pants and took out a wad of money. He counted out the correct amount.

Collins had secretly drawn out \$1,500 earlier in the day from his "private safe." A private safe that consisted of a hollowed-out section on the underside of the bottom log of the woodshed. There was a trap door that swung a peg only after one dug away dirt and reached upward and gave it a ninety-degree turn. In addition to cash, he kept gold nuggets and silver bars that he mined himself on his land, and eighteenth-century Spanish pieces-or-eight that his daddy's generation used sixty years ago. He was well off and almost nobody knew it.

"You know, Harry, I have always hated banks. Besides, the only one within a day's ride is at Sneedville, and I don't think any banker deserves to know my worth. Do you Harry?"

"Of course not, Claude. One of the reasons we get along is that we're cut out of the same bolt of cloth. And we're discrete."

"'Course, Harry, you spend more and show it off with your horses and houses, but up here, I would stick out too much if I flaunted it."

"Oh, Claude, nobody would pay any attention."

"Oh, yes they would. I would be an easy target."

Harry yawned. "Thank you very much. Guess this just about does it for this trip, don't you think?"

"Yeah, let's get on up for supper and then you can bed down."

Collins blew out the lamp and the two men walked back to the house, each feeling smug for the good dealings that had transpired.

SPENCE LAY AWAKE in the loft that night. Harry was asleep. Mrs. Collins had changed the summer straw-tick mattresses for winter goose downs, and had brought the hot bricks and placed them under the covers at the foot of the bed. Through a small window made from rippled glass, Spence could see a lazy quarter-moon over the crest of the mountain. A hoot owl was asserting himself over in the hollow. How pretty Lochsley looked tonight at the dinner table.

He wanted her to look at him more than she did, but he reckoned she was just being coy. Most of the talk was about the abolitionist movement up North, the new preacher over at Newman's Ridge Free Will Baptist, and the hog-killing season coming after first frost.

How he loved this afternoon. I wish I could kiss her right now, right up here in this loft, he thought. He fantasized how he would hold her, how he would feel the warm moisture of her inviting lips . . . his eyes became heavy and he drifted into a deep sleep.

AT DAWN, MRS. Collins softly awakened her guests.

Harry had instructed her at bedtime that he wanted to get an early start for their trip home. Eliza Collins apologized that the children were still asleep. She explained that the children needed their sleep because her husband would have them working in the fields all day, and Lochsley would be helping with the canning in a hot kitchen.

After breakfast, Spence went to the barn to hitch the team of horses to the wagons. He was feeling better and knew the return trip would be faster with empty wagons.

The thoughts of yesterday and the events on the hillside perked him up even more, and he was looking forward to recapturing those warm memories on the trip home. For now, they were his secrets, which nobody had to know about ever, unless he was willing to share them. He reveled in the power of that possession.

Harry lingered a moment to say final farewells and climbed aboard and took the reins. Shortly, Spence crawled in the bed of the Conestoga to nap on some empty grain bags.

Two hours passed before Spence awakened. He stretched and yawned and thought of Lochsley, missing her already.

He climbed over the seat and took the reins from his grandpa.

"Did I tell you we're having a guest Sunday afternoon?"

"No, you didn't, sonny boy. Good nap?"

"I feel much better. Guess sleeping on the floor of that loft—well, I'm just not used to it, even with the mattress."

"Who's the visitor?"

"His name is McGlothen. He's a professor at the college and he knows something about everything. He came from up North years ago. He hunts ginseng in the deep woods. His family came from Scotland, and you'll like him."

"Whoa, son, one thing at a time. Why don't you start at the beginning and tell me how you met this man—and God love ye laddie, I don't know if I can stand another Scot."

Spence spent the next twenty minutes recounting the story of his chance meeting with the professor in the forest. Harry listened intently.

Chapter Five

"More sausage, Heinreich?" Gerta asked as she forked over the last patty from her black cast-iron skillet.

"Thank you, thank you," Storch said, his voice garbled by a mouth already full of eggs and bread.

"You know, Gerta, you can really make the good sausage: just the right amount of cayenne peppers to make my eyes water."

"Oh, ya, I like to cook like we did in the Homeland."

"By the way, when do you think we'll get the first frost? Got to think about killing those hogs soon. Those Durocs out there in the lot are fat enough now to be slaughtered what with our meat supply getting low." He gulped warm beer followed by coffee. Grease fell from the corner of his wide mouth and onto the bib.

"Ya, I know the meat is a little low, but there's plenty to last through November. That reminds me—I was over at Rose's yesterday buying sugar and coffee and I was talking to some of the other people in the store. Did you hear about McAlpin's wound?"

"No," Storch replied as he downed the last of the sausage.

"Wound?"

"Well, early this week, he and Chamons were talking by the fire, and just as McAlpin got up, somebody shot him through the window and rode off. They said McAlpin thought he was dead."

"Is that the truth?" Storch asked as all chewing came to a halt. "Who'd they think did it?"

"Nobody has the foggiest idea. Of course, they were drinking and it was pitch-black dark, and they were all confused, with all that broken glass everywhere and Harry moaning and screaming. I hear his arm is all right, but he'll have to wear it in a sling for a while. I would love to have been there, wouldn't you, meine Herr?"

"Oh, definitely. The old rotter had it coming. Did anybody find a clue? A trace of anything?"

"Chamons and the sheriff found bullet casings on the ground, but nobody knows who might have owned that kind of gun."

"What kind was it?"

"A Maynard carbine," Gerta stated. "They also found a long pheasant feather on the ground."

Gerta expelled a breath of exasperation and slapped her dress. "All this untamed violence around here." She began to scrub the skillet with a loofah sponge. "People shoot, rob, and loot without any fear of punishment, and I tell you Heinreich, it seems like it's getting worse since all the talk of secession got started. They wouldn't get away with it in Prussia for long. I know that. Our organized culture and strict sense of propriety wouldn't stand for it—"

"Stop it, woman!" Storch screamed." "Stop it now. I've told you a thousand times to leave it alone. Forget Prussia. That place is behind us. I don't want to hear about it. It's no longer a part of us since we escaped and I'm damned glad to get out alive, and you should be too.

"If you don't like it down here, you can go back to Boston. Of course, Forbes would find out about it and we would be ruined—extradited back for prosecution and probably the firing squad because of that murder charge against me. Of course, you know that, so just be a good wife and mother and keep your fatuous mouth shut."

"I'm sorry, I just can't help it sometimes if I miss my heritage? That Prussian blood runs deep, and geographic moves don't dilute it out. We're different from all these other people around here—"

"Be hanged we are!" Storch countered. "We fit in these mountains. Our boys are just as backward as everybody else and talk with the same mountain twang as everybody else, and besides, who says one has to be Scotch-Irish to belong and be counted? Look at the Germans up in Morgan County. They run the place and the other people around there respect them.

"So, like I said, just be content. We have no choice. And I'm sorry, but that includes getting along with McAlpin too, as bad as I hate to do it, but that was Forbes' rule. He finds out everything sooner or later, and he'll know if we break the contract."

There was a noticeable silence. "All right, all right. Let's change the subject. I've been meaning to talk to you about Virgil. Here lately, he's been wild and rambunctious and mean; he goes off for long periods of time—"

Someone was knocking at the door. Storch walked over and opened it. In front of him stood a short, knotty little man aged beyond his years. He had no teeth and the creases leading away from his mischievous eyes made deep furrows in his tan skin.

"G' day, Mr. Storch? Name's Willis. You wouldn't happen to have any work for a man, would you?" he said, shifting from one side to the other.

Storch closed the door behind him and stepped onto the porch.

"Who told you I could use help, Mr. Willis?"

"Just 'Willis,' sir. That's my first and last name, I reckon. Never known anything else. But, uh, some of them fellers over in Maryville said you had a big operation, and couldn't get all the work done even with several sons. So I thought I'd ride out here and was hoping you might let me help."

"Don't you have a family?"

"No sir, I don't." He held his hat in front of him with its dried ring of sweat around the band.

"Where do you come from? Have you worked for anybody I know?"

"Uh, I was born in Arkansas, and uh, well to tell ye the truth, I reckon I'm just a drifter. Can't stand to settle down too long nowhere. I ain't worked for anybody this side of the Cumberland Mountains and I was headed up to Virginia when I had to pull up in Maryville to get a new shoe for my horse. I was talking to some of the men around the blacksmith shop when they told me you might be hiring. Mr. Storch, I'm stone mother-lovin' broke and I need a job in the worse way. I'm a bloody good worker and I wouldn't bother you any and I sure don't need much, just some food and a bed." There was a pause. "Kind sir, do you think you could help?"

"Let me see your hands."

The little man flopped his hat back on his head and opened his hands. There was a row of calluses.

"How'd you lose part of that finger, Willis?"

"Got careless with an ax, sir." He grinned.

"All right, we could probably use you around here. You'll start this afternoon. Pay is twenty dollars a month plus food and room. Got extra rooms over in the bunkhouse. Two of my boys stay there too. The youngest one stays in the house with us.

They'll tell you about where the coal is for your stove and where things are in the barn. You can get your food out back in the cookhouse, but we don't have any more room around the table, so you'll have to eat in your room."

"That's just fine, Mr. Storch. I'll do a good job. Thank you very much, sir," Willis stuttered as he gave a little half bow and reached up to tip his hat.

"Dinnertime is at eleven o'clock."

"Thank you, thank you," he said, nodding his head up and down. He led his horse over to the bunkhouse. He couldn't help smiling. One thing at a time—getting the job is first. Shoot man, this may not be as hard as I thought.

"I SEE YOU boys met the new hand," Storch stated. He stomped out on the back porch to wash for dinner. "Go on in and sit down. We'll make room at the table today, but he'll take his meals in the bunkhouse from now on. Now sit down and eat while it's hot."

Willis stood with his plate as the family gathered. Boots shuffled and chairs scraped before a temporary quiet. As usual, no prayer was given.

"Virgil, take off your hat when you're at the table," Gerta said.

As Virgil tossed his hat on the floor, Storch stared at it.

While Willis ate with his gums, he glanced at the two oldest sons. You two are going to be very useful to me, he thought.

Virgil was gaunt with deep mutton-chop sideburns that framed a face with high cheekbones and sunken cheeks. And those eyes. They showed all of him—almond shaped, slanted down with heavy eyebrows. The pupils were dark and penetrating; the iris a green color and totally visible within the whites. Oh, they were sinister.

J.D. was fleshier with a sallow, bloodless face and thick lips. Both older boys had Kaiser mustaches that turned down. Willis figured neither of them had many redeeming qualities.

Then he observed Moody, the youngest. Square jaw and rosy cheeks with no facial hair made him look as though he had a modicum of honesty and trust. He's still a Storch though.

And I don't give an old whore's crack about the whole lot of 'em, but I have a job to do, so I'll gain their trust and friendship, what little they have.

❖ ❖ ❖

IT WAS LATE afternoon when Storch went to the front porch to cool off. He had been in his study doing paperwork for the next corn shipment. He sat down in a rocking chair, fanned a little, and dizzily observed the beauty of the setting sun over the stand of hickories in front of the house. He drifted off to sleep and began to dream of his time spent in Boston years ago.

"Listen, you rotten Dutch," Harry McAlpin spoke in the dusky closeness of the booth in the tavern, "I told you the Marble Godwit had to be repaired by Saturday. Forbes said the owners already had hired their crew and were to begin payroll Friday."

"No way it can be done, McAlpin," Storch said.

Harry stared into Storch's cold eyes. "That's as plain as it gets. Forbes will be onto me something fierce if it's not done, so when are you going to get that damn part fixed?"

"But—"

"I mean, Storch, tomorrow is Saturday. That crew will be sitting around cussing and spitting and drawing pay and loving every minute of doing nothing while Forbes stands up there on the fourth floor and watches the whole sorry lot of them. I mean . . . what would you think if you're the customer and that rudder assembly isn't working?"

"I can't help it what they think, it—"

"I can tell you my carcass will be thrown all the way down from the fourth floor to you and your sodden excuses for repairmen. We'll all be begging for our next meal over on the commons—"

"That's enough," Storch yelled. "You never earned the right to be yard foreman anyway, besides, my crew is the best in New England and you know it. 'Gott in Himmel' man, I told you Monday we couldn't have the rudder and the mizzen stay sails fixed by Saturday, but you bilious bullhead, you wouldn't listen or even go ask Forbes for other arrangements."

"Other arrangements, me eye," McAlpin yelled back. "When a big trading house like ours is dealing with important clients, then we must perform. That's the stuff from which reputations are made—being reliable and trustworthy—something you wouldn't know anything about, Storch."

Harry leaned over the table that was carved with the initials of sailors and traders from four decades. He pumped his fingers into Storch's chest.

"I'm saying we needed help since this client was so God-cursed important and his blessed Saturday sailing date was—"

"Like what?"

"Like calling down a crew from Marblehead. They've helped us before and—"

"Shit! Storch. You know bloody well it's the beginning of whaling season up there and they haven't a man to spare. In fact, you shouldn't even be here tonight. You ought to be down there on the Godwit with your crew getting it done."

Storch's fist rammed into the Scot; a hard right to the head sent him backward into a table of Irishmen, who had been trying to ignore the loud confrontation. Harry dropped to the floor in the tobacco juice and sawdust. Two Irishmen rushed Storch. Storch countered as best he could, but a pint bottle to his head sent him reeling. Harry looked around confused at the others entering the fight. They crashed over chairs and whiskey glasses. From the floor, Harry chopped one of the Irish with his boot. All the patrons in the place were out of their seats to surround the fighters wanting more action. The little Jewish tavern owner was flailing his arms and yelling, but no one would let him through. He realized he was helpless, so he just watched as his drinking room was riven with chaos.

Storch felt the blood and glass in his hair. An extra rush of power took over. He staggered around, but hands from the crowd turned him to the thick of the fight. Storch grabbed the nearest Irishman and slung him to the ground. He fell full weight to the man's chest and began to choke the man with his own kerchief. The Irishman's face flushed crimson and his eyes bulged from their sockets. His legs quivered, total quiet, nothing.

Death scattered the crowd. Men rushed the doors trying to get away before the law arrived. McAlpin and Storch headed out the back door, and for them the remainder of the day was a blur. They skulked in the shadows until they reached the shipyard and hid in a dry-docked boat. Late that night, Forbes's men found them and forced the two to face the boss.

Storch remembered being seated in front of Forbes and watched as Forbes paced the floor and chewed on his cigar. Both men were a sorry sight. Cut, bruised, hungover, exhausted. Forbes yelled at the two, "You caused $175 worth of damages at the tavern, and you both realize one man is dead and two others are critical. The police have been here twice looking for you. The word is out that the dead sailor's twin brother has formed a gang to hang you both. I hear the name is O'Conroy and you better look out."

❖ ❖ ❖

HEINREICH STORCH AWAKENED in a sweat, the past was behind him. He walked directly to his office, sat down, and yanked open the bottom drawer of his desk. He unlocked a small strongbox. There lay his copy of the original contract from Forbes. He lit a cigar and began to read.

"...a farming operation will be set in motion as a front to the opium business. You will plant, reap, gather, mill, and go to markets as other farmers, except you will deal in more distant markets than your neighbors.

"Mr. Storch and McAlpin and their families must get along and cooperate. . . . Failure to do this will endanger the operation and subject the offender to penalties and extradition.

"Any acts of malice, bodily harm, or breaking of civil laws that might jeopardize the business will immediately void the rights and privileges of the offender. . . . Upon the death of a principal stockholder, a period of six weeks must be allowed for verification of cause-of-death to reach Boston. Then other stockholders could buy the vacated portion subject to my approval."

Storch fanned his red face with the sheets of the contract, then skimmed through the pages until he reached the last one.

"...Bearer bonds to be at par of one thousand dollars each; fifty bonds will be senior debenture to the stock, which you will purchase and will act as mortgage bonds. In the case of default, Mr. Forbes will take possession of all assets, such as houses, barns, horses, wagons, and land. These bonds are non-callable and will be extended to ten years from date of original signature, and whose coupon will be at eight percent per annum."

Storch threw down the cigar and crushed it under his boot. "Eight percent . . . eight percent . . . damned usury."

He sat back in his chair and crossed his arms. He stared at the wall at first and then his gaze drifted to the hatrack. Virgil's hat was hanging there. Storch thought of the attempt on McAlpin's life, and that a feather had been found outside Rose's Tavern. He thought of Virgil throwing his hat on the floor at lunch—without the feather.

Storch screamed and bounded out of his chair and hit the wall with his fist. He stomped to the front porch, down the steps, and kicked dust with his boot. Where are they working? he wondered. The barn? No. The granary? The cave? Smithy? That's it. He quick-stepped in the direction of the blacksmith shed.

Storch threw open the door and stepped inside. He squinted his eyes in the dim room. The fire in the forge cast a glow. J.D. was pumping the bellows, stoking the red-orange heat to greater and greater temperatures. Virgil was pounding thin iron strips into hasps for a pasture gate.

"Virgil," Storch bellowed. "I know you did it. Think I wouldn't find out?" His fists were clinched. "You were stupid enough to shoot McAlpin and then drop your hat feather on the ground so the sheriff could track you down."

Virgil froze.

"You trying to ruin me?" Storch yelled. He charged Virgil with arms reaching.

"I'm under a contract you know nothing about, and your attempt to kill McAlpin could make me loose everything I have. In fact, you sorry excuse for a son, you could force my wealth into the hands of the McAlpin family! I would be destitute and it's my money! Do you hear me, it's mine." There was scuffling and deflection of arms. Storch wrestled himself into position over Virgil who was pinned against a support post. Storch's strong hands were squeezing and shaking Virgil's neck.

"And where were you, J.D.? Tell me it was not you!" Storch squeezed Virgil's neck more.

Virgil's hand wildly flew backward, grasping, and found one of the iron rods lying on the hearth, its end glowing white hot in the flames.

Virgil swung the rod in an arc. The searing tip made a thump and a hiss as it hit Storch's rib cage. The big German screamed in pain and surprise, released his grip, and reeled backward against the wall. Virgil pursued his advantage and ran with the poker held high. Before he could bash his daddy with the poker, Virgil felt the pricking pain of the tip of a hunting knife in his midsection. Storch had pulled his knife from his hip scabbard with the full intent to use it. Their eyes met.

"Now, stop it," Storch yelled.

Virgil shrieked and recoiled to a standing position with his hands in the air.

"Drop that poker, now, or I swear I'll kill you."

Virgil dropped his arms and pitched the poker in the dirt. The fight was over.

"Now I want to know, did you fire that shot?"

"Well . . .," Virgil stammered, he looked toward his brother. "Me and J.D. were in the cave mine looking for that silver vein we found last year. And, uh, a chunk of ore broke off and fell into the water—right where the river runs into the mountain from that cane thicket."

"Go on, go on."

"I eased down into the water to get the ore and saw a strong-box in that cut-out section of rock. J.D. and I pried it open, and found some papers. All that was there was some stupid contract between you and Mr. Forbes."

"That's my duplicate box. And just what did you make of it?"

"Well, I figured that with McAlpin gone, his shares would go to us, or I mean to you, and . . ."

"You figured wrong, Virgil. Since you think you know so much, did you read the section about the bodily harm, or that the breaking of civil laws would void all rights—"

"Aw, Daddy, words on paper don't mean nothing. Who'll catch me?"

"I'm responsible for everything you do to those people. Gott, I wish somebody would kill him but not us."

"But I thought being so far away from Boston, and if no one proved who shot McAlpin, then his shares could go to us."

Storch paced back and forth across the hard, black earth. The brothers glanced at each other and then back to their daddy.

"You two boys have probably gotten us all in trouble. Your mama says the Maryville sheriff is looking around. I've got to think about this. Now I want you two to finish getting those wagons loaded for the trip south. Corn and opium. My man down there is expecting us in a few days. And, not a word about any of this to that new man. What's his name?"

"Willis," J.D. said.

Crouched outside the window, Willis turned to run back to the woodpile to resume chopping. There was a smile on his face. He had heard it all.

"And Virgil," Storch said, "you better find another feather for that hat."

Chapter Six

I<small>T WAS A CLEAR</small> Sunday morning in autumn. The glowing sun was just appearing over the crest of the mountains to meet the morning crispness. Spence and Blue John were milking.

"You seem excited about that professor coming to lunch," Blue John said.

"Yeah, I wish I could remember some of the long words he used. Let's see, Panex quin . . . Panex ginggi? Can't remember exactly, but I know it means ginseng. I'll listen better when he comes."

"I'll probably enjoy it too," Blue John said, "I've never been around a professor."

"There's only one problem—and that's church," said Spence. Then he thought to himself, I'll have to wash and ride over there and listen to Reverend Mayhew—he is longwinded and boring and the benches are hard.

"Spencer." The shrill of his mother's voice broke his thought process. "You had better get in here and wash up. Don't want to be late for church. You know how your granddaddy gets if we're late."

"Coming, Ma," he yelled back. He bent over and picked up

the bucket of warm milk with the bubble still breaking on the
surface, his biceps showing taunt from under the rolled-up shirt
sleeves.

Inside the house the aroma of meat greeted him.

"What's on the stove, Mama?"

"Venison. I'm going to let it simmer while we're at church.
Blue John will watch it. Now get dressed and get that Bible,
so we can get just as soon as we finish with breakfast. Oh, and
strain the milk, please, before you do all that. But hurry."

Within half an hour the foursome was loading the buggy.
In sight of the white clapboard church, the family could hear
the large bell kneeling from the belfry high atop the roof
over the front door. The wheels of the buggy made their
own furrows in the dusty road leading to the church nestled
into a grove of cedar trees.

There was a cast-iron water pump twenty yards from the
front door. Spence had always been fascinated by the modern spigot. It could be revolved so that in one position, the
well water would fall into a trough leading to a cistern so the
horses could drink. The other position led the water into an
iron tube that extended out ten feet to the horizontal. Ver-
tical supports held the tube over a trough that caught water
from the eight holes bored into it. When the handle was
pumped, eight arcs of water would spew upward into the
mouths of as many Big Pistol worshippers. Of course, Harry
had financed this project, buying the unique pump from an
ironworks in Cincinnati on one of the trips. After all, nothing was too good for the parishioners of Tuckaleechee Cove.

The family parked the wagon and hitched the horses to the
post beside the cistern, and proceeded toward the front door.
Mary Clay had to lift her dress so the dust wouldn't soil her
laced hemline. Greetings were exchanged with people milling
outside the front door. Two elders took the last drags before

dropping their cigars in the dust and extinguishing the fire with their boot sole.

They walked slowly and pompously to their customary pew on the second row, right side. Spence could feel the stares of the congregation upon his family.

Standing tall in the pulpit was the very Reverend Finas Rhodes Mayhew. Over six feet tall in his black suit and string tie, his ivory complexion told that he had spent no time in hot fields, or little in the out-of-doors. Harry McAlpin liked him because he was educated at Princeton Theological, knew scriptures, and had a flowing delivery, which, upon arousal, could rattle the rafters. Most of all, Mayhew knew who controlled the church money and would frequently allude to Brother McAlpin in his sermons.

Reverend Mayhew looked somberly down at Mary Clay and nodded. She took her seat at the piano to play the first hymn. The man in the alcove to the left of the front door stopped ringing the bell. A hush fell over the congregation. A few of the better prepared, at least those who could read, had already identified the hymns to be sung from the block-lettered sign above the piano and had inserted markers at the proper pages.

"Let us pray," Mayhew bellowed.

Spence bowed his head, but opened his left eye, as was his custom, so when the preacher got rolling with the prayer, he could turn and look out over the crowd.

"Oh, Lord, our Lord, how excellent is thy name in all the earth! Who hast set thy glory above the heavens. When I consider the heavens . . . the moon and stars . . . what is man, that thou art mindful of him? Yes, we gather here this Sabbath morn to give thee thanks for the bountiful blessings which thou has bestowed upon us: our freedom, the beauty of the mountains, the clean air . . . We place our minds and hearts in your care. In the name of your Son. Amen. Will the congregation please remain standing for our first hymn."

Spence had spotted her midway through the prayer. Strange he had never noticed her before. She's a visitor, he thought. She's sitting next to Mr. Chamons. Hum! She's pretty.

"For our first hymn," the reverend said, "we shall sing one of Robert Robinson's old songs written in 1758, 'Come thy Font of Many Blessings.'"

Mary Clay came down hard on the dominant major chord of E-flat. Mayhew held up his arm so all voices would be ready: "With gusto." And everyone sang, "Come thy Font of Many Blessings, tune my heart to sing thy grace, Praise the mount I'm fixed upon it, Mount of God's unchanging love."

Spence watched the girl sing and could see the dimples in her cheeks as she said "streams of mercy." Look at that little turned-up nose. Does she have freckles? Can't be sure—too far back. Love her hair tied back with that red ribbon.

He felt Fletcher nudge him in the ribs. He glanced back at his songbook and joined in with the chorus of the final stanza.

"Be seated," Mayhew ordered.

While the collection plate was passed, Harry, being chief elder, came to the front with the usual announcements: "There will be a dinner-on-the-ground next Sunday after church, followed by our quarterly grave decorating ceremony. Sister Minnie Sue Stalcup has been ill of late . . . Brother Titus McPhail is bedridden after being thrown by a mule. . . ." Harry sat down and Mayhew took over.

"This week's assignment for the young people will be to read the book of 2 Samuel, then next week at Sunday school, we will discuss it."

"Now, children, you must read your Bible daily, for it is God's Holy Word and it pleases Him for you to study the Great Book, and you know you want to please God. Only sinners don't want to please God. Parents! Make your children do their studying, for the Apostle Paul says in the epistle of 2 Timothy, 'Study to shew thyself approved unto God, a workman that needeth not be ashamed, rightly dividing the word of truth.' And you know you want to be approved by God, so study hard.

"Now, brothers and sisters, today's scripture lesson is taken from the Book of Acts, chapter five, verses one through ten." He paused for the few who brought their Bibles to find the reference. He heard only a few parishioners leafing through the pages. He thought, I hate it when my flock depends upon me to spoon-feed them on Sunday, rather than dig out the meat of the gospels themselves. He made a note to reprimand them for not bringing their Bibles to church.

Reverend Mayhew extended his arms, grasped the sides of the lectern, and looked out over the audience.

"The title of today's sermon is 'Deception and Deceit— the Devil's trick.'"

The reverend proceeded with an abusive, bitter, and lengthy diatribe of the deceitful nature of man, the sinner, and how the Devil contrived the artful hoax to trick man and God. He pointed out that it wouldn't work, and for all Satan's cunning and baffling schemes, God only laughs at man when he tries to trick other men through Satan's works.

Watch him steeple his fingers, Spence thought. He always does that when he wants us to think he's seriously pondered a subject. Now watch him point his bony finger up to the sky . . . yep, there he goes. I'd hate to be up in the rafters—they're getting a beating. Why is Big Pa shifting and sweating?

I wonder what Lochsley is doing? She should be proud of my being in church today, enduring all this. What would it be like right now kissing her up on the hillside?

Mayhew's hand slammed the surface of the lectern.

"And I beseech ye brethren, folk who put on one type of face, or pretend to be doing an honest day's work in one kind of calling, and are, in fact, sneaking around behind the backs of God's people and doing clandestine things, will not be honored by God.

"Suppose a man ran a feed store and was a deacon and in church every Sunday, and he fasted and prayed daily, but then was discovered to be running a gambling operation at night in the back of his store.

"Or if he were a farmer, or even a preacher, and he was found to be selling whiskey for financial gain—yes, for filthy lucre!

"This shows perfectly the dual side of man, the side the Devil inflames and encourages.

"Satan knows that in time those base deeds will crowd out the word of God, and will ultimately lead a man to some kind of crisis, maybe a break with his family, or the law, or financial ruin. So, brothers and sisters, stir up the gifts that are in you and nurture those good and godly traits and shun those seamy inordinate affections and stay in the straight and narrow. Let us pray."

Harry wiped a bead of sweat off his forehead with his handkerchief and took his hat from the seat and fanned his face. He wondered if his opium operation would fall into the category of inordinate affections.

I've been generous with the money I've earned over the years by giving large donations to the church. Why did Mayhew preach on that anyway? Harry thought.

While the worshipers were leaving the church, the preacher said, "Good morning to you, Mr. Harry. Tell me now, did you like the sermon today?"

"Oh well, preacher, you did your usual good job," Harry mumbled.

"As a minister, I have noticed that facade with mankind and his earthly dealings, and thought it would make a good theological point. Do you agree?"

"Oh, I do, I do," Harry said, relieved. He released his handshake and turned to walk down the steps. "See you next Sunday."

Harry stopped on the bottom step to gaze over the church-yard. He stared at the rows of picnic tables to the side of the building. He thought of the fun that people had pitching horseshoes at the pits he built. He looked up at the sturdy outdoor privies partially hidden by a grove of mountain laurel. Then he admired the water pump.

Yes, he thought, it is good to have money and authority to finance things that people enjoy. I know I'm a big frog in a tiny puddle and I know this isn't center stage at the Edinburgh Symphony, but through my efforts, I've carved out a sweet existence in these mountains. If only I had Kate back. I miss my wife.

He watched Spence drink water from the pump. Polly, a new young lady, bounced down the steps to get in line for a drink of water. She boldly approached Spence and said, "Are you going to read that Bible lesson this week?" She peered into Spencer's eyes while he wiped his mouth with his shirt sleeve.

"Uh, yeah, I guess so—haven't really thought about it. You?"

"Nothing else to do in this place. Been here two days and I'm bored stiff," Polly said. She jerked her head. "What's your name?"

"Spence McAlpin."

"Pleased to meet you, Spence," Polly said, with a curtsy. "I'm Polly Chamons. Where do you live? Maybe we could study together and save some time."

"Uh, Aberdour. How 'bout you?"

"At Rose's Tavern now. Mr. Chamons—he's my daddy."

"Sure, sure. One of my grandpa's best friends. Our farm isn't far away."

"Very well then, Spence McAlpin, if you'll come over after supper Saturday night, we can study together. I like to be organized and have things done on time, don't you?"

"Sure. I guess so."

"Anytime after supper. Would seven be all right?"

"Yeah, that's fine."

Spence got in his buggy, and Fletcher flapped the horses' rumps with the reins.

"That new Chamons girl is pretty, isn't she, son?"

"Well, she's got some nerve coming all the way over to the pump just to meet someone," Mary Clay said. "You reckon boarding school makes all their girls that forward?"

"Boarding school, Mama?"

"Well, son, I was going to tell you once I learned she had arrived day before yesterday. See, Mr. Chamons used to live in Baltimore years ago. His first wife died giving birth to Polly, but he always treasured his little girl and considered her a gift from the Almighty, even though Betsy, or the former Mrs. Chamons, died bringing the gift."

"Sorry to hear that," Spence said.

"Yes, it was terrible and Chamons was crushed, but he tried to be the best father he could. After awhile, he couldn't stand living in the same house with the same friends and surroundings, so he figured he would get away from it all. That's when he moved down here."

"What did he do with Polly?"

"He gave her to Betsy's sister to raise until she became old enough to be boarded in a school of Mr. Chamon's choosing, that would teach his daughter knowledge as well as social grace.

"He got a land grant down here and farmed for a while and I understand was very good at it, but he lived like a hermit and saved every dime, that is, what he didn't send back to Maryland for Polly's education and expenses." Mary Clay watched some Meadowlarks light on the telegraph wire above. "Birds have it so easy."

"And then?"

"He met Rose at a barn dance over in Cades Cove and they married. He's waited this long before arranging to have the girl come down here. Fletcher, could you drive a little faster so I can start on dinner."

"What kind of child is she, Mary Clay?" Harry asked.

"No one knows yet, except Rose said she was about what you could expect coming from a big-city girl's school."

"And what is that?" Fletcher yelled.

"Oh, wise to the ways of the world, more grown than the children down here. She'll hate every minute of it. That's my guess."

The carriage made the turn into Aberdour and pulled in front of the small McAlpin house. Blue John was waiting on the porch so he could take the horses into the barn.

"Mrs. Mary Clay, the meat and the cornbread is about done," Blue John stated proudly. "Anything else you all want me to do?"

"No, John. Thank you very much. Just come on down after you get through in the stables and wash your hands."

"I will, ma'am." He took the lead horse by the reins.

THE SOUNDS OF hoofbeats came from a distance. Professor McGlothen cantered up the hill leaving a trail of dust.

After he dismounted, he turned and shook hands with everybody. Harry came out the front door, but not in much hurry. He was grunting and huffing and tugging at his pants and suspenders, agitated because he had to leave a soft chair in front of the fire.

"Pleased to meet you, McGlothen—nice of you to ride all the way out here. Spence tells me y'all met up in the mountains last week."

"Oh yes, Mr. McAlpin. The boy and I met while looking for ginseng. I know you're proud of him."

"Oh, we are," Mary Clay interjected. "Shall we all go inside."

As Harry turned, he saw a man's figure behind a log in the thick underbrush high above his own house farther up the hill.

Must be imagining things. Who would be watching us eat Sunday dinner? But then, who would have shot me through a window. Some cursed abolitionist probably, from up North sent down here to see if I was treating everybody right, or worse yet, somebody nosing around my opium, or . . ."

"You coming in, Daddy?" Fletcher asked, standing inside the door. "What do you see?"

"Aw, nothing, son. Thought I saw a deer on the ridge."

Blue John bounded down the hill from the riding room where he had been putting up bridles. "Time to eat, Mr. Harry?"

"Yeah, John, they're trying to get us all inside, so let's oblige 'em John. Have you seen anybody looking suspicious in the woods over the last day or so—like they're watching or maybe spying on the farm?" The two men rounded the corner of the porch.

"Nope, haven't seen anyone—everything has been going pretty smoothly. Why?"

"Just thought I saw someone behind the big house. Let's get inside and eat."

"Big Pa, you sit here at the end; Fletcher, next to him; Professor, on the right; Spence, beside the professor. Let's pray."

Mary Clay passed around the food and poured fresh apple cider.

"So, Professor, Spence tells me he has been excited about your knowledge. We've never seen him this way before. You must have made quite an impression," Harry stated.

"Well, sir, he seems to be very bright and in my opinion, one who should be encouraged to study and learn—to even go to college."

"Humph, I don't know about that," Harry said. "I firmly believe too much book learning can damned near ruin a man if he isn't careful. With all the work needed on a farm of this size, and his being the only blood kin around here, I think we could teach him about all he needs to know about planting and seasons and all. Then he could run this place and make an honest living off the land by hard work and thrift."

"But of course," McGlothen said. "Honest living—I like that—may I ask if you think my teaching and anything else other than farming should also be considered an honest living?"

"Oh, Professor," Mary Clay said, "I think it's just grand that you have such a high opinion of our son. Do you really think he could go to a college? Fletcher, don't you think it would be exciting to have our son be a college graduate?"

"Mary, the boy's only eighteen. College cost money and young people go off and study things that sound good, but won't teach 'em how to do anything," Fletcher said as he looked at Harry. "Maybe Daddy is right. We'll know when the time comes."

There was a pause in the conversation because Harry had his mouth full of corn on the cob. He swallowed forcefully. "Well, it doesn't matter much what y'all decide, I'm against all this education beyond reading, writing, and arithmetic. He needs to know how to figure the acreage and bills of sales, counting money and interest. But, even if he did want to go study, and if we were in agreement to send him, it all could come to naught, what with all this talk of secession. There could be conflict—who knows, even all-out war. I hate to hear folks talk about it, but they are. Tell me, Professor, what do you hear? What do you think?"

"Hum." He paused and threw his head up and looked pensively at the ceiling. "Now, that's a topic for you. I get *Harper's Weekly* and—by the way, do you get *Harper's?*"

"Certainly do," Fletcher stated. "Me and Pa need to know what they're thinking up North, even though our little farm isn't affected much by what goes on up there."

"Well anyway, *Harper's* loves to play up the South Carolina delegation and what a bunch of flaming state's righters they are, and what agitators they are in—"

"Well, they ought to be, by God," Harry interrupted. "All they hear from the North with their high 'n mighty industrialists is what a bunch of ignorant backwoodsmen and planters we are down here and how progressive and enlightened they all are up there. Of course, they love to buy our cotton for their textiles, and love to eat the rice from our lowlands, but then they curse to the heavens the labor we use to make it all possible."

"Yes, yes, that's true," McGlothen said. "I can see South Carolina's point, and of course those abolitionists are just as rowdy and belligerent—"

"A curse on all poxy abolitionists," Harry roared. I hate the academic bastards—uh, excuse me, Mary Clay."

"You're forgiven, Big Pa," Mary Clay whispered.

McGlothen looked at Blue John and thought, I can't figure out the relationship with Harry and the Negro. "Sounds as though you sympathize with the South," McGlothen stated, looking back toward Harry.

"Tell you what, 'fessor. John over there can answer how I feel. Coming from a Negro will make my position much more creditable, even though I don't have to prove anything to you or anybody, at least, not today, not at this table."

All eyes shifted as Blue John stopped eating, wiped his mouth, and shifted his chair back.

"Well, what Mr. Harry means is that he's sympathetic toward the South's predicament, but that doesn't mean he's ready to take up arms and fight for their position. Mr. Harry's a worldly and forward-thinking man and doesn't believe that a man should own another man like so much chattel. He and his family have been very good and fair to me and, well, you wouldn't even find a person of my race eating at the same table, or even in the same room as we're doing here, in most places in the Southern states.

"In fact, it would be the same in the North for that matter. I work for this family for fair compensation and—"

"Hell, Blue John, with your discipline and brain, you'll have more money than any of us in a few years," Harry interrupted.

"What he means, Professor McGlothen, is that I get a salary I use to buy necessities and make modest investments. I have plans for my life and I am free as a bird and can walk away from here any time I want, but it pleases me to stay here. I love the mountains, the hunting, the weather, the people. Mr. Harry just wishes the slave trade had never started and nobody would be faced with making any of those difficult decisions. Of course, he knows the problem just won't go away."

"Now, John, what do you think should be done—I mean, if you were President Buchanan?" McGlothen asked.

"Can't rightly say, sir," Blue John answered. "The country has a real problem, doesn't it?" There was a pause, then all nodded.

"No, professor, I'm naturally dead-set against slavery and bondage of any kind. Here in East Tennessee, we have small merchants, riverboat trade, and subsistance farming. Our economy doesn't run off large operations requiring large numbers of workers. Most of us don't understand the thinking of the plantation owners down in West Tennessee or the lower cotton states."

"Oh, yes, yes, of course. The people at the college are for the Union and have always had the philosophy that every man has an equal chance to work, have a family, and pursue happiness just like the constitution says," McGlothen said. "But I'll tell you this much. If a conflict were to come along, it would wreck the economy down here; I know a lot of people who do business up North. They would loath the mess war would present."

"Fletcher, pass that plate of cornbread down this way," Harry asked. "Let us hope that this discussion is nothing more than mere academics and nothing serious will ever come to pass."

There was silence as everyone at the table realized what a war might bring to their valley, to their fields, to Aberdour. To another state, yes. To another city or town, certainly. But to think of horses, cannons, and men moving over their own pastures and fields was sobering.

"Well, hummph!" Harry cleared his throat. "Professor, you've been asking all the questions, how 'bout telling us how you would vote."

"Oh, well, you see, I'm afraid my mind is concerned with bionomial theory, cosines, logarithms, ontogeny, and pnyla. . . not politics. In fact my hero is Linneaus, instead of Senator Douglas or that Lincoln fellow." He paused and sighed.

"Oh, come, come now, my good man," Harry interrupted. "I know all that interests you, but surely you have an opinion on how the country is going and what you like or dislike about it. Don't tell me you just sequester yourself off in you little cubicle and ponder sine waves and such."

"And how do you know about sine waves, Mr. McAlpin, may I ask? You said you were against higher education."

"I studied music theory years ago at Edinborough."

"Oh, my, from Scotland, eh? My parents were from there."

"Really?" Spence asked. "Big Pa, I'd bet you and the professor might know some of the same people. Where were you from sir?"

Harry tugged at his collar and a bead of sweat came to his temple.

"Spence, I told you I was born in New Hampshire, and I have only been to Scotland one time. It is a place with large family clans, seps, and infustions of Saxons, Norse, and Irish, so I'm afraid there would be no way we would know if we had folks in common. Besides, I was young when I left years ago." The professor paused. "Now my father still has business contacts in Edinborough and Glasgow. What was your father's name, Mr. McAlpin?"

"Excuse me, gentlemen," Mary Clay interrupted cautiously, "the apple cobbler is hot on the stove and needs eating. Let me take your plates." She quickly left her chair, her long dress fanning the air.

Both McGlothen and McAlpin's head lowered; they knew the conversation was over for now. Harry was grateful.

Chapter Seven

CHAMONS CRANED HIS HEAD in Uncle Wade's direction, "Wade, you got the pit ready for the fight?"

"Yes, sir. She's all ready—swept out and tidy. Got some chairs 'round. When we starting?" Uncle Wade had been Chamon's steward for years, along with Wade's wife, Aunt Jessie.

"Soon as this lunch crowd is gone. One of my night guests has a pair of Irish Gilders we kept out back of the smokehouse, they'resupposed to be unbeatable. Can't wait to get 'em in the main," F.L. said. "Wade, just keep on serving and they'll leave soon. Probably start 'bout 2:30."

Inside Rose's Tavern, twenty people had eaten Sunday dinner. There was one long table where Chamons and his family sat, along with seven others, sometimes special guests, sometimes not. No liquor was served on Sunday. That is, not until after dark and in the drinking room in the back, so respectable folks, who at least outwardly scorned whiskey and brandy, could bring in their children after church and not have to worry about the young people becoming tainted.

The Chamons, their ten-year-old daughter, Becky, and the lively Polly, had finished eating.

"Mother Rose," Polly asked, "how old is Reverend Mayhew?'

"Lord, I don't rightly know, child," her stepmother said. "Why on earth would it matter?" She turned to her husband, "F.L., how old is Reverend Mayhew?"

"Goodness Rose, don't rightly know. Maybe twenty-three, twenty-four. Harry hired him a couple of years out of school," Chamons said.

"He's mighty elegant looking for a preacher. I can't wait until next Sunday. I've heard some of the older girls in Baltimore talk about older men." Polly rolled her eyes.

Chamons was thinking about the cockfight.

"Polly, if you're through with your cobbler, why don't you get your Bible and go out back and study those lessons. I've just about had enough of your boy-talk."

"Well, if that's what you want me to do, I'll just have to do it, that's all."

"Hey, wait a minute, Polly," Becky yelled. "Wait for me."

The two half sisters took wide steps through the kitchen door and slammed it behind them, continued out into the grassy backyard and into the living quarters sixty feet away.

They stomped up the stairs to the second floor and pounced on the bed. Polly put her chin on her fists and her elbows on the bed and fumed.

"I just hate it when people do me that way. It isn't fair. They just don't understand. I have feelings like everyone else. I know girls at school who were married when they were sixteen, and that's what I am . . . and down here, where are all the boys?"

"Polly, I'm sorry," Becky whispered. "You begin school next week. Maybe there'll be some handsome boys over there."

"Well, maybe, but then maybe not. Don't they ever have any dances down here? I'll probably not meet anybody and grow up to be an old maid, and then where will I be? Lonely, fat, gray, and an old hag." She began to cry.

Becky scooted sideways across the straw mattress to comfort her new sister. She put her arm around Polly's slumped shoulders.

"Polly, now don't say that. Somebody as cute and pretty as you are—you'll meet the right man one of these days."

"What do you know?" Polly blurted out. She jumped off the bed. "You're just a little girl with big front teeth and I bet you haven't even been out of this county, much less to a big city. Oh, I'm beginning to hate it down here." She picked up a locket from the nightstand.

"I tried to comfort you, Polly, and you bit my head off in return. You're not being very nice to me." Becky rose from the bed and started toward the door.

"No, wait, Becky. I'm sorry about what I said. You were only trying to make me feel better, and I guess—I know I hurt your feelings and you didn't deserve it. Please stay and talk. I apologize for what I said and . . . and how I said it. Can you forgive me?"

Becky sniffed her nose and wiped her eyes with her sleeve. "I forgive you," she whispered.

"Thank you. Becky, have you seen this little gold locket Daddy gave me? He sent it while I was at school when I was twelve. Isn't it pretty?" She fastened the chain behind her neck and spun around.

"Oh, Polly, it's beautiful. May I look at it?" Becky stepped forward and examined the gold heart. "Wonder where Dad got it? Maybe he'll get me something like that when I'm twelve, but—"

"But, nothing! You're his daughter, same as I am. Of course he will get you pretty things. I love the two dolls that he bought you last year."

"I hope so," Becky said. "I want to grow up to be just like you."

"Well, I still have a lot to learn: get the right man, build a house, maybe have horses, and then of course, babies. Do you know where babies come from, Becky?"

"No. 'Course not. Do you?"

"Sure, I know all about it. We used to talk about it back at school in the dark, after the headmistress turned out the lights."

"Oh, tell me, tell me."

"Listen, I will one of these days. You may be too young now, but I will, I promise. Speaking of having a lot to learn, I need to start studying those verses Reverend Mayhew gave us."

"Polly. Tell me about babies now."

"No, not now. I wish I had never mentioned it." Polly's mind was already on the verses. She could change directions as often as a clock ticks. "Unless you want to learn this too, give me some privacy, for maybe an hour. Come back up and we'll talk more. OK?"

"All right. One hour, but I still want you to tell me where—"

"Don't worry. I said I would."

POLLY HAD BEEN sitting for an hour in a straight-back cane chair studying her Old Testament lesson. She had been sitting beside the room's only window where the light was strong. Her mind drifted from the scriptures and her eyes were glazed with fatigue. She stared at the yellow pine walls. She took off her locket and laid it beside the kerosene lamp standing on the nightstand.

I am thankful Mother Rose went to the trouble to make these curtains, Polly thought, those yellow and red roses are nice. Didn't she say she ordered the material from Cincinnati?

Good to finish 2 Samuel. Better than I thought it would be. I'll memorize some verses tomorrow.

The low October sun was casting shadows from the hemlock and beech trees outside her window. She laid her Bible back on her pillow and got up from her chair. She stretched, yawned, and peered out the window.

"Oh, my God!" Below her, in the yard, were at least forty men in a circle waving their hands and shouting; slapping each other's backs, and focusing their attention on activity in some sort of ring.

"Becky! Becky, are you down there?"

"Yes, what do you want? I was taking a nap on the rug. Do you want me up there?"

"Yes, I want you up here—right now—hurry!" Polly screamed.

Becky tromped up the stairs, still in a daze.

"Becky, quickly, what are they doing down there?" Polly asked without turning from the window.

"Cockfighting. You haven't seen it? They do it every Sunday—at least in the fall. Don't do it much in the winter."

"I have never seen anything like that, ever. Look at that white bird lunge at the red one—it has it by the neck."

Blood was visible on the red one's neck, but the white one began to thrust and shake its head, not relinquishing its grip. The powerful legs of the white were digging into the loose dirt as it pushed the red against the wall of the pit. Now the girls could hear the roar of the crowd through the window and walls of the room. Cold chills traveled up and down Polly's spine. She gasped as she watched the white give several shakes of his head while the neck of the red was still in its grasp.

Suddenly a man jumped into the pit with arms outstretched and pulled the white bird off the red. The legs and spurs of the white were still pumping, but the owner was careful to hold the bird away from his own body.

Another man slowly entered the pit and bent down to pick up the lifeless body. Some of the men watched him, as he climbed out and made his way through the crowd into the area where the buggies and horses were parked.

Then, all eyes saw the somber figure of Reverend Mayhew riding slowly toward them.

One by one, the men in the crowd stopped their loud talking and betting and turned to watch the minister approach.

"Uh oh!" Polly said softly.

"Polly, what do you think he wants?" Becky asked.

"I don't know. Lord, don't let him look up here and see me," Polly prayed. The two quickly kneeled on the floor and peeked over the window sill. "Becky, how do you get this window open?"

"Like this." She pulled the latch and nudged open the window. "Whew, that breeze feels good. I've never noticed preachers outside the church."

"Oh, Becky. Something bad is going to happen."

Just look at Finas Mayhew sitting straight as a poker in that saddle, Polly thought. How refined he looks in that black suit and hat. Wonder how he looks striped down with no shirt—maybe chopping wood and sweating . . .

"Gentlemen!" Mayhew said. He tipped his hat. "Ah, Mr. Chamons, what do we have here?"

"Reverend Mayhew, to what do we owe this pleasure? My friends and I were . . . I mean these men were just testing some of these chickens to see who could raise the best ones. Nobody meant any harm." Chamons thought, how dare you ride in here and call me down. I own this land—you broke up a beautiful fighting main. Pompous preacher!

"Don't you remember inviting me to supper tonight? One day last week. Thought I'd come out a little early and visit a spell—didn't know I would run into this, this abomination unto the Lord. I know full well what you're doing and you know it's against the law?"

"Shoot, Reverend!" Chamons looked down and dug at the dirt with his boot. "Lots of men higher'n you pursue this sport: Andy Jackson for one."

"Andrew Jackson is dead," Mayhew yelled.

One by one, the men in the crowd began to walk away.

Chamons watched the men leave. You caught me this time, preacher man, Chamons thought. You're also tougher than I thought. But before sundown, you may mature even more after I get through with you.

"Reverend, why don't we go inside and have tea and then supper. Might as well end the day on a cordial note, don't you think?"

"Thank you, sir. I believe I shall," Mayhew said, dismounting.

"Uncle Wade," Chamons yelled toward the smokehouse.

"Yes, sir!" Uncle Wade poked his head out the door.

"Take the reverend's horse over to the stable and care for him."

"Yes, sir, governor," snapped Wade.

Chamons and Mayhew walked into the side door to the dining room.

Upstairs, Polly was still staring at the scene, still trancelike. Her fingernail nervously played with her teeth.

"Did you see what he just did?" Polly said, talking to no one in particular. "That preacher just broke down that whole bunch of men. He stopped all that betting and all that animal cruelty—and did you see how he stood firm on the top of that horse? Now, that was brave."

"Were you talking to me?" Becky asked.

OTHER THAN THE two men, the dining room was empty. The faint smell of cigar smoke lingered from the lunch crowd, but the feelings between the two men became less onerous. They exchanged pleasantries.

I've got to keep after him—another volley just to keep him on the defensive, Chamons thought.

"How do you like it down here in these mountains, Reverend? You've been here for—what—almost a year, haven't you?"

"Ah yes, Mr. Chamons, almost a year." Mayhew drummed his fingers on the table. "Having a pastorate is not at all what I envisioned it to be. I guess I thought the Lord's hand would gently be placed in the minds and hearts of God-fearing, church-going people."

"You find that it's not?"

"Well, no. Not exactly. I mean . . . it seems that people need to be pushed more than I thought—almost as if they enter God's house only as a token of decency rather than with that white-hot desire to learn the scriptures and use them for their lives."

Chamons reached into his vest pocket and pulled out a cigar.

"You having a tough time motivating your people, are you?"

"Frankly, yes. Don't get me wrong, Big Pistol Presbyterian has been good to me. Even the pay isn't bad. It's a good place for a man right out of school to begin his life's work."

"Now, Reverend, you're not using our congregation as a stepping stone for a big city church, are you?"

"No, no, sir. Nothing like that. I'm quite happy here. I think one learns more about his field from that first job than he does at later positions. I've learned a lot on this one. Sometimes more than I can find comforting."

The kitchen door swung open as Aunt Jessie bounded through it carrying a silver tray with two cups of steaming tea.

"Good day, Reverend. Have you been talking to the Lord today?"

"Why yes, Jessie, I have, as a matter of fact."

"Me too!" she said, and turned to hurry back into the kitchen.

"Anyway, preacher, as we were saying—I believe we were talking about motivation and your not finding much comfort in your job."

"Yes."

"I can tell you, Reverend, you ain't going to find a lot of comfort around here. You must get used to discomfort, disappointment, gossip—you'll probably even be the brunt of people's jokes and slurs.

"They'll talk about you meanlike, but when they get sick or hurt and are lying in bed aching and retching, I tell you they will expect you to be right there by their side while they pretend they're living at the foot of the Cross."

"Yes, I know," Mayhew agreed. "When it happens, I retire to my cabin and pray for those people who malign me."

"And?"

"Sometimes I feel better and sometimes I don't, but at least the bitterness is gone. I just turn it over and it's His problem."

"That's well and good," Chamons remarked, "but sooner or later you're going to have to learn to fight and be mentally tough and defuse those people. Then you can go and pray for 'em."

"But that would be putting me on their level," Mayhew argued.

"Reverend, get your tea and let's walk outside. You need to learn some things."

The two men got up to walk out of the dining room, their shoes sounding loudly on the oak floors. As they walked out the back door, the aroma of a late-blooming tea olive bush smelled sweet and succulent. Their boots popped the fallen fruits from a persimmon tree.

What would the preacher think if he knew I had $5,000 of gold bullion buried under that bush? Chamons thought. He isn't real. Chamons turned and walked past his house until they came to the Little River.

"Look west, sir. Do you see the swinging bridge?" Chamons asked.

"Yes, sir."

"Now look over there across the road—those stables, the silo, the henhouse. Now look over all that land, the barns, and the crops."

Keep going, he thought. Don't let him reply.

"What you see is what motivates me. It's economic security. How men go about getting it varies with the person and where he happens to be positioned in life at the time.

"But for us down here living with the brutality of the wilderness, and with nothing else to rely on except one's own mind and hands, and those of his family, land is the answer. Can you think of other motivations, like love and sex?" Chamons stated. "Those things inspire men to move on their personal initiative. They make us do a great deal more than is expected. Now what do you think?"

"Horrible," the preacher said. "Blatant humanism. Animalism I say—"

"I'm not through yet . . ."

"There's more?"

"Many others, like self-expression. Things like art, writing, music, engineering, teaching, medicine—any number of things that are gifts from the Almighty. Then, the freedom to move around from place to place; the freedom to create, to think, to speak one's convictions. Finally, there's revenge, life after death, and fear, which should appeal to you because they're so obviously scriptural."

"Scriptural?"

"Sure," Chamons responded. "Faith and fear cannot exist in the same heart."

"Yes, yes, that's right." Mayhew snapped off the top of a red staghorn sumac bush. "Enough! Where did you learn all those lofty facts? And where did you learn so much about the Good Book?"

"I learned those 'lofty facts' from observation, reading the Book myself, and . . . talking to Reverend Stonington."

"Who is he?"

Chamons became pensive. He looked out at the splotches of blue asters and green amaranth along the road.

"Who was he?" Chamons said. "He was the man who preceded you. He was retired here by the Synod after being in a larger church in Roanoke. Brilliant soul, he was. We spent many a night beside my fireplace discussing life and how strange it was."

"What happened?"

"Couldn't hold his liquor."

Mayhew drew in a gasp audible to Chamons.

"See, Stonington was a man of deep conviction, but one who had a worldly side as well. Unfortunately, with his family background and the pressures of a larger church, John Barleycorn entangled him and he never found freedom. They sent him down here to finish out his life with a little peace and dignity. Great friend and teacher, but never understood by our people. Perhaps he was too deep for the mountain people and their primitive hellfire and brimstone."

"Are you trying to tell me something?"

"Look! Why don't you preach simple, basic sermons. Be a friend of your flock; visit them more and help them with chores—harvesting and planting. They'll love you for it. Who knows? You might even find a woman someday. Life is hard down here without help and love."

"You think I should warm up more to people? Is that right?"

"That's right, especially McAlpin. Listen, I know where you're coming from. I know McAlpin paid your way through school and is subsidizing your salary here. If I were you, I wouldn't preach sermons that hit him too close."

"Meaning?"

"Meaning the one like you preached this morning."

"But that was strictly a stock sermon, not meaning to—"

"Did you see Harry sweating and squirming? Many of us have little businesses on the side other than his raising millet and my running a tavern. That's nobody's business, not even yours, and since the long arm of the law doesn't often extend into these mountains, there are few pursuits considered illegal, or even 'devilish' as you put it."

Chamons removed his boot from the fence rail and turned to cross the road and head to the tavern.

"These little deals are just ways we feed those basic instincts I talked about—maybe you should stay out of the way."

A graceful brown and tan pair of foxhounds ran from around the back of the tavern to meet Chamons. He patted them both. "Ahhh, look at those dogs, Reverend. I'll always know that at least two spirits love me."

Mayhew paid no attention to the loping animals. "You won't tell anyone will you?"

"About what?"

"About McAlpin subsidizing me and all."

"No, of course not. But what difference would it make?"

"Well, it might undermine my authority to the congregation."

"Still worried about your authority, aren't you?"

They reached the door of the tavern. Darkness was falling fast on the valley. The smell of food wafted through the dining room. Uncle Wade and Aunt Jessie had supper ready.

"Look, Reverend, your daddy worked under McAlpin on the docks in Boston. I know you're grateful for what McAlpin did for you, but I'd guess you're resentful—that you will always be in his debt."

"Could be."

"Then listen to your own motives."

"How?" Mayhew pleaded.

"Ask God."

Chapter Eight

THE BLAST FROM SPENCE'S muzzle-loaded rifle abruptly broke the afternoon solitude. The noise echoed back and forth between the steep escarpments of the steadfast mountains. A gray-black fifty-pound turkey collapsed a hundred yards away. Feathers fluttered to the ground from the impact. Spence screamed with victory and ran into the edge of the woods where his prize lay.

Game abounded here: foxes, pheasants, quail, eagles, hawks, falcons, bears, possums, raccoons, squirrels, deer, grouse, and turkeys.

McAlpin and McGlothen sat on their horses atop a bare knoll watching the action. Foxhounds stood at bay between the two. The dogs were there for the exercise since they weren't needed for turkey hunting. But what was needed was deadly aim, ability to use the homemade reed to simulate their call, and patience.

"He's a damn good shot, Professor. Going to be a fine hunter that boy," Harry said. He reached for a cigar. "I've worked with him since he was eight. But I've got to give his daddy credit for teaching him accuracy—well, that is, 'till Fletcher got the shakes, then I worked more with him.

"But still, accuracy—things like squeezing off, windage, breath control—that's what bags 'em.

"I'm impressed. My daddy was a good shot. Never had time for it myself," McGlothen said.

"See, I'm training him in practical things. The rest of that stuff is useless. He doesn't need Homer and Linneaus."

Spence rode toward the men and held the bird high.

McGlothen scratched his nose and sighed. "Mr. McAlpin, there's something I don't understand."

"What's that?" Harry asked, his closed teeth held the cheroot.

"It's none of my business, but since we were discussing education at the table, and since the boy is showing an interest in it, why in the world would you want to hold him back? Anyone can tell he worships you. Why are you interested in only those basics you talked about? There's time for that too."

Harry thought about the time limit on the contract Forbes had drawn years before and how it allowed that after twenty years, the whole opium operation had to be passed down to one heir, to be voted upon by the stockholders and Forbes himself. For his part, he knew who he was grooming—no time for higher education.

"I've already told you—he won't need all the other things for what he's going to do." Harry eyed the squinty-eyed little man and perceived his thoughts. "I know you two have become pals lately, but this is family business—know what I mean? I've got plans for him that I don't care to discuss with you or anybody . . ."

"Oh, good man I did not mean to meddle, I just—"

"I know," Harry interrupted. He shifted in his saddle. "You see a spark in the boy and would like to nurture it. I understand that, I appreciate it. But you do understand?"

"Oh, yes, yes, I do," McGlothen responded. "Guess I got pushy."

"You're forgiven," McAlpin grunted. He watched Spence approach. "Good shot, son. You were still as a rock—hit him in just the right place. I'm proud of you."

"Thanks. My hands are still trembling. Is that normal?"

"Yeah, it's normal. Not everybody can bag a big one like that," McAlpin said. Turning to the professor, he asked, "Have you ever seen something shot, Professor?"

"I'm afraid not." He reached for his pocket watch. "Gentlemen, the sun is going down and I must be getting back."

"Spence, tie the turkey to the pommel and let's start in. Maybe we can get your mother to dress the thing. Blue John can help if he's through milking.

"By God, there he is again!" McAlpin shouted. The figure moved high on the ridge on the other side of the creek. He fired.

The man ducked for cover as the bullet tore through tulip popular leaves nearby. He slid down an embankment, untied his horse, mounted and rode into a dry creek bed and onto a wagon trail and disappeared.

"I want to know why somebody is watching me. That's the second time today I've seen him. Sooner or later I'll hit him."

THE THREESOME WOUND their way back to Aberdour from the meadow to the west gate of the grazing pasture. Spence jumped down and opened the gate.

Harry was the first to speak. "Professor, take a look at those Hereford cows. I love to watch 'em graze on the red clover. Went up to Kentucky in 1850 and bought my first bull and heifer from Henry Clay. Remember him?"

"Oh, how well. What a man—lawyer, statesman, even ran for president."

"Yeah, well, he imported his first Herefords from England and amassed a large herd. I wanted to be the first down here to import progeny from Clay's stock." Harry gazed lovingly at their roan bodies and white faces, chests, and undersides.

As Spence opened the gate of the second pasture, he had the same gnawing fear of the cattle that he developed when young. One of the bulls gored him in the back, and knocked him against a fence. He was always glad to click the hasp in the gate.

The fence between the pastures contained a ten-yard-long feed rack that Blue John had stocked with hay for winter feeding. Lombardy poplars were planted along the fences to provide shade from the searing summer sun. The Herefords and Red Polls had all the comforts they could want in order to get fat.

Aberdour creek tumbled rapidly down the tall slopes forming the north face of Rich Mountain. Along its banks were the ever-present flint and silver-barked sycamores interspersed with river birches and swamp privets.

As the horses made rumbling sounds crossing the wooden bridge, Spence glanced at the flowing black water with its foamy-white breakers bursting over the rounded boulders like sunlight reflecting across clouds. How many hours have I spent along that stream? thought Spence.

Once across, they traversed the dusty cuts between eighty acres of millet and milo with their brown tasseled tops. Mocking birds and partridges lived here. The clean smell of the harvested grain met their nostrils with sweet solitude. Corn grew to the left of the riders, but it was the millet and milo that Aberdour was about.

The gray barn appeared. Its use was more functional than esthetic. It was a working area and Harry never bothered to paint it. Nobody else in the area had the money or the time to paint barns, and being practical and occasionally frugal, he had decided to skip that luxury. A fenced area for the horses to roam and a riding ring for their training were behind the barn. Inside the fenced area was a rain pond. "I never wanted to fiddle with dairy breeds," Harry said. I keep those four fawn Jerseys and the Guernseys for our own milk. Imported them from the Channel Islands."

The barn had a milking room, saddle room, stalls, a corncrib, a henhouse and covered chicken pen, and a large threshing floor.

The massive granite chimney on the west wall of the big house caught the eye first. Being autumn, the stout trumpet creeper vines that covered the chimney had long since lost their funnel-like orange and red flowers, which, in hot weather, made it alive with bees and hummingbirds.

The big house that Harry and the late Kate McAlpin had built in 1854 was white clapboard Greek revival. It was two stories with double porches supported with six tall, round, and fluted Doric columns. There was a stand of white oaks behind the house with their beautiful shapes and stately trunks and fissured bark. Acorns were falling and the leaves were turning crimson as the breezes washed through the boughs. The front porch was three feet off the ground supported with brick pilings and abutted with English boxwoods. At the corners of the portico were Italian cypress; narrow, deep green, and reaching beyond the second-story porch due to cold winters and long summers in full sun. Forty feet from the steps, in the middle of the driveway turn-around was a blue spruce with its cool, crisp silvery aura, giving the place a milieu of stateliness, yet perfectly suited to the majestic environment.

The fresco above the capitols of the columns extended the width of the house. There were no gables in the roof.

"Professor, I see you're looking at that roof. Never did like gables. I know most houses like this should have them, but I consider them useless. Reminds me of some of the affectations I saw when I lived in New England," Harry said.

"Yeah. They sure like 'em up there. They don't serve much purpose unless the family is so large, one has to bunk them in the attic," McGlothen said.

"Don't pay attention to the grass either. My wife used to keep it all nice and neat—beds of zinnias, marigolds, dahlias. But we don't have time now. Blue John turns loose the goats and lets them graze out there. Satisfies everybody."

When the trio reached the front of the house, Spence said a quick farewell as he turned to lug his prize turkey down to the little house.

"Professor, he won't be young much longer," Harry said. "The thoughts of a war make me sick. Think about it, that fine boy could be gunned down and his dreams snuffed out as fast as the morning sun withers the grass."

"Aye, 'tis true. So sad, so sad. Well, Mr. McAlpin, daylight is fading and I'd better be getting on toward Maryville. School has begun and I need to prepare a recitation for tomorrow. It's been a distinct pleasure meeting you and your family." He leaned over and shook hands with Harry. "Hope I didn't push too hard about the boy's education, sir."

"Take no mind of it," Harry said, relieved to be getting rid of this intrusion in what would have been a peaceful Sunday.

Chapter Nine

MAUD PERKINS STARED AT the leaded Waterford glass holding the 1851 Clos De Vougeot.

She gazed at her ecru-colored chimney piece from the Adams period with its sienna marble panels and center fresco of Diana—seated with dog and bow. In her remembering, she thought of the time when she had bought the statuary at Litchfield's on the corner of Bruton and Bond Street, London. She had just learned her husband had been killed at the Battle of San Jacinto, so she had gone on a buying spree.

She remained in Maryville and watched the United States grow and unfold. She got her news from *Harper's*, the Boston Globe, and local gossip. Maud read, tended flowers, and taught piano to the handful of children whose parents believed music important for upbringing.

Her personal fortune continued to grow, although no one knew it except Forbes, her nephew in Boston. The little house on College Street with its white clapboard and black shutters looked no different from any other in her neighborhood, until one looked inside. She had artfully assembled world-class finery about which she could detail the craftsman's history and the period through which he worked. This was no affectation, no pompous vainglory; it was her sweet spot, her heartthrob, her good pleasure.

There was a tap on the door.

She slowly arose and opened the door. "Hello Clint." She bent forward and kissed him gently. "You look a little tired from the ride."

"I'm fine. A wee bit weary, but fine. How are you?"

"I've had a wonderful day, but first things first. I've opened a nine-year-old bottle of Vougeot and it's about perfect. Let me pour you a glass."

"Thank you, my dear," McGlothen said as he took off his riding coat and hung it on the old English coatrack.

She poured the wine the proper one inch from the rim so the nascent vapors played enticingly back and forth above the nectar.

"Ahh, delicious," McGlothen said, after the fruity liquid rolled by his palate. "Now, Maud, where did this one come from?" They took their seats facing each other on matching mahogany Hogarth chairs with their claw-and-ball Chippendale legs.

"I'm glad you like it, Clint. This comes from a vineyard in the Côte de Nuits area in the larger Côte d'Or region of Burgundy. We've discussed this region before. The soil is rich in iron and it's chalky and rocky. The hills take their name from the burnished gold appearance they present in the late fall when the leaves fall off the vine and the ground is exposed. It means golden slope. This bottle has all the right color, body, bouquet—just an infinite grace."

"I agree," he said.

"Legend says that after the Little Corporal Napoleon became emperor, he heard of the excellent wines made at Vougeot. He sent word to one Dom Gobelet, the last clerical cellar master prior to the French Revolution, that it would please him to taste these superlative wines. Guess what Gobelet replied, Clint?"

"What, Maud?"

"He said, 'If he is that curious, then let him come here to my house and taste it.'"

They both laughed at the temerity of the Cistercian monk.

"All right, enough history for now. I always enjoy your conversation," McGlothen said. He poured another glass.

She told him she had gone to the Baptist church that morning and had taken a long walk in the woods after lunch.

"Now, Maud, you better be careful. If those Baptists ever get wind of your love for wine, they're liable to excommunicate you and sentence you to eternal hellfire."

"Oh, I know that, Clint, but what they don't know will not hurt them one bit, and you know how private I am and how few people so much as see the interior of this house, much less know what I do in my personal life."

After dinner and a glass of Amontillado sherry, the two were again seated and talking.

"What did you think of your visit to your new friend's house? What's the family name?" Maud asked. She coyly pretended she knew nothing of the McAlpins.

"McAlpin, and the farm is Aberdour. Oh, it was an interesting day all right. The mother is pretty and has ambition for her son. His daddy has a limp and I think a stroke or something because he doesn't seem quite right. Anyway, he doesn't say much. It's the big granddaddy who is the peacock.

"Says he couldn't be bothered with higher education for the boy; that all he needs is knowledge to grow grain—got irritated at me for pushing the matter. Of course, I could see he was serious, so before I rode away, I apologized for digging deeper than the old man thought I should."

"So, Clint, what can you do about it? And why are you so interested in the boy in the first place?"

"He's a nice lad, a handsome lad, who I think has potential that I hate to see wasted. Besides, I'm in the business of recognizing potential, don't you think? There is too much wealth there for it to have been made on some grains."

"Really? What makes you say that?"

He told her about the huge house and barn, the pastures with the cattle, the fine horses, and the land. "Oh my, the vastness of land."

While he spoke, Maud thought of the fourteen years she had been a silent partner of McAlpin, Storch, and Chamons, and the many reports she had sent on to her nephew in Boston. Yes, she thought, they've done very well. For the most part, they have been civil to one another and I'm glad to have procured the land previously so they could buy it back, thanks to my nephew's brains, acumen, and ruthlessness. Yes, it took somebody like Forbes to keep them straight—subdued, if you will.

But, what is he getting at? Maud thought. After all these years, I don't want an outsider to mess things up. Especially someone I care for. Don't want any conflict. Not now.

"The hour is late, Maud, and I really must be going." He thanked her for the wine and the ham and they said farewells.

He mounted his horse, and looked at the house, expecting to see Maud blowing out the lamps. Instead, he thought he saw her at her desk writing a letter. It was hard to be sure, since it was dark and sheers were drawn across the windows.

SATURDAY NIGHT, SPENCE rode down to Chamon's house to study Bible lessons with Polly. Mr. Chamon's was in the tavern mingling with his customers and Rose was supervising the cooking. Spence and Polly were in the house behind the tavern seated at the table.

Spence became sleepy studying the trials and tribulations of David in the book of 1 Samuel until he felt Polly's leg touch his during their discussion of Abigail and Nabel. He couldn't help being impressed with how bright Polly was.

But the soft glow of her cheeks, the warmth of her golden hair, and the enticing cleft in her chin impressed him too. His heart skipped when he felt her hand on his thigh as she leaned forward to make a point in the story. He could only stammer in agreement as she pointed out what they needed to know.

"Uh, Polly, I think my brain can take no more of this Bible stuff. I'm tired."

"Oh, I'm sorry," Polly said. "I guess we have studied enough."

Just doesn't seem fitting, Spence thought, to be studying the Good Book and thinking of carnal things.

"Yeah, guess I best be getting home." He got up, stretched, yawned, and awkwardly gathered his belongings.

"I'll walk you to your horse." She held his arm all the way to the hitching post. "Good night, Spence."

"Night, Polly. Thanks for your help." Should he have tried to kiss her? Hold her? Bet she's disappointed, he thought.

"See you tomorrow," she yelled. He turned his horse and rode away.

Spence tossed and turned in bed most of the night.

ALTHOUGH THERE WERE winds from the northeast and steady rain, the McAlpin family loaded the buggy and went to Sunday school and church.

Reverend Mayhew was glad that all but two of his pupils had their King James Bibles with them when they took their seats along the back pews of the church.

After a halfhearted attempt to sing "Faith of Our Fathers" a cappella, the group got down to the serious business of discussing 1 Samuel. After questions and discussions on the parting of David and Jonathan, David saving Keilah from Philistines, Saul pursuing Dave, it then came Polly's turn to comment on the story. Polly accurately and crisply related it. Spence felt smug since he felt he was responsible for Polly's good performance. This euphoria was short lived.

"Excuse me class—Polly, keep going—I'm stepping out back for a minute," Mayhew said. The class was silent.

"Is he out of earshot?" Polly asked one of the boys.

The boy looked out the window. "He's almost to the outhouse."

"Good. I want to tell all you children about another fact in the story. Do you know how many times the words 'piss or pisseth' are mentioned in the Old Testament? She paused and waited. There was stoned silence, then some shuffling of feet, and then some snickers.

"Eight times. Right here in this story, twenty-fifth chapter, twenty-second verse: . . .to him by the morning light any that pisseth against the wall. Then—"

"Polly, maybe you had better stop," Spence suggested. By now, the naughty side of the children reacted in unabated enjoyment and laughter.

Polly continued, "Then in 1 Kings 16:11 . . . 'drinking himself drunk and Zimri smote him and left not one of the house of Baashe that pi—'"

"Polly—Oh Lord, help her to shut up," Spence pleaded.

"Polly, I believe that was just an expression among Hebrews for males and just got translated from the old English that way," Mayhew shouted. He had slipped in by another door and was greeted by the growing bedlam. "It just means no males would be left alive, and would you please sit down young lady!"

Polly fell backward onto the bench and smiled in victory.

"You, you woman-child of sixteen have just desecrated the Lord's house with vile thoughts and language. And at the same time you have displayed an apparent godly gift of magnificent recall ability."

"We tried to get her to stop," yelled the boy beside the window.

"If only your talent could be turned toward the positive, Polly, why, did you wreak havoc in my church?"

Mayhew spun around. His face was crimson and the veins in his neck stood out.

"Class is over." He stumbled out the door past two girls and headed toward the water pump.

"Lord, have mercy on them all and please help me to remember the sermon Thou hast given to preach in forty minutes."

Chapter Ten

By DAWN MONDAY, BLUE John had the wagons loaded for their trip to meet Thick Neck Wehner in Cincinnati. The rain had stopped, but the weather was cold and raw. Spence brought two sacks of hot bricks to warm their feet.

"When can I expect you three back?" Mary Clay yelled.

"We'll get to Covington Tuesday, ferry the Ohio, then . . ." Harry paused. "We're driving the wagons back, so expect us first of next week."

"Be careful, and don't worry about a thing. I'll see that the stock gets fed while you are gone," Fletcher yelled. He thought, you old impudent sod. I hate your maggot-infested opium powder and all the wealth it has brought to you and not me. I deserve my share. Fletcher saw Orvil Lee hiding in the shadows by the barn. I'll go talk to him after Papa leaves. Maybe my dad has something to worry about, after all.

The wagons pulled out of Aberdour. Harry had to get to Knoxville to catch the 3:15 P.M. to Lexington. They took the mountain road to Wear's Cove; then onto the Sevierville Pike into Knoxville in time for a late lunch at a boarding house near the depot.

The train was only twenty minutes late. The men boarded once the wagons were loaded in freight cars. As the train reached traveling speed, in the remaining afternoon light, Spence saw wild and rugged terrain where only bear and cougar felt at home. Darkness came at half past five. A porter came around and lit the lamps in the passenger cars.

Harry made his usual glance to see if anyone was paying any undue attention to his Negro foreman. Two card games had commenced along with idle chatter and cigar smoking. He looked across the aisle at Spence. He leaned over and mumbled something to Blue John.

"I am interested in seeing how this daughter has turned out now that she is coming of age. Her beginning is some story. I wonder if Johanna has been told."

"Told what, Mr. Harry?" Blue John asked.

"You mean I never told you? Well, Thick Neck sowed some wild oats when he worked on the docks in Boston. You know, Olga is not much to look at and Thick Neck was pretty strapping in those days. His playing around caught up with him one day when the baby, Johanna, was left on his back porch. A note from his mistress was attached that pleaded for the baby's life. After many bitter fights with Olga, she agreed to take in the beautiful blue-eyed bundle. How would you like that for a predicament?"

Spence heard only a few scattered words over the roar and the clacking of the train. ". . .Thick Neck's daughter . . . new experience . . ." He couldn't hear the rest. Blue John laughed.

Despite his excitement, Spence slumped in his seat and fell asleep. He awoke as the train pulled into Lexington and the sun was rising.

"Hurry! Off-load those wagons, feed and water the horses, then put 'em all in boxcars on the feeder train. Leaves in ten minutes for Covington," Harry yelled.

Harry walked to the window, rented two boxcars, and went toward Blue John. "We're riding with the car carrying the single wagon—saves money. No need to buy tickets in passenger. Only takes three hours. Shouldn't be so cold that we can't stand it."

"I'm freezing," Spence said.

"Lie down there. We'll all cuddle against the horses' belly. Spread that blanket over us, John."

Spence saw through a crack in the siding that there were no evergreens up there. The leaves had fallen from the deciduous trees on the rolling landscape. The fields were empty save for a few corn stalks left for silage. Snow was on the ground. The barrenness gave him a naked feeling. At least back in Tuckaleechee there was greenery scattered among the drab hardwoods.

"Covington in five minutes," Harry yelled.

They off-loaded the horses and wagons. Blue John took Spence to the end of the depot to view the giant expanse before him.

"That's it, man," Blue John said with reverence. "The mighty Ohio . . . and it don't stop 'till it gets to New Orleans. Thrills me every time I see it. Over there is the Queen City, Cincinnati."

HARRY WASTED NO time ordering Blue John and Spence to get the wagons down to the landing to board the ferry.

"He always knows what to do," Spence said.

"That he does," Blue John replied. "He has wisdom and pride in what he does. Comes from those years of studying and thinking. Gives a man authority."

"Maybe I can be like him some day."

"You will, you will. Work hard, study, and do what he says.

Bet you didn't know he sent a telegram from Lexington to
Mr. Wehner letting him know when we'll cross the river."

"No, I didn't."

"Your granddaddy works in strange ways sometimes, but
he thinks ahead; doesn't tell people what he's doing either.
Now Spence, look yonder. Probably twenty-five steamboats at
the landing. They make them boats right here—got all the
passengers and produce they can handle. Cincinnati merchants do business all over the United States."

"And, Blue John, look at the church steeples. I can see
nine from here. Makes our little steeple at Big Pistol look
puny. When will we meet Thick Neck?"

"In a moment—he's on that dock somewhere. But you
call him Mr. Wehner. Nice man, unlike the German we know
back home. When we stay at his house, you'll feel as if you're
in another country. All the people in that section speak German, eat German food, and drink German beer. They love
their festivals, too."

The ferry approached the landing. Over forty people were
waiting beside buggies and wagons. The ferry driver expertly
nosed the craft into the moorings with only a gentle bump.
Colored dockhands ran to secure the boat with ropes.

"Grundig!" Harry yelled. He bounded from the quarter-
deck.

Greetings were made and within minutes the Tennesseans and their wagons were following Wehner in his buggy up
the hill.

"There's the granary. Corner of Third and Sycamore—in
the heart of it all. Look south, you can still see the river."

Wehner motioned Harry to follow his carriage around the
back of the building. Wehner got out and opened the nine-
foot-wide door. The wagons entered into a large packed-
earth area inside.

"Fellows, move those wagons all the way to the back wall— get your baggage and put them on my carriage," Wehner yelled. "Albert will take care of the horses. Tomorrow, we'll take care of business. Let's get home now. Olga has been cooking all day."

A large black man came out of nowhere and began tying reins to posts, and filling feed troughs with oats.

After they left the granary, the carriage headed west. It crossed the Miami canal. Wehner was busy instructing Spence.

"The canal flows north and empties into Lake Erie at Toledo. We send and receive cargo via that route.

"Spence, now we're entering the Over-the-Rhine section. Most of us Germans who came here in the '30s live over here."

Grundig Wehner's house was one of a dozen row houses of four stories. It had heavy oak doors and upper-level flower boxes. His street was Unter den Linden Strasse complete with thirty-foot linden trees planted down the middle of the double lanes. Parallel to that was Leipziger Strasse, then Friedrichstrasse, both named for streets in Berlin. There were flower stalls, beer gardens, and smaller shops reflecting German life and trade.

The carriage parked under a covered enclosure and the foursome walked around to the front of the house and through the door.

"Olga, here's Harry and Blue John. I don't think you know this fine-looking young man. Meet Spencer McAlpin from Tennessee. Spence, this is my wife, Olga."

"Pleased to meet you, ma'am," Spence said, in his best manners.

"Good to meet you too," Olga replied in guttural English. She turned and yelled up the stairs. "Johanna, kommen sie hierein, schnell!"

Spence heard soft footsteps coming down the steps. She bounded into the room and captured his attention immediately. She wore a long medium-gray dress hemmed in red, a white blouse with puffed shoulders—everything perfectly starched. Long blond hair and blue eyes, her skin was flawless. His heart beat rapidly like the time with Lochsley.

"Spencer, this is Johanna."

She says it so smoothly. Yoh-hahn-ah! Spence thought.

"Johanna, this is Spencer McAlpin."

"Nice to meet you," she said, giving a half curtsey.

Harry winked at Thick Neck.

After a supper of pork, sauerkraut, noodles, and bread, Thick Neck, Harry, and Blue John announced they were going down the street to the tavern.

"Olga, let the young people go to the drawing room and get acquainted while you wash the dishes. We'll be back in a little while."

Johanna looked at Spence and beckoned him to follow her upstairs.

Her dress made a swishing sound reminding Spence of prissy cleanliness. Once on the second floor, they sat on the love seat.

She told him of Stephen Foster and how he wrote "Oh Susannah" in Cincinnati, how John James Audubon had lived up on East Third Street, and how keelboats plied the river until only a few years ago 'till they gave way to steamboats. She described the Vista as being the first steamer built in the Queen City, but that the Natchez was faster.

"Spence, in earlier days, pigs would roam the streets, and from the pigs came soap and candle making. Poor pigs," Johanna said.

They laughed.

"Farmers up and down the river had no way to get their corn to market, so they fed it to their hogs and sent them into town, so we had a pork industry. I love that, don't you?"

"Yeah. Funny."

"Someone got the idea that the salted pork needed to be shipped, so the barrel business began. Hides from cattle produced shoes, harnesses, and saddles. After that, wagon makers, carriages . . ."

"Business is booming in this city," Spence commented.

Olga brought each of them a glass of white Mosel wine.

"Spence, a man named Nicholas Longsworth owned the land on Mount Adams, east of downtown. He encouraged the German immigrants to help him grow grapes up there." Johanna said. "In time, Cincinnati became the wine center of the whole country."

"This is another world. Am I living a dream?" Spence said under his breath.

And aren't there any dumb females? Spence asked himself. Seems like I'm always around smart ones.

Johanna's hand touched his arm. "Spence, I'm sleepy. If you don't mind, I'll show you where you'll sleep. Third floor."

"Where do you sleep, Johanna? I mean, how many floors does this house have? What I meant was . . ."

"I know what you meant. We sleep on the forth floor. My brothers slept on the third, but they're gone now. Work at Mr. Longstreet's winery. Now we use that floor for company. Come on."

THE SNOW WAS falling outside Boarshead Tavern. Inside, a big fire raged. Most patrons were German-Americans, some of whom had only been in the country a year or two. Beer was brought to the tables in large pitchers by aproned barmaids. Jovial and loud was the mood. At a round table in the corner, there came a chorus of "Du, Du, Ich mir im Herzen."

Harry, Thick Neck, and Blue John sat drinking. They laughed, joked, and stared into the fireplace, their eyes glazed.

"Now Grundig, what's the recent scuttlebutt about secession?"

Grundig leaned forward, snapping the mood like a knife. "It doesn't look good, Harry. The folk here are scared on the one hand and mad and aroused on the other."

"What do you mean by that?" Blue John asked.

"They're scared they will be invaded and punished for their part of the Underground Railroad," Wehner answered.

"Underground Railroad?" Harry asked.

"A system, Harry. Gets the slaves out of the South to places in the North or Canada. It's neither underground nor a railroad, but its activities are conducted in secrecy and railroad terms are used to conduct the system.

"Your beloved friends, the abolitionists and philanthropists are the ones behind it. Then too, the Quakers have contributed. It's done a lot to arouse Northern sympathy for the lot of the slaves. Cincinnati is one of the funnel points. Then there's Harriet Beecher—"

"Who?" Blue John asked.

"Harriet Beecher Stowe, my boy. Brazen old wench." Wehner stopped long enough to guzzle down the remaining beer in his glass. "She wrote *Uncle Tom's Cabin*. Lived here years ago while her daddy has head of Lane Theological. The book is hotter than ever here, Harry. She went to England and was damned near lionized. That is, until she wrote about their precious Lord Byron and his incestuous love for his sister, then the English turned on her."

There was an exhausted silence as each man finished another glass.

"Harry, if hostilities ever break out, I think we can still get our opium down the Erie, but I just don't know about New Orleans and the Mississippi route. We'll all have to work harder. On the other hand, armies need morphine and laudanum. We might get filthy rich."

"Grundig, sounds like you've been using your devious German brain," Harry said.

SPENCE AWAKENED AND washed his face from the basin beside the bed. He pulled on his clothes and went downstairs. "Good morning, Spence. The men have already eaten and have gone down to the granary," Johanna said. "After breakfast, I'm to take you around the city to see the sights."

"That'll be fine," Spence mumbled, rubbing his eyes. "Is it cold outside?"

"It's not bad, twenty-five degrees, but the snow has stopped. If we bundle up good, I think we can stay warm in the buggy."

Afterwards, Spence took the reins behind the one horse and Johanna began giving directions. They toured along Lower Broadway south of Fourth Street and viewed the city's most fashionable residential area. Then they went by the Pike Opera House, which had just opened the previous year. "That's where the men will go tonight to see the play Martha. Over there is the Burnet House Hotel. The London News called it the finest hotel in the world," Johanna said.

"Stop the buggy a minute," Johanna continued. "There is the beautiful Saint Peter in Chains Cathedral. I think the steeple goes over two hundred feet up. Across Sycamore Street is the Plum Street Jewish Temple. We call them the Twin Towers. Not too many places in the world where you'll find Jews and Catholics worshipping across the street from each another."

"I don't know a thing about the Jews and Catholics."

"Now the building beside the cathedral is Saint Xavier College. Behind it is the medical school." There was a pause. "Spence, have you ever thought about becoming a doctor?"

"Not really. My granddaddy doesn't even want me to go to college. Says outside of arithmetic and business, the rest of the knowledge is rubbish."

"Rubbish? For what reason? And just what does he want for you?"

"To run Aberdour I guess," Spence replied, his voice trailing off in tone and conviction.

Spence felt Johanna move closer to him. She put her hands under the flap of his coat and came to rest on his leg. She leaned over and lightly laid her head on his shoulder.

"Well, maybe you should think about making yourself into something besides a farmer—like maybe a doctor—and you may even want to think about coming up here to medical school."

The freshness and warmth of her breath against his ear felt good.

Spence started the horse moving. "Who knows? That's awhile away. I must first get through Coker Hill."

"Coker Hill? Is that your school?"

"Yeah."

"What's it like?"

I knew she was going to ask that. Why is my education so important lately? thought Spence.

"Aw, it's a one-room building up in this draw at the end of the cove—run by Baptists. Has a potbellied stove sitting in the middle of the floor and a chalkboard—"

"I just love to hear you talk, Spencer. It's so cute." She wiggled even closer and kissed him on the cheek and giggled. "I could listen to you all day. Is that the way everyone talks there?"

"Yeah, I reckon 'bout everybody talks like I do." This attention feels good. "Some say that forms of Old English was trapped in our hollows a century ago and never left. Elizabethan, I think they call it."

"Well, I love it." There was a pause. "Spence, would you like me to show you the granary. Your granddaddy and Blue

John will be doing business in the front office and you don't want to miss the part where all the work takes place." By now, the couple was holding hands under the blanket. Each could feel the other's warmth, despite the temperature.

"Sure, Johanna, just tell me how to get there." He tried to conceal his breathing, but knew he couldn't. At an intersection, he stopped the buggy to let another carriage pass. He rolled his head to look down at Johanna and met, instead of her eyes, her lips. What is happening here? I get the feeling she has things planned.

They rounded the corner of Third and Sycamore and pulled the buggy through the door in the back of the granary.

"Tie the horse to the rail and I'll show you the upper stories first." They got out, but before they took two steps, Johanna said, "Why don't you take that blanket."

He grabbed the patchwork quilt in one hand and reached out for Johanna's hand with the other. He did notice Big Pa's wagons where Albert had put them the night before. It was late in the afternoon and the workers had gone home. He saw Wehner's head through the glass in a closed door up front. He hoped they would be doing business a long time.

"Shhh! I don't know where Albert is," Johanna whispered. "No need to arouse his attention. Come on up these stairs."

They walked up the wide stairs with their arms around each other. On the second floor, they maneuvered around feed sacks and climbed the second flight of stairs. They were both breathing hard. There was an overwhelming aroma of grain, some loose in bins and some in course feed sacks. It was a pleasant, clean smell. When they reached the third floor, Johanna pulled him to an isolated area. Feed sacks were everywhere, some stacked on one another six feet high.

Johanna reached and put her arms around him. Their lips met and held. Her knees buckled and her body sagged.

He followed her and they collapsed on feed sacks filled with millet. Neither was interested in reading the labels, but they did notice the sacks gave way and conformed to every bodily contour.

"Pull the blanket up," she whispered. Their hands explored. She began to undo her buttons. In no time, they savored their youth; lips parting and tongues touching, flicking and playing. They explored, caressed, and teased. The quivering of excitement took his breath away. Johanna made soft sounds while bodies billowed with the rhythm of the ages. Joy was riveted into orbits of a higher plain. In the crescendo, the explosion hit both with such force that spots came before their closed eyes.

Time ceased as Spence explored this new world. The soft skin and those enticing breasts. Five minutes of speechless interlude passed. Then they heard the noise. Startled, both peered around the edge of the blanket. Albert, the steward, was plodding the steps from the floor above. They looked at each other.

"Could he have seen us?"

As the paddleboat ferry pulled away from the dock, the two McAlpins and Blue John waved to Thick Neck, still standing beside his buggy.

"Did ye have a good time, me boy?" Blue John asked.

"Oh yeah, John, I feel like I've learned much—I'll never forget this trip."

Chapter Eleven

Upon reaching the Kentucky side, the drive to Lexington was long and grueling. Since each man had a wagon to drive, Spence had no one to talk to and it was difficult to stay awake. The cold weather didn't help either.

In Lexington, they saw banners and signs hanging out of windows and on the front of buildings admonishing citizens to vote for the Union or to vote to secede from the Union. It was unsettling and a reminder that the nation had a problem to solve, and the rumblings and debates were getting louder and more frequent.

They spent the night at a stand, or tavern, at the Cumberland Gap, a hiatus in the mountains between Kentucky, Tennessee, and Virginia.

Later the next day they stopped for water. Harry was talkative.

"Spence, you must set your goals and go after what you want. There are always people out there who are always after you and your money. Every man owes it to himself and his family to never be poor. Don't depend on somebody else to support you and always keep something laid back, like cash or gold. It's a terrible thing to depend on the results of a coming crop to determine whether your family goes hungry or not. Do you understand what I'm talking about?"

"Yes sir, I think so."

"Blue John, tie that team to the back of your wagon and let Spence ride with me for a while. We need to talk," Harry said.

Blue John nodded.

"Spence, I've been doing a lot of thinking. You know what I told your Mama about my being against formal education for you—anyway, I've changed my mind. I think that after you finish this term at Coker Hill, you should go over to the college. Maybe McGlothen is right. Get started on a higher education. Personally, I think fighting is going to break out and for some reason, it might pay to be in school, although no one can be sure. How would you like that?"

"I would like that," rubbing his hands together to keep warm. "Will Mama and Papa agree?"

"Aye! Your folks will be pleased you're going to get more learning."

Harry reached into his vest pocket and got a cigar.

"You've been everything an old man would want in a grandson. You're kind, tough, smart, and you're blood. You're all I've got, except Fletcher."

The wagon jolted on while the two rode in silence. The sun was going down and wetness in the cold air made their bones shiver. Spence looked to the brown mountains ahead punctuated by an opening. "What's that?"

"Sharp's Gap. When we get through that cut, we'll have only six miles 'till Knoxville. We'll spend the night, and be in Aberdour tomorrow afternoon."

"I'll sleep well tonight," Spence said.

A mile or so from the gap, Spence noticed smoke lazily drifting upwards, but said nothing as he thought it was nothing more than hunters. "Big Pa, how do you like your Le Mat?"

"Oh, son, that is one fine pistol, I tell you." The wagons kept slowly trudging onward. "Here, look it over, but be careful, it's loaded."

Spence felt the cold metal on his hands and rotated the object slowly, inspecting every detail. He looked at the underside and saw the swivel lanyard ring in the butt, the spur on the trigger guard, the octagonal barrel with a cartouche engraved in the metal with the letters L and M enclosed. Following this was the number 24. He counted nine cylinders that rotated around a second, central barrel—a barrel that fires a .63-caliber grape shot much like a single-barrel shotgun. The one hammer takes care of both barrels just by shifting the hammernose up or down.

"What do the markings mean?"

"The L and M letters mean the patent was given to my old friend, Colonel Jean Alexander Le Mat, who invented the thing. The number means it was the twenty-fourth to be made under the patent."

"When we get to that clearing up yonder, we'll stop for a minute and you can try it. Here, take my holster and bullet belt and fit it to your waist. I've got my carbine. Never like to go without being armed. One never knows when some idiot might—"

A shot rang out from the hillside and splintered the upright board inches from Harry's arm. The horses went into a fury and reared up before they sprinted forward. Masked men came down the hill in twos toward the group.

Blue John and Harry had rehearsed many times what to do in the event of an attack on their wagons. They had drawn on paper the pattern of the wagon's positions if there was one in a trailing situation with no driver. Harry pulled his lead wagon to the left, away from the second wagon, then to the right back to the third, forming a protective triangle.

The riders were whooping and shooting. The pairs split. Harry shoved Spence onto the ground between the wagons, shouting and cursing. Blue John rolled off his seat onto the ground and was returning fire.

Spence saw one of the attackers in a blue coat jump onto the horses of the third wagon. He looked at Blue John, then realized he had Harry's pistol. He jumped, ran three steps, aimed and fired. He had no idea which way the hammernose was positioned. He found out. The recoil of both shots almost took away his right arm from his body, and spun him around. He heard a dull thud, even amidst the yelling and shouting.

He jerked his head to see the man in the blue coat, twisted and bent, lying on the cold earth, his face blown off.

"I've killed a man, I've killed a man, I've killed . . ." He stared at the smoking pistol. Rage came over him. Instincts took over. He began firing, skillfully dodging and weaving behind wagon wheels, then falling and rolling to the ground until his nine shots were spent.

Then he saw him. A second man in a long black coat and kerchief jumped on the horse tied to the second wagon. A move that had cost one man his life already. Spence's heart pounded; he sweated despite the November chill, but he loved this fearless emotion. He bolted forward.

Four skips and he left the ground to land on the back of the man in black. Spence grabbed his neck and locked up a vice grip. The man was shifting, cursing and yelling, trying to throw the boy. Finally, the elbow of the man in black found Spence's stomach, making him almost pass out with pain and shock. Spence lost his grip. The man held his gun in his left hand, and seeing his advantage, he slammed it into Spence's temple, knocking him unconscious.

❖ ❖ ❖

THE FIRST IMAGE he saw was his grandfather's face bending over him. His mind raced back to when the Storch boys beat him so unmercifully.

"Wake up son, wake up. Are you all right? Say something," Harry begged.

"What happened?"

"Never mind that now. Take a little nip of brandy. Blue John and I are all right."

Harry tilted the bottle to Spence's quivering lips. He exhaled deeply and saw darkness again for a few more seconds before opening his eyes.

"Where are they? The men? Did they take anything? Spence felt the soft, swollen tissue of his throbbing temple. He brought his hand down and peered at the congealed blood.

"You'll mend fine, boy, but you're mama ain't going to like this one bit. I'll have hell to pay, but it'll pass. What won't pass so easily is the loss of my wagon. Damn bushwhackers! How did they know we would be coming through on this day and at this time?" He choked and tears welled in his eyes. He looked at Blue John. "How are we going to explain this to Chamons?"

John was mute, but then said, "Somebody told 'em. What are they going to do with the wagon?"

Harry arose and spread out his arms to the heavens and paced the ground aimlessly. "Oh, I'll tell you what they're going to do. They'll get good and drunk tonight with my whisky. They'll be sitting around some campfire drunk and gloating about their victory over me and what I stand for. Oh, I can't stand it, Blue John," he bellowed.

Harry twisted away; he wanted to be alone in his agony. Then he turned and faced the other two.

"I'll tell you this much. It cost 'em. It cost them two lives. Spence, you got one of them. With my Le Mat no less. I'm proud."

"Mr. Harry, what are we going to do with those dead 'uns?"
Harry walked over and stared at the body. He spat on it.
"Bury the bastards."

THE SUN WAS setting over Aberdour when Spence awakened.
Harry and Blue John had driven the wagons all night to reach
home. Spence's head wound had been cleansed and dressed
and he had been given the mandatory laudanum dose, and
put straight to bed.

Mary Clay quietly peered into the boy's room and saw that
his eyes were open. "Spence, are you all right?"

"Throbs a little, but mainly I'm hungry."

"Oh, I just hate it when things like this happen to you,"
Mary Clay said. She reached down and caressed his forehead.
"If you weren't so tough, you would be dead by now. Tough
as a hickory nut hull. Now, one more tablespoon of medicine
and then some hot chicken soup that I cooked. Then it's
back to bed."

"Did anything particular happen while we were gone?"

"No, not really, except . . ." Mary Clay looked up at the
ceiling as if she were thinking. "At church last Sunday, Polly
asked me if you could come to the square dance?"

"That would be fine," Spence said. He slid down under
the covers.

"Open your mouth and take the laudanum."

As the medicine took effect, Spencer closed his eyes and
exhaled heavily. "Anything else interesting?"

Mary Clay paused and thought. "Oh yes, I almost forgot.
There's a letter downstairs to you. Who do you know in
Sneedville?"

Spence opened one eye. "Sneedville what?"

"Sneedville, Tennessee, of course. Isn't that near where
you and Big Pa went last month?"

Spence sat up in bed. "Where is it?"

"Just a minute, I'll get it. I'll need to light your lamp. I'll bring up your soup." She tiptoed to the kitchen. In no time, she was arranging a wooden serving tray holding a soup bowl on Spence's lap. She lit the lamp and handed him the letter.

"Thank you, Mama."

"Call out if you need anything."

Spence tore open the envelope with its two-cent stamp and begun to read.

> Dear Spencer,
>
> Thank you for coming to see me last month. Nothing of interest has happened except that Daddy has visitors every week. They go down to the barn and, as he says, do business. Sometimes he gets in the wagon and goes on trips for a night or two at a time.
>
> You will be glad to know the hens are laying a lot and the rooster that flogged you so badly is behaving himself. Daddy says he is going to send me to Porter Academy in Maryville for the short term in the spring. I've been asking questions about the stone. Getting interesting answers. Must go now and milk. Why don't you write me.
>
> Your humble servant,
>
> Lochsley

Despite the medicine, Spence had a difficult time drifting off to sleep. *Of all the good fortune, I get an invitation to a dance with Polly, and a letter from Lochsley. Life is picking up.*

"I'LL BE A mother-lovin' son of an Irishman—you mean to tell me they got the whole sodden wagon? And it full of our whisky and opium? Jesus Almighty Christ!" Chamons bellowed. He picked up a rock from the ground and threw it across the river in disgust. He took another sip of Scotch.

"Now, now, F.L., don't let it give you apoplexy," Harry said. "I know I was fit-to-be-tied, but looking back, we're lucky to even be alive. Those men were shooting to kill, I tell you."

"You mean they were hiding on Sharp's Gap waiting for you to come along? Did you recognize anybody? How 'bout those two you killed—ever see them before?" asked Chamons.

"They were wearing kerchiefs, F.L."

Chamons paced back and forth in his shirt sleeves in the late afternoon winter air, impervious to the temperature. "How in hell would they know you all were coming along on that day—and at that time in the afternoon?"

"I just don't know, F.L., but they knew what they were doing, and . . ." Harry stopped talking and yelling as if a light went off in his head. "Come to think of it . . . yeah, it's true."

"What's true?"

"It was as . . . as if they were shooting for Blue John or me, but any one of them could have shot Spence several times, but didn't. One of them paid dearly for that. It was as if they had been forewarned not to harm Spence."

"Interesting, Harry."

"Of course, Spence wouldn't agree, seeing's how he's wearing the print of one of 'em's pistol on his face."

"Then that settles it," Chamons said. He flung another rock across the river.

"Settles what?"

"Harry, it was an inside job. Somebody who knows us or even works for us planned the raid. They had enough decency not to shoot an eighteen-year-old boy. Here's another possibility. Whoever informed them as to dates and times cares about the lad and didn't want him harmed. That person insisted on that in exchange for his squealing. No doubt the informer had his palms greased in addition to obtaining the looter's promise of protection."

Chamons stopped ranting and was holding his glass in deep contemplation, staring at the river while the raging water made its timeless, indifferent course northwestward to join the Tennessee thirty miles away.

"Sounds logical, but what were they after?" Harry asked. "Do you think it was the whisky? Would they kill over a few jugs of liquor?"

"Shoot, Harry, you know men have killed for far less than that. But you have a point. It wouldn't surprise me if it was the powder. Someone had to know it was aboard."

"Yeah, yeah, I know."

"Harry, we must be careful. Furthermore, we need to think far beyond that lawless bunch. Who put them up to it? There is more to this than meets the eye.

"And remember, you and I must keep perfectly quiet—as if nothing went wrong, nothing was stolen, and that you returned from a trip as if nothing had happened," Chamons warned.

"F.L., listen! Remember my telling you about the letter that Widow Perkins wrote some weeks ago from Maryville?"

Chamons nodded.

"It was to tell me that the professor at the college had paid her a visit after he had spent that Sunday at Aberdour. She warned me that he was inquisitive and couldn't figure out why I was so wealthy by growing corn and millet. McGlothen's his name and Spence thinks he is wonderful. Could he be a suspect?"

"Anybody could be the culprit. We'll watch every little thing, like a fox. One of these days, they'll overplay their hand and we'll be there."

"Huh! I just hope they don't kill us first while they're overplaying their hand," Harry said.

"I'm getting cold and my glass is empty. Let's go inside."

The two men turned and headed into the tavern. Chamons put his arm around Harry. "Does a man good to blow off steam now and then, doesn't it old friend?"

"Yeah, you're right," Harry drawled. "I'm looking forward to the dance. I should be able to cut a fast jig, now that my dander is up."

"Yeah, I've hired fine pickers and fiddlers for that purpose."

THE DREARY RAW winter of 1860 saw the nation spiraling deeper into conflict over slavery and the states rights question. Among the people of Tuckaleechee Cove, activities slowed. Milking and cooking still had to be done, tools had to be sharpened and repaired, and firewood had to be cut and stacked.

"You still like to fool around with that 'hog ball,' don't you boy?" Blue John asked.

"Since I was little," Spence replied. He kicked the ball against the side of the barn.

"Think about it, Blue John—blow up some poor animal's urinary bladder, tie it off, and we have a ball. Amazing!"

"Sho' is. But it should be perfect hunting tonight. Had that cold snap, and now we're about forty degrees—with a good moon. You ready, son?" Blue John asked.

"Yeah, I'm ready, so is my Airedale. Let me get Daddy."

"Make sure he has his pint. That way, you'll get in more shooting."

An hour later, Blue John, Fletcher, and Spence sat by a roaring fire along Middle Prong Creek that flows down Meigs Mountain, east of Tuckaleechee. The dogs were out in the night—working the possum. Their unique bark and howl would signal that a possum was treed. Fletcher had his bottle, so all three were having a good time.

"Mr. Fletcher, how you going to go if'n war comes?"

"Hate to think of it, John. From all the talk, a war would split these coves wide open like a burnt chestnut. Neighbor will hate neighbor and families will be divided, but there are more Unionists up here than there are Secessionists.

"Most of them have no use for them lazy planters down yonder in South Georgia and South Carolina with all their slave help. We believe in killing our own meat, cutting our wood, building our own houses, making our clothes, picking our own berries."

"Yes, but . . ." Blue John tried to interrupt.

"Everything we do, we do with our own family, or with our neighbors right up until they lower us in the ground."

"Yes, sir, but if war came tomorrow, which way would you go?"

"Why, John, I'd go the Union way, no doubt about it."

"What about Mr. Harry? What do you think he'll do?"

"Oh my, I don't know what to say about Daddy." Fletcher turned the bottle up for another swig. His tongue was getting loose and the hour was getting late. "He has his own mind about everything and he is stubborn. If I could guess, he would be a Secessionist if he couldn't stay neutral."

"Why would he do that?" Blue John asked. He drew little patterns in the dirt with his boots, and watched the fire flicker on his brown face.

"He hates the idea of a bunch of politicians in a distant place making rules for everyone in the country. I tell you this, he loves the Southern politicians like nobody I've seen. Says they have guts and insight, and can charm the horns right off a billy goat."

"Shhh, listen to the dogs," Spence said. "They may have treed something." There was hushed silence. For over a minute, nobody spoke, their heads cocked and listening.

"Naw! False alarm," Fletcher said loudly.

The older men talked more and even got Spence to talk about his school and his lady friends. They noticed him blushing, even in the faint light of the campfire.

Thirty yards away, sinister eyes watched the three men in their conversation. Eight men drew guns as they sat erect in the saddles, their coats buttoned high and their hats pulled over their eyes. One of the men motioned the others forward. They began firing and shouting as they plummeted down through the fallen leaves and thick underbrush toward the startled hunters.

Quickly surrounded, Spence thought, my God, everywhere I go, men are coming out of nowhere trying to get at me. What have I done to them?

"Well now, what kind of party do we have here?" the leader asked, snarling. "You boys doing a little huntin'?" All the men had guns pointed at the three hunters.

"Yassir, we're jus' trying to get a few possums, sir," Blue John stammered.

"Quiet, nigger, I ain't talking to you. You there!" He nodded at Fletcher, holding his bottle. "What you got to say?"

"Like he said, we're hunting. Any law against that?"

"Listen to that, boys, we got us a smart 'un there. You that boy's daddy? You ain't setting a very good example—drinking that whisky and all. Why don't you just hand me up that bottle."

Fletcher put the bottle in his coat. Seven pistols cocked.

The leader spurred his horse to move closer to Fletcher. The man took his leg out of the stirrup and kicked Fletcher in the chest, sending him falling over a log. Blue John took a step and three of the men pointed their pistols at him with arms extended.

Blue John froze and looked toward Spence.

"Daddy, get up from there and hand me that bottle like I told you," the leader teased.

Fletcher pulled himself up slowly, holding his chest. He handed over the bottle.

"Now then, that's better." He turned the bottle up. "Ahhh! good bourbon. Makes a man warm on a cold night, right, boys? "In case you're wondering, me and the boys here have been doing our rounds of the settlers up here on Meigs, just to see how they're voting. We want to make sure everyone is Union Blue." There was a pause. The man took another drink. "It's to your advantage too, see! You don't want no secessionists bothering you, now do you?" Another pause. "Well, do you?"

Fletcher, John, and Spence looked at one another. "No!"

"Good. Good," the man said. "You see, we've been listening to you talking around the campfire. Daddy there, I know how he stands, and I reckon the boy feels the same way, and the darkie there, I know how he had better feel, if'n he likes living."

Spence felt his anger swell. He knew Blue John was furious and was considering lunging for his carbine. But he knew Blue John realized this was no time for heroics. They were beaten. Fletcher was too drunk to care, one way or the other.

"Well, it's late men. Why don't you hunters head right back down the Prong and go home. By the way, who was that Mr. Harry you were talking about? The one who loved Southern politicians?"

"Harry McAlpin," Blue John said.

"Where does he live?" the leader asked, taking another drink.

"Aberdour Farm. Down in Tuckaleechee."

"I'll remember that. Now get on your horses and head out."

"Hey, what about the dogs?" Fletcher slurred, waving his hands.

"Damn your god-cursing dogs," the leader shouted. "If'n they can't find their own way home, they're not much punkin', now, are they? Oh yeah, I'll relieve you of those two possums."

On the trail home, Fletcher fell off his horse. Spence rode double and held onto his daddy while his own horse trailed behind.

When they arrived at the house, Blue John and Spence made a clatter trying to get Fletcher on the porch and through the door. Mary Clay came into the front room carrying a kerosene lamp.

"What's the matter? What . . . what happened? My Lord, is he all right?"

"Yes'um, I think he'll be up and around in the morning," Blue John said. "He had a pretty rough time up there."

"Like what?" Mary Clay asked. "Spence, honey, are you—"

"Yes, ma'am, I'm fine. Just mad. Let's get Daddy to bed and then we'll talk, but not for long. I'm worn out."

They carried him into the bedroom and laid him on the bed.

Mary Clay put down the lamp and began to pace in front of the fireplace. "Now you two sit down and tell me what happened?"

Spence and Blue John related the story, painful as it was. John excused himself and left for his room in the big house.

"Mama, what's the matter with Daddy? I'm worried about his drinking. Has he always done that?"

Mary Clay reached and pushed the hair out of her son's eyes and stroked his temples. "Spence, Spence!" she whispered. "One of these days you'll understand—I'll tell you one day."

"No, Mama, I must know now. Tell me."

"Oh, very well, guess now's as good a time as ever. You see, your pa was born with a limp. The doctors in Boston said nothing could be done about it. Even though Fletcher was muscular and comely to look at, he despised his affliction. Harry didn't help either—always criticizing Fletcher, always wondering out loud whether it was Kate or him who had passed on the trait. Sometimes he would accuse God of punishing him for certain things that happened in Scotland a long time ago.

"When they moved to Tennessee, your dad grew to be a fine-looking man—a person who captured my heart. He worked hard, went to church, and provided the best he could for me. Well, let me say that differently, he provided according to what Harry would pay us." Tears streamed down Mary Clay's cheeks.

"Look at this magnificent land. Look up there at that big house, the livestock, the crops, wealth everywhere."

"Won't you and Dad get it all when Big Pa is gone?" Spence asked.

"We'll have ample provisions, Spence, but no, we won't get it all. There's much about Aberdour you don't know, can't know. Not just yet. Maybe never. The ownership is complicated and I don't want to go into that tonight, but if your grandfather would allow his own blood a chance to run Aberdour, then that would be fair, but he won't. Never will. Your father has been made to feel he is only half a man. It has affected his thinking, his health, and now . . ." Her voice faded.

"I can't finish—I just can't." She was crying.

"Mama? Please?"

"No. Another time, maybe. Leave me along." She turned to dry her eyes. Silence. "I'm sorry son that I spoke to you that way. Go to bed now. Tomorrow will be another day."

Chapter Twelve

Fʟᴇᴛᴄʜᴇʀ ѕᴛᴏᴘᴘᴇᴅ ᴛʜᴇ ᴡᴀɢᴏɴ in front of Rose's Tavern and let everybody climb out before he drove the team to a cedar tree for hitching. Spence saw Polly look his way as he entered the tavern. The tables and chairs were moved from the dining hall leaving room for the band and dancers. Corn stalks and pumpkins decorated the corners. Liquor jugs and apple cider were on a table.

Uncle Wade and Aunt Jessie had prepared an ample supply of breads and other dainties to satiate hungry appetites.

Spence beamed when Polly showed proper concern over his bruised face.

F. L. Chamons halted the festivities by stopping the band and holding up his hands until the crowd was silenced.

"Ladies and gentlemen, welcome to the annual Cove Harvest Dance. In the light of recent tension between sections of our great country, tonight is special. Rose and I order you to talk no politics tonight, but rather to eat, drink, and enjoy yourselves. May I introduce the band? All the way from Galax, Virginia, come the 'Mountain Ramblers.' They'll play Irish

jigs, Scottish ballads, Old English one steps, and mountain fa-
vorites you know and love. They may take a request or two, so
have fun."

A cheer rose from the crowd as the band lit into "Chilly
Winds" that featured a poker-faced boy of twenty who had a
flowing, three-fingered claw style on the five-string banjo. His
nimble fingers danced up and down the fretboard. The crowd
stood, sipped, and listened. After he finished to the roar of the
crowd, a guitar player in a checkered shirt stepped to the front.

"Thank you. That was E. P. Herndon on the banjo. May I
introduce the rest of the band? We are from Galax, passing
through here on a goodwill tour to nurture respect for our
glorious heritage; to honor our Norman-Saxon lineage, and
preserve our way of life, the way of our forefathers." That
said, he introduced the others. Only moderate applause came
from the crowd.

Spence saw Orvil Lee in the darkest corner standing with
another man whom he didn't know. He tried to get close
enough to hear them. Orvil cut his eyes toward Willis, from
the Storch farm—momentarily blank—then a smile broke
across his face.

"They ain't nothing but a bunch of secessionists trying to
whip-up support," Willis whispered. Orvil nodded and began
to clap.

After an hour, the band took a short break. Polly and
Spence had danced feverishly. She looked him in the eye as
if she was searching for something. He wondered who she
was looking for? Maybe nobody. She put her hand on his
arm, whispered in his ear, "Spence, get your coat, but don't
make a to-do about it. I want you to see something."

Shortly the two of them were in the night air walking toward
the barn. Inside, it was quiet and dark. The animals were silent
in their stalls; the smell of hay was strong but welcome.

"Good to get away from all those people," Spence said.

Polly lit a lantern and took Spence's hand to lead him to an isolated corner stall.

"Get down and brush the hay from that spot." She pointed.

He looked at her, then bent over, felt the hard wood of a secret door counter sunk in the packed dirt of the barn floor. He opened the door, took the lantern from Polly, and started down. After ten steps down on a ladder, he hit the level floor of a room.

The room was dry and the temperature seemed constant. The lantern cast light on multiple shelves holding curious brown bags stacked on one another. Two tables held chemical makings: flasks, burners, mortar and pestle, water jugs, measuring spoons, and glass bottles. A hole in one of the sacks exposed a brownish-white powder.

"How did you find this place, Polly?"

"Stepped on the door while grooming a horse last week."

"What is that powder?"

He didn't wait for Polly's answer; he put some of the powder in a spoon and tasted it. He grimaced. Then he turned to inspect the other items in the room. Soon, the warm glow hit.

"Polly, taste that. I feel so good, and I promise you I haven't been dipping into the bourbon."

The two of them were soon as giddy and flighty as two June bugs on a summer night. Inhibitions gone, Spence and Polly embraced, warm and tender, then more intense.

Polly twisted away. "Let's get out of here and go up to the stall."

Guilt and caution to the winds, Spence thought. God has no doubt made me gifted with the girls. He turned, grabbed the lantern and led Polly up the stairs. The door was closed and the straw replaced.

He knelt on the ground and drew Polly to him. As in Cincinnati, he and another were passionately exploring . . . Then the winds of good fortune changed their capricious direction. Polly tore away and jumped to her feet.

"I'm attracted to you, but Spence, back there a few minutes ago, I realized something."

"Yeah, what?"

"There's someone else."

"Someone else? Now's a fine time to tell me."

"I know. But only now did I realize it fully."

"So, who is it? And anyway, couldn't we have a little fun together, tonight? You've got years and years to settle on one man."

"It's Reverend Mayhew," Polly said firmly.

"Mayhew? Ha!" He broke into a rolling laughter.

"That's the wildest thing I ever heard. He's too old for you and after the stunt you pulled in Sunday school, he wouldn't dare look your way. Pure foolishness! Anyway, what kind of preacher's wife do you think you would make?'

"I can help him. He needs someone like me. He just doesn't know it yet. But I intend to plant the seed someday that will show him why he should get a girl like I am. Someone spirited and knows what she wants and not a sweet little drippy milquetoast kind."

"Not to mention he might bring you in line—tame you. Deep down, you want him to impart some of his spirituality— something you're sorely lacking."

"I want us to be friends. Good friends. Tonight I've seen a big change in you. You seem . . . more mature, different."

Spence turned and leaned against the wall.

"Why don't you tell me about it?"

"About what, Polly?"

"About your trip to Cincinnati."

He told her the whole story about Johanna. He told her he knew God would fling down lightning and strike him dead

for such blatant sin. Then he related the story of the ambush
and how he had taken the life from another person. He went
back and told about his beating by the Storch brothers.

As they talked, each realized a new and different kind of
bond was forming between them, honest, candid, and loving. After Spence's exhausting monologue, there was silence between them. They heard the band music through
the night air.

Polly broke the reverence. "What do you really want,
Spence?"

"Polly, I might want to be a doctor—to help people. I want
money and power, and I want a girl to love me and have my
children," Spence replied.

"I want to leave this cove," said Polly. "I want a city where
there's more people. I don't share the love for the mountains as I think you do. I can see my reverend behind the
pulpit of a congregation and hundreds of parishioners are
seeking his advice for their poor miserable existence. Of
course, I'd be by his side.

"Spence, here's what we should do—there's a church over
in Wear's Cove where they speak in tongues, shout and pray,
and fall all over the floor. This is a perfect time to go."

"Not I. I've heard about those kinds of places—they scare
me. I'm just fine over at Big Pistol. Your reverend may shout
a little, but none of that other stuff."

"Oh come on," begged Polly, "it'll be sporting. We'll have
fun. Besides, we need to bare our soul. We can't do that at
Big Pistol. You need to ask God for forgiveness for your killing. We need forgiveness for our carnal lusts . . . possibly a
few other things too. Is it a date?"

"Maybe.

"Good, then it's a date. Ride over here about half past
three tomorrow. I think they get started about dark."

"Polly, you know there's a war coming?"

"We'll pray about that too," she replied. "Come on, let's get back in the house before Daddy comes looking for me."

THE SWIFTLY MOVING clouds covered the moon as rain approached. Hours after the last guest left the tavern, the last liquor drunk, and the last note sounded, a cold quietness settled over the valley.

Two figures crouched under Chamon's persimmon tree, dressed in black and wearing handkerchiefs over their faces. They walked to the window and raised it. They crawled up and over into the dining room, found the stairs and made their way to the second floor where members of the band were sleeping.

They slowly turned the knob in room four and entered. The smaller man in black cupped his hand over the one in bed while the larger man in black clicked back the hammer on his pistol and pointed it into the temple of the band's leader.

"Make one peep and I'll blow your brains through the floor," Orvil Lee said. The man's eyes were gorged with terror.

"See! Me and my friend here didn't like what you said tonight about 'the preservation of our way of life, the way of our forefathers,' during the introductions. You're making your tour to stir up the fire-eaters in our peaceful valley, a Union valley at that. Put your hands behind your back and roll on your side." He did as he was told while his hands were tied. Willis took a handkerchief and gagged the victim.

"Where's the banjo picker?" Orvil demanded, before the knot was stretched and tied tightly.

"Two doors down."

"Get up and walk real nice and quiet to his room and show me. Don't forget, one sound and you're dead."

They entered room six and found him—in a deep sleep. Orvil, holding the gun, nodded to Willis, who drew out his

Bowie knife, muffled the boy's mouth and slit his throat. Only a muffled moan commemorated the passing life force.

"You can now go and visit the 'way of your forefathers,' since that's so god-cursed important. Now you! Get on the floor and put your feet around the bedpost." He tied him around the post in a way he couldn't bang his body to awaken the others.

Orvil got down on his knees to whisper in the man's ear.

"Listen, partner, in the morning when they find you and start asking questions, you should know you're in a hotbed of Union sympathizers. We work hard in East Tennessee and got no use for the fornicating aristocracy with their big homes and fields full of slaves. If you should go into Georgia, tell 'em what happened here tonight. There's more up here like we are and we ain't going to stand for your kind. Understand?"

The man nodded and fainted. Orvil and Willis shut the door and went down the stairs. After climbing out the window, they broke a branch from the tea olive bush and brushed away their tracks.

The pair said nothing until they reached their horses. "I think our man up in Knoxville will be pleased when he finds out about what we did tonight," Willis said.

"Not half as pleased as he'll be when he sells that wagon of whisky and opium," Orvil replied. "Besides the money, think about how much medicine can be made from the opium. Why, that'll provide the medical needs of Union bushwhackers up and down these valleys for a year. Now be quiet when you slip in over at Storch's. Our work is too valuable to get caught now."

SPENCE AND POLLY rode along the east side of Bricky Branch so as not to be caught on Storch's land. Even though the path was firm and well traveled, Spence didn't relish the return trip in the black of night with Roundtop and Cove Mountain casting their pail and blocking any moonlight that would otherwise be available.

After crossing the Sevier County line, they forded a creek and headed west. After two hours, they were in sight of Clear Prong Pentecostal Prophecy Church. A dreary-looking log building with tan chinking between the logs, a square resemblance of a steeple with no bell.

"Doesn't seem fitting to not have a bell."

"I know. You seem nervous."

He didn't answer.

They tied the horses alongside the others and slowly opened the door. Services had begun. The crowd was mournfully singing "Rock of Ages." A man motioned for them to follow him to the second row.

Spence knew everyone in the house was staring at him as he and Polly slid into position. A woman behind them handed them a songbook.

What would I give to be somewhere else?

Everyone had their arms extended heavenward while they sang. Spence looked up from the songbook at Polly—then at the congregation. He hunched his shoulders down his jacket, trying to disappear. The song leader had them singing another fifteen minutes.

Polly nudged his ribs and by craning her own neck, indicated she wanted him to straighten and stand tall. The singing ended and the congregation sat down.

The preacher was bland looking with pale, sagging cheeks, hair combed backward from a high forehead. He began his delivery innocently enough, but holding his Bible in one hand, he move from one side of the congregation to the other and even up the center aisle, his voice getting louder all the time.

The audience would punctuate vital points with loud "amens." The man told the crowd he would be taking his text from two little-read books of the New Testament, the epistle to Titus, and Jude.

Polly surprised Spence when she pulled a small Bible from her dress pocket. Finally, they found Titus and began to follow the sermon. As it progressed, Spence thought that God Himself must have led them to this spot.

The preacher ranted: "For a bishop must be blameless . . . not self-willed, not soon angry, not given to wine, no striker, not given to filthy lucre; but a lover of hospitality, sober, just."

"Fletcher should hear this," Spence whispered to Polly.

"Young men likewise to be sober-minded . . . denying worldly lusts . . . for we were foolish, disobedient, deceived, serving diverse lusts and pleasures. . ."

He knows—he knows! Spence thought. Oh my, my, he's preaching straight at me. Oh, God, please get me out of here. I'll be good. I promise I won't hate the Storchs, or go near another woman. Please release me.

The preacher showed no mercy. He directed them to Jude. Spence was sweating, the air stagnant.

"For there are certain men crept in unawares . . . turning the grace of our God into lasciviousness, and denying the only Lord God . . . Even as Sodom and Gomorrah . . . giving themselves over to fornication, and going after strange flesh, despise dominion, and speak evil of dignities . . . for whom is reserved the darkness forever."

Spence dropped to his knees in a prayer of repentance.

Polly shifted in her seat, nudged him again and rolled her eyes when he looked over at her.

Spence and I are both going straight to hell and to the darkness forever, I know it, Polly thought.

"Repent! Repent, ye sinners!" the preacher said. He held a pudgy finger up toward the ceiling.

A woman began speaking in unrecognizable words that sounded like a foreign language. A titter of moaning spread over the crowd. The "amens" came when she finished. A man on the front row sprang to his feet, and with both arms extended, began speaking in his "unknown tongue."

The congregation lifted their collective voices, shouting to the rafters in a miasma of droning and wailing. Then quietness.

The preacher stood in the center aisle. "All of you who repent of your wrongdoing come to the front. Oh yes! Come on—absolve your guilt, clean your hearts and souls, my brothers and sisters. Don't wait. Do it now. Jesus is calling."

People came to the front. The preacher reached and put his hand forcefully to their foreheads. Six collapsed. Singing began. The lady beside Polly turned with a grin. "I love it when they get slain in the spirit, don't you?"

Polly smiled and nodded, then to her embarrassment, an old man placed his hand on Spence's shoulder, pushed him toward the aisle and motioned him forward.

Spence plodded to the front dragging Polly with him. The preacher put his hands on their heads and mumbled. A man in the back began a solo in tongues. The preacher interpreted what the man in back said.

"Be still and at peace, my daughter and son. I, the Lord God Jehovah Jira who created you, I, Eloheim, the Creator of the Universe, love you, and My spirit moves on your troubled hearts, and My breath is here to cast a shroud over you both and remove your shame, guilt, and sin.

"So rise up, stand tall with the covenant I made with Abraham, Moses, Isaiah. 'So magnify me. Be sanctified with the spirit of grace, peace and forgiveness that will last all the days of your life, then you can fellowship in the House of the Lord forever and ever,' so sayeth the Lord. Amen."

There was great jubilation and clapping. The preacher laid hands on Spence and Polly's head again. His eyes looked heavenly.

"Do you repent of your sins and wish the Lord's forgiveness on your poor wretched souls?"

They both nodded as best they could under the weight of the preacher's hand.

"Brother Hester, do you have a prophecy for these people?"

"Oh yes. The Lord gives this message, my son. Success and riches will be yours one day, but not in a way you would imagine and not of your own efforts. First you will go down into the realms of darkness. You'llbe doubtful and cynical of My love and grace. You will deny me. It takes faith for the miracles of my word. Then walk in the light. Remember those who help you. I am thinking of one person in particular. Do right and fight to stay alive during the trying times to come soon. So sayeth the Lord."

Again, the crowd flew into screaming and clapping. Tears flooded Spence's eyes. He was not aware the man had moved on to Polly.

"Young sister, you have strayed from the narrow path. You too will fall from My grace and then embarrass Me. But, study of My Word and your new spiritual surroundings will benefit you and you will become My servant. Remember you are my beloved child. So sayeth Yahweh."

The crowd roared and then broke into smaller groups for more prophecy.

Polly and Spence wandered out the door. They mounted their horses and walked them down the path into the night's cold darkness. The sound of Clear Prong Pentecostal Church faded in the night.

Chapter Thirteen

COKER CREEK SCHOOL WAS a one-room white clapboard school-house, that had three rippled glass windows on each side, a split wood shingled roof with a steeple on the top. A rim of red-brown dirt was always visible around the house from the rain pouring off the roof.

This January day began Reverend Mayhew's winter term, with eighteen young people in attendance. Spence was front and center, for he was always eager to learn. Today was Polly's first experience outside her boarding school. Heinreich Storch convinced Moody to attend the school but Virgil and J.D. had refused any formal schooling. Moody had previously been taught by his mother at night by fire light.

At first, Spence didn't recognize Moody until Mayhew called roll. Hearing the Storch name kindled those bad feelings toward the boy, and Spence was unsure how to act when lunch came. He and Polly sat on the same log. As Moody walked by, Spence unexpectedly offered him half his apple.

Moody's first words to Spence were, "You know that my daddy hates your granddaddy, don't you?"

"Yeah, I know something about that," Spence said. "How are your brothers?"

"Fine. This time of the year, they're fixing equipment—when they're not in the mines."

"I'll never forget those cretin brothers of yours or the time they shot my horse and beat me up."

"Listen, they are meaner than snakes. Think what it's like to live with them. I stay out of their way as much as I can. Remember, they would have killed you if it hadn't been for me."

Listen to him. Just another pompous Storch, Spence thought.

"Papa nearly killed 'em both the next day after I told him about their getting drunk and making it hard on you. Took away their pay, too." Moody looked at the girl with Spence and said, "Who are you?"

"I'm Polly Chamons, and my daddy runs Rose's Tavern."

"Well, didn't I hear you moved here from up North somewhere? Went to some fancy school, correct?"

"You heard right, if you consider Baltimore 'up North.'"

"You his girlfriend?" Moody asked. He nodded toward Spence.

"We're friends, just leave it at that. I have goals set on things, and Spence has his, and they're not necessarily the same. What are you going to do with your life, Mr. Moody Storch?"

"I don't know yet, but I want more from life than my brothers do, maybe run the farm for my dad."

"Ha! You'll be waiting a long time for that with those two older brothers in front of you. From what I hear about them, they'll not even leave enough table scraps for you." Polly broke into a laugh. "Stay in school and learn something so you can make something of yourself, since you'll be eighty years old before you get the farm."

"If that Lincoln fellow is elected, there ain't going to be anything for any of us since his Yankees are going to come down here and take it away."

Mayhew rang the bell signaling the end of lunch break. The three arose from the log and trudged inside.

For the remainder of the term, Moody was cordial enough, but distant toward Polly and Spence, except when Polly took a notion to get his dander up about something. But they all knew after April, when the term ended, they would not see each other again for a long time.

DESPITE THEIR ISOLATION, Harry made sure Aberdour received *Harper's Weekly* out of New York, as well as the *Knoxville Whig*, published by a fiery little Methodist minister, Parson William G. Brownlow, East Tennessee's most outspoken Union supporter. In the middle of a row of corn one day, Spence smirked at the thought of how much his granddaddy hated both papers. Seems he subscribed to them as a form of masochism guaranteed to work him into a furor.

Then one hot afternoon in July, a thought hit Spence. His daddy Fletcher would be Union and his granddaddy would be a Secesh. The thought chilled him in spite of the 105 temperature. His would be a divided family. Which way will I go? he wondered. He placed his hands on the slick handle of the gooseneck hoe and started down the row again. Sweat dripping and feet hurting, he stopped and rested.

His mind went back to that cold night when he and Polly went to Clear Prong Pentecostal and heard the prophecy. He remembered the bearded man say, "Success and riches will be yours one day, but not in a way imagined and not as a result of your own devices."

So see there, God is in command and there is nothing I can do about it, so I'll let things come as they will.

But whom would he go with if the opportunity came? He remembered seeing a squadron of Secesh sympathizers ride through, members of a home guard across the mountains in North Carolina. Although they had no uniforms, they wore gold sashes around their waist, and had hats bent up and tied to one side. With Van Dyke beards and carrying their Enfield rifles pointed upward with butt resting on saddle, the squad had an air of cocksureness and authority that he liked.

Lochsley had written five letters to him, the latest coming only last week. She, too, was going to be in Maryville to enroll in Mrs. Porter's Female Academy. He was excited beyond belief over the prospects of seeing her again. He remembered her sultry face and handsome body.

IT WAS A long, dry summer, but the crops turned out better than expected. Spence was thankful that, for once, he wouldn't be there to help with the harvest.

On September 10, 1860, Blue John swung his trunk in the back of the buggy, and Spence and his family began the trip into town to begin his college training. Professor McGlothen had arranged for him to board with Dr. Ernest Gaunt, a local physician, and to work in his office after school, mostly sweeping and cleaning.

Harry gave him $50 to pay his first term tuition, buy books, and place a down payment on his piano lessons from the Widow Perkins. Fletcher and Mary Clay said their good-byes and left their son standing on Dr. Gaunt's front porch. Mary Clay cried all the way back to Aberdour.

THE SECOND EVENING he was in Maryville, there was a knock on the door of the Gaunt home. Supper was finished.

"Spence, there is a young lady here to see you," Dr. Gaunt yelled after opening the door.

Spence got up from the table and walked to the door. It was Lochsley. She wore riding boots, pants tucked in the top of the boots, a white linen blouse buttoned to the neck around which was the stone.

Her wide-brim hat and long hair to the waist made her look more mature than he remembered, but alluring and beautiful.

"Hello, Spence," she whispered. "I spent the night at the inn and have asked all over town where you might be. Luckily I ran into someone at the college who knew where you were. How are you?"

"Good to see you too, Lochsley. Spence stepped out on the porch and closed the door. It was almost dark.

Inside, Dr. Gaunt whispered to his wife about who was at the door. Mrs. Gaunt was putting away dishes in the cupboard.

"She's a beautiful girl, Molly, with big brown eyes. I wonder how they know each other?"

"Just never you mind, Ernest. As long as the boy does his studies and is properly helping you in the office, then we needn't meddle. Don't you remember when you were young?"

Back outside, Lochsley asked if they could take a walk. They started up the dirt road toward town. "Lochsley, it is so good to see—"

"Spencer, I rode down here to tell you that . . . You see . . ." Her voice trembled, her face flushed, "Mama died two weeks ago."

"Oh, God, Lochsley, I'm sorry."

"Thank you," she whispered. "The doctor thinks it was a fever. She got sick and couldn't hold anything on her stomach, and the sweating . . ." She couldn't go on.

Time passed without either of them saying anything.

"It's all right. I'm all right." She took a deep breath and sniffed several times before speaking. "She slipped into a coma and then she was gone." Lochsley threw herself around Spence.

Spence was visibly moved. He remembered when they buried his grandmother three years ago on the hillside. He cried. Now, after all the things he had been through the last year, he felt different. But he realized it had left him more vulnerable to human suffering and loss.

"Spence, I won't be going to school this year. Maybe not any year, for that matter. I must go back and help Papa raise my brothers and look after the house. Lord knows, Papa can't cook for himself, or wash, or anything like that. He told me to go on to school anyway, but I can't. He needs me more than he realizes, and I can't let him down."

"Oh my!" Moments passed as Spence's mind whirled. "Lochsley, Big Pa told me that your daddy had more money stashed than he could rightly count—he could hire a women to come in and—"

"I know, I know. He might do that one of these days. But for now, this year, he needs me and I guess I need him."

"You said in your last letter that you would be in school at Porter Academy," Spence said.

"I did. I really looked forward to this fall. Were you glad?"

"Yes, of course I was glad. Why would I not be?"

"I just didn't know how you felt—I mean, if you remember your visit to our place last year as well as I remember it, as being . . .," she paused and searched for words, "as being something special."

"Lochsley, yes, I've thought about it many times. All summer long in those hot fields, I've wondered how good it will be having the next school year together in the same town. I don't mind telling you that I want to get to know you better."

"Really, Spence? I'm glad you feel that way. I was beginning to wonder . . . I haven't heard from you for a while. I know you went to Cincinnati, and Lord knows how many pretty girls you saw up there. You might have forgotten about this mountain girl."

They held hands and walked before finding a bench under a magnolia tree. He looked her in the eyes—those mysterious, beckoning, almond-shaped eyes.

"I wanted you to hear directly from me that I would not be in school here this year. I've already cried a thousand tears, but it won't bring Mama back. I must help him now, but I wanted to here from your lips if you thought about me. If you cared about me."

"Well, yes, I wanted us to be together this year, but . . ."

"I came because I wanted to see you again. It may be the last time with the possibility of war and all. I'm being forward, I know—please forgive me. Time is short."

"Don't talk that way, Lochsley. Listen, things will work out. A new president will be elected in a few months; maybe he'll make peace with both sides and life will go on as usual." He knew better than that and felt ashamed that he would consider softening the reality that Lochsley was facing so well.

"Spence, last year, you were quite taken with the stone I wear."

"I had never seen anything so pretty."

"I want you to have it," Lochsley whispered softly. She bent her head down and pulled the leather cord over her hair.

"Lochsley, I can't take your stone. My God, your grandmother gave it to you, and who knows who gave it to her. I mean, it's a keepsake—no, more than a keepsake. It's a treasure. It's yours."

"You take it. Think of me with sweet memories. Stare deeply into the stone and embrace its value and honored past.

And then, Spence, become what you can dream. I just feel you should have it."

Spence slowly took the stone. He put it around his neck and then stroked the side of her forehead gently.

They kissed, passionately and deeply. Then they held onto each other, feeling the imminent separation of their lives. The moon passed behind clouds and it became dark. The two had only a hint that their worlds were connected by their families, but they both felt a personal link to each other.

The couple paused in front of Dr. Gaunt's steps.

Lochsley turned, untied her horse and rode to her family duty. Spence walked back to his new world of school, but he felt a part of him ride off on that horse.

Chapter Fourteen

"THAT BILIOUS, COCKROACH SCOT has put his grandson in college and has him taking music lessons from Maud Perkins. I'll guarantee McAlpin has more in mind than furthering the boy's music abilities. He's trying to gain the widow's favor, that's what," yelled Heinreich Storch.

"So Heinreich, what difference does that make?" Frau Storch asked as she looked down at the floor.

"What difference? I'll tell you what difference. Next year the bylaws allow any one of us to sell out either to our offspring or any of the other members. At worst, we could sell out to Forbes for fifty cents on the dollar and he would take everything we own. Of course, nobody in his right mind would want that, but it could happen."

"Why do you care if Spence McAlpin goes off to college?" J.D. asked.

"Ah, my middle son, it just might mean that Widow Perkins could find such favor in McAlpin that she might sell him her shares."

"And with what money would an eighteen-year-old boy buy out the Widow Perkins?" Virgil asked, drumming his fingers on the table.

"His grandfather would give it to him, you moron! Then he would control everything and nothing would be left for you."

"So, Papa, what can we do?" Virgil asked.

"I'll think about it because Harry McAlpin will stop at nothing to get the upper hand."

"Moody, what do you think about that McAlpin boy? You went to school with him."

"Well, Papa, he told me he shot a man on the trip home from Cincinnati. Of course, I didn't believe him. He's also in tight with Chamon's daughter. Don't know if they court or not, but they're good friends. Another thing he told me, he would never forget the beating he took from Virgil and J.D."

"See there, I knew it. Everybody in the operation is against me. They're all ganging up on my family and me. We're blood and we must fight!"

THE COLLEGE TERM opened in that pivotal year of 1860. Spence handled himself very well with the subjects of grammar, rhetoric, math, history, Greek, and declamation. He studied by the light of a lamp in his room until late at night to keep his grades high.

By mutual agreement with his mother and grandfather, he was to further his music studies to help round out his training.

Harry knew so many doctors and men of letters in Scotland who made their living doing one thing, but buttressed their soulish realm with fine music. His mother had taught him along the way, and he enjoyed it, so it only made sense to let Widow Perkins take Spence under her wing while at school.

During his twice-weekly sessions in Mrs. Perkin's house, Spence couldn't help but notice the finery. Her 1848 Broadwood grand piano occupied a prominent spot in the living room.

Every Tuesday and Thursday afternoon found him rehearsing chromatic scales and other exercises intended to teach him a forceful touch, disciplined technique, and a grasp of ear training to work in various tonal motifs. By the end of October, he had mastered two of Chopin waltzes: the "Number Two in A-flat" and the difficult "Number Six in D-flat," or the "Minute Waltz."

Mrs. Perkins was proud of her pupil and realized he seemed to appreciate the higher things in life. She spent extra time giving background information on the composers.

One Thursday afternoon in October, Maud said to Spence, "You've come a long way in seven weeks with your music. Do you like the tone of this piano? It was made in London in 1848 and I've had it for ten years. This model is an exact duplicate of the one they made for Chopin in that year. It was their finest: Has iron tension bars with a fixed iron string plate—their first model with a complete iron frame. Allowed them to get sixteen tons of string tension that the older wooden pianos could never deliver."

"Can you keep a secret?" Maud asked.

Spence nodded.

"I'm giving this one to the college as soon as my new one arrives. I'm having a 1859 Steinway shipped with three pedals and seven octaves, probably the world's finest."

Spence was impressed with Maud Perkins' grasp of so many things.

"WALTER. WALTER," MAUD yelled to her houseboy who was in the kitchen cooking.

"Yes, ma'am? You called me?"

"Walter. Stoke the fire and add more coal and wood. There is a northern coming in; I don't want to get cold tonight. Got one more pupil and then I'll have supper."

"Yes'um. The beans and turnip greens are almost ready. I'll be out back getting the wood." The little man plodded out through the kitchen and out the back door.

As Walter uncovered the tarp that kept the wood dry, two figures with handkerchiefs over their faces stepped from behind the pile. One grabbed him around the neck and smothered his nose and mouth. The other snapped a 1857 Kerr London Armoury .44 revolver to the petrified Walter's temple.

"You're Widow Perkin's houseboy, aren't you?" the man who held the pistol said.

LEAVES RUSTLED ACROSS the small yards of the village as Spence hurried along to the Perkin's house. Once there, Maud opened the door exhibiting a warm smile. She had invited Spence to afternoon tea and conversation about the upcoming election.

"Come in, young man. I've been looking forward to your visit. Have a spot of tea and a cake or two. How much do you know about the election process? You know that the Democratic Party met in April in Charleston?"

He nodded and listened for almost an hour.

". . .We need to remember the Republicans were formed four years ago from the old Whig Party and came to be known as the Free Soil Party. The leader was your grandpa's friend, Henry Clay of Kentucky, who holds slaves. Lots of them. But he was not slavery-propagating. They dreaded the advance of slavery more than the breaking up of their Whig Party. There are many men like Clay and I must say I don't understand them. They want their Negroes to be with them as long as they're living and working their farms, but they don't want anybody else to have them in the future. Such hypocrisy!"

Walter entered the room to clear the table and he made pretense to dust the furniture.

"Thank you, Walter," the widow said, who turned back to Spence to renew the conversation, not paying any attention to Walter. Time passed.

Spence reluctantly said, "Thank you for your insight, I'll go and study now—see you Tuesday." He got up, picked up his satchel, and opened the front door.

Maud went into the living room to read. Her discerning eye immediately discovered the absence of one of her favorite pieces: a Chinese porcelain vase fired during the Sung dynasty.

Since Walter had gone home, she ran out the door to the shed and saddled her two-year-old gelding. She was furious, disappointed, and frustrated, and rode straight to Dr. Gaunt's house, dismounted and knocked on the door.

She explained her dilemma once Dr. Gaunt opened the door. The two marched up the steps to Spence's room and barged in without knocking.

Spence was lying on the floor, reading by the light of the fire. As Maud scanned the room, she saw the vase on the bed.

"You are in a lot of trouble, young man," Gaunt yelled.

"I have never been so let-down in my life—when I had come to admire and respect you so much—now you steal one of my prize antiques. How could you?"

"The vase? It was in my satchel. I don't know how it got there—I mean, I didn't take it. I know you think I did, but I didn't." His face flushed. "I intended to return it to you immediately, but I'm perplexed as to how and why it was in my satchel?"

"Yes, I bet you were." She took two steps and slapped Spence's face. "I've never had anything done to me like this in my life. I want the sheriff!"

Spence held his hand to his face, his eyes staring at the floor.

Widow Perkins carefully took the vase from the bed. She held it up for Gaunt's scrutiny. The vase had a lovely design of three peacocks.

"Look at this. It was fired at Tzu Chou 700 years ago. The kilns are still working. Bought it in Dresden on my honeymoon in '36."

"What do you have to say?" Gaunt asked. "Because if you don't come up with something in a hurry, it will be to the provost you'll go in the morning and you'll be out of school and back in Tuckaleechee by sundown tomorrow."

"Nooo! I've never stolen anything in my life. I don't think that way and I wasn't brought up that way." There was a moment of silence as the boy walked back and forth across the floor.

"Walter! Mrs. Perkins, what about Walter? As you were talking this evening, he came in to clear the table, didn't he? Then you talked some more while he went about dusting furniture, or pretended to dust. That's it. Don't you think that was a strange time to dust furniture? While you had a houseguest? He could have blocked our view with his body as he slipped your vase into my satchel."

Maud looked at Gaunt, then back at the boy, her countenance softening. Still she said nothing. Spence walked across the room.

"He did it, Mrs. Perkins. You know it and I know it. But why? Only Walter can answer that and I suggest we all find out now—before we go to bed, otherwise, nobody will sleep for worrying about it."

Gaunt looked at Widow Perkins. "Well, what do you think?"

"I don't know. I want to believe him. And if I can remember back to when I was his age, stealing a vase would not have been in my thinking either, that is, if I ever had a mind to steal, which I didn't. A knife, gun, or money . . . but a vase? No!"

"Shall I get the sheriff?" Gaunt asked.

"No. If the boy could borrow one of your horses and ride with me over to Walter's house, we'll get this thing straightened out."

Within five minutes they were at the home of Walter and his invalid mother. Pounding on the door brought Walter, wearing a long coat over a nightshirt, to see what the commotion was about. The trio barged in and got a quick confession.

"Walter, I am disappointed in you; you must give me some explanation."

"Two men told me they'd kill me if I didn't."

Then Maud closed her eyes and prayed. "Lord, have pity of Walter's poor soul and forgive him of this sin that he's most surely done."

Back on their horses, Maud said, "That still leaves the question of who those men were and why their strange demand?"

THE NEXT WEEK, Spence walked to the Wallace Hotel to buy a paper, the *East Tennessean*. Across the front page were the words: "Lincoln Wins Big!"

The article stated that the electoral vote was: "for Lincoln, 180; for Breckinridge, 72; for Bell, 39; for Douglas, 12."

At his piano lesson that evening, Mrs. Perkins said, "Spence, this election will bring the country to a boil in no time at all."

FARMERS OF THE Appalachian and Cumberland Mountains were bracing for a long winter. Hogs had to be killed, hams had to be cured, lard and soap had to me made. Wood had to be split and stacked. Quilts had to be fetched from cedar chests. Anticipation and dread were in the air. Once home from college for the Christmas holidays, Spence plunged into the chores. He had missed hog killing, but he helped make candles from the boiled pig fat.

Mary Clay had Willamae spend Christmas Day with the McAlpins at the big house to serve the festive family meal. Aberdour had not looked so pretty since Kate had died.

There was a knock at the door. Harry opened it.

"Merry Christmas, Harry."

"Merry Christmas, Rose. Come on in, F.L. Good you could come too, Polly, Becky."

"Thank you for inviting us," Rose said. "It's been a long time since I've been up here." She looked around at the McAlpin's beautiful furnishings. There was a low chest with brass fittings, cabriole legs, and ball and claw feet made for the Dutch market in the East Indies. She looked at the Hepplewhite sideboard—tambour front—and that gorgeous mirror with those carvings. She said to Harry, "I remember Kate told me that chest was done around 1740. Didn't it come from a manor house outside Sheffield?"

"That it did, Rose. Your memory is still good."

"Your Christmas tree is pretty," Becky said.

"Thank you, my dear. Blue John did it all. Cut it, ran the popcorn strings, and tied the candy to the boughs."

"Blue John. Start us off with a little libation, please sir. Yes, Rose, I enjoy our fine things, but give the credit to Kate."

CHRISTMAS DINNER OF turkey and dressing, biscuits, cranberry sauce, and pumpkin pie was eaten on a late George III 1820 dining room table.

Afterwards, gifts were distributed as a gentle snow fell outside. Raw and cold, darkness would come early. Political discussions were kept to a minimum. Deep in their hearts, both families knew this would be the last normal Christmas for quite some time, so they wanted to savor it the best they could.

Spence received a carbine rifle from all the family. He took Becky and Polly outside in the snow so he could try his new piece.

Once outside, Polly couldn't resist questioning Spence. She rubbed her hands.

"What is that stone around your neck? You never wore it before."

"Oh, it's just what you think, a stone," he said, and fired a shot at no particular object.

"Spence, now don't be coy with me, your friend. Did you buy it in town? In Maryville?"

"No, I didn't buy it in town. I went there to study, not to buy frivolous rocks. And Polly."

"Yes, Spence."

"Drop the subject."

"Becky, look at that thing around Spence's neck." Polly reached and pulled the stone away from under Spence's shirt.

"Spencer McAlpin, did some girl give it to you? Yes, Becky, look at the color of the thing. It's beautiful and I know a girl gave it to you. We're just dying to know who she is. You're not in love are you?"

"No, Polly, I'm not in love," he answered. He pulled away from Polly's prying hands and questions. "I met someone a year ago and she wanted me to have it to wear. That's all! Can't somebody wear a gift without being in love with them?"

"Yes, of course. Becky, have you ever seen anything as beautiful?"

"Sure is pretty," Becky said.

Spence shot his carbine a few more times and held it out in front of himself to admire the rifle.

"Oh, Spence, stop shooting that thing and answer. I won't sleep tonight if I can't find out who and why she gave you the stone."

"Well, you'll have to not sleep. Besides, it isn't your business." He wheeled around so his body was between Polly and Becky.

"Spencer, you make me so mad sometimes, I just . . . I just want to spit!"

Polly marched back into the house with Becky not far behind.

Spence stayed another twenty minutes and shot his rifle.

Chapter Fifteen

ALTHOUGH IT WAS PITCH-black dark, and so cold that no one in his right mind should care, it was still strange to see horses and Widow Perkin's buggy parked deep in the thicket of cane break across the stream from Rose's Tavern. Their times of arrival weren't the same, but their purposes were: the business of the opium operation for another six months. They would sneak into Chamon's barn and go down into the underground room.

Harry sat smugly with a cheroot in one hand and a bourbon in the other. Widow Perkins sat primly with a wool shawl around her shoulders and a glass of burgundy in her hand. Storch had brought his own schnapps. Chamons was standing beside the worktable. He had lit a pipe.

Harry and Chamons were friends, Widow Perkins was all business and neutral to the other three, nobody cared for Storch, so conversation at these meetings was always restricted.

Chamons called the meeting to order. McAlpin gave his accounts of the past six months, including his Cincinnati trips and client sales. Storch gave accounts of his corn sales to agents in Georgia.

Storch also stated his guano sales were improving as various militia units from the South needed niter for gunpowder. He reported his best year ever on his runs into Polk County, Tennessee, and into North Georgia. He and McAlpin each handed Widow Perkins a check for $4,000 from which she would take a cut, send her brother in Boston his share, use a portion to amortize the land debt, and another to help retire the indebtedness of the bonds.

Chamons gave his report of how much money he had paid McAlpin and Storch for opium and how much he had collected after he compounded the powder into laudanum or other products.

They discussed the nearby ending of the debts and the potential turnover of the operation to one person. Storch was noticeably agitated as he differed on every point brought up by the others and drank more schnapps as he spoke.

"This chair is uncomfortable," Storch said, "and I think my ulcer is acting up." He looked at Widow Perkins.

"With what you put down that gut, anybody's stomach would hurt," Harry said.

"Listen you, I didn't ask—"

"Our last topic this evening," Chamons said, "is discussing our allegiance when hostilities break out. Since I've talked with you separately, I know each of you thinks there is no avoidance of war, so it isn't a matter of if it comes, it's a matter of when. It seems to boil down to what the boys down in the Palmetto at Charleston do against the Lincoln bunch at Fort Sumter. My bet is it will start there. I want feedback from you. Storch, you first."

"Now I can tell you the Southerners are serious about this thing," Storch continued. "They think the North is afraid to fight and they figure one Rebel soldier is equal to four or five Northern boys. Anyway, my routes are in Georgia, so I would

be inclined to side with them. It's all they talk about—almost
a spiritual thing, this rebellion."

Chamons looked at McAlpin. "Harry?"

"Staying alive is terribly important. I'll stay neutral as long
as I can. I'll even take the oath for the Union as a last resort."

Chamons tilted his chin and looked at Widow Perkins.
"Maud?"

"Well, gentlemen, by virtue of birth and culture, my incli-
nations are Union. I have a strong suspicion that we are in a
veritable 'hotbed' of Unionists. I tend to advise us to first
remain flexible and be able to go in the direction of whomever is in power at the time.

"But, gentlemen, I don't think your neighbors will let you do
that. I wouldn't be surprised if there weren't interfamily kill-
ings. If Governor Harris held an election today, I guarantee
that East Tennessee would vote overwhelmingly to either stay
with the Union or form another state separate from Tennessee.

"So, I urge you men, being up here in this insular cove, to
sympathize with the Union. If you want to cut some deals
with a few secessionists on the side, then slip and do it, but
for God's sake, go on record as Union men."

"Are we all in agreement now?" Chamons asked. "How
about you, Storch?"

"We're surrounded by Union people, but my boys—I'm
afraid they're Rebel through and through. I can proclaim
my allegiance all I want, but my sons will never lie down and
give in. For business, I'll do my part to maintain a Union
stance, but it seems mine will be one of the divided."

"There will be many of those families," Maud whispered.

After a few moments, Chamons cleared his throat.

"Let's call it a night. Oh, one more thing. Night after
tomorrow at my tavern, there will be an open meeting for
everybody up and down the cove to discuss the war. I'm sure

you will be there, except maybe Maud, so then we'll be able to get an idea of how the people are thinking. I'll see you then.

"Be careful and be quiet as you leave. Remember, one at a time."

Storch came away from the meeting with the distinct impression that his boys' plan to divide Maud and Harry as friends did not work. The two were still speaking. The planting of the vase in Spence's possession did not have the result he was after. Why was he, Storch, the outsider and not McAlpin? I must think about another plan to increase my power in this group, he thought.

IT WAS WEDNESDAY, January 2, 1861. The sun had shone brightly in the early morning, but was now alternating in and out with some low, heavy-looking clouds. Snow was predicted by mid-afternoon. The December 29, 1860, *Harper's Weekly* had arrived and Spence settled before the fire to read. Besides the lengthy ninth chapter of *Great Expectations* by Dickens, *Harper's* had advertisements for things such as Burnett's Cocaine, India Rubber Home Gymnasium chest expanders, Patent Improved French Yoke Shirts, Military Field Glasses, Yeast Powder, and finally an ad for Steinway & Sons' patent overstrung Grands and Square Pianos, "now considered the best pianos manufactured." He tore out the ad and made a point to take it to Mrs. Perkins when he returned to school.

TONIGHT, THE STARS of the winter solstice were out in force and the air was crisp and clear. Despite muddy roads, Rose's Tavern was crowded. People from miles around jammed into the large dining hall and into the side rooms.

"Ladies and Gentlemen, I want to thank you for coming. We don't want to drag this out too long, so we will have open speeches for one hour. I'll remove the speaker from the stage if he gets long winded. Limit your topic to the points concerning whether Tennessee should secede on February 9 and why? Please use the spittoons." Chamons took out his watch. "Who will go first?"

Harry watched Spence shift his weight from side to side as the meeting progressed. Then he stretched to look at Polly in the kitchen.

"I'm bored, and it's stuffy in here."

"Pay attention and get your mind off that girl. You need to hear all of this because it's going to affect you, like it or not," Harry whispered.

Ten speakers took to the podium during the first hour, seven were staunchly pro-Union. Chamons skillfully kept crowd noise down and each speaker limited to five minutes.

Harry realized soon which side the majority of Cove residents were on. Maud was correct two nights ago. Yes, we must support the Union cause, no need to rock the boat, he thought.

After Chamons concluded the formal part of the meeting, the crowd stayed and visited and vented their opinions. Discrete sources of bourbon and brandy were available. Scattered arguments flared from time to time, but that was to be expected.

Spence got up and wandered toward the barroom, and ran right straight into Storch, coming out.

"Guten Abend, young man. Aren't you the McAlpin boy?"

"Yes, I am."

"And I believe you are in school over at the college?"

"That's right." He turned from Storch and walked away.

"Damn it, boy. I'm talking to you," Storch screamed. He took a step to get in front of Spencer, grabbed his shoulders and began to shake him.

"I know what you're up to. I know what your mean grandfather is up to. It won't work, trying to shut out my family and me as well."

Fletcher, wiry of build and half drunk, leaped from his chair, knocking over whisky glasses, and flew into Storch's back, pushing him off Spence and sending him sprawling onto the floor. Fletcher pounded the German with both fists before other men pulled him away.

As the men pushed Storch out of the room, he looked over his shoulder at Spence. I won't let your family do this to me. It's not right. Just not right."

Harry couldn't believe his eyes. He smiled from knowing that someone of his own raising, his own flesh and blood, had bested his oldest nemesis.

SPENCE RETURNED TO college in January. The excitement of the impending conflict was almost more than he could stand. Yet he knew that any war was an impediment to the serious nature of fulfilling his goals: getting an education and gaining freedom to support himself without depending on his grandfather or anyone else.

Professor McGlothen told Spence earlier that Rebel troops were being recruited in Knoxville. An infantry company called the Mitchel Guards, named for John Mitchel, a fiery Irishman of the mountains, was training at the fairgrounds two miles east of Knoxville. Another unit was already encamped on College Hill, home of East Tennessee University, most of whose students had already deserted the campus to join the Confederate army. Since Tennessee was still neutral and a convention to secede had not even been called, Spence thought it all incredible. He plunged into his studies once back on campus, in spite of the distractions. Tennessee Governor

Isham Harris called for a convention to secede. The move was defeated handily with East Tennessee casting the largest vote.

That evening McGlothen climbed the stairs to Spence's room, and knocked.

"Professor. I must have dozed off—didn't hear you."

"Sorry to bother you. I know you're studying for exams, but I won't take a minute." He sat down on the bed.

"I've come from a meeting with the president and faculty, and I regret to say we must close the college."

"Oh no," Spence said.

"If fighting comes here they would most likely requisition College Hall for billets or hospital use. The students are leaving anyway for duty with one side or the other."

Spence listened to the devastating news. His plans were extinguished by forces beyond his control.

"How much longer do we have, Professor?"

"Five days. You take your exams and then that's it. April 12 to be exact."

"And what are you going to do?"

"Me? I'm heading to Kentucky to join General Thomas' troops."

"You're going with the North?"

"Yes," said McGlothen. "Other faculty members and I have discussed it at great length. I believe in the Federal Union. I was born up there. There is no room for neutrality. All of us must take a stand, so I'm taking mine. I wish you God speed. I'll write to let you know where I am. Maybe the war won't last long and we'll be back together again, because God knows, I love this part of the country."

In the early morning hours of April 12 the militia shore batteries of South Carolina, under the command of Brigadier General G. T. Beauregard, opened fire on Fort Sumter and its Federal troops commanded by Major Robert Anderson.

These shots were to usher in the largest amount of blood-shed in American history; homes and farms wrecked, crops depleted, and lives changed. Young men Spence's age, with their hopes and dreams of a career and family, would be dashed on some forlorn field or mountaintop.

As Spence studied Latin the previous night, the lamp flame flickered from the breeze coming through the open window. Spring had arrived, and his life was in danger from now on.

THAT SAME NIGHT in room thirty-one of the Lamar Hotel on Gay Street in Knoxville, Orvil Lee, crop foreman at Aberdour Farms, and Willis, hired hand of the Storch farm, stood side by side in dusty work clothes in the middle of the room.

Behind them sat two guards beside the closed door. Each had pistols and a frown. In a corner of the room, there was a table with a man sitting behind it. Across the front of the table hung a long sheet, tacked between the walls, to disguise the identity of the man. A kerosene lamp outlined the silhouette of the man's head; it illuminated a Colt 1849 Pocket Revolver on the table. He finally spoke.

"I, Re Erenn, King of Ireland . . ." His Irish dialect was thick and deliberate, but muted and somber.

"I give my thanks to you men. For two years, you have been able to pilfer more than two wagonloads of whisky and 242 piculs of opium from the Storch-McAlpin business. More importantly, the proceeds of our efforts are used to help our countrymen who land on American shores. Do either of you have any news?"

Willis and Orvil looked at each other and back toward the figure.

"Yes, sir, we do, or I do," Willis stammered. He held his hat in his hands and grinned. "Looks like Mr. Storch and his boys are making a trip to Georgia Thursday. They'll have four wagons of corn and hidden opium.

"How do you know that?"

"Because the other night I heard a noise at two o'clock in the morning. I got up and sneaked up to the ridge in front of the main house. That colored man who works for McAlpin was unloading what looked to be little bags from his wagon into a cloth sack that Storch was holding."

"Then what happened?"

"Then the Negro rode away and Storch dragged the big sack down the hill into the barn."

"He was making a transfer. So! You men know when to intercept?"

Willis and Orvil both mumbled and nodded.

"Now I want your complete attention. As you leave tonight, my men at the door will give you both a twenty-dollar gold Double Eagle to show my appreciation. But men, we now have a bigger job to do and a change in mission.

"As you know, our beloved Union is threatened. As war comes, the army will need pain killers and laudanum. I, Re Erenn, have arranged to supply certain government agencies with white powder to be made into medicines, so our brave men in the field can be treated properly."

Orvil and Willis turned and left the room, collecting their gold pieces on the way out. They had the long ride back to the cove. The phantom man, dressed in black, clasped his hands, paced the floor and laughed.

"Now I'm closing in. Won't be much longer before I have those two families completely under my control. They will rue the day they brutally killed my brother."

IT WAS SATURDAY, April 13, 1861. As Spence and his daddy loaded the wagon with his belongings, a feeling of gloom and sadness prevailed at the Gaunt house and the Maryville community as well. Fletcher used Harry's money to pay the remainder of Spence's board money. They climbed in the wagon and headed out of town.

Spence slept on a blanket in the back of the wagon. The examinations had taken their usual toll. Before he drifted off, he thought that he was too sad and depressed to even be awake.

I have no idea what I'm going to do. Another summer of hoeing and chopping corn? I can't bear to face it now. All I want is sleep, thought Spence.

Excitement increased among the peoples of the now-warring nation. That Monday, President Lincoln in Washington issued a proclamation declaring that an insurrection existed, calling out seventy-five thousand militia from the various states. Some of the so-called border slave states, including Tennessee, were infuriated with this pronouncement, equating it to a call to suppress the South.

Throughout the North and the South, papers continued to scream the news. Writers penned flaming editorials; people at public gatherings sang patriotic songs, and heard flamboyant speakers. All the same, it was hard to comprehend that war had actually begun.

Spence helped Blue John with chores the first week home, but he went about it with somber and mechanical economy sparing few smiles. No spring in his step; no smile in his countenance.

Despite their isolation, the McAlpins still received *Harper's Weekly* and the *Knoxville Register*. Harry wanted Southern papers like the *Charleston Courier*, but with gossipy postmen and nosy neighbors, he refrained from divulging his true leanings. The family read about Southern merchants repudiating debts to the North until after the war.

Then they read about the riots in Baltimore. It seems that in response to the call of President Lincoln, the Sixtieth Massachusetts Infantry had left home and moved through New York toward Washington. At Baltimore it had to detrain to transfer to the Washington depot. Pro-secessionists greeted them with stone throwing, hooting and jeering. Four soldiers and nine civilians were killed. Although the governor of Maryland was furious that he had not been consulted about the troop movement, it was he who later influenced his state to cast its ballot with the Union, a heavy blow to early Southern excitement.

More importantly, President Lincoln summoned Lieutenant General Winfield Scott for advice. General Scott had been the hero of the Mexican war and although too old and too fat to mount himself in a saddle, his strategic mind was as sharp as ever.

He drew forth a master plan because this would be a long, drawn-out campaign, and the Union must institute a blockade of the ports of all the belligerent states along the Atlantic and Gulf shorelines. Their chief staples of cotton, rice, and tobacco must not readily be exported for cash. Moreover, European items contributing to both military and civilian use must not get into the area—something the South desperately needed.

This masterful concept of strangulation became known as the "Anaconda Plan." In the months to come, both Southern and foreign vessels became adept at evading the naval blockades, but not without cost and effort. While events were sporadic in other fields of war, the blockade went on relentlessly, day after day, making its partly unsung contribution to the results of the conflict.

The men and women of the secessionist South built an army, a navy, and ammunition factories; they developed a constitution, a congress, and a treasury; and then issued bonds to finance it all. It was a time of joyful expectation before the grim realities approached.

The call for troops by Lincoln greatly influenced Tennesseans to reverse their previous vote against secession. Governor Harris told his legislature that he had agreed upon a military league with the Confederate States of America and submitted it for ratification by the legislature. Both senate and house approved, so to all intents and purposes, Tennessee was now in the Confederacy as of May 7, 1861.

In Knoxville, that day, Unionists held a rally and defiantly raised the American flag to the top of a pole at the corner of Gay and Main. Among those listening to the speakers were Major Washington Morgan, of the Military League state troops, and a Charles Douglass, a familiar figure around town with a fondness for homemade liquor.

Douglass was peaceable enough during sober moments, but these were infrequent. When the beginning of the war was announced to the public, Douglass was sitting on Gay Street in front of the Lamar House Hotel, beating a bass drum.

During the rally, an argument arose between Morgan and Douglass, and Morgan fired at Douglass as he entered a store, wounding him slightly and killing a passerby. Major Morgan went to the military camp, gathered several hundred state troops, and marched back up Gay Street. Although there was rioting, violent conflict was prevented by Colonel David Cummings, a leading Confederate citizen, along with two Union citizens, who together persuaded the soldiers to return to camp.

Several days later as Charles Douglass sat by a window in his house, he was mortally wounded by an unknown person who fired from a hotel window a hundred yards distant. The angry Unionists were determined to make a martyr of a man who might have passed on unattended otherwise. Once again, minor clashes of citizens who had once been friends were of little importance in the long war. But they indicated force would be necessary to whomever wanted to control East Tennessee.

Chapter Sixteen

COLLINS HOUSE, NEWMAN'S RIDGE

"Papa, now you sit down in front of the fire and I'll bring your best bourbon and branch water. You've worked hard today; it's my time to take care of you. Your boots too!"

"Oh, Lochsley, my, my, you're too good to me. Yeah, we did put in a tough one today—can't seem to bounce back like I used to," Claude Collins said. "Since your mama died, I haven't had the mind to do much."

"I know, I know," Lochsley whispered. She got the liquor bottle from the cabinet. "But, Papa, you still have Jep and Sam and me. We all love and need you." She poured the whisky; took the dipper from the water bucket and filled the glass.

"Here you go. Now sip on that and rock in front of the fire."

Lochsley sat down beside him in the other rocker.

"Lochsley, I've been thinking about you lately. You're nineteen, now, and you need to be in a place where there are young gentlemen around, boys who would pay attention to you. Not too early to begin looking for a husband, either."

"Oh, Papa, hush now. We've gone over that before. I have plenty of time. Now, it's you and the boys who need me the most.

"Papa, I suppose one of these days, if the right man came along, there's a chance he would take me from here. But my heart would stay."

"That's wonderful, of course, but you're so pretty—and so smart and fine. You'll make a fine wife, Lochsley Collins.

"What have you heard from the McAlpin boy? Surely he hasn't gone off to war?"

"I hope not for his sake, but I'm not sure Spence wouldn't love to go. I got a letter from him a month ago. He seemed bored and confused. His college closed and all there is to do is work on that farm.

"Said there were groups riding through Tuckaleechee every week, Union and Confederate. He said they'll sometimes stop and beg for food and drink and inquire about his age and ability to handle a rifle. But he said his mother always came out and ran 'em off."

"Oh, yes. I'm sure either side would love to have him."

Rain had fallen since supper. The patter of drops on the wood shake roof made the fire all the more pleasant and cozy. The burning hickory logs flickered and hissed.

Lochsley rocked and thought and watched her daddy doze.

The neigh of a horse outside made Collins open one eye. The clatter of boots on the front porch made him jump from the rocker. The knock on the door was soft but forceful.

"Who could that be at this time of night?"

"Maybe it's one of the neighbors—maybe somebody's sick. Do you want me to answer it?" Lochsley asked.

"No, I'll do it." Claude reached for his pistol lying on the stone mantle, and cautiously opened the door.

On the porch stood a man in Union blue covered with a white canvas raincoat and wearing a black brimmed hat. He held a rifle in his left hand, pointed downward. Rain dropped off his hat, and his face had a tired, blank expression. Behind him were a dozen men on horseback hunched over their saddles.

"Evening sir," the stranger said. He tipped his hat.

"Evening. What can I do for you, young man?"

"I'm Lieutenant Hansen, sir, serving with Lieutenant Carter at Camp Andrew Johnson up in Kentucky an—"

"Camp Andrew who?" Collins asked.

"Andrew Johnson—named for the vice president—the Union vice president, sir. My men and I have been out for two days doing scout patrol. Got caught in this rain and darkness, so I wondered if you might have room in your barn for us to spend the night and dry out?"

"Johnson. That's what I thought you said. Grew up not far from here. Did you say you were with Carter? Isn't he forming an army of runaway Tennesseans up there?" Collins asked.

"Yes sir, that's right. He gets 'em coming across that state line every night. About the other, we wouldn't bother anything and would be obliged if you could spare that barn."

"Very well, son. Will you be moving on in the morning?"

"Oh, yes sir. We still have much ground to cover."

"You wouldn't be hungry, would you now?" Collins turned his head toward Lochsley.

"No sir, we're fine for now. If you could just show us the barn, and where we could hang out wet clothes, then that'll do. We could use a little something in the morning though."

"I reckon we can muster up some food for breakfast. I'll get the lantern and go with you down to the barn. Wait right there." Collins left the room and went to the back porch.

Lochsley stood with a hand on the rocking chair. She glanced at the man on the porch, then smiled and looked down.

Wonder where he came from? Even with that raincoat, I can tell he's handsome. Maybe I can fix him something special for breakfast. That uniform does something for a man. But, he hasn't even noticed me—too busy thinking about his men and sleep.

"Ma'am, I'm Lieutenant Hansen of the Twenty-eighth Ohio Infantry."

She looked up and smiled. "I'm Lochsley Collins of Newman's Ridge, Tennessee." Claude rambled back into the room with the lantern and a raincoat slung over his arm.

"Be back in a minute, Lochsley. Come on, Lieutenant. The barn is down the hill a bit. It should be dry as a chip."

"LIEUTENANT HANSEN," LOCHSLEY said, "you've been pesterin' me for thirty minutes to let you help, so here's your chance. Slice the bacon. The skillet is over there. You can cook bacon, Lieutenant?"

"Yes, ma'am. I was raised on a farm at Granville. Ohio, ma'am. And I would be obliged if you would call me John."

"Well, I don't know why. We've hardly met. Down here in the South, it takes awhile before we get that familiar. Just the way I was brought up."

"My regiment has been stationed up at Camp Johnson for a month now, helping organize that ragtag bunch of refugees. I expect we'll be there awhile. My captain is sending the boys and me on scout trips all the time, I could always stop by to say hello?"

Lochsley didn't answer, but turned to set the table.

Breakfast was served to the grateful men, now dry and rested. Afterwards, Hansen mounted his horse, spun around once, tipped his hat and rode away with his men. Lochsley, her two brothers, and her daddy stood on the front porch, waving good-bye.

"We're going to see a lot more soldiers before this war is finished," Claude said. "Isolated as we are up here on Newman's, they'll still find us.'

"Why is that, Papa?" Sam asked.

"Lincoln knows this area is pro-Union and it would be a feather in his cap to get it into Federal control as soon as possible. Also, the Confederate army gets most of its pork and corn from this area. Then, there's the railroad. If the North can control the East Tennessee & Virginia, that would cripple the South. Confederates control it now, but that Yankee army will be lickin' chops to come back and take it. Our little mountain won't be left alone."

That night Lochsley sat down at the table and began a letter.

Dear Spence,

Last night a scout party of Union soldiers stopped to get dry and to sleep in our barn. They were led by a lieutenant from Ohio serving in Kentucky training East Tennessee runaways. He was educated in New England and was a 'smarty pants' who thought he knew everything. Don't they say most Yankees are that way? I would hardly talk to him . . .

SPENCE RECEIVED THE letter from Lochsley, so he was in a good mood. He walked through his chores with ease, almost enjoying them. As the sun went down, Spence and Blue John carried two buckets of fresh, foamy milk to the house. They heard horses and stopped.

Spence could see his mother on the front porch making gestures, her voice he couldn't hear. A group of men on horseback were gathered at the front porch. Spence saw one man standing in front of Mary Clay. He wore a gray jacket lined with gold piping. He had a feather in his wide-brimmed hat.

Mary Clay turned toward Spence and Blue John with terror written all over her face. The men turned and two of them stepped aside so the leader could view Spence and Blue John.

"Blue John, that's the man who broke up our hunting trip up on Meigs mountain," Spence said.

"Ah, that it is boy. What's he doing in that gray uniform? Wasn't he a member of some home guard checking on people to see if they were 'Union Blue'? I believe that was how he put it. He done gone and switched colors, like a lizard."

"Spencer McAlpin. Is that you?" the man yelled. "Come on over here. I'd like a word with you."

Spence slowly walked down the hill and stood before the man.

"Spencer, your mother and I were talking. My name is Jeremiah Stewart, Jeremiah Polk Stewart. I've been commissioned to lead these cavalrymen to do duty and honor to the glorious cause of the Confederacy. Your fame as a marksman and a true gentleman has been made known to me, and I'd be pleased to invite you to ride with us."

"You're the man who beat Daddy and stole our possum on Meigs Mountain a year ago."

The man looked Spence squarely in the eye, but had a puzzled look on his face. Stewart didn't utter a word.

"You were checking on whether people were 'Union Blue' that night, sir. And now you're riding for the South? What is this?"

"Well, humph, certain things happened that I would be happy to tell you once you're riding with us. For now, suffice it to say, I saw the light."

"Why would I want to ride with a person like you?"

"Why you would make a grand contribution toward our grand effort to repel this area of Northern aggressors and Yankee swine. We're destined to merge with larger cavalry units. They'll be led by the most gallant and brave leaders this country has ever produced. What say you boy?"

There was a pause and a hush. A mockingbird was singing from the althea bush. A crow flew overhead. Every ear heard the breezes gushing through the rhododendrons and the pines.

Spence's boot made a crescent pattern in the dust. Then he looked up, "How much is the pay?"

"No, no, Spence!" Mary Clay wailed.

"Twelve dollars a month for regular enlisted, that is, privates."

"I'll do it!"

"Spencer, don't. This is your mother begging you, don't!" Mary Clay winced and then twisted ever more tightly the handkerchief in her hand. She turned away and hid her face in her hands.

"Good, my boy. You'll not regret it. Now, here is how we'll work it: My assistant on that dark horse will check by every couple of days. If we have a mission, or in that case, if you hear of dangerous Union activity, the information can be conveyed then."

"I come back here for dinner every day about 11:30 A.M.," said Spence. "Have your man be in the orchard at the back of the house."

"Very well, then. Size him for a jacket and we'll be off."

The man mounted and the group disappeared down the road.

THE CONFEDERATE STATES of America assumed all the characteristics of an independent nation: agents were in control of the civilian governments, an army was being raised, and its diplomats were casting about for allies and world recognition.

Some success was achieved in overtures to England and France, but no progress was made in securing the loyalty and support of the mountaineers of East Tennessee; only people of the larger cities of Knoxville and Chattanooga willingly joined the move for Southern independence. To these cities, the Confederate government dispatched armies led by forceful but tolerant commanders.

The first regiment from the southwest to pass through Tennessee, the Third Alabama Infantry, had been greeted with wild cheering and gifts of food and clothing at every stop—until it reached Knoxville. Here it was greeted with threats from Parson Brownlow himself, the fiery little Methodist and the editor of the Whig newspaper to which Harry McAlpin subscribed, but personally hated.

At Strawberry Plains, a regiment of Southern troops being transported by train, fired on a mass meeting of Unionists as they passed, the fire was returned. Hatred intensified.

MARY CLAY HANDED Lochsley's letter to Spence on a cloudy November day. As he fumbled with his knife to open the envelope, he walked onto the porch and leaned against the post. His face flushed and his heart pounded as he sank down on the steps to read her letter.

> My Dear Spence,
>
> Papa and I stay in a state of upheaval. Not a week goes by without troops, blue and gray . . . May God pardon me if I tell you this . . . I overheard men talking . . . Parson Brownlow urged the Carters up at Camp Andrew Johnson to consider burning the East Tennessee railroad bridges. General Thomas took plan to Washington . . . Lincoln approved and sent $1,000 for this destruction on the Twenty-first instant. Had to tell someone.
>
> Your most humble servant,
>
> Lochsley

Spence stared at the rhododendron thicket. He read the letter again, got up, and wandered into the orchard.

He knew Blue John was in the barn.

"Blue John, could I speak to you a minute?" His boots pushed through the dust and hay on the floor.

"Of course. What's wrong?"

"Listen, I've just heard that the Yankees are going to try to burn all the railroad bridges between Virginia and Alabama tomorrow night."

"I want you to know I'm not fighting for slavery. Don't know anything about it. I don't believe in it.

"For me, on the other hand, I don't want somebody far away telling us how to run our lives. I believe that is what the federal government wants to do. That's why I signed with the Confederates."

There was a silence.

"Don't go get yourself killed."

"I won't." There was a pause. "Blue John, what are you going to do?"

"Lay low. Stay around and protect your mother and grandpa. I'm not going to let a little old conflict mess up my plans. You go do what you have to. Old Blue John will work and keep the home front protected."

"Thanks," Spence whispered, affected but relieved. He turned and walked toward the door. He stopped.

"You mentioned you would stay and protect Mother and Grandpa. Did you mean to leave out Daddy?"

Blue John looked up. "I don't think he'll be around much longer."

"Why not. What's wrong with him?"

"He's got that sugar," Blue John said.

"Got what?"

"Diabetes. Spence, you're dad's slowly dying."

"Dying? You sure?"

There was silence. "Nobody knows how long it will take to kill him. That's why your mama don't scold him about his drinking."

Spence walked out of the barn saddened. It was time to meet his cavalry contact, who was crouched under a pear tree in the orchard. He walked to him.

"Have you heard anything?" the man asked.

"I've heard from a lady friend in the upper east—says the Yanks will burn all the bridges between Virginia and Alabama, all through the Great Valley, nine in all, tomorrow night."

The man raised one eyebrow. "Now that's news. Pray tell how this lady knows such a thing?"

"Seems a Federal officer on scout duty has been stopping by her house. He leaked the news."

"You better come on with me; we'll meet Jeremiah in the mountains. He'll figure out what to do, but time is short. Get your stuff."

Spence ran to the barn to tell John to ready his horse, then he ran to the house for his knapsack, the new jacket, and his carbine.

"DADDY, YOU'RE PACKING. Where are you going?" Spence asked.

"I could ask you the same thing. Your going against everything I believe in."

"It's something I must do."

"Oh, God, deliver me!" Mary Clay yelled. She sat at the kitchen table and sobbed. "They're both going."

Spence faced his father and held out his hand. Fletcher stared at his son, and refused to shake hands. Spence turned to his mother, hugged her tightly and kissed her.

"Good-bye, Mother."

"Spence, I made a red kerchief—packed it in your duffel." She watched as Spence walked from the house and into the night.

"Why do you suppose he's leaving tonight, Mary Clay?" Fletcher asked.

"I don't know. Ever since he got that letter . . . from that girl."

"What girl? What letter? Where is it?"

"Under his mattress, but it's not right to read his mail. I never would . . ." Of course I would, she thought. Any God-fearing mother should read all letters.

Fletcher went to the loft, read the letter, and stormed through the kitchen.

"Where are you going?"

"To the big house. After that, Kentucky," Fletcher yelled.

"DADDY, I AIN'T goin' to stay down here and fight a plantation war for them rice and cotton farmers. They can have all the Negroes they can afford. That ain't got one hoot in hell to do with the way we operate in these mountains," Fletcher said.

Fletcher and Harry were both standing and pacing the floor, each with a glass of bourbon in hand.

"Yes, but think of your family, the mountains, your land. You're going to ride out of here for the cause of Yankee manufacturers who could care less about you?" Harry yelled.

"And you thought you were going to send me over to the North to fool people about your personal convictions."

"I know, I changed my mind," Harry said.

"Admit it, Pa. That was your plan and now you're afraid you'll be left alone so you want me to stay here?"

"Well, maybe. But a hot ball in the gut doesn't care whose flesh it rips open. Stay at Aberdour." Harry was perspiring, despite the thirty-five degree weather.

"Stay? Never! Enough Confederate sympathizers are around to make life miserable for me. As for Aberdour, you've never given Mary Clay and me land. You just want me to work your land. Had Mama lived, I think she might have changed your ways. But after she was buried, you got even worse."

"You're wrong about that," Harry said.

"I'm nothing more than a hired hand to you, sweating and straining all day out in those fields. If you think I'm going to fight for that, you're crazy."

"You and Spence could meet each other on a battlefield."

He turned and stared into the fire. He stroked his beard. He fought the tears, but they came anyway, running down his face. He rallied strength before he turned to face Fletcher, again. He took a cigar from his pocket and lit it. He wiped his face with his sleeve.

"Tell you what, son, I'm going to change my will. Right away. We'll set up different compensation rules, if you'll stay. I'm an old man. As God is my witness, I don't want to face Him with the thought I had cheated you."

There was a pause. "I'm overwhelmed. But it's not believable."

"Why not?"

"Too little, too late. If this war was not pressing us, it might be different. I'm leaving for Kentucky tonight."

"Oh, my dear God in Heaven, don't say it."

Fletcher sat his glass on the table. "Now with that, there is one more thing."

Harry appeared as if he had been shot. He braced himself for the next volley.

"I have been leaking information to your enemies about your opium."

"What enemies? What do you mean my opium?"

"About how much you trade, when you ship, and who buys."

"Oh no!" Harry fell backwards into a chair. "I feel faint. Right under my nose. I've suspected someone . . . You? Did you have anything to do with that . . . that ambush up at . . . at . . ."

"Sharp's Gap. Yes, I was there. That's why Spence was not killed. Unfortunately, those others had to be."

"Who else is involved? Where are they?"

"I wanted to tell you before I left. I got paid handsomely for my part, and I have no remorse. I must do my part to preserve the Union, and to preserve, or regain some of my dignity. I'm leaving now. Don't bother to follow me."

Chapter Seventeen

JEREMIAH STEWART FINISHED giving his cavalry the instructions for their exercise against the bridge burners. Spence heard horses approaching from his position in the last row of formation. He turned his head and to his horror, Virgil and J.D. Storch appeared.

"Boys, them two riding up are the Storch brothers, the last of the Rebel men from Tuckaleechee Cove," Jeremiah announced.

"J.D., you all ride up front with me for a while and I'll give you the assault plans that you missed. We're leaving now and with this full moon we ought to get well into Sevier County before midnight. We'll sleep then. Our objective: to save the railroad trestle at Strawberry Plains."

Spence was able to keep his presence unknown to the Storchs by riding in the back during the night. He knew that in the morning at daylight, they would recognize him and his reception wouldn't be cordial.

They stayed in Wear's Cove to camp because it would be useless to leave the cove with its dense underbrush for protection at night. The clouds obscured the moon's light.

Jeremiah told the men to drop their bedroll. No fires were
to be made. Spence rolled and tossed until 3:00 A.M. before
sleep finally came.

At dawn, two swift kicks to the ribs were Spence's awaken-
ing bugle. He was rolled out of his blanket, his swollen eyes
focused on the two sneering faces.

"Well now, don't we have a nice, close little gathering from
Tuckaleechee with Mr. Stewart? McAlpin, why don't you ride
on back home to your mama."

Spence slowly got to his feet. His side ached and his body
was stiff. "I'm sorry boys, but the time has come."

His fist hit Virgil squarely in the plexus of the belly, bending him over enough to take Spence's knee into his face,
uncoiling him backward. J.D. grabbed at Spence but Spence
gave him a swift kick. Virgil staggered and coughed and approached Spence. Spence squared off to meet their next
attack. J.D. made his move by grabbing Spence at the neck
and jerking the coveted green stone from him.

"Look here." He laughed. "Take it Virgil, I don't want no
jewelry."

"My stone, now. Thank you very much," teased Virgil.

Spence broke loose by jabbing an elbow into J.D.'s ribs.
Jeremiah rode up.

"Cut that out! Save your strength for those Unionist bridge
burners. And keep your mouths shut. Now, mount up."

Jeremiah's group rode most of the day. They veered west
of Sevierville and crossed the Little Pigeon River at a shallow
ford to avoid the Knoxville Pike traffic. They came to the
deep and winding French Broad River. The ferry driver asked
no questions, but took the money for cross passage. They
heard far-away shots and road faster toward their mission.
They knew the attack had begun.

A small, but powerfully built bridge guard was the sole pro-
tector. Unionists got up on the platform of the trestle to

torch the bridge. The guard got off a few shots and wounded two raiders. But the fire was started. Jeremiah's Cavalry forced the Unionist to scatter, and a bucket brigade was formed to put out the flames. They watched the bridge through the night.

At noon the next day, they heard gunshots to the south and they rode a half hour to Underdown's Ferry on the French Broad River. A heated battle was in progress. Jeremiah's scout met them on the road with the news: "Jeremiah, on this bank we've got Confederates and a bunch of citizens from Knoxville and Strawberry Plains. There's 400 Unionists from Sevier County on the other side. The Rebel down there said the Union sympathizers felt the Federal army was going to invade East Tennessee due to the success of the burnings, so they had taken it upon themselves to help with an uprising."

"How many bridges were destroyed?" Stewart asked.

"Got six out of nine. Thank goodness they didn't get the big ones at Loudon or the one at Bridgeport, Alabama. There were too many of us Rebels around."

Jeremiah swallowed hard. "Six of nine. My God! We've got to move."

He barked orders to his group and immediately the cavalry rode to take cover alongside the others on the north bank. After three hours of shooting, Spence could see the battle was taking its toll; he saw wounded or dead bodies on both sides of the bank.

Each group had tried to storm the other by way of a ford fifty yards downstream, but the attempts produced nothing but bloody carnage lying face down in the dark waters.

The sun was beginning to sink in the western sky. Spence knew Virgil was only ten yards from his own position. A thought came.

The ground leveled out right behind where Virgil was posted behind a swamp willow. His horse was tied to the same tree. Spence thought back three years—to his beating—and the killing of his fine horse.

He looked all around, up one side of the bank and then the other. The shooting was increasing, each group trying to get in its licks before dark.

Now is my chance, Spence thought. He loaded his carbine.

From Spence's angle, he could see the reins of Virgil's horse—a black line against a silver-gold background of the setting sun's reflection on the river. He raised his rifle and braced it on his knee. He isolated the reins in his sight and squeezed the trigger. The ball snapped the leather reins and scared the horse. The horse reared upward and bolted.

Virgil instantly swung around, yelled, and plunged forward to capture the chestnut gelding. As he did, he left the protection of the tree and exposed his backside to the enemy on the other bank.

As if thrown from a single firearm, three mini-balls pierced his body, bringing three round blood spots to his tan shirt.

Virgil Storch's body collapsed in a heap in the mud and green moss.

Bullets flew inches over J.D.'s head. He crawled an inch at a time and dared not rise up; he heard the dull sounds of the balls hitting the dirt of the riverbank.

Virgil's lifeless body was thirty feet away. J.D. saw Spence about the same distance on the other side from the body. J.D.'s head was swimming, his thoughts were blank, his brain numb; he was acting on raw instinct. He began to crawl on his elbows. Muddy and exhausted, he moved, but saw Spence also advancing toward the body. Why?

"He's trying to get his blessed stone back, the son of a . . . He'll not do it. Old J.D. is coming. Ain't gonna' let nobody pick your body bare. No sir!" J.D. said aloud.

He doubled his efforts, but saw Spence quicken his. Spence got to Virgil's body first, and Spence began rifling through Virgil's pockets. J.D. came at him screaming and clawing. They were both on their stomachs in the mud with Virgil's cold body crumpled beneath them.

Spence freed his hand and swung wildly at J.D.'s face. The blow knocked him downward into the water. Quickly Spence searched both of Virgil's pants pockets. No stone.

J.D. elbowed his way upward again with gravel and algae covering his clothes. They began to grapple again.

J.D. slid his hand down to his holster. The pistol came out of nowhere and slammed into Spence's face.

"You'll never get your stone back, you dung-offal Scottish filth. You'll have to kill me first," J.D. screamed.

"Come on Virgil. I'll carry you out of here—we're going home to Papa."

❖   ❖   ❖

SPENCE'S VISION WAS blurred, but he saw the reflection of sunlight dancing among the high branches of the willow oaks. He saw the blue sky between the leaves, now amber and orange. His head roared and throbbed with every beat of his heart. His wet clothes gave him a chill, which meant he was still alive.

There was silence. No shooting. No screams. Hundreds of blackbirds exited the canopy above him with their miasma of chirps.

He began to reconstruct the events as best he could.

"Virgil! He jerked his body to an upright position and looked around. Bodies were strewn along the riverbanks on both sides, but no Storch brothers. He slumped back to the ground and covered his head with his hands.

Something was hard under him—his carbine. He raised up to a kneeling position and fondled his rifle. His body began to wretch and he discovered he wasn't too old to cry.

Soon, he was able to pull his way up the bank to a clearing. He was barely able to see Jeremiah. He was talking to three other men.

"Spence. My God, son! They told me you were dead. Where were you?

"I think I'll live. Anything to eat?"

Someone got him meat and hardtack and water. After a few sips and bites, he felt better.

"What happened?"

"Well, son, we've been here on this river for thirty-six hours. The other side gave up and vanished. Most of our side left to go protect the Strawberry Bridge. I think we can go home now."

"Storch. What happened to them?"

"J.D. put Virgil over his horse and left last night. Took him back home to bury him."

POLLY AND BECKY CHAMONS bent over Spencer, who was lying on the living room rug in the Chamon's home. He stopped here before going to his own house. Polly gently rubbed the bruised and swollen side of his face with ointment.

"I must say, Spencer McAlpin, you seem to like all this attention. Becky and I feel privileged to be the anointed ones to treat your most holy wounds. But won't your mother feel cheated?"

"Polly, why must you be that way? Why can't you be nice?" Becky demanded, now fifteen years old.

"Why, I wanted to give you young ladies the pleasure of treating a brave, daring soldier of my caliber," Spence said. "Besides, you need the practice. There will be more of this later if the war heats up like I think it will, and the others might not be as nice as I am. Probably nasty old Yankees.

"Ohhh, that feels good. Now do the other side, will you?"

"No, that's enough. You think we're doctors or something? And I guess you think we should work for no fee?" Polly asked. She gave a shoving gesture on Spence's shoulder, got up and went into the kitchen. Spence looked at Becky.

"You sure are growing up," he said, "and getting to be as cute as a speckled pup under a red wagon."

"Thank you. Polly is terrible, Spencer. I apologize for the way she acts, but she is still my half-sister, and I must admit, she has been good to me lately. Says she expects hard times, so I guess she wants a friend."

"Becky, has she behaved at church? I haven't been for a while."

"Oh yes, yes. She wants to stay on the good graces of Reverend Mayhew. I think she has a . . ." Becky stopped and put her hand to her mouth.

"You mean, she likes him?"

"Well . . . yes. Promise you won't tell her I told you."

"I promise."

Back in the kitchen, Mrs. Chamons was washing dishes. "Polly, I still say that boy would be a good catch for you."

"Oh, Rose, we're the best of friends, but well, uh, he wants to live here in the cove and I want to get away from it. Why don't we put Becky on him later on?"

Rose Chamons stopped what she was doing and gazed into the bucket of dishwater.

"That is a splendid idea. I'll remember that."

Polly came back into the main room with a tray with teapot and cups.

"Where is that precious stone you wore around your neck?"

"Don't have it."

"Don't tell me you lost it? No? You didn't give it to another girl, surely?" She and Becky snickered.

"No, it was taken from me before one of the battles—by one of our own men. I'll get it back. Polly, tell me, what kind of people have been coming through the coves lately? Any blue devils?"

"You mean Northern soldiers dressed in blue uniforms? None so far. Papa says they're still in Kentucky, but he says that these bridge burnings have the whole countryside so fired with hope that surely General Thomas himself will invade East Tennessee any time now and drive the Confederates out," Polly stated.

"And that means you, Spence. Better watch out," Becky warned.

"Well, they're not here yet, so I have time to get a good night's sleep, eat some ham and biscuits, and get back to my unit. Anyone else unusual?"

"No, I don't think so. Nothing but the mountain men with their mules and muskets, and their solemn old wives with their hair wound up under their bonnets tighter than an eight-day clock," Polly said.

"Now that you asked, there was this man who spent the night at the tavern a couple of nights ago. Big man! You remember him Becky. Never took his hat off. Kept the brim turned down over his eyes.

"He spoke almost nothing. He just sipped brandy in the bar until midnight, so Papa said. He asked about everything. I mean, he would ask where one road led and where certain mountains were, and who lived in what houses? Strange!"

"Maybe he was just being friendly. What was his name?"

"See. That's crazy too. He called himself the 'King of Ireland.'"

Chapter Eighteen

THREE DAYS LATER, IN a clearing deep in the looming spires of Meigs Mountain, Stewart's cavalry finished their afternoon exercises of sprinting horses, dismounting, shooting, loading, and retreating.

The trees were bare, except the hemlocks, the spruces, and pines. Long shadows reached to the east, so the drill field was without sun. The men buttoned their jackets.

"Attention! Fall into formation," Stewart shouted. Shuffling sounds and curses were heard and then silence fell.

"Men, I have announcements to make. I've received word that General Carroll has been named as successor to Colonel Wood at Knoxville. He organized trials for the bridge-burning suspects. Yesterday, three were convicted by the military tribunals and executed. A fourth, a Mr. Self, was spared by no less than Jefferson Davis after a telegram that the man's daughter sent to the president pleading for her father's life."

A loud shout went forth from the men that bounced around each mountain peak. "Up at Greenville, two others were convicted by drumhead court-martial and sentenced to execution by hanging." Another shout. "Their bodies were left suspended for four days near the railroad tracks so that our good Southern sympathizers riding by in the trains could reach out and beat the bodies with sticks."

There were muffled groans from the men.

"They have the gallows standing in Knoxville as a deterrent to all who might contemplate further action."

Jeremiah continued. "General Zollicoffer has now returned to Knoxville and has relieved the city of martial law. Many important Unionists of the town have left for Kentucky. But the worse thorn in our side, this Parson Brownlow, who runs that Whig newspaper, is still around. Since October, he has been hiding up here with friends. Now we know he is nearby in Wears Cove.

"We're being split up. Half of us will arrest the good parson and take him back to Knoxville for trial. While we're at it, we will pick up J. D. Storch, still in morning for his beloved late brother.

"The rest of you are to go on into Knoxville for deployment elsewhere. Men, I've been honored to ride with you for the good of the glorious Confederacy, for the principles of state's rights and self-government. Be tough, be mean, fight hard and survive."

Jeremiah turned his horse and led his group down out of the mountains into the lush clearing of Tuckaleechee Cove. Half the men kept west toward Maryville and Knoxville. Half crossed the bridge on the Little River.

An hour later, Jeremiah saw the Storch house. J.D. had his saddlebags packed and, without saying a word, mounted his horse and joined the men.

Jeremiah watched a large, drunken figure stagger out the front door of the house and climb a hill.

Storch fell on the ground in a stupor beside a freshly dug grave. Storch uttered words in German, slurring his speech and drooling on the dry ground.

Jeremiah looked at J.D., kicked his horse, and together they rode onto the trail toward Wears Cove.

Before nightfall, the cavalry located Parson Brownlow in a cabin behind the house of a known Union sympathizer.

Jeremiah told the parson that he had orders from General Carroll to persuade him to return to Knoxville to surrender. He reaffirmed the promise that no bodily harm would befall him and that when he reported to Command Headquarters, a passport would await him that would entitle him to safe passage into Kentucky.

Brownlow accepted the terms. So, finally, one of the Confederate's peskiest problems had been harnessed. With his newspaper office in Knoxville being used as an arsenal for Rebel gunworks, Parson Brownlow's vituperative attacks against the Southern cause was silenced, at least for the time being.

By noon the next day, William Brownlow was locked in Castle Fox, the Knox County jail.

MAUD PERKINS LAY in her bed staring at the ceiling.

"What in God's name has happened to my country? She thought of childhood trips to the coast of Maine. Her mind vividly recalled the crashing green and white surf wrapping millions of tentacles around black, slick boulders, and then being released to recline backwards into itself and the rest of the azure abyss. She remembered laughter at picnics under the lighthouse at Pemiquid Point. The smell of newly painted whaling ships wafted into her nostrils.

Yes, she could recall perfectly those visits to Marblehead and how she sensed the excitement of the captains as they discussed their trips. She imagined the ship in front of her resting in a distant romantic port, the warm waters lazily lapping the sides, making a hollow smack. It was painful to realize than many of those places would be used to make provisions

for war against their own countrymen. Her mind flashed to
machine shops now making cannons and muskets rather than
anchors and harpoons. It hurt.

She winced at the horror. Her mind began playing tricks.
She could see brown-haired boys, freckled faced, arm touching arm, pacing across a green field. One would fall first,
then another. Then she could see puddles of blood on fresh
grass, which disturbed the crisp air of a new morning. "Oh
God, forgive us," she whispered.

"You wanted cream in yours, didn't you, my sweet?"
McGlothen yelled. He walked into the dim room carrying two
cups of steaming coffee. He had stopped to say good-bye.

There was no answer.

"Maud?"

"Oh, Oh! I'm sorry, let me put on my robe."

"Were you asleep? You were dreaming weren't you?"

"Clint, promise me you'll be careful. I know you'll probably be a surgeon's assistant, or something medical, but Clint,
if anything happened to you, I would never get over it. I've
already lost one man . . ."

"Drink your coffee Maud. You'll feel better. I have a feeling we might not be able to get it much longer down here.
Prices are starting to climb."

"But, I care about you, not coffee. Don't do it. Don't go."

"We've been through that. You have your man, Walter,
look after my house. I'll be back before you know it and I
promise to be careful."

She walked him to the door. His horse stood outside, two
saddlebags tightly tied around the flanks.

McGlothen took one long look around the room. It had
provided him much pleasure, visceral and metaphysical. He
gazed at the haughty Steinway—staunchly planted on three
carved posts, waiting for a virtuoso to sit in front of its keys.

Yes, Maud decorated this room, this spot on earth. Something he never had. She brought him to know peace, contentment, and the elevation of the soul. He would never forget. He hoped for a return to this joy, to his classroom, to his ginseng patch, and to his mountains.

"Maud, it's time. They're to meet me in Sevierville at midnight. Then it's Kentucky. I promise to write."

They kissed and Clint McGlothen, fifty years old, rode off to help fight his war.

THE WINDS AND rains came and signaled the end of fall. The mood of the people, whether Union or Confederate sympathizers, was somber like the landscape.

The bridge burnings of November did not produce the massive uprising that was feared. But in Kentucky, General Sam Carter and his loyal Tennessee regiments, supported by General George Thomas and his troops from Indiana and Ohio, were indeed ready to march into East Tennessee now that the destruction of the railroads had been accomplished.

General Thomas, commanding at Camp Robinson, was not impressed with his troops, and had no confidence in the raw recruits, who seemed more moved by speeches of visiting politicians than commands of officers. The camps had become a rendezvous for exiled Horace Maynard of Knoxville and other politicians, more impetuous than wise in military affairs.

But General William T. Sherman, commander of all Union forces in Kentucky, put a stop to any idea of an invasion at this time. He had other things to do over in western Kentucky that were to occupy his time and emotions.

Carter's troops threw down their rifles in disgust, and many left. Some pleaded, some wept, and some shouted abuse against Sherman for halting their return to their native East Tennessee. Andrew Johnson was furious. It required all the

restraint General Thomas could muster to keep from arresting Johnson for inciting the troops. Johnson and Maynard
immediately left for Washington to plead their case with
Abraham Lincoln.

Christmas Eve, the first of the war, many hearts were torn,
North and South. Many a soldier on a lonely, inactive post
dreamed of home and fireside. In the U.S.A. and C.S.A.,
Christmas would not be the same this year. The year 1861
ended in sorrow, consternation, and doubt.

The dawn of 1862 was dismal, uncertain, sobering. For
those at home in the North, conditions were not yet too bad,
except when casualty lists came, or regiments had to leave
for battle. To those at home in the South, the harsh realities
of war on their own homeland began to hit home. Many asked
themselves if the battle for their rights was worth it? Were
they even correct? There were still songs, rallies, and cru-
sades, but the glitter was dimming.

In the White House at Washington, a worried and anxious
Lincoln took command of his own army, since his top general, George McClellan, was seriously ill, and had accomplished nothing in five months other than organizing a few
troops. General McClellan's propensity to march a lot and
rarely attack annoyed the president.

In the White House at Richmond, an equally worried
Jefferson Davis watched his armies diminish in manpower.
Many went home to repair things so they could return in the
spring. The Federal blockade wouldn't go away, or be beaten,
and the shortages were grinding down the people's will with
the passing of every day. There was not enough of anything
at times, except valor.

With headquarters at Louisville, General Carlos Buell created the Army of the Ohio. Buell agreed with Sherman that
his troops were not in shape to invade East Tennessee and

had plans of his own to sweep south on the Tennessee River and open up the entire Mississippi valley to Union forces.

But Buell had not reckoned with the political pressure the Unionists from East Tennessee would place on President Lincoln. Representative Maynard and Senator Johnson went to the president. They obtained his promise that an advance toward Knoxville would be made immediately.

In his annual message to Congress, Lincoln stated: "I deem it of importance that the loyal regions of East Tennessee and western North Carolina should be connected with Kentucky and other faithful parts of the Union by railroad. I therefore recommend, as a military measure, that Congress provide for the construction of such a road as speedily as possible." Congress took no action on this request, so Maynard wrote Buell a curt letter intending to prod him into action.

Buell paid no attention to the politicians and kept his forces idle. He conferred frequently with General Thomas at Lebanon, Kentucky, and in January advised Thomas that Zollicoffer was advancing from Cumberland Gap toward Mill Springs, a few miles southwest of Somerset.

Corporal Spence McAlpin, now twenty-one years old, rode in a cavalry regiment in Zollicoffer's army.

President Lincoln became impatient and telegraphed to ask, "have arms gone forward to East Tennessee? Please tell me the progress and condition of the movement in that direction. Answer!"

But the Federal forces still made no movement. Buell did write to his president that any thrusts made in this direction would be done "more for my sympathy for the people of East Tennessee and the anxiety with which you and the general-in-chief have desired it than by my opinion of its wisdom."

Abraham Lincoln was not alone in having troubles with generals. For some time, Jefferson Davis at Richmond had had doubts about the military abilities of General Zollicoffer. Consequently, he assigned Major General George Crittenden to take his place.

In the cold and wet of January, Crittenden learned that General Thomas was approaching Zollicoffer near Mill Springs, Kentucky. He ordered a surprise attack.

Spence and his cavalry encountered Union pickets early. The rider to his right took a ball through his neck, sending fear among the others. They scrambled for cover to the rear.

"What do you think Corporal? Can the Fifteenth Mississippi hold?" asked an unknown Rebel on his horse beside Spence.

"Naw! Watch 'em drop like flies, one by one, over and over."

"I'm scared, Corporal—my first fighting an—"

"Shut up and move. We're going to the front," Spence yelled.

AT THE CREST of the hill, Spence reloaded and looked at the ground behind him. Dead and bleeding boys lay everywhere. Fear jolted his body.

Suddenly, a bolt of firing came at close range. General Zollicoffer fell. Spence's horse threw him to the ground. He looked up from the mud and saw the smoking gun of a Union lieutenant. On a horse Spence would know anywhere, sat Spence's daddy, Fletcher, in Union blue. A cloud of smoke briefly obscured the scene. Spence jumped up and ran for the cover of a tree.

Lieutenant John Hansen of the Ohio Twenty-eighth carefully aimed.

"I'm going to get that one. Look at him run. Got me a general already—might as well get me a corporal."

Fletcher was shocked to see the red kerchief on the Rebel's neck.

He quickly reached over and nudged Hansen's barrel, just as he squeezed off the shot. The bullet snapped a branch from a tree above Spence's head.

"What the hell?" Hansen screamed.

Fletcher sat stiff in the saddle—mute–staring ahead.

"McAlpin! What on earth? Why did you–whose side you on?" Silence.

"Answer me. Now! Or you'll find yourself before the general."

"I know him," Fletcher mumbled.

"You know him? So? Good God man, this is war! When are you going to learn?"

A BIG MAN wearing a black coat and hat stood in front of his blacksmith shop on the north end of Gay Street. He watched the exhausted swarms of battle-weary Rebels drag themselves into town. He walked beside Spence's cavalry friend and stopped.

"Son, how many Rebs fought up there?" the man asked.

"'Bout four thousand," mumbled Spence's friend, as he trudged along beside his horse. A torn gray blanket covered his head.

"How many deserters? Fugitives are all over."

"Who knows. You write for the paper, stranger?"

The man in black ignored the question. "Word has it that one Rebel ain't superior to five Yankees no more. What about it?"

"I wouldn't know." The soldier stopped, stretched, and turned to check Spence's reaction.

"Do you know if Generals Crittenden and Carroll were drunk the night before the—"

"Go to hell!" Spence shouted. "Leave us alone!" The two Rebs and their horses started walking again. The man in black fell back.

He could not conceal the smile as he watched the turmoil and dejection.

"This bunch is going to need a lot of laudanum and morphine," he said under his breath. "After I make sure the Rebs are comfortable, I'll ride up to Mill Creek and check on the Yanks. They'll need some medicine too."

"Why don't you put down that *Harper's Weekly,* Big Pa. Don't you get tired of the Northern press?"

"Touchy, touchy, Spence. Yeah, I get tired of it, but I need to know what they're thinking. Says here 'this victory inaugurates the beginning of the end of the rebellion . . .' treason draws a great deal of sustenance from Kentucky and Tennessee. Conquer the Border States, and the rebellion is mortally wounded. Our generals know this. Rebel generals know this."

The big fire at Aberdour roared and crackled. "Thanks for letting me come here. I know it could be dangerous for you, but I needed to collect my thoughts and rest."

"Why don't you tell your grandfather just what did happen?"

Spence took a sip of warm brandy, lay back on the couch, and began to talk. He told of troop movements on both sides, the incompetence of the officers, the poor logistics of artillery, the harsh weather, the utter failure of the surprise attack.

"Then General Zollicoffer thought Colonel Fry's Fourth Kentucky was part of his own brigade and ordered the Nineteenth Tennessee to stop firing because he thought they were shooting their own men. Zollicoffer rode to the front in this white raincoat—smoke was everywhere—until he was knee to knee with Colonel Fry. The colonel didn't even know who the general was. Then my commander and I realized what was happening, so we rushed Fry. Unfortunately Fry woke up and shot the general. Some lieutenant shot him too. Poor stupid man—didn't stand a chance. Then my horse threw me, so I ran away on foot."

"First Tennessee general killed," Harry said. "Still, it was nice of General Thomas to send the body back to his family in Nashville."

RECENTLY PROMOTED TO Captain, John Hansen was awarded three days of furlough. He wasted no time in riding to Lochsley Collin's house in Hancock County, sixty miles away.

Chapter Nineteen

THROUGHOUT THE LONG history of warfare, there probably has never been a soldier who didn't believe God was on his side— at least, those who believed in a Supreme Being. Then there were pragmatists, many of whom loved his God no less than the next man, who believed that God didn't care who won battles.

In the spring of 1862, God was indifferent to war, showering East Tennessee with His most beautiful manifestations— springtime in the mountains.

On April 6, His red flaming sun peered over the top of Clingman's Dome and saturated the spaces between the level strata of clouds with lessening intensities of chroma until the blackness of the night was encountered. In time, the consistency of His power lit up more and more of the land until the darkness was shoved into the Pacific Ocean. Crocus and jonquils broke through the icy earth and sweetened the gray mist surrounding the bare forests.

Harry and Mary Clay were at church. Reverend Mayhew finished singing the hymns, had the offertory, and in no time was into his sermon, but not before he took occasion to look

down at the increasingly attractive Polly Chamons. Their eyes
met. A discreet smile registered on the reverend's face, and
then he looked at his text.

"Brothers and Sisters, for those who have their Bibles, turn
to the first chapter of James in the New Testament. Reading
from the second verse: 'If any of you lack wisdom, let him ask
of God . . . and it shall be given to him. But let him ask in
faith, nothing wavering. For he that wavereth is like a wave
of the sea driven with the wind and tossed. For let not that
man think that he shall receive any thing of the Lord. A
double minded man is unstable in all his ways.'

"Now listen, my flock, our nation is wavering—double-
minded. Most of you know my affection for our glorious
Union. Most of you have already suffered because of this sad,
unholy war. It is sad to allow that the clergy, yes, men from
within the ranks of my own profession, have had a great deal
to do with the fracture of the Union. Secession in the church
was a natural prelude to secession in the state.

"When John Calhoun noted in his last formal speech, in
1852, that the bonds of unity between North and South were
beginning to snap, he undoubtedly had in mind the spiritual
cords that had bound together the Methodists and the Baptists.

"Religious fire-eaters, such as Thornwell, the preeminent
Presbyterian in South Carolina, held a fast day only a fort-
night after Lincoln's election. Of course, he called for secession, even 'though our path to victory may be through a
baptism of blood.'

"Then of all things, Presbyterian Palmer of New Orleans,
in his Thanksgiving sermon 'Feeling impelled to deepen the
sentiment of resistance in the Southern mind,' struck fire
with God's plan for the South—to perpetuate slavery—and
the sublimity of the Southern position: 'If she has the grace
given her to know her hour, she will save herself, the country,
and the world.'"

Mayhew paused and looked over the congregation. Except for a few men in their late fifties and older, he was talking to a smattering of women.

"What a pity," he continued, "to behold a rebellion that has claimed our youth. The products of the birthing and the nurturing that you women out there in the congregation propounded. It is wrong I tell you. Wrong, wrong!" He pounded his fist on the lectern.

"This dependence on religion in the Confederacy may be one more reason for associating this vile war with the age of chivalry. You tell me. Is it chivalrous to murder and hang Union-loving ministers of the gospel? Is it? This has been done."

Toward the end of the sermon, the tolerant congregation was becoming fatigued with the reverend's harping. Harry McAlpin, while agitated, couldn't help but notice that Mayhew seemed to be getting tired of hearing himself and was making eye contact more with Polly.

Mercifully, dismissal was pronounced and so ended another Sabbath service at Big Pistol.

While the parishioners were going home, 350 miles to the west, the Confederate army under General Albert Sidney Johnston was battering Ulysses S. Grant's Federals around another church called Shiloh. The church sat near Pittsburg Landing on the Tennessee River.

Areas like the Sunken Road, the Hornet's Nest, the Bloody Pond, and the Peach Orchard would ring down through infamy. Heroes were being made on both sides and few cowards were revealed.

TUESDAY EVENING, APRIL 8, 1862. After supper in the big house only two sounds could be heard: the muted crackling of the fire, and the sound of Blue John polishing boots. Harry McAlpin sat with a homemade brandy and read *Harper's Weekly*.

Mary Clay sat knitting her son a shawl in the gray and cream colors of the Confederacy.

A member of the church, whose husband raises sheep, was able to supply her with wool since it had become impossible to buy the yarn at the markets. Another neighbor boiled sumac stalks for the gray and Queen Anne's lace for the cream colors. Her mind drifted back to the red scarf she had knitted for her husband. That dye came from the boiled cochineal insect from the New Mexico Territory and cost thirty-two cents for an ounce. Very expensive, she thought.

"Tell me what's happening with the war," she asked in a monotone.

Harry looked up from his paper.

"I know exactly what they're trying to do. They took Forts Donelson and Henry in February and in two days were in Nashville. They've split our state open as ice ruptures copper pipes.

"The folks in Nashville must have been terrified—to know that the Yankee army was coming. I read that Governor Harris himself carried all the state records out in boxes. That is, all his wagon could carry.

"Then they took some places where Tennessee, Missouri, and Kentucky come together. Memphis will be next, then Natchez, then Vicksburg. They're using the navy—frigates, gunboats, and those gruesome ironclads."

"Ironclads?"

"The usual gunboat, but altered with iron plates. Cannon shot can't pierce 'em. Got revolving gun turrets on top too. Powerful weapons. Got us blocked around our coasts. Now they're sealing the Mississippi River. Going to strangle the South like a snake does a rat."

"Doesn't seem fair," Mary Clay whispered.

"Fair? Huh! All that Northern power and industry. Our Southern boys are half-starved, without shoes, sorry weapons, cold—and yet we still come at 'em. The same bunch of Feds who took Nashville will keep on moving until they get into Mississippi. You know what they want? That railroad. The Memphis and Charleston."

"Wish I hadn't asked," Mary Clay said. "Big Pa, do you think Spence will like this scarf I'm knitting. If I do say so, it will be pretty as well as warm."

"But Miss Mary Clay," Blue John said, "it done getting warm now. What's he going to do with a wool scarf wrapped around his neck with it being 100 degrees in the shade?"

"Blue John, don't be silly. He won't be wearing it. And we don't even know when he will be able to stop and get it now do we? Never you mind, this war will be going on come fall, and he'll use it then."

There was a pause. Harry went back to his reading. Mary Clay was deep in thought as she continued knitting.

"You and Blue John going to plant this year?" Her mind raced.

"Oh yeah, got to. With prices what they are, we have to be depending more on ourselves than ever. But, with them renegades coming through and stripping our fields as they did last year, we'll need to go to the fields at night I guess, just to get something to eat. Even then, we'll have to bury the crop, or hide it some way," Blue John said.

"Of course we'll plant, Mary Clay," Harry said. "The worst part is that I can't get my opium from Thick Neck. Somebody has also been stealing the opium we had hidden here. I tell you, nothing is safe anymore, not property, not food, not life. This is terrible."

Loud pounding on the door brought Blue John to open it. F. L. Chamons barged in.

"Evening, Blue John," he said in a perfunctory manner.

"Evening, sir, what brings you out this time of night?"

"Big news. Evening, Harry, Mary Clay. They've been fighting on the Tennessee at a place called Shiloh. Sunday the Confederates routed them and damned near ran Grant into the river 'till it got dark.

"During the night the Yankees got reinforcements from Wallace and Buell. Yesterday the Feds took back most of the ground they lost Sunday. The South is retreating back to Corinth without a victory."

"Was it bad, F.L.?"

"It was considered a standoff—one that cost the Federals over 13,000 killed or wounded, and cost the Confederates 11,000 killed, wounded, or missing. The South lost General Johnston is the worst part. Got shot in the leg and simply bled to death. Beauregard took over, but with all those extra men on the other side, the South couldn't pull it out."

Harry paced in front of the fireplace.

"It's looking bad out there in the West. Hell, it's looking bad here. I haven't had income in a year. Chamons, we've got to get some opium down here."

"It won't happen, Harry," Chamons said. "Not until the South pulls out and the Feds come in with a supply line from Kentucky and Ohio. Maybe Thick Neck could bribe people in the quartermaster corps to stash a few piculs under a wagon and get it to Knoxville. Then, maybe we could pick it up. In a way, I would hate to see Unionists running all over these parts, but we must be flexible."

"Yes, yes, you're right," Harry said. "Guess we'll have to bide our time and try not to starve. Just have to wait and see."

❖ ❖ ❖

JULY 1862

"I don't see God's justice—making someone with ambition and schooling as I have be behind this . . . arrgh! ole hoe! Oh, I hate this. Hate, hate, hate!" Polly said. She pounded her hoe into the caked soil to rid the pole beans of bull nettle and jimson weeds.

"Polly, now, I don't blame God for putting us in this field," Becky reasoned. She was one row over and ten feet behind. "Think of those poor men whose misfortune caused them to die in battle, do you blame God for that?"

"Oh Becky, shut up! I'm tired of your religiosity. You're too nice, and much too soft on God who put us here."

It was late in the morning, but the sun seemed to be at its zenith, in position and intensity. The humidity was stifling.

Two months ago, on April 16, President Davis approved an act of the Confederate Congress calling for conscription of every white male between eighteen and thirty-five years of age for three years of service. Most of the field hands hired by Harry and Storch were gone. Women and children took to the fields for survival—profits and commerce had long been forgotten.

Willis at Storch's farm, and Orvil at Aberdour managed to stay and work by day and steal opium by night.

Storch even hid Moody in a root cellar when a squadron of Confederates came snooping around looking for men. Martial law had been declared in East Tennessee the week after Shiloh in anticipation of a Federal invasion as well as increased threats by pro-Unionists civilians.

Polly wiped the rolls of sweat from her brow with an already-wet sleeve. A circle of perspiration radiated from under her arms. Polly and Becky's billowy long dresses were wrinkled and filthy. The rows never seemed to end. When they finished hoeing in a patch, they got to return to the first row and do it all over again.

"It's punishment you know," Polly said.

"God is making me go through all this because of my thoughts about men. Or maybe because I told you where babies came from. Or maybe because of the time I said all those bad words in Sunday school."

"Don't be silly, Polly. We have to do what Papa tells us to do. Trust him. He knows best. We'll be all right and we'll have enough to eat as well."

"And, Becky, when we get our little meager plants to grow, ruffians will come through and strip everything bare. How is that for justice? If we don't bury everything, we'll be looted."

Storch had wisely planted carrots and sweet potatoes in a small clearing hidden in the forest. They had underground roots and would not be noticed. He hid his pigs in the cave, but had given up on the cows. Too big to hide, they were constantly being slaughtered and eaten by roaming hoards.

He had also given up on mining his silver vein since gold and silver disappeared from circulation. He and Moody would slip into their nitre mine at night and harvest that. They could sell the nitre for gunpowder to the Rebels in Maryville, but they had to accept Confederate paper since banks had withdrawn their own notes from circulation.

Debtors had a windfall, as they could pay in depreciated bank notes, or better still, Confederate notes. The creditor was in an uneasy position. If he refused Confederate currency, he was subject to suspicion and abuse. By April 1862, the military authorities held that any persons refusing to accept these notes would be guilty of political offense and punished accordingly. Prices rose as a result of speculation, profiteering, and genuine scarcity. Coffee and salt became the most wanted items.

❖   ❖   ❖

"POLLY, POLLY. LOOK up. Guess who's here?" Becky asked. She dropped her hoe.

Polly stopped hoeing. From a distance she saw Reverend Mayhew riding around the corner of the tavern. The girls gathered their dresses and walked through the field toward the house.

"Morning, Miss Polly—Miss Becky," Mayhew said.

Both girls beamed.

"Thought I'd ride over and have lunch with your daddy and mama. Been visiting around with members of the flock trying to encourage them, trying to make them believe that all this hardship isn't willed by the Almighty and to remember the words of our famous New Englander, Ralph Waldo Emerson: 'Our strength grows out of our weakness. Not until we are pricked and stung and sorely shot at does it awaken the indignation which arms itself with secret forces.'"

Becky glanced at Polly. She stood sweating, legs aching, and feet numbing. Polly crossed her arms and thought, This is the man of my dreams? He is sitting up there on that horse in the shade of our oak trees with his clean suit, lily-white skin, and soft hands. I'm worn-out from fieldwork. He'll want to come and eat some of the beans that I've helped put on the table—and for free! I still say he's handsome and oh, so learned. Why, oh why have I fallen for him of all people.

Mayhew continued. "A great man is always willing to be little. Whilst he sits on the cushion of advantages, he goes to sleep. When he is pushed, tormented, defeated, he learns something. He puts on his wits, his manhood. He has gained facts, learned his ignorance, has been cured of the insanity of conceit. He has got moderation and hence, real skill."

There was silence. Mayhew was in a trance. His being had translated back to his college days when he fell in love with the words of transcendentalist thinkers, like Emerson, Thoreau, Whitman, and Longfellow.

"Oh. That's so beautiful," Becky said.

"Yes, my good Reverend, it's beautiful all right, but do you think you could take some of your 'moderation and skill' and get out here in the hot sun and help us weed the beans? It's not fittin' that a lady should have to do all this," Polly stated.

"Uh, no, ma'am, not this time. After we eat, I must see two more families up on the Middle Prong; by the time I get back, it'll be dark. Perhaps the madam Chamons would like to take a ride in the country one of these days?"

"Reverend, we are in the country. Deep in it." She paused. "All right, anything to break up the monotony around here."

"Very well, one of these days I'll come calling. Now let's go inside and eat lunch." He turned and walked toward the tavern.

Becky waited until he was inside and then she put her hand to her mouth and beamed. "Did you hear what he said?"

"I did, but don't you dare tell a soul, Becky Chamons."

Chapter Twenty

LOCHSLEY FANNED HERSELF WITH the writing paper, exhaled, and placed it on the table.

Dear Spence,

Just a short note before I fix supper . . . Union men stop constantly—know some very well, one Captain especially. He is with General George Morgan at Cumberland Gap. Recently, General Kirby-Smith's Rebel army skirted the Yankees at the Gap and then invaded Kentucky. Papa says he is trying to link with Bragg's army and drive into Ohio. Must crush Buell's army first. If successful, it will force Grant to call off his siege of Vicksburg, run to Ohio and defend the North.

Spence, are you with Kirby-Smith? I know you're busy, but a note from you would be appreciated. Looks good for the Confederates now . . . frankly tired of them all.

July 12, 1862

Fondly,

Lochsley

Bragg delayed too long, and Buell's Yankees slipped right by him into Louisville where he received reinforcements. Kirby-Smith was ordered to evacuate Lexington, and the two invading armies did not unite.

Lexington was looted, and everything that could not be carried off was burned. An immense cavalcade of wagon trains, filled with ammunition and captured artillery, headed the procession southward. Trains of merchandise and army stores followed, including 20,000 captured rifles. Farther behind came refugees, fleeing with their families and servants, women and children in carriages, stagecoaches, express wagons, ambulances, and every available vehicle at hand.

Finally came the brigades of Rebel soldiers, thousands of herds of cattle, horses, and mules, and 4,000 shiny new United States wagons. The procession was forty miles long.

By October 23 the two armies were entering Knoxville, where 15,000 men required medical treatment. They had marched 1,000 miles, fought battles, and were back where they started two months before. The campaign had been conducted over more territory than any other of the entire war, but the results amounted to nothing of strategic significance.

Entering Knoxville, Spence rode two columns behind General Kirby-Smith. Snow was falling and nobody spoke. Spence saw the man in black and two men with rifles come out of the blacksmith shop at the foot of Gay Street. Kirby-Smith stopped.

"Evening General," the King of Ireland yelled, grabbing the bit of Kirby-Smith's horse. "Y'all are about the lousiest, dirtiest, ragged looking bunch of Rebels I ever saw."

"I'm sorry my friend, but we've never met. I really must get my men some medical—"

"What happened?" the man in black asked.

"General Bragg lost his guts and lost Kentucky—let Buell slip by into Louisville. We never linked up. Looted the hell out of Lexington for our troubles. The men love those Yankee blue wool blankets. Excuse me, I need to keep going."

Ireland let go of Kirby-Smith's horse. "Aren't you glad you aren't still teaching math at West Point?"

"Yes, and good day."

"General, bet you're sleeping at the Cowan house where it's nice and warm."

"Mr. Cowan serves the finest coffee in the world," yelled Kirby-Smith as he rode away.

Spence rode to catch up with his general. "Who was that, sir? I've seen him before."

"Some agent—claims to run a blacksmith shop—likes to poke fun at the Confederacy and our efforts."

"Agent. What kind of agent? Do you know him?"

"Never met him, but I've seen him around the sick bays. I think he sells medicines. Forget him. Where will you be for the next few days? Don't tell me—Tuckaleechee Cove."

"Was planning on sleeping there tonight, sir, if it's all right."

"It's all right, young man. We didn't turn the tide, but at least we kept 'em out of East Tennessee for a while—still kept our railroad, too. See you in a few days?"

"Be back soon," Spence said, as he broke from the column.

"SPENCER. ARE YOU all right?" Mary Clay whispered. "You've been asleep fifteen hours now . . . Blue John has a little food downstairs. Don't you want to get up and eat something?"

"All right, Mother," the young man groaned. He rolled over. "I'll be down in a minute or two."

At Harry's insistence, Blue John had boarded up the small house in which Spence was reared. With the roving bands coming through the cove, Mary Clay was safer to join the men at the big house.

"Good morning, son. Food is on the table." Mary Clay watched Spence slowly make his way downstairs. "Sure is good to have you, even if it is for only a few hours. Here's country ham . . . eggs . . . cat-eyed biscuits, and sorghum molasses."

Harry came in the back door and greeted Spence. "Son, tell us about that march into Kentucky and back. Always proud to get a personalized account of the war."

Spence used the next twenty minutes to relate the lack of the large-scale victory the Confederates hoped for.

"Boy, where's that stone you used to wear around your neck?" Blue John asked.

"Lost it . . . it was stolen." Spence put molasses on another biscuit. "Guess you want to hear about that too?"

As he finished his story, Mary Clay snapped her fingers and jumped from the table. She returned from the living room, "I almost forgot this, Spence. It came a month ago—the same time you were on your way to Kentucky with Kirby-Smith."

Spence looked at the two-cent stamp and return address. He excused himself from the table and walked into the orchard to be alone.

Dear Spencer,

Although we haven't experienced battles around Newman's Ridge, I hear war is an awful horror. It gets so lonely up here . . . maybe Papa is right . . . I should get off this mountain . . . lack of people my age, the scarcities . . . Spence, we have been close, our emotions strong, even though we have been far apart. We both felt the future might hold something for us, that is, until this dreadful war.

All this has worked on my mind . . . I think I have changed, truth is, I have met a wonderful man who asked me to marry him, Captain John Hansen from Ohio, served with Generals Thomas and Morgan around Cumberland Gap. Spence, I told him 'yes.' Don't know when we'll be wed as he had to leave the gap with Morgan. Keep the stone, think of me, become the man of success and means and influence that I know you can. I will never get over you, but it has been so long since I've heard anything, who knows, you may be dead. If you're alive, I wish you Godspeed and His richest blessings. September 16, 1862

Your obedient servant,

Lochsley

Spence wandered aimlessly among the pear and apple trees. He kicked the dirt and smacked an apple still hanging from a low limb, stuffed the letter in his pant's pocket and charged back into the house.

He got a pint of brandy from Harry's liquor cupboard, packed his few belongings, said his good-byes and climbed on his horse for the ride to Knoxville. He turned around. His mother was leaning against one of the columns, crying.

"THERE THEY ARE," Jeremiah Stewart yelled. He yanked his horse away from the creek.

"Who? General Buckner?" Spence yelled back.

"Yeah, General Simon Bolivar Buckner. Ex-emperor of Knoxville."

The cloud of dust and a covey of dove rose to announce 8,000 marching men arriving at the Tennessee-Georgia state line. Buckner's Corp had been ordered to evacuate Knoxville and join Bragg's army below Chattanooga.

"You scouts have anything?" Buckner asked.

"Yes sir, they're 'bout ten miles away," Spence said.

"Thank you son. We've missed you two for the last two days. Ride up here at the head with us. When will we get there?"

"By dark, sir."

"Forward, March!" yelled a nearby officer.

"Coffee Spence?" Jeremiah asked. He turned from the campfire.

"Not tonight. Too hot. I'll take my water."

"Wonder what she's doing tonight . . . oh, my little Knoxville girl."

"You spent too much time in that river tavern, Jeremiah. You know you'll always be leaving somebody, or something. That's why I try not to get involved. Speaking of leaving, I'll bet Burnside has already marched into Knoxville. Left it wide open for him, why wouldn't he?"

"Listen Spence, there's a dentist working over there at that wagon. I need to see him. Besides, he has morphia. Be back at taps."

Spence wrote a letter home and went to bed. Sleep wouldn't come.

"Spence. You awake?" Jeremiah shook Spence's shoulder.

"We're being transferred tomorrow—to Gist's Brigade."

"Who's he?"

"States Rights Gist—Harvard man."

"Who said?"

"A captain said—while I was at the dentist. Know what else he said?"

"Who?"

"The dentist. I'll swear, he knows everything. He was with our men at Vicksburg. Rations of parched corn were being counted out by the kernel. That's per day. Says they ate vermin, too.

"He said that General Burnside has been in Knoxville three weeks. The loyalists are feeding him cakes and pies. Burnside thinks he's their savior. Won't leave, either."

"Good night!"

"One more thing. Rosecrans will attack us any time, now. The dentist says Rosecrans thinks he's Napoleon."

"Go to bed, Jeremiah."

"ATTENTION! ROLL CALL. Quiet!" screamed the sergeant major.

"How do you feel being a new first lieutenant," Jeremiah whispered from his horse.

"Hush, Jeremiah. Pay attention—you're supposed to be at attention."

"Isn't that Forrest's Cavalry over there?"

Spence turned to look. A minute passed before he brought his head back to the front. "Forrest isn't the only one I'm interested in," he whispered. "Third squad, second man—J. D. Storch."

"Really! He doesn't deserve to be with that group—with all their prestige. What are you thinking?"

"I knew God had a reason to bring me to Chickamauga Creek."

"You're not going to do anything dumb, are you?"

"When the attack comes, Jeremiah. Watch and see."

EARLY ON THE morning of September 19, 1863, Rosecrans' Army of the Cumberland and Bragg's Army of Tennessee faced each other.

A major battle developed before either commander had prepared a plan. As dusk came, little progress had been made by either side, although the casualties were heavy.

"Jeremiah! This is it—now's the time," Spence yelled.

"For what? And keep your bloomin' head down."

"To settle an old score with Storch. Remember, I told you about it? This is the perfect opportunity."

"Spence, don't be stupid. We've become friends—I hate to see my friends get killed."

"I won't get killed, especially if you'll cover me. Do it, Jeremiah—I'll forgive you for what you did to us up on Meigs Mountain that time."

"All right. Stay low and move fast."

Spence broke from his group, changed jackets with a dead Confederate captain, smeared mud on his face, then rode toward Forrest's Cavalry position.

He approached J.D.'s squadron and yelled, "General Forrest wants y'all to take that breastwork over yonder."

In his haste to obey the orders, J.D. led his troops into a grove of trees occupied by hidden Federal artillery. Amongst wild yelling and excitement, J.D.'s horsemen charged, thinking it was theirs for the taking. At a range of fifteen yards, a mighty burst from a cannon spewed forth. The ball ripped through J.D.'s leg, tearing it in half. Other men of the squadron, recognizing the trap, retreated backwards. Spence disappeared back to his regiment and changed into his own jacket.

He felt no guilt—only extreme satisfaction to know the next-to-worst of the clan was now gone. One of these days, he would take care of Storch and Moody. He roasted his meat over the fire that night and smiled.

THAT EVENING, UNDER light of kerosene lamps, Union surgeons worked feverishly in the regimental medical tent. Stretcher-bearers and their ambulance-wagon drivers had the task of circulating among the dead and wounded of both sides. Moans penetrated the night stillness. The air was heavy and warm. Many were calling for their mothers. All who had any strength left were begging for water.

Lanterns of the ambulance crews bobbed up and down like fireflies. When a wagon filled with litters, the driver would make way to the busy medical tent. As wagon number eleven unloaded, the driver jumped down and checked the pulse of each man as they were being put on cots—just to make sure the soldier had not died since being picked up from the field. As he checked the weak pulse of his last patient, the driver looked up into the gaunt and fatigued face of Clint McGlothen.

"This one's about gone. Took a ball through the leg. Damned Rebel! I wouldn't waste a lot of time with him."

"I'll make that decision," McGlothen snapped. He dismissed the driver to return to the night for more body retrieval. He placed two fingers on the ulnar artery of the man's limp right arm and peered into his face. He looked hauntingly familiar.

"Mama . . . Papa . . . Virgil, I'm coming to be with you. Water!" J. D. Storch groaned, the life ebbing from him. In a moment he was gone. His eyes dilated.

McGlothen looked over his shoulder to see if he was being watched. He wasn't. He began to search through J.D.'s pockets.

DURING THE NIGHT, General Longstreet, on loan from General Robert E. Lee, arrived from Virginia, with five of his nine brigades. His Corp was assigned to the Confederate right wing.

The next day, the Confederate army resumed the attack at dawn. Neither side made progress until eleven o'clock. Longstreet found a breach in the Federal lines and broke through to the rear of the demoralized Federal brigades. As Longstreet's men poured through the gap, sweeping forward like the flood of a mighty river, the entire Union line crumbled.

As General Bushrod Johnson's troops and General Simon Buckner's troops joined with General Leonidas Polk's men near the Chattanooga road, a mighty roar swelled across the countryside, not as the burstings from the cannon's mouth, but in a tremendous swell of heroic harmony that seemed to lift from their roots the great trees of the forest.

The whole Federal line was taken. Rosecrans' headquarters was overrun, and he fled to Chattanooga. At four o'clock in the afternoon, he rode to the door of the adjutant general's office, faint, ill, and hysterical.

Longstreet ordered General Joseph Wheeler's cavalry to dash forward and cut the fleeing Federals to pieces.

General Nathan Forest climbed a tree and observed the disorganized masses swarming over the fields, though no one was in pursuit. He shouted to an aide, "Tell General Bragg to advance the whole army, the enemy is ours."

But the obstinate Bragg halted his generals and ordered them to pick up arms and stragglers.

General Longstreet shook his head and was teary eyed. "Bragg seems to be the only man who doesn't know a great victory has been won."

ROSECRANS, NOW GIVEN time to calm down and regroup his forces, wired Burnside that night. "We have met with disaster. Please bring assistance from Knoxville."

From Washington, General Halleck sent fifteen telegraphs to Burnside urging him to assist Rosecrans, all to no avail. At one juncture, Burnside wired back to Washington that he was moving to Jonesboro.

"Damn Jonesboro!" Abraham Lincoln shouted, a man who rarely cursed. He dictated a reply to his stubborn general: "Yours of the Twenty-third is just received and it makes me doubt whether I am awake or dreaming. I have been struggling for ten days to get you to go to assist General Rosecrans in an extremity, and you have repeatedly declared you would do it, and yet you steadily move the contrary way."

Rosecrans' army was in actual danger of starvation, and the railroad to his rear seemed inadequate for his supply. George Thomas replaced Rosecrans in command of the Army of the Cumberland. Sherman replaced Grant in command of the Army of the Tennessee. Grant was made commander of the newly formed Military Departments and Armies of the Cumberland, the Tennessee, and the Ohio. Burnside retained command of the Army of the Ohio and stayed in Knoxville. General Grant at once began steps to rescue Thomas' troops trapped by Bragg in Chattanooga.

Chapter Twenty-one

GENERAL GRANT BELIEVED THAT if he stalled long enough in Chattanooga, his adversary, Braxton Bragg, would make a mistake that would change the whole picture. And on November 4, 1863, General Bragg, prodded by Jefferson Davis, made the mistake.

While the Federals were concentrating their forces, Sherman joined Grant and Thomas in Chattanooga, and Bragg suddenly decided to divide his forces. From Atlanta on October 29, President Davis suggested to Bragg that he "might advantageously assign General Longstreet, with his two divisions, to the task of expelling Burnside from Knoxville." Davis hoped by this move to separate his two quarreling generals. Furthermore, if Longstreet could move with the swiftness and decisiveness of a Stonewall Jackson, defeat Burnside, and return to Chattanooga before the arrival of Sherman, the move would be a stroke of genius. Should the move against Knoxville fail, there could not be a worse mistake.

Longstreet had only a sketchy map of the roads and streams near Knoxville. No quartermaster or engineering officer was detailed to the expedition. Nevertheless, 17,000 intrepid and seasoned men marched into the teeth of one of the coldest winters in years.

The bloody fight at Knoxville lasted only twenty minutes. Bushrod Johnson's support brigades got no closer than 500 yards from the ditch below Fort Saunders when the first wounded were brought back by their comrades. The dripping blood from the litters, the groans of their mangled occupants, apprised Spence of the disaster. He also knew that 500 more Mississippi boys lay dead or dying in the moat.

General Johnson turned to Spence, "These are they who have passed through great tribulation."

Spence felt nauseous and knelt on the ground. He covered his head with his jacket and his thoughts went back to last night when he saw General Longstreet make assault plans in his comfortable quarters in the Armstrong House on Kingston Pike. Longstreet's aides were cursing and wondering why twelve days of siege wasn't enough to starve General Burnside's Federals.

Spence saw the row upon row of Southern men assembled in assault formation at 3:30 A.M.—thinly clad and barefoot, their suffering incalculable as they stood clasping with numbed hands the cold barrels of their muskets. The night was wretched with freezing temperatures and falling mist. He thought of the stout hearts that beat hopefully beneath each ragged gray jacket.

Spence saw the swinging lantern from Longstreet's headquarters at dawn used to signal the cannons across the river to inaugurate the battle. He heard the high-pitched yells and jerky canine yelps of the Rebels as they stormed the parapets of the fort.

Spence remembered the cold terror he felt when he and General Johnson realized General Longstreet had underestimated the depth of the ditch in front of the steep dirt bank. The Yankees had baited it with picks and strands of wire, and had poured water down from the top of the fort. This promptly froze, making the ditch a deathtrap of horrors for the invading Rebels.

Spence saw and heard the cannon and canister that the Federals poured into the storming party. The Confederates, with their battle flags of red with cross of blue floating defiantly above their heads, now lost the aspect of an assaulting column and became merely a mass of men who could not go forward, but were determined not to fall back. Many attempted to use bayonets and swords to hack out footholds in the slippery mud. The dead and dying were piling on top of one another.

He saw the assault degenerate into a frenzied trial of individual strength marked by beating, gouging, taunting, and swearing.

He saw the Rebel officer climb to the top and stand in front of the muzzle of a twelve-pound Napoleon gun. Spence still heard the echo, "Surrender, you damned Yankees!" He also heard the retort, "Yes, we'll surrender this to you," the Yanks responded as they yanked the lanyard and blew the Rebel into a thousand pieces.

Then it was quiet. Spence jumped up and flung his jacket to the ground. In a rage Spence yelled, "I'll bet the general is planning another attack. Old Longstreet hasn't hurt enough--wants some more of us to die. He got impatient? He guessed the depth of the ditch wrong? He should have sent me in there first. I put ten of 'em in the ground at Chickamauga, myself."

Jeremiah grabbed Spence. "Shut your mouth, it's not one man's fault. Nothing is going right for us. Besides, here comes a major . . ."

"Men! General Longstreet just saw a telegram from a courier at Rogersville—from President Davis. Says that General Grant has broken out of the Chattanooga encirclement and driven General Bragg's army from Missionary Ridge. You men have been ordered to abandon Knoxville and join Bragg near Ringgold, Georgia."

As the major rode away, the men looked blank. "What does that mean?" Jeremiah asked.

"It means we stop this nonsense, and head toward Virginia," Bushrod Johnson said.

"Virginia?"

"Remember men, Longstreet hates Bragg and will never again work with him. Longstreet is part of General Lee's army—that's where he'll return. You two men go and help with body counts."

❖ ❖ ❖

"Hey, Reb!" came the voice from atop the parapet. "Swap 'ye a pair of shoes for a twist of tobacco."

Two of the sharpshooters were beckoning to the exhausted Southerners below doing the "body work." The truce had been extended until seven o'clock in the evening so the Confederate dead and wounded could be carried to the rear. Spence and Jeremiah were each in charge of a squadron of men.

Spence looked around and saw none of the field officers were near enough to notice his activity, so he and several other men accepted the invitation to climb the hill and enter the fortress—so impenetrable two hours before—the fortress whose occupants had rained down sheets of hot lead into Southern flesh.

"Come on in boys—get yourselves warm by the fires," said a knotty man, older than those around him. His hands were weathered and cracked, his face smeared with gunpowder.

"Captain Hansen over there won't let us talk to you long—
got work to do. Lieutenant, you think old Longstreet will try
to whip us again?"

"He thought about it, Sergeant, but he got a telegram—
said Grant drove Bragg from Missionary Ridge," Spence said,
feeling awkward standing in the enemy's middle. Most were
busy cleaning cannons and tending to wounded to pay much
mind to the men in gray.

"Whoopee! Captain, did you hear that? Grant beat Bragg.
Makes our victory all the sweeter, wouldn't you say?" the man
said.

The captain wiped blood from his sword. Looking up, he
sheathed the sword in his scabbard and walked toward the
visitors.

"Good day, Lieutenant," John Hansen said. He returned
Spence's salute. "Nice to have you boys for a visit. You must
excuse my battery sergeant. He's a little loud, but a good
fellow. Can I do anything for you men?"

Spence shuffled his boots in the dust. He looked at the
Yankee sergeant being handed a twist of chewing tobacco
from a Confederate. The sergeant ran to scrounge a pair of
shoes for the barefoot Rebel.

"Yes sir, Captain, you could do something. Tell me how your
men held out twelve days and still have the energy to fight?"

"Of course, I'll tell you. Every night the Union sympathizers up river would float food down the river on rafts. We
caught the boats by lifting a submerged cable stretched across
the river below the fort. By the way, I'm John Hansen, Twenty-
eighth Ohio, and you're Lieutenant?"

"McAlpin . . . riding with Wheeler's Cavalry, attached to
Johnson's Brigade."

They shook hands.

"Have we met?" Hansen asked. Is it your name? That look in your eyes? Or the haughty way you walk—proud, cocky, defiant. Do I see myself in you? Yes, that's it, he thought.

"No, Captain, I don't think so. I've been to Cincinnati one time, but it wasn't up there. Probably someone else," Spence said.

It hit him like the butt-end of a cannon rammer jabbed in his stomach. Captain John Hansen. Fiancé of Miss Lochsley Collins. He is the one. Must remain stoic and unaffected— keep my secret.

"Captain, I must get these men back down there for body work. Your men are busy too," Spence stated. He braced to salute.

Hansen returned the salute. Spence turned to get back to his men.

Spence got as far as the stack of cotton bails on the edge of the parapet when his emotions overwhelmed him. He turned.

"Captain! Hansen! I believe you know a Lochsley Collins? We know each other through her."

Hansen heard the remark and turned. As Spence disappeared through the embrasure and down the embankment, Hansen yelled, "Wait!"

Too late. Spence was gone.

On December 3, 1863, Longstreet's army packed, and by the next dawning, was gone from Knoxville, headed northeast toward Virginia. They were an exhausted, dejected bunch of ragtag veterans of many battles. Time for them to lick their wounds, rest, and forget.

This is what they wanted. This was the way they thought it would be.

Chapter Twenty-two

MAUD PERKINS WALKED OUT the front door of the Maryville post office with a Boston newspaper in one hand and a letter from McGlothen in the other. She settled on a cold wooden bench on the front porch.

A month had passed since she had heard from the professor, but she knew it had been a busy time for the medical detachments of the Union army in Chattanooga.

She missed him, but knew he was keeping men alive —working deep into the night, catching sleep when possible, then back to work around the surgical tables. She hated it, but she understood. She buttoned her coat and read.

My dearest Maud:

Truly, I apologize to you for not writing, but as you can tell by the papers, we had our hands full. The Rebels had us pinned down and could have starved us if only their General Bragg knew how well he had us trapped. Daily we thank the Almighty that Grant opened a supply line out of Alabama into Chattanooga. As I'm sure you've read, Generals Hooker, Grant, and Sherman drove the

Johnny's off Missionary Ridge into Georgia. Chattanooga is in Federal hands for good. It was a double dose
of good fortune for Burnside to hold Knoxville. Sherman
left to help. I was transferred out of Thomas' Corps into
Sherman's. Yes, I'm coming home—at least for a little
while . . . can't stop in Maryville. Miss you and our lively
conversations. Have feeling the McAlpin boy fought at
Chickamauga—can't say why . . . am in possession of the
green stone he used to wear around his neck . . . eerie
occurrence. Will tell more later. Save a bottle of Medoc
for me.

My love,

Clint

"The utter futility of it all . . . ," she whispered. She picked
herself up from the bench and fought back the tears. "The
needless lives lost. And for what?" She walked across the
muddy street in a crooked line like a drunken sailor.

"Of course, nobody cares—I'm all alone." She took out
her handkerchief and wiped her eyes. "And those nasty, horrible soldiers! God curse 'em all. Oh Lord! I didn't mean
that. Just curse the ones who used the college as barracks and
carried off that Broadwood piano I donated, God-cursed, savage
thieves."

She looked down the ravine at the depot and thought how
Big Pistol Presbyterian Church was on that spot at one time
before Harry McAlpin got rich and bought the church and
moved it to Tuckaleechee. It had been named after Pistol
Creek that flowed through Maryville on its way to the Little
River, and Harry wanted to keep the name.

Why am I thinking about Harry right now? Maybe because
of Spence who may be dead. Dead! All that potential and
talent could be lying in the cold ground.

She hastened her steps and walked home. Even though it was only midday, she poured a brandy, stoked the fire, and sat in front of her mantle and hearth and said nothing.

GENERAL LONGSTREET MOVED his weary army eastward, out of Knoxville, along the northern edge of the valley, to Rutledge. By December 8 he was less than four miles from Lochsley's home, in Hancock County.

Spencer pined away, knowing of the many miles traveled, of the many battles survived, how ironic to be in the same county as Lochsley.

Strange, he thought. I think of her as "my Lochsley" with one part of me and the other part knows she isn't mine at all. I've lost her to a Northern soldier. She seems so near and yet so far, even though I'm riding through her county.

Am I in love with her? Naw! I'm feeling this way because someone else has her. It's just fatigue and loneliness.

No matter . . . it's over. She's over. Probably the war's over. Oh, to be back at Aberdour . . . running through fields . . . coming home to Mama's good meals.

His mind drifted . . . His horse plodded along effortlessly without being guided. Spence knew he was near his lowest point, maybe his breaking point. He feared he might do something irrational.

There was little talking among the ranks. Just one long gray line. Longstreet halted near Rogersville on December 9. He held his army here for a few days to forage for badly needed supplies.

That Longstreet was voluntarily leaving the area to rejoin Lee in Virginia was the consensus of the Federal authorities. Burnside, having the same opinion, did not accept Sherman's offer to remain and help drive the Confederates farther away—a serious mistake on his part.

He did, however, retain 10,000 of Sherman's men near Knox-ville as reinforcement. Included was a small field hospital unit employing one Clint McGlothen, surgeon's assistant.

Burnside thought a force of cavalry at Longstreet's heels would be sufficient to keep him moving until out of the state, and ordered it forward under General John Parke on De-cember 7. Annoyed at such inhospitable treatment by a force hardly one-fifth the size of his army, Longstreet turned on his antagonists at Bean Station on December 14. He soundly defeated the Federal forces and sent them in retreat toward their base at Knoxville.

With the pressure relieved, Longstreet decided to go into winter quarters here, and rest his army. On December 20 he moved his army across the Holston River at Long's Ferry, into a beautiful valley with farms now rich in forage. He selected a position along the railroad near Russellville for his camp.

Longstreet was content to settle into a strong defensive position, forage for supplies, and let the Federals make the next move. His decision was a sound one as it forced General Foster, Burnside's replacement, to take the offensive to remove him.

For the people in the valley, however, this decision spelled disaster. Knoxville was the nearest the residents of the valley had come to experiencing actual warfare. The citizens were to become victims of a military situation unplanned by either side. Regardless of which side they favored, their enemy was nearby.

Forage parties from both sides constantly came in search of food for their hungry men and animals. They came at all hours and took anything in sight that they needed or wanted. To resist was futile.

❖ ❖ ❖

THE NIGHT OF December 21 was clear and cold as the constella-tions above were twinkling their heavenly salutations. Spence and Jeremiah spurred their horses to ascend the banks on the east side of the Holston River that gave off an eerie fog that the men had to penetrate.

It had been a season of unprecedented bounty in East Tennessee. The fields groaned with the teeming abundance of wheat and corn. Pumpkins were on the ground like apples under a tree. Cattle, sheep, and swine, poultry, vegetables, maple sugar, and honey were all abundant for the immediate wants of the Southern troops.

What would the tender-hearted Lincoln have thought if he had known that nearly one-half of East Tennessee, which he thought freed of the enemy, was still in its possession. That the Rebel enemy was eating out the very life support of the loyal people, leaving them as destitute as if they dwelt on the plains of the Sahara. Longstreet's infantrymen constructed huts of logs and fence rails, and many were resting beside warm campfires. They built up a storage of food, and made shoes at the rate of 100 pairs per day. Efforts were made to find cloth to make blankets and clothing.

The Federals assembled a strong force of 6,000 cavalry for the purpose of removing Longstreet, but they would have to wait.

The weather was cold, and the river swollen and full of floating ice. The Federals began gingerly penetrating the icy waters at McKinney's Ford. The ford was tricky even in calm weather because it changed direction part way across.

Suddenly a horse and rider of the Twelfth Kentucky Cavalry were swept away. Comrades watched helplessly as still another was carried off struggling, then disappearing beneath the swirling water. The long line of riders could but move on. It was a dangerous undertaking, but accomplished before dark.

Spence and Jeremiah were assigned under the handsome General Frank Armstrong. Armstrong had pickets guarding the railroad and Knoxville road for miles ahead. His position was directly in front of the advance.

As the Federals moved through New Market, the enemy pickets were spotted, and for a few moments confusion reigned. Everywhere the Union troops took cover and prepared for a big fight. But the Confederates kept hidden, offering no resistance. As dark approached, the advanced regiments camped. That night, General Sturgis, commander, pondered what his next move would be. General Palmer visited him at headquarters at New Market and advised Sturgis of the latest Confederate positions. Both realized more time was needed to determine the strength of the enemy. At the same time, Sturgis was a man of action, and delay did not suit his purpose here. Therefore, he split his forces, one leg toward a Rebel movement at Dandridge, and the other leg to advance from New Market to Mossy Creek, where Spence and General Armstrong's cavalry were in waiting. Federal artillery pounded the Rebels into falling east of the creek. Jeremiah and Spence dodged canister and shell, fighting for their lives as they retreated backwards, not yet willing to play their hand as to their strength.

Federal artillery moved farther along the road toward Mossy Creek to the house of a Doctor Peck, and his home was ransacked, yielding fishing tackle, guns, and a piano.

On December 26 a steady, cold rain fell. The Federal camp was up at daybreak again with still no enemy in sight. They threw a few shells at Armstrong's men, but the Confederates keep well under cover.

Since no action developed, large fires of fence rails and logs were built along the Federal line to dry clothing and to keep warm. The smoke of these fires hovered in a blue haze across the fields as the rains continued.

The rain still fell on Sunday, December 27, and the whole valley became wet and muddy. All was quiet and both sides got some rest.

But at 3:00 P.M. the Union troops were ordered out to force the Rebels to do something. Back into town and across Mossy Creek they moved through the rain. The Confederates retreated, keeping a mile between the two forces.

Neither side did any harm. As dark approached, the Federals bedded down in the field at the point to which they had advanced. They had moved forward three miles without resistance and were only a short distance from Talbott's Station along the railroad.

The roaring campfire at General Armstrong's campsite was made from railroad ties, Yankee saddles, and slabs of oak and hickory. Spence and Jeremiah had a blanket apiece and shoes on their feet, a luxury in the Longstreet army.

General Armstrong walked to the fire and secretly handed Spence a pint of whisky. He and Jeremiah each had a sip and handed it back to Armstrong who then trundled back up the hill and disappeared into his tent to think.

The other officers dozed before the fire leaving Spence and Jeremiah alone with their thoughts. For once, there was the awesome sound of silence, save for a slight hiss of the wind high above the trees. The silence was broken by a faint sound of a harmonica with singing. Beautiful harmony filled the air and came from a distance away.

"Where's that music coming from?" Spence whispered.

"Don't know," Jeremiah answered. "Maybe it's coming from the pickets."

"Yankee pickets?"

"Yeah, maybe. Let's go see. I haven't sung in a long time. Maybe they would be glad to let us join 'em. Come on!"

"We can't go into Yankee lines to sing a song. If the enemy didn't shoot us, Armstrong would."

"Don't be silly. Get some tobacco and let's go."

The two men walked west for half a mile until they came to another large fire, this one occupied by Yankee sharpshooters. Two of the men jumped up until they saw that Spence and Jeremiah meant no harm; they motioned for them to sit down with them on the log. The men shared the tobacco and swapped stories; then the harmonica player began another song—a mournful one frequently sung by both sides.

"Just Before the Battle, Mother," the harmonica player said. "Key of B-flat."

While up on the field we're watching,

With the en-e-my in view.

Comrades brave are round me ly-ing,

Filled with thoughts of home and God:

For well they know, that on the morrow,

Some will sleep beneath the sod.

Fare-well Mother, you may nev-er,

Press me to your heart again;

But oh, you'll not for-get me, Mother,

If I'm numbered with the slain.

There was solemn silence. Several men had tears streaming down their faces, shining like silvery strands from the reflection of the fire. All wondered if tonight would be their last.

"Well, goodnight, gents. Enjoyed the songs. Gettin' heavy-eyed and need my rest," Jeremiah murmured. He slowly rose.

Spence stood with him, tipped his hat and turned to walk away. "Hey, Reb, what's old Armstrong gonna' try to do in the morning?" Spence turned around to face the Yanks, but kept walking backwards. "Who knows? Too cold to try to figure him out. But when I do, I'll let you know."

His answer brought a low round of laughter from the Yanks. They waved their hands in farewell. The harmonica player began playing "Battle Hymn of the Republic."

The two men walked along the Morristown road. Spence broke the silence.

"Jeremiah, we've been riding for two years, but you've never told me about yourself—where you come from. Forgive me if I'm nosy, but . . . well, what if something happened to you? What would I do? Who would I contact—and where?"

"You've never asked before. I never talk about it, but well, maybe it was the singing, or the weather . . . but OK"

"Good! I'm a little 'down' tonight, discouraged, tired of fighting," Spence said. They reached their campfire. Muffled snoring could be heard from the amorphous heaps beneath the blankets. Jeremiah took a stick and stoked the fire and the two of them sat down on their saddles.

"What do you mean you're discouraged, Spence? I've never said this, but you're the fightingest, and when you want to be, the meanest soldier a person would ever want to serve with. I've heard the generals talking—Wheeler, Gist, even Longstreet. Word gets around. They've watched you. I've watched you. When battle comes, something inside you must . . . must 'go off!' You become animal like—fearless, determined."

"Haven't thought about that part of it much. It's true I like the action."

"Like it? You love it! You thrive on it. If this war keeps on and if you stick, you're in for a lot of advancement. Who knows, you could be the youngest brigadier in all the Confederacy. Wouldn't that make your mother and grandpa proud?"

"Maybe so, but that's not my aim. Besides, my rotation is about up, so tomorrow when we meet Sturgis' Yankees, may be my last.

"And another thing, I don't think the South can last much longer. Look at our men. Many don't have shoes—in this kind of weather. The South can't even clothe its own.

"And, Jeremiah, how many hills have we taken, how many divisions have we routed, only to have to give it all back because we ran out of ammunition? The longer the war goes on, the more hardware those bastards get from all that industry. I'm beginning to think the United States Army could fight us with one arm tied behind its back and still grind us into the mud."

"I hear you."

"Our men have been baptized under fire so much— Manassas, Sharpsburg, Gettysburg, Chickamauga . . . and yet that blue army keeps coming."

"Hey, I thought you wanted to hear my story? We're going to need everything in you, tomorrow. Concentrate on what we're doing here and try to stay alive to fight another day. Let Jeff Davis and Judah Benjamin worry about the large details. They'll let us know when it's time to lay down our arms."

"Yeah, you're right."

"Well!" Jeremiah said, taking a breath. "You wanted to know about me?"

Spence nodded.

"I didn't really come from the other side of Meigs Mountain. I grew up in Baltimore. My daddy owned a saddle shop, but his real love was the theater. He was assistant stage director for the old Grafton Theater and spent much time there.

"I had a brother who joined with a Dutch merchant ship on its way around the horn bound for Sumatra; haven't seen him since.

"Anyway, I grew up around that theater. Papa loved Shakespeare; read it all the time. I grew to love it too, but as a spectator, never an actor. Mother died when I was eight, so it was all Papa could do to run that shop, direct plays, and be a father to us boys. There was something missing in our home, and I always stayed in trouble at school.

"When my brother left, Daddy seemed to believe he had failed us, and set about finding a wife to round out the household—only it was too late. He found a lady willing to marry him if he would move her to New York. He thought that was all right since he could be around even more stage plays."

"What did you think?"

"Listen, I wasn't about to go to New York. Too cold and crowded. Baltimore, in fact, was feeling that way to me, so I was old enough to strike out on my own, and that's what I did.

"Many folks headed to Kentucky, Tennessee, and farther west, so I decided I would do the same. When I got as far as these mountains, I had seen enough. Didn't need to go any farther. Papa had given me some money when he sold his business, so I bought a few acres on the North Carolina side, and learned to farm. Built a cabin too."

"How did you know what to do?"

"I didn't. But my neighbors took time to teach me and I took time to listen and ask questions.

"But still, I was a loner. Always had a chip on my shoulder. I was nice to the few neighbors nearby, because it was the thing to do, but I was mean. Still am. Seemed like I always attracted fights.

"Looking back on it, my only outlet was through the theater. I would watch the actors and carry through plots and pretend I was part of it, but in reality, I didn't want any part of it. Never was good with the women either; never knew how to do all that small talk you've got to do with a woman. The frontier was perfect. This war was even better."

"Don't you miss the hustle of a city? Don't you miss—"

"The plays?" Jeremiah slid forward off the log onto the ground. He leaned back and shut his eyes.

"Ah! Those plays. Papa helped direct *Hamlet, Troilus and Cressida, Henry VIII, The Taming of the Shrew.*"

"That's funny," Spence said. "I'm always learning something new about people. You always seemed like a tough, unfeeling person. Who would have thought you had a cultured side?"

"You never know, do you? About people, I mean."

"No, you don't. Would you think I play the piano and love Mozart and Schubert?" Spence asked.

"You? Never!"

"What was your favorite play?"

Jeremiah thought for a few seconds. "Oh, I don't know...maybe *The Tempest*. We had this actor named Arson Lee who worked for the company. He had the part of Alonso, the King of Naples, and he—"

"Who?"

"Arson Lee. Great actor. Could act any part Papa asked."

"What did he look like?" Spence jerked upright.

"Oh, he wasn't tall, had little squinty eyes, his belly stuck out, his shoulders slouched a bit, in a way, he reminded me of a little mole—"

"My God!"

"What's the matter? You don't know him, do you?"

"Maybe. I mean, I don't know. What happened to him?"

"Don't know. I left Baltimore while Lee was still doing the theater. Papa said Arson was bad to use opium, but as far as I know, and from what Papa reckoned, it never affected his performance.

"Do you really think you know him? Surely he wouldn't have made it down here to these mountains . . . 'course, I reckon anything is possible."

"Yes, anything is possible," Spence said. "Goodnight, Jeremiah. I've had enough. Thanks for sharing with me."

"Goodnight, Spence. We'll give 'em hell tomorrow."

Spence's mind was reeling. Could this actor from Baltimore have made it to East Tennessee? Could he be his grandpa's field foreman at Aberdour? What a coincidence if true. Too much of a coincidence to believe, he thought. But why?

Then he remembered the dance when he and Polly slipped to the barn and into that below-the-ground room. That powder—was that opium?

The barn belongs to Polly's daddy. Big Pa and Chamons are best friends. Naw! Maybe! Could they have something to do with opium?

Why else would Orvil Lee, or Arson Lee, find his way to such a remote and insular spot? And how or why would a successful actor want to work as a common laborer spitting snuff and chopping corn?

He pulled his blanket and closed his eyes. Pieces of a puzzle were beginning to fall into place.

Chapter Twenty-three

On the morning of December 29 orders were given to form ranks. Today they would fight on foot. Two thousand men advanced with eight pieces of artillery and passed Talbott's Station before nine o'clock. Federal pickets were encountered and brisk rifle fire broke the morning stillness.

Across the front, Federal generals saw lines of dismounted Confederates advancing. The pickets were being driven in toward main camp where they had but two regiments of cavalry and no artillery. This was not simply another skirmish. Union infantry had orders to resist, but fall back to the place General Sturgis had chosen to defend Mossy Creek.

Armstrong's artillery opened with four guns firing. Spence and Jeremiah each had a platoon of men who were firing on Federal regiments, the First East Tennessee and the Second Michigan. The Confederates drove the Federals to a wooded area behind a brick house. The Second Michigan troopers dismounted and ran into the yard for cover as the First East Tennessee remained mounted to the right of the house.

The Confederates were coming through muddy fields in long lines. Their artillery opened fire again, and shells burst all about the house. The Confederate infantry made a charge, shouting and waving their battle flag: they were nearly upon the yard.

Breaking cover, the Second Michigan stood and fired a tremendous volley from their Colt revolving rifles. At the same instant, with a shout, the mounted East Tennesseans charged with sabers drawn.

Men fell all about the brick house. Both sides were losing heavily, but for a few moments, the Confederate charge was halted.

Another Federal attempt to stand was futile. They fled the scene, moving across the road into the mouth of a long valley. Fierce charges and battles were raging in every cornfield, valley, and hillside as the morning hours wore on.

Armstrong's men, including Spence and Jeremiah, were advancing along both sides of the Morristown Road. The gun crews were struggling through knee-deep mud of a freshly plowed field. They pulled on the lead horses' reigns, and manually pushed the artillery forward, a foot at a time. Finally, the first four guns reached the road and moved toward the front. The other four guns remained in the mud.

At Mossy Creek, Federal General Sturgis sent for reinforcements. The 118th Ohio Infantry was camped on the other side of town. Their commander had called his officers, including Captain John Hansen, together to defend their camp.

"What is it, this depression? It won't go away," Hansen said to no one. He felt better talking out loud. "How many battles have I faced? But still, something seems different about today. God, have mercy."

"Activate! Activate! ll8th Ohio. Support Mossy Creek," the rider yelled.

Panic stricken, the citizens of Mossy Creek were on the road walking, riding horses, or in buggies or wagons moving west, away from the front.

On a conical-shaped hill, with a hollow in front, stood Eli Lilly, head of a small artillery battery with three-inch Rodman rifle guns in position. He could see for a mile and could command all the rolling fields in his front. Shelling from his battery kept the whole of Sturgis' Federals from being overrun.

General Armstrong knew that Lilly must be dislodged, but as Rebel shells burst around them, Lilly's artillerymen seemed to work all the faster, loading, firing, then pushing the guns up the hill once more.

Suddenly, a shell hit one of Lilly's guns, glanced off the trunnion, and took off the head of the man sighting the gun. It exploded with a flash and a roar, and another man went down, part of his head blown away. But others nearby pitched in and helped push it onto position for another firing. The position was held.

Jeremiah, Spence, and Armstrong had moved their forces down the valley north of the Morristown Road.

The 118th Ohio and Captain Hansen moved through the forest, full of sulfur smoke, to check Armstrong's advance. The Ohio men took cover behind trees to return fierce fire from Armstrong's Regiment. They were quickly routed. Hansen was furious and heartbroken. His mood changed quickly, however, when it became obvious Armstrong's men were running out of ammunition and were forced to grudgingly give back the ground taken. Hansen led a move to drive the Rebels back through the trees and out of the woods into the valley.

So furious was the Federal charge that it not only shattered the Eleventh Tennessee regiment, but also ripped a huge gap in the line of the Eighth Tennessee, positioned nearer the woods.

For the first time in his life, Jeremiah Stewart and his platoon had to turn tail and run.

To the west, Spence's troops slowly moved from tree to tree trying to outflank the 118th Ohio. For a moment, there was silence in the woods and no visible resistance was offered. The crouched Rebels knew the Federals were up ahead somewhere, but where?

"Come on, where are you?" Spence muttered. He stood and motioned his men to advance to the top of a wooded hill.

As the platoon reached the crest, two men on horses and a dozen men with bayonets came running down a ravine toward the Rebels. Spence fired, killing one.

The Rebels engaged in hand-to-hand combat. Men fell from the hot lead fired at close range. Some were killed with the swinging stock of a rifle to the head. Some were bayoneted.

As Spence reloaded, a Federal jumped from a log and ran a bayonet through his body. He fell in the leaves as the grizzled Union veteran left him for dead.

Spence slowly awoke and tried to raise himself up to lean against a sapling. His vision returned. Dead bodies, blue and gray, were all around. The only remaining men left alive in the area were one blue soldier on horseback and one of foot. Both turned toward him as Spence moved and the leaves rustled. They ran toward him a few steps. Both wanted to place the bullet that would put him away forever.

Spence drew his Spiller and Burr revolver with his right hand to fell the man on foot—the bullet piercing his heart. His left hand held the carbine that took down the lone horseman with a ball through the stomach.

"Ah! The most beautiful shot of the war!" Spence said, and fainted.

Minutes later, Spence awoke again. His first thought was how good he felt. He knew he was wounded, perhaps badly, but his mind was alert and bright. He had no feeling in his abdomen and hip. He put his hand down to the gooey bloody slick around the tear in his shirt. Then he looked. There was a rip through his thick coat.

He spotted the horse loyally waiting near its fallen rider. Spence crawled in that direction. If I could get on that horse and ride out of here, he thought.

Moving through the brown leaves, he heard a moan from the man he shot. Peering into his face, he recognized him, John Hansen.

Hansen's parched throat uttered one gasping word— "Lochsley." There was silence in the cold woods. The fight was over.

All through the rolling fields were the results of war—broken equipment, dead horses, hundreds of dead and dying men.

My war is over, but I need to do one last deed, Spence said to himself. If I can stay alive, I'm duty-bound to take Hansen's body to Lochsley for proper burial.

They made it to the road and headed northwest. Spence slumped on the horses' neck and slept, awakened, then slept again. He rode all night.

At daybreak, Spence was deep into Hancock County and started up Newman's Ridge. Miraculously, he remembered every turn of the road, every landmark. Upon approaching the house, Spence fell unconscious onto the ground.

IT WAS WEDNESDAY morning, December 30. Lochsley had been up at dawn to get firewood and awaken her brothers. The kitchen stove was beginning to warm when she heard the dogs barking.

She threw a blanket over her shoulders and ran to the front door, opened it, and peered into the dim, gloomy winter mist. What she saw would stay with her the rest of her life. The war had brought death to her front yard. She gasped and felt faint.

"Papa, wake up!" she yelled. "Oh, God, what has happened?" She ran onto the porch and into the yard. She instantly knew the one on the ground was Spence. She carefully lifted his head and discovered he was breathing. She looked down and saw the blood.

Spence came to and opened his eyes. He smiled as he looked up into her face: "Good morning," he whispered.

"Spence! How badly are you hurt? What happened?"

"Lochsley . . . you have lambs ear?"

"Of course, we've got lambs ear. Yes, I'll take care of you! You'll get well." Suddenly, she looked at the limp body hanging from the horse.

She moved across the cold ground to look at the body. She saw the face. Her arms buckled; she fell face down, sobbing, heaving.

Her daddy watched saying nothing save, "One gray must be fed and put to bed, and one blue must be buried. Lochsley, honey, try to get up so we can get Spence's side dressed; then we'll put him down to sleep—that one on the horse can wait."

Days passed and the wound began to knit. Spence thought, thank you, Lochsley, I'm grateful for your help. After all, Hansen was the one you were going to marry. Not me. I want out of here—to go to my unit, to Aberdour, anywhere but here! Besides, Lochsley needs to be with her thoughts and bereavement.

His wound wasn't mortal. The bayonet had been slowed by the thick coat and deflected into the flesh and muscle layers to the side. The wound hurt greatly when he moved, but the laudanum dose took care of the pain.

"I don't think I like Lochsley anymore," he whispered. "But I don't hate her. The very idea of her rejecting me in favor of that, that . . . Yankee."

Spence mused, a bird in the hand is worth two in the bush—that must have been what she thought. Probably what they all think when left at home deprived of security, or children, or whatever it is they want. They're likely to panic and marry the first man to come along.

He threw off the blanket and put on his boots. Out into the kitchen he trudged, only to view Lochsley crying with her head in her hands.

"Lochsley, I'm leaving. I want to thank—"

"You can't go, Spence—you're not in any condition to do anything but rest several more days," she said shaking her head.

"Where is your papa? I've got to get my horse from the barn and get back to General Armstrong. I'm missing in action."

"Spence, believe it or not, I've missed you. These long, cold, winter nights I've longed to hold your hand. I didn't hear from you, so I thought you weren't interested anymore, or were busy, or dead!"

"I know. You wrote that in your letter, remember?"

"I know. I guess you think badly of me now. I wouldn't blame you. Thank you for doing what you did, what with your own wound."

"I would have done it, wounded or not. I really must go."

Don't give in to her. Get out, Spence thought.

"You really are going, aren't you? Stubborn boy! You know you need medical attention. Spence, I know you better than you realize. I expected you to go as soon as you woke up. I was right. So, if you must, who am I to stop you?"

There was a silence.

"Good-bye, Lochsley." Spence walked toward the front door.

"Spence," Lochsley yelled. "Do you still have the stone?"

He stopped at the door, but didn't turn. "It was stolen from me at the start of the war, but I'll get it back."

"Spence," Lochsley continued, "you know I love you. I think I always will."

"You're just saying that because . . . because of him and you're upset," he said without turning around.

"No! I mean it. I mean it with all my heart," she said, knowing he was gone, perhaps forever.

The door closed and she heard the sound of boots on the porch, down the steps, and then she heard nothing.

Chapter Twenty-four

A ways from the Collins' house, Spence felt sick, not only from the wound, but from emotions as well. He rode faster and faster.

It should have felt nice when she said she loved me. I should have been happy. No, I can't feel that way. It's no good, he thought. Actually, I conquered her. I had the upper hand. I won over her . . . Anyone could tell she spoke in a moment of weakness, and sorrow too. Naw, she didn't mean it. How could she? He rode on.

Has battle hardened me this much? Spence wondered. I don't care anymore, I don't care about anything anymore, except finding my unit and killin' Yankees.

The pain in his side became a throb. He stopped beside a small branch to give his horse water. He plunged his hand into the saddlebags for food and a pint. He unscrewed the cap and downed a slug.

"Old Mr. Collins knew what I needed," he said out loud. "Thank God he did. It's so cold out here."

"I might not make it back to my unit," he yelled. He pictured himself falling off the horse and literally freezing to death. The thought scared him. Many a battle he had entered, and yet all he could think of was when the battle would begin. He loved the action, the yelling, the suspense, the thrill of seeing blue coats running away from him. He took another drink and began to feel the warmth and the tingle.

Spence drank most of the pint, and was delirious with pain and cold. He knew his wound had opened because he felt the wet and warmth of blood oozing down into his pants. He was too scared to put his hand down there.

By the morning of December 31, the temperature continued to drop and the harsh wind was unbearable. McGlothen was up early in the surgical tent. A report came that more dead Confederates were found. Many were shod only in stockings or shoes of beef hide. They were buried in the corner of a church graveyard that was also used for the Federal dead.

Reverend Honnell, of Wolford's cavalry, spoke to McGlothen.

"I know that church building well; I slept on its front pew the last two nights. My men froze to the ground in their own blood before I could reach them down the line. After we drove 'em back, we gathered the dead of both sides for burial. They were as stiff as blocks of ice."

Suddenly, a medic raised the flap of the surgical tent. "Doc, I need you outside for a minute," he said.

McGlothen excused himself from the reverend and stepped out into the cold.

"The pickets of the Twenty-third Infantry saw this Rebel being dragged along with his foot caught in the stirrup. They put him back on his horse and brought him to me since he looked wounded—and drunk too," the medic said.

McGlothen looked at the pitiful sight. He instantly recognized his friend, but said nothing to reveal it. The back of the boy's head was filthy—matted with blood and mud. Leaves and sticks covered his coat. His face was pallid.

They carried Spence inside the tent to one of the cots. McGlothen dismissed the medic and began the examination. He washed his head and stomach wound and dusted sulfur powder in the flesh puncture. He wrapped him in blankets and nudged him to drink the hot, black coffee. Spence began to come around.

"Where . . . where am I?" He rolled his eyes around the periphery of the tent until his glaze came to rest on McGlothen. "Professor?"

"Shhh, don't say anything. You're lucky they brought you here instead of dumping you with the others. We're officially out of laudanum, but I have it in my private stock."

The professor got up and walked to the hidden knapsack and brought out a small glass bottle. He gave Spence a teaspoon. Then he called for another medic to get his patient some food. Afterwards, Spence dozed off and on. As the gray aura of winter dusk settled over the valley, McGlothen walked over and smiled. Nobody had paid Spence any attention, even though he was a Confederate. It was too cold.

"I'm feeling better, Doctor," Spence whispered.

"I'm glad, although I've been worrying about you. One of these days after this mess is over, perhaps you can tell me how it's been with you. Especially how you got yourself in this predicament, being dragged right into the heart of the enemy. But enough! We won't go into that now, we have other things to talk about."

"What is in laudanum? I've never known, even though it has been around the house all my life."

"Why, it's opium and alcohol, my boy. Good for what ails you."

"Have you any idea where yours came from?"

"We ran out during your siege in Knoxville, but I looked around there and found a man had plenty."

"Who was the man? Do you remember?"

McGlothen sat on the edge of the bed and leaned closer. "He called himself the 'King of Ireland.' Strange man who wore all black. He fetched a pretty penny for the opium, but my Lord, Burnside's army needed it, so it was worth it to relieve the injured's pain and suffering."

Spence closed his eyes, aware that another piece of the puzzle had just fallen into place.

Loud groans came from across the tent. Thrashing around on his cot, his shirt wet with sweat, his face pale, the patient screamed as he grabbed the back of his knees.

"What's the matter with him?" Spence asked.

"Got soldier's disease. Funny this happened as we were talking about opium. Since our supply is exhausted, he is in withdrawal. He'll be miserable for days, maybe weeks."

"And that's what opium does?"

"I'm afraid so. It's awful when the medicine is taken too long. Opium use is widespread, not only in our country, but everywhere. England has terrible problems with its abuse."

"I think Big Pa has been trading opium for years. I think Chamons is in business with him.

"Do you remember when Big Pa took me to Cincinnati? Well, it was to buy the stuff from Thick Neck, his German friend. Even though we brought back whisky, I'm convinced that opium was on those wagons somewhere. Right under my nose. I was almost killed because somebody wanted those wagons.

"As for the 'King of Ireland,' I've heard of him too. Haven't figured out where he fits in, but I will."

"Hum, that's an interesting story. Yes sir, we've got a lot to talk about after the war. A lot!" McGlothen said.

"I don't think the South can last much longer. Our resilience is remarkable—fighting against such odds, so the war may drag on awhile because of our resolve."

McGlothen bent over and fumbled in his knapsack. He grasped the precious green stone.

"Spence, I believe you've lost this," he said. "I have been hiding it in hopes I could give it back."

He looked around to make sure they weren't being watched, and then placed the object in the man's hand.

Spence knew what he held. "How on earth?"

"Shuush. You've got to get out of here right now. At first light, Sturgis' adjutant will come through here for a medical report. It wouldn't do to have a Rebel here. Do you think you can walk?"

Spence nodded. He looked up and down the surgical tent. Even the soldier recovering from addiction was asleep.

McGlothen leaned closer. "Your horse is outside. I'm going to drape you over the back and lead the horse down the hill toward the grave site at the church. I'll tell anybody who asks that you died."

They slipped away easily enough. Only one sentry was passed before they entered deep woods. A brief farewell was exchanged and they parted. McGlothen gave Spence back the pistol and carbine he had when he entered the Federal encampment.

They both knew McGlothen must return with the horse, so as not to arouse suspicion.

Spence traveled by foot at night and lived like an animal, surviving on whatever he could steal, strangle, or forage.

He alternated between rage and tears. He fell into holes, got cut on branches and briars, and was desperately cold. During the next three weeks, his instinct to survive ruled. He grew bitter thinking about the life he left behind and the girl who left him.

He floated the French Broad River at night on a log, and covered himself with dirt and leaves for warmth when he rested. He stabbed two Union scouts who were about to discover him. Finally, on the night of January 22, 1864, he crawled out of the rhododendron thicket and onto the front porch of the big house at Aberdour.

Chapter Twenty-five

For the next few months, Spence hid in a cave on the back edge of the Aberdour property. As reluctant as Mary Clay was to allow this kind of existence, she knew it was for his own safety because scouting parties left every ten days out of Maryville and Sevierville to hunt the mountains for stray Rebels and their own Federal deserters.

Harry McAlpin continued to be an enigma to the Federals. They were sure he was a Southern sympathizer; they just couldn't prove it. Federals tried to bribe the members of Big Pistol Church to say that McAlpin's grandson had indeed ridden with the Confederates. But to be sure he didn't turn up at Aberdour, scouting parties always made it a point to visit Harry and Mary Clay at the big house. Searching every room of the house and barn, as well as the root cellar, wasn't above Union army etiquette.

Mary Clay had memorized every step from her back door to the cave. Food, water, and bourbon were Spence's fare. He had changed drastically. He was distant, aloof, and never talked of the future or his plans. He drank too much and carved objects out of wood with his Bowie knife. He was angry and ill tempered.

Mary Clay brought newspapers to Spence, but most were used to start the small fire he made at night.

February, with its icy winds and frigid nights, gave way to a tempestuous March. The few times Spence ventured outside the cave, he could see the wild jonquils in the meadows. Beauty—that was his past. So many men he had killed. They had hopes and dreams too, but now they lay beneath the jonquils themselves. To what avail?

"For what shall it profit a man, if he shall gain the whole world, and lose his soul?" he muttered loudly.

In the early morning fog, he walked to the creek to drink. He angrily kicked a clump of blue crocus out of the ground. A warbler sang its bursting song in a nearby bush.

As he paced back to the cave, a Bible verse from Ecclesiastes played in his mind: "To every thing is a season, and a time to every purpose under the heaven: A time to be born, and a time to die; a time to kill and a time to heal; a time to break down, and a time to build up . . ."

He entered his cave and went for the bourbon bottle, and lay down on his bedroll. Hours later, he felt a hand shaking him.

"Spence, Spence, wake up! I've brought a friend to see you," Mary Clay said, holding a kerosene lamp.

"Spence, I knew you were alive." Jeremiah fell on his knees and clasped Spence's hand.

"Jeremiah, what are you doing here?"

"Listen, Spence, I don't have much time. Your mother took a lot of chances bringing me down here. Yesterday, Jeff Davis sent orders to rejoin Lee's army in Virginia. Armstrong gave me time to come to Aberdour in a last attempt to find you."

Spence didn't react to Jeremiah's offer. "What's going on up there, Jeremiah? How is the war going?" Spence asked.

"Who knows," Jeremiah replied. "Seems like nothing but skirmishes going on. We've fought 'em at Maryville, Knoxville, Sevierville, you name it."

"You remember what I said at the campfire before the Mossy Creek battle? My time was up and I said I thought the South was doomed. I still believe it. So I won't go—I'm just not able."

"No! No! Not if Lee can whip 'em in Virginia, God rest his dutiful soul, and if Joe Johnston can hold Sherman in Chattanooga and keep him out of Georgia, then we can turn this thing around. Nathan Forest is on Sherman's ass like a duck on a June bug—oh, sorry Mrs. McAlpin. I'm so used to army talk, I completely forgot."

"Forget it, Jeremiah. Look at me! I'm whipped. I have nothing better to do, and don't want to have anything better to do."

"But, Spence, come out of it. You have lived to fight another day. That's what every good soldier dreams about—to live to fight. There's always a fresh start, a new begin—"

"Want some whisky?"

"No," Jeremiah murmured, looking at Mary Clay.

"Just go." Spence rolled over on his bedroll with his head on his hand. He gazed at the moss on the wall, faintly visible with the light of his mother's lamp. Jeremiah turned and left. With the Bible verse in mind, a time to weep . . . a time to mourn . . . and a time to . . . Spence grabbed the bottle.

POLLY CHAMONS WAS preparing to scour the mountains and streams for cresses, toothwort, or wild leeks. She knew these herbs thrived in the hills, so she volunteered to search for them instead of digging for radishes in the hot sun. As she saddled her horse and got her hoe and sack, Reverend Mayhew rode into the barnlot.

"Good day, Miss Polly." He tipped his hat. He wore riding boots, and a plain white shirt, open at the collar. He looked younger today than when he donned the clerical collar and other ministerial paraphernalia.

"I told you one of these days, we might take a ride together, so this being a lovely day, I thought I'd ride over and see if you were agreeable. What do you say?"

"I've sweated and toiled in that hot kitchen and in those hot fields. I am ready for the cool mountains. Of course, let's be on our way. I must stop along the way and fill my sack, so don't mind me."

After riding awhile, Polly noticed Finas Mayhew's perspiration-soaked shirt. He appeared more rugged on this wild setting. She felt stirrings within her. After filling her sack, they rode down the steep path homeward through rhododendron thickets whose flowers were bursting with crimson colors. Rain began to fall, making the leaves shimmer and glow. At first, a sprinkle, then a downpour.

The pair, feeling the urgency to hurry, spurred the horse to move faster, but instead they slowed in the soft, sodden creek bed. They heard a thunderous roar. To their horror, they saw a spring freshet, a tidal wave of water crashing around a bend from the combined waters of Bricky Branch and Little Cove Creek. It quickly engulfed and swept them out into the dangerous swirling center. Polly disappeared.

Mayhew saw her arm appear and managed to pull her to the surface. They made it briefly to one of the horses, but slid off and were clutching each other. As the raging waters soared, Mayhew grabbed a small tree branch. They clung on for dear life. As fast as it had come, the waters abated and they were left on a sandbar. Polly's blouse was in shreds as she lay on her back, her breasts heaved up and down. They gazed at each other. In a wild moment of abandonment, they melded together like drops of water join to make a pool.

"Do you mind now, if I called you Finas?" she asked with humor. "After all, we have become, can I say, intimate?"

"No, I don't mind. I feel somewhere between joyously triumphant and woefully guilty."

"We did a beautiful thing," Polly said. "Most of all, we lived. We saved each other. We survived."

"Yes, you're right. I hope you know that for a long time you have been my beginning and my end, my alpha and my omega. Please, never forget this day."

"We won't, my love." There was a pause. "Will you take me away from here, Finas? Far, far away? You're my hope, my inspiration."

They held each other into the night. At first light, they swam to shore and trudged toward home. Few words were exchanged.

Chapter Twenty-six

SPENCE REACHED FOR HIS pistol when he heard the bushes rustle at the opening of the cave. Then he saw him. Reverend Mayhew stood erect, with his hands on his hips. His large black hat and long coat cast a ghostly apparition.

"Is that you, Preacher?" Spence yelled.

"That it is, son. I heard your pistol cock. You can put it down now."

"What are you doing here?" Spence laid the pistol on the blanket.

Mayhew slowly walked into the cave, letting his eyes become accustomed to the dimness. "Came to have a little talk with you."

"So talk! You can see I'm not too busy. Guess I might be able to spare a little time with a man of the cloth." He lit the lamp. "How did you find me here?"

"Polly told me. She pressed your mother to tell of your location. See, there's a rumor out that you're back home; just nobody has been able to find you."

"Including those damned Yankee scouts, right?"

"Yes, including them. Don't worry. I'm not about to let them know anything. I would be within my rights; you being a Rebel and all.

"I first wanted to just see you," Mayhew said. "Now, I wish I hadn't. Look at you! Look at this place. Whisky bottles all over, you and your clothes stink. You are the epitome of a defeated Rebel, the conquered animal."

"Well, that's what I am, a conquered animal. I had to have time to heal, to think—"

"You've done enough of both. Is this what Southern glory, honor, laissez-faire, states-rights supremacy has now come to? Yes, I think so. Your grubbing around here in the darkness is a small example of the whole Confederate cause. I'm glad. I'm delighted and can truthfully say, I could have told you so, and if I didn't care—?"

Spence charged the preacher, both fists flying, but his speed and powerful reflexes were gone.

Mayhew easily landed a fist underneath the boy's chin, sending him reeling into the dirt.

Spence sat there, bewildered. Where did that come from? he wondered.

"I've never hit a minister before," Spence yelled. He got up. "But I've never been talked to like that. What gives you that right?" He charged again.

This time, Mayhew gave him a powerful backhand fist, sending him back down into the dirt again. His head was spinning. He slowly leaned forward on his hands and knees in the dirt. He bolted forward again, but Mayhew kneed him in the throat.

Spence realized how badly out of fighting condition he was.

Mayhew stood there with his feet apart and firmly planted, arms folded.

"How does it feel to be beaten? You and Polly had a yearning for each other at one time. I watched you in church casting sheep's eyes at each other. How would you feel if I told you that Polly and I are to be married soon? Eh? I don't know how you feel about her now, but she loves me and I deserve her.

"Spence McAlpin, I've known you for over five years. The Devil himself successfully led you to this private hell, but there is a way out. You must give yourself to God. You must repent.

"Ask for His guidance. Instruction will come if you listen. You must.

"This war will be over soon, and I believe it will be within the year, and you'll mature and remember these times as just a distant memory.

"So, as your pastor, I say arise and make something out of yourself and be useful. Now, I must be going. There remains a lot to do." He turned and walked to the entrance of the cave.

"When is the wedding?" Spence asked. A trickle of blood ran down the corner of his mouth. His legs were weak, his head hurt.

"Day after tomorrow," Mayhew stated. He stopped and turned. "I've asked the Baptist minister to officiate, but we'll be married at Big Pistol. It would be a favor to everyone if you weren't there, not in the state you're in. Besides there's too much controversy, with you—"

"I know, I know."

"I'm moving Polly to Knoxville and will preach at the Methodist church. First Presbyterian is still being used as a hospital. Good-bye, son, maybe one day, we'll cross paths again. May God go with you." He turned and disappeared into the night.

Spence stood silent and dazed.

"A time to cast away stones, and a time to gather stones together . . . a time to get, a time to lose. . . ."

He straightened to gather what little pride he had left. Something was happening. His mind returned to Brother

Hester's words from the night he and Polly spent at the Pentecostal church.

"You are a child of mine . . . Success and riches will be yours one day, but not in a way you would imagine . . . you must first go down into the realms of darkness . . . like people in Jude: brute beasts, raging waves, foaming out their own shame, escape the darkness and walk in the light. . . ."

Spence lay down on the bedroll to think. He didn't reach for the whisky bottle.

Polly Chamons and Finas Mayhew were joined in holy matrimony. The Baptist preacher pronounced the vows to a packed house. A large reception was held at Rose's tavern where the couple later consummated their vows by spending their first legal night together.

The same day, General Sherman began his march on Atlanta.

Mary Clay smiled when she left the cave. Her son was different. He was washed, his color was coming back. He still doesn't talk much, but that's okay, she thought. She had not seen him sharpening his Bowie knife with the whetstone she had brought him.

At dark, Spence sat looking into the fire. He thought he had an old score to settle, but he needed to be strong, sharp and accurate.

He left the cave to visit Blue John at the big house. He wanted to avoid his grandfather, so he waited until he knew Harry was asleep. Blue John told him the whereabouts of Confederate cavalry units near Aberdour.

He returned to the cave to study his plan. A soft rain fell outside. He smelled the nascent aroma of the wind. He was glad to be alive.

❖ ❖ ❖

ORVIL WAS BENT over the basin in the wash house at Aberdour. His galluses dropped off his shoulders and his underwear was unbuttoned to his hips. As he splashed cool water in his face, he felt cold steel piercing into his flesh of his neck.

"What th' hell?" He jerked upright and reached wildly for a towel.

"One sound out of you and you're a dead man," Spence murmured. "Just turn around slowly and walk into your cabin. If you think you might get away from my Bowie, you surely won't get past this .36 caliber in your back, so take it nice and easy."

Orvil recognized the voice. He tried to look around.

"McAlpin . . . Spencer. Is that you? What are you doing? Is this some kind of a joke?"

"Just march and shut up," Spence whispered. The men entered the cabin. One lamp was lit. Spence tied Orvil's hands behind the chair, then stood in front of him. He calmly stroked Orvil's face with the side of his knife and stared into the squinty little eyes.

"Well now, Mr. Arson Lee, or is it the 'King of Naples?'"

"I don't know what you're talking about. What has gotten into you? I heard you were back—"

"Hush! I'm the one asking questions here. I believe you had a career as a Shakespearean actor at one time in Baltimore, but your performance at Aberdour for the last four years wins the prize."

"How did you know about that? Who told you?" Orvil asked. He squirmed in the chair. Beads of sweat formed on his brow. "Why are you doing this to me, Spence? I thought we were friends—all the hours we worked and sweated in the fields together. All the things I taught you—"

"Like swallowing snuff so I could be accepted?"

"Aw, that was just a joke. I was just teasing. You were young and I thought the boys could stand a laugh or two—surely this isn't about that?" There was a pause. "It isn't, is it?"

"Orvil, you are going to tell me about the opium. Let's see, the way I figure it, you took this job so you could spy on my grandfather and his opium business."

"I don't know what you're talking about."

Spence arose from the bed, walked to Orvil and placed the sparkling-sharp edge of the knife against his throat. Orvil froze.

"I'd just as soon leave you up here bleeding to death. How would it feel to die that way, Orvil? They say your whole life flashes by—as you're dying, rivulets and spasms of blackness just . . . just come upon you—and then nothing. It may be easier than you think."

Spence moved the knife, drawing blood.

Orvil jerked and howled.

"Want to try it now, Orvil?"

"No, no, God no! What do you want to know? You have gone off loco, friend. Just hold off with that knife."

"Remember the ambush at Sharp's Gap? Did you hire those thugs to attack us on the road? Was there opium in the wagons? You caused me to kill for the first time that day, didn't you?"

For the next hour Orvil related how he spied on Harry McAlpin and followed every opium delivery. He confessed to the murder of the banjo picker at the dance at Rose's. Try as he might, Spence could get no more information. He jerked Orvil up and the two of them walked down the mountain to the big house. Harry was getting ready for bed. Blue John answered the door.

"Big Pa, I've come out of hiding to introduce you to one of your enemies. Orvil here's been tracking your opium production and stealing the stuff as long as he's been here. Yes, it has taken this whole war for me to learn what this family is all about, and hiding under the guise of grain farming."

"You good for nothing, lying snake. I'm going to rip that lying tongue out of your mouth." Big Pa grabbed Orvil by the throat.

Blue John interrupted, "Mister Harry, remember your heart. Spence and I will take care of him."

Harry fell into a chair, took a deep breath and turned to Spence, "Son, I was going to tell you about everything, in my own sweet time—when the war was over. What do you know and how did you find out?"

"Actually, no one told me; I just finally figured it out. I even tasted it one night by mistake. Polly led me to a trap door in the barn where Chamons has his pharmacy. That was the night the banjo player was killed. I have Orvil's confession to that murder."

After a few moments, Harry stated, "Well, the Maryville sheriff will be happy to solve that murder."

"That's not the tact I want to take with this man. I want him in a Confederate prison where he'll get what's coming to him. With the Federals in control of government, Orvil might not be punished since he killed a Southern sympathizer. Isn't that right, Big Pa? A Yankee court wouldn't be fair. No, I'm going to take you to a good Rebel group nearby."

"No, Lord no! It'll be the end of me if you do that. I'll do anything you say, but please don't give me to the Rebs," Orvil cried loudly, while his body shook with fear.

Spence gave him no reply. His mind was made up. He walked over to his grandfather, "Now what's the real family business?"

"I can't tell you who the principals are, but I'll tell you the history of how we got down here from Boston years ago, and how Aberdour came into being. I want you to know that your

college, the piano lessons, your clothes, the horse, the carbine, were all a product of money—the money opium gener-
ated, so you needn't be all that ashamed or sanctimonious
about it. Also, there's a good chance you'll inherit the place
when I'm gone."

"I don't care about this place anymore."

"Yes you do, young man, you just think you don't now. In
case you haven't figured it out, you cannot stay here any
longer. Too many Unionist in the cove—when somebody dis-
covers you're here, you'll be murdered. You must leave at
once. You're my flesh and blood and I want you to live a long
time. Your heart will ache for this land. You'll return someday. In other words, you'll find a way home. I'd lay money on
that."

Spence looked at Blue John who gave him a half smile and
nodded.

Harry asked, "So now, my young Turk, where would you
like to go?"

"I'd like to go to medical school, maybe in Cincinnati. I
saw the university when we were there. How would that be?"

"Perfect," Harry replied. "Thick Neck will love that. It'll
be magic enough to get a Rebel through Federal lines under
the guise of higher education, but to actually get you enrolled
in a Catholic university—why, that'll be near impossible. Give
me a few days to reach Mr. Wehner, and I'll show you what
money can do."

"Thank you." Spence stood tall, sensing a new start.

Harry cleared his throat, "Now, if you and Blue John can
get rid of this piece of scum." He nodded at a wild-eyed
Orvil Lee.

"We'll do it, Mr. Harry," Blue John said. "We'll ride at first
light. You'll not lay your eyes on this thief again; we'll take
care of that."

"Now, Spence, I'll begin to tell the history of Aberdour."
Blue John poured from a decanter holding France's finest brandy. Harry swished it around in the bulbous glass of Irish Waterford crystal. With the opulent aroma engulfing his senses, he took a sip and began.

An hour passed as Spence finally received the information he had been seeking. Tears ran down his cheek as Harry related Fletcher's life, as he learned why the only son would never be the heir-apparent of the large land holdings.

"Yeah, being born with the limp, then coming up with the 'sugar' . . . I blamed myself a long time for his defects," said Harry, "then I begun to blame him . . . punished him for it, hated him for it. No wonder he drank. Of course, I wanted my son to inherit Aberdour—dear God, why couldn't it work out?

"The night before he left, I had a change of heart. Offered to change my will if Fletcher would just stay. Maybe his problems weren't so bad after all—maybe he'll live longer than we expect, I thought, but it was too late. He left, and I can't blame him," moaned Harry.

"So now, Spence, it's open to you."

The clock slowly struck midnight. Spence got up, walked over to Harry, bent and hugged him.

"Thank you for believing in me. I'm sorry, sir. I wronged you in my heart. Now I know all the facts."

"It's all right, lad! You've always been the apple of my eye. Don't worry about me. I've had dreams—thoughts out of nowhere—that I won't be around all that much longer."

"How can you say that, Mr. Harry?" Blue John asked.

"But I've made a few enemies here and there, and I've dodged a few bullets along the way, but don't worry. I'm not afraid to die, and who knows," Harry yelled as he slapped his thigh, "I'll probably outlive all you bastards! Now, let's get to bed.

"Blue John, make sure Mr. Lee is tied up tightly so he'll still be here in the morning." Harry arose, put down his glass, and trudged up the stairs.

Blue John led Orvil to the barn; bound his feet and arms to a post, then came back inside. He blew out the lamps and retired.

SPENCER WAS IN his Confederate uniform before sunrise for the first time in months. It looked the best it could look considering all the wear it had. Willamae had pressed it. Spence couldn't help feeling proud as he climbed into the pants.

Old memories flashed through his mind as he buttoned the blouse. Today, he must convince an unknown group of fellow Southerners to take his prisoner and haul him away to their own kind of justice.

He donned the uniform to appear legitimate. Most Rebel units were thin in the ranks. It was hard enough to save one's own skin at this stage of the war, much less take on extra baggage in the form of one lone prisoner; feed him, transport him, try him, and then meet out the proper justice.

Spence, Blue John, and Orvil began the long, arduous journey east across the mountains into North Carolina, following the north bank of the Little Tennessee River. Their objective was the railroad running south into Augusta and Macon. Since General Sherman had begun his push through Georgia, Blue John knew that North Georgia would be crawling with Federal troops, so that area was to be avoided.

Once into North Carolina, it took only a half day to run up with a Confederate regiment. They were led by a blond man in his thirties, named Swaim, wearing tall boots and long riding gloves.

Introductions were made and papers were completed giving the reasons Orvil Lee should be in a Confederate prison rather than face a reconstituted court system in Tennessee, one highly biased toward Unionists—especially a Baltimore Unionist suspected of only stealing something as trivial as a little opium from a possible Southern sympathizer.

"Captain Swaim, what can I expect to happen to this prisoner?"

"Well, Captain McAlpin," he drawled, turning his head to the side to spit tobacco, "you can expect him to ride with us until we get into South Carolina. Then I'll turn him over to the authorities at Greenville. I imagine they'll put him in a boxcar and send him to South Georgia where we have a brand-new prison. You ever heard of Andersonville?"

"Can't say that I have."

"Been open since February. Friend of mine named Wirtz is the commandant—not the kind of prison you or I want to be in, but it's no worse than those hellholes up North they put our boys into, so your man here should be in good hands."

"Thank you, sir. I'll be heading back into Tennessee now, if you don't need anything else."

"Fine. Speaking of good hands, you wouldn't want to sell me your 'darkie' you got there, would you?" Swaim asked. "He's a mighty fine-looking specimen."

Spence acted like he was saying something inaudible to Blue John. He turned his back to Swaim; eased his revolver out of the holster and placed it under his jacket that was draped across the saddle's pommel. Then he turned back to Swaim, kneeing his horse so the two men would be closer.

"Captain Swaim," Spence said, in a low voice, "if you look closely under my coat, you'll see the barrel of a pistol. Another remark like that and I'll blow your ass clean over into Albermarle County. He's a free man and damned-near family, so for now, you'll apologize to Mr. Nelson for your impertinence—then we'll be going."

Swaim squirmed in his saddle, there was a pause, and he tipped his hat toward Blue John.

"Sorry, Mister . . . uh, Mister Nelson. Didn't mean no harm. I can see you mean a lot to Captain McAlpin, so I take back my remark."

Blue John made a tipping gesture toward Swaim.

"Apology accepted, Captain. Please take good care of that prisoner. He don't look like much, but he is an actor of the highest order, and can be quite dangerous; cut a man's throat."

The cavalry group rode off heading south. Spence and Blue John turned to go back across the mountains into Tennessee. They both knew they would never see Orvil Lee again.

Neither of them would ever know that 'Arson Lee of Baltimore', one of the stars of Shakespeare's *The Tempest*, would weaken after four months of dysentery at Andersonville, and be strangled by a corporal from Michigan. They both wanted to eat the same rat that Orvil had caught.

Chapter Twenty-seven

ON HIS RETURN FROM disposing of Orvil, Spence took the Oath of Allegiance to the United States government and began his new life. As soon as he and his grandfather could pack, they took their wagon to the river village of Louisville, ferried across the Tennessee, and headed west toward Nashville—long under Federal control, where order was established, and the trains were running.

Spence stepped on the train in Nashville on Wednesday afternoon with a gnawing, empty feeling in his stomach. He was leaving the people who had nurtured him, the mountains that had sustained him, and the cause that had matured him.

Harry McAlpin stayed in Nashville long enough to buy a new suit and two bottles of whisky. He was in the autumn of his life, his wife was dead, his son was no telling where, and now he had packed his only grandson on a train to take him across the Mason-Dixon line.

His beloved South was being slowly bled to death, and only God knew when the end would come. His mind drifted . . . his wealth didn't assuage the pain he was feeling.

❖ ❖ ❖

THICK NECK WEHNER'S steward, Albert, met Spence at the train station in Louisville, Kentucky. They took a steamboat upriver to Cincinnati where Thick Neck had arranged for Spence to board at a Widow Dunkum's boardinghouse near the university. Albert told Spence that two years ago Johanna Wehner had married a Union major and had moved to Cleveland.

The $100 charge had been paid so that Spence could begin an apprenticeship with one of the professors. He learned to press pills, mix powders and potions, and attend to the professor's patients as a male nurse. He also had to attend to the professor's horse.

His room with bed, chair, and fireplace also cost $100. He began to study anatomy and soon learned the 200-plus bones in the human body. November came and school started. Fees for medical jurisprudence and physiology were $15 each. The other subjects of anatomy, pathology, midwifery and gynecology, surgery, chemistry, medicine and materia medica varied a dollar or two from the $15 depending upon the number of professors in attendance.

Bodies were difficult to find for dissection. Graves would be robbed by night at the pauper's cemetery. Albert also had a connection down at the docks wherein he would claim unknown dead river workers. There were classes by day and homework by the fireplace by night. Spence learned quickly and did well.

Harry wrote Spence informing him that his old commanding officer, States Rights Gist, had been killed at the Battle of Franklin, Tennessee. Spence couldn't study that night after he read the letter. He sat in his room and stared at the fire until he fell asleep.

Two days before Christmas, Spence received a letter from Mary Clay. At the Battle of Nashville, Fletcher had been wounded by a minnie ball. It shattered his femur and required amputation. Fletcher was discharged and returned home.

Spence had ambivalent feelings about his father, who had left him and his mother to take the side of his mind's dictates. It now appeared that Fletcher had chosen correctly.

As 1865 arrived, peace was in the air to the North. Reality in the South could not be escaped, though wishful thinking remained. President Lincoln was inaugurated on March 4. Before the tipsy Vice President Johnson took the oath, he made a rambling, incoherent address that shocked many. It was an inauspicious beginning to the day that Lincoln made great by words of conciliation, which echoed far beyond that hour.

In April of 1865, General Grant knew that he had trapped General Lee's Army of Northern Virginia, and sent Lee a note asking him to entertain thoughts of surrender. On Palm Sunday, April 9, 1865, a clear spring sun rose in Virginia. When that sun fell that same night, with it fell the hopes of a people, whose prayers, tears and blood had striven to uphold the flag of the Stars and Bars. Robert E. Lee surrendered the Army of Northern Virginia to Ulysses S. Grant.

That week, Spence became Dr. McAlpin. He sat in his room by day, then took walks along the river by night. I hate it—hate not knowing—what to do?—where to go? Maybe the dean can help, he thought.

"Dr. Forney, I won't take much time . . ."

"It's all right son, I've little else to do. What's on your mind? Not sure what to do now?"

"Uh, yes sir. How could you tell? Seems the other men have definite plans."

"Son, I know about your past with your mixed feelings about your home. I know you have to continue your life in a new place. Mr. Wehner and I have been old friends for years.

Why, he even had notions of you and his daughter . . . what's her name?"

"Johanna. But I thought she was in Cleveland."

"I don't know . . . I'm not at liberty to speak about her to you."

Spence rubbed the back of his neck and slumped.

"Now, back to the point. Yes, the school needed your money, and no doubt you're the only Rebel soldier to study medicine while the war was going on. Hell, boy, you've made history."

Forney leaned back in his chair and folded his hands.

"Do you know of Dr. Goforth here?"

"I've heard his name," Spence said. "Some of my classmates—"

"Excellent man. Fifty years old and works all the time. Do you know what some of his fees are?"

"No idea."

"Bleedings, twenty-five cents; office visits are fifty cents; a dollar for sitting up all night with a patient."

Spence sat erect in his chair.

"He might get twenty dollars for an obstetrical case, a dollar for an office prescription, fifty dollars for an amputation, maybe two dollars for a vaccination, and a dollar for a blister procedure. Of course, he must collect it—nigh on impossible. Goforth hasn't accumulated a dime."

"I had no idea . . ."

"You need to hear more? Cincinnati has 200 physicians, one for every 400 residents, and about as many lawyers and preachers. Put bluntly, the vast majority barely eke out a living from medicine."

Spence stared at the floor. "I thought I could do better."

"Listen to me. Go see Mr. Wehner. He's worldly and has connections all over. He got you up here, so he can help you get out."

"I'm not sure he wants to see me."

"Why do you say that?"

"Well, I've gone by the granary twice during the past year. They always say he's out—out of town—or out of the country."

"Try again. Try him at his home. Maybe now, the time is right."

"I shall, sir. Thank you."

They shook hands, and Spence left Forney's office.

Forney sat back down at his desk and smiled.

SPENCE QUICKENED HIS steps when he entered the Over-the-Rhine section. His shirt was damp from the heat of the April sun. He smelled the knockwurst and sauerkraut. He turned up Schildergasse Street and walked past the flower stalls and small shops. He slowed his pace to step around a parked buggy.

The lady stepped down out of the buggy with the help of an extended hand of her driver. The rustle of the dress made him look up, but only too late. He still ran into her.

"Excuse me ma'am. I'm so sorry. How clumsy . . ."

"No, no, I wasn't looking . . ."

She straightened her hat and veil and stared.

Spence looked at her. There was something . . . "Johanna?"

THEY STOOD TALKING in the empty parlor of the school building. Spence could see the buggy and driver through the window.

"I didn't hear a word from you during the war, Spence."

"Johanna, if you only knew of all the times I saw your face. In the fire of a cannon blast, in the sunset, in the dark of the rivers . . ."

He pulled her toward him. She raised her veil. They kissed, long and silently.

"You've been here all the time?"

"No, I married a Union soldier not long after you visited Cincinnati that time," Johanna whispered. "We settled in Cleveland. But I have been here waiting for the war to end."

Loud noises from around the corner interrupted them.

"Mommy! Mommy! Where are you? Guess what we've been doing?" The little girl screamed and ran the length of the hall and into the parlor. A middle-aged lady trailed behind.

Spence and Johanna released and straightened. Johanna gazed from Spence to the child. This surprise meeting caught her off guard. Should she? . . . could she? . . . , she wondered.

"Bretta! Now what did you do today, my sweet? You must tell mama all about it." Johanna knelt and picked up the girl. She turned to Spence. "She's five." She fumbled with her veil and pulled it down over her face.

"Mommy, we've been making cornhusk dolls. See, here's one." Bretta turned to look at the stranger, paused, and handed the doll to Spence. "Would you like to have my doll?"

"Please, Bretta let's go, it's time for your nap." Johanna, with the little girl, turned and walked to the door; she looked back, paused, then walked out to the waiting buggy.

Spence heard, "Mommy, who was that? He looks like a nice man."

He walked out, but he could feel the stares of the German lady teacher. Outside, he turned around to read the sign on the window: "Frau Schneider's Kindergarten."

"May I help you?" the lady asked, standing at the door.

"Mr. Wehner's house?"

The perplexed teacher said, "Go down five blocks, turn left, two blocks—the name is on the door chain."

"Thank you."

Chapter Twenty-eight

SPENCE STOOD AGAINST THE railing on the third deck aboard the *Rob Roy*. He was pensive—he had a lot to think about. A week had passed since he had learned another shocking secret. This time it was a secret that originated because of his actions.

Mr. Wehner had agreed to see Spence to discuss ideas for finding a job. Spence had walked into the house carrying the cornhusk doll. As Spence began the story of his chance meeting with Johanna and Bretta, Mr. Wehner became furious. He said he couldn't stand it any more, he cursed and raved at Spence. Wehner was enraged to tell Spence that Bretta was his baby. He said that Johanna had indeed married a Federal major, and that Spence was not welcome in their lives.

Spence felt it best for now to do as Wehner bid. Through one contact and then another, Thick Neck got the U. S. Government to invent a position for the young doctor to work; his salary split between the Freedman's Bureau and the army.

He would still be a civilian since the government was, at best, tentative toward hiring a former member of the Rebellion to care for the sick. His location would be Memphis. His pay: $500 per annum.

The Rob Roy was just over 200 feet long, drew only seven feet, had the typical dual smokestacks, a large boiler room on the first deck pushing a stern wheel thirty feet in diameter, and an elegant hurricane deck, atop which sat a pilothouse with a red roof. The saloon and restaurant on the second deck was plush with imported oil paintings from Europe and heavy red curtains on the windows. Although privately owned, the Rob Roy's largest customer was the government, which used it for movement of troops and agencies from Cincinnati to New Orleans.

Spence felt hopeful about the trip and his assignment. He had a small berth on the third deck. He would need the next four days to enjoy the scenery of the river and let his overworked brain rest.

After dinner that night he entered the saloon area. There were eight tables for cards in the center of the room, then smaller ones along the walls for drinking and conversation. The spittoons were polished brass, the mirrors ornate and shiny, and the gas-lit chandeliers added a warm glow to the people taking their leisure under them.

He ordered a whisky and stood against the bar. No wonder they won, thought Spence. If we had machinery like this, then . . . He watched card games until time to go to his berth.

The next morning, he walked up to the pilothouse to meet the captain who told Spence to look around all he wanted. Spence noticed old newspapers lying crumpled in a corner, and picked one out. It was the *Memphis Daily Appeal* of January 2, 1863. It was printed only on one sheet with a classified section in the column to the far right. Spence looked at the paper and turned to the captain.

"You know a lot about the city?"

"My wife and I lived there during the'50s, but smelled the war coming, so I bought a farm down river in Arkansas. Took the oath early so I could keep my job on the river," the captain said. There was silence as the pilot negotiated a bend in the river.

"Guess you could call it a typical riverboat town. Liquor, brothels, gambling, and shootings say a lot, except for one thing."

"And that is?"

"Business," the captain continued. Back in the 1830s Memphis was in the middle of westward expansion. Everybody was moving to Texas and they had to go through Memphis to get there. I was there the night Davie Crockett pitched the biggest drunks ever in Bell's Tavern—told the whole state of Tennessee to go to hell! 'Course he died out there fighting the Mexicans.

"But anyway, many fine businessmen either brought their companies to Memphis from the East, or they started from scratch. Millions of bales of cotton are bought and sold at the exchanges, and shipped for Europe or our East Coast. When you arrive, you'll find wealth and culture beyond the bawdiness of the river trade.

"Oh, Memphis still has its wild side. Fact is, my sources say underneath the facade of reconstruction and putting up with the Yankees there's smoldering hatred in many die-hard Rebel sympathizers."

"Yeah, I would think it's tough on them," said Spence.

"Sure. It's getting tiresome to Memphis folk, and you mark my word, they ain't taking to it kindly. Something will happen, rioting or looting, or who knows what?"

Spence checked his pocket watch. "Time the lunchroom opened, so I'll let you get on with your business."

After lunch, Spence leaned against the rails watching the never-ending alluvial cornfields of southern Indiana.

A voice spoke from behind him. "We'll reach the Wabash River in an hour—probably be ice floating out into the Ohio. Hope the pilot isn't hung over."

Spence turned and looked into the steely gray eyes of one of the most handsome men he had ever seen. He was dressed in a blue suit over a white high-collar shirt, complete with French cuffs and a little band of lace at the edge. A maroon Kentucky colonel tie hung from his neck. He wore a top hat on black, wavy hair.

"Good morning, sir."

"Were you talking to me?" Spence asked.

"If you're here and you heard it, then I guess I was talking to you. If you played like you didn't want to hear it, then count it as talking to the wind," the stranger said.

"You said something about the Wabash, I think."

"The Wabash River, son. Cuts all the way down Indiana. When we get there, you're at the corner of three states, Illinois, Indiana, and Kentucky. Sounds like this is your first time down this way."

"Yes, sir. Going to Memphis to do some doctoring down there."

The man looked him up and down and paused while he sucked on his long cigar. "Some doctoring, eh? You didn't get that mountain accent in Ohio?"

"No, sir, don't reckon I did." I don't owe him any explanation, not out here on this riverboat, Spence thought.

"Anyway, I didn't mean to interrupt your thoughts. I must be going down to the dining room to meet a lady. If you have nothing better to do tonight, come down to the saloon and sit at my table. I understand the captain is going to pick up a small band and an Irish singer when we stop at Paducah tonight. Maybe it'll be worth listening to. Good day."

"Good day, sir." He watched the man walk away.

Look at that cocky walk—bet he has ice in his veins, but then, he did invite me to sit with him, didn't he?

"YOUNG MAN, I don't believe we met this afternoon. My name is Flynn."

"Good evening, my name is Spencer."

"And this pretty little thing—her name is Abigail. She'll be getting off at Cairo in the morning. Nice of you to join us."

"My pleasure, sir."

"Care to join the game?" Flynn asked. Three other men were shuffling chairs at the table, jockeying for poker positions.

"No, thank you. Don't play. Don't know how. But you go ahead; I'll sit here and sip a little brandy."

"Very well," Flynn muttered indifferently. "I think the band will be out shortly, so I hope you aren't bored. If so, just strike up a conversation with Abigail here—don't distract me when I'm working on my game."

Spence enjoyed the intensity of the crowd, as well as, the ambience. Halfway through his second glass, he felt bored.

No, that's not it, he thought. Maybe my spirit has left me and is looking down on all of this and wondering what my body and soul is doing way out here, so far from everything I've ever known. And how old is Bretta, Johanna's daughter? my daughter? Five?

Flynn leaned over. "Let me teach you something, Spence. I play a lot of cards and often stop at the cotton exchange in Memphis. I've seen fortunes lost and gained at the tables. I've been on packets on the Vicksburg and Natchez routes and have seen whole plantations lost and gained by big-doggin', blood-thirsty braggarts. Greedy, filthy men who are deluded—they'll risk everything to show off and satisfy their insatiable ego.

"But, I tell you, you've got to be cool—have self-mastery. Let winnings run up to a point. Watch the traders at the cotton exchange. They'll set limits and then get out. Cut your losses quickly. Get up, go to the bar, or back to your room. Get away so you can play another day. You hear?"

"Yeah, I hear you. I'll remember that," Spence said. The band appeared and launched into Irish jigs and ballads.

Most of the gamblers at the tables hardly noticed their presence. The Irish girl singing was pretty. Nice figure, long fragile neck, short dark hair, eyes almost too large for her face, thin nose and a small but tightly shaped mouth.

When she sang, the sounds were like tinkling crystal. Her music was taunting and mysterious.

Spence got another glass from the bar and settled deep into his chair to listen.

Cold as the northern winds in December mornings
Cold as the day that rings from this far distant shore.
Winter has come too late, too close beside me,
How can I chase away all the fears deep inside?

I'll wait, the signs to come
I'll find a way,
I will wait, the time to come.
I'll find a way home.

Spence realized his eyes were moist. It was the last line. She's singing to me, he thought. I shivered at the first lines; the last lines made me glow. I'll find a way home. Beautiful.

After finishing his drink, he stayed for two more songs, excused himself, and went to bed. He couldn't sleep for hearing the echo of the song.

Two days later, the boat rounded the bend at the fourth Chickasaw bluff: Memphis.

Chapter Twenty-nine

JEREMIAH STEWART WAS SOAKED to the bone. He slid off his horse in front of the hitching post at Rose's Tavern. Jeremiah figured there would be a warm fire and a touch of whisky to be had inside. He was tired from the ride over the mountains. Although his aim was the McAlpin house at Aberdour, he thought it would be good to stop and meet F. L. Chamons, the man he had heard so much about from Spence.

"Come in, my man. Come in," Chamons said. He took him by the arm and pulled him into the barroom. "Nasty weather out there."

"Mighty nasty. You must be Mr. Chamons."

"Am I suppose to know you?"

"Not really. I rode with the McAlpin boy during the war. I thought I'd stop and see how he's doing."

"Come in. Let me get something to warm your spirits."

"He's . . . he's all right, isn't he? I mean, he's still alive?"

"Yes, he's alive. Not exactly sure where he is right now, but his mother can tell you later. Right now, take your glass and go upstairs.

"Uncle Wade! Would you bring this man a robe?

"Now, you go on up and change. Take off those wet clothes and bring 'em down here. I'll get my daughter to hang them in front of the fire to dry. Before you know it, you'll be good as new, then you can ride down to Aberdour and pay your visit."

"That's mighty nice of you," Stewart said.

Shortly, Becky Chamons, now seventeen, lithe and pretty, was arranging the wet clothes in front of the fire. Jeremiah sat in the robe sipping his bourbon.

He noticed how fresh and cute she was. Her countenance was light and the life in her shown like the North Star. He, on the other hand, felt that his spirit was bankrupt from too many lonely nights and too many battles. His heart was hardened after the war. Walking all the way from Virginia to his home in North Carolina had cut deeply into him.

"There now, Mr. Stewart, it won't be long before your clothes will dry. Will you be staying the night with us?" Becky asked.

"No, ma'am. I'll be leaving soon to ride to Aberdour."

"Oh! How do you know the McAlpins?"

"I have been to their home twice. Once at the first of the war and another time two years ago. Spence and I fought together. I wanted to come see how he was doing now."

"Oh, yes, Spence is our good friend. My half-sister and I used to be his secret admirers—well, it was hardly secret. Actually, we grew up together. I think he took the oath and headed up North to school. Don't know where he is now, but Mrs. McAlpin will tell you." There was a long pause. Then Becky broke the silence.

"Mr. Stewart, you look sad. Is something wrong other than being cold, wet, and tired?"

"Oh, no ma'am, I don't . . . well actually, I was just thinking how lucky you and your sister . . . what was her name?"

"Polly."

"Yes, Polly. I was thinking how lucky y'all were to grow up in a place like this around good people—and a boy like Spence who was kind to you. I never had that. Here I am nearly thirty, and I feel worn-out and useless."

Becky laughed out loud, but it wasn't a laugh of condescension. It was a laugh of warmth and confidence. She took two steps and placed her hand on the man's shoulder.

"Don't worry, Mr. Stewart. The war is over now and times are changing. Look on the bright side and be willing to change. There's always a light and a dark, a thorn and a rose, a bitter and a sweet. It's just what you choose to focus on."

He couldn't believe the ease of speaking and the authority coming from the mouth of this young lady. He also couldn't believe he spoke so freely to her.

"I'm sorry, ma'am. I'm just indulging in too much self-pity. I think the war affected me more than I care to admit."

He stood up and felt his clothes. They were dry. He liked the emotions he was feeling, but he needed to go.

"Guess I'll go up and change, then get on my way. You've been most kind to tend to me, Miss Becky."

"My pleasure, sir." She turned and went into the kitchen.

Jeremiah paid Chamons for the whisky. He walked through the dining room toward the door, paused, and turned around. Becky was on the other side of the room, leaning against the wall.

"Hope you'll come back, Mr. Stewart. Don't worry. Things will get better," Becky said.

"Thank you, ma'am." Jeremiah tipped his hat. He walked through the doors feeling like a jolt of white light had pierced his tough exterior. He rode the half-mile to Aberdour. His heart was lightened and his spirit buoyant.

It was because of that girl—plus a little whisky.

He turned his head to the sky and laughed loudly. He couldn't remember doing that since way back before the war.

❖　　❖　　❖

Now discharged and back in the little college town of Maryville, Professor Clint McGlothen was a Unionist by birth and loyalty, but a reconstituted Tennessean by choice. He looked forward to doing what he loved best: teaching and influencing minds. He rode to Widow Perkin's house to have their usual Saturday night dinner. He slid off his horse and walked toward the door, but slower than four years ago. Maud threw open the door and hugged him.

"Clint, my wine supply is quite low, thanks to the embargo, but on this occasion, I'm going to break out my only bottle of Trockenbeeren Auslese. My brother sent it from one of his trips to Hamburg—scarce as hen's teeth!"

They talked about the war. Maud told McGlothen about Spence living in the cave, taking the oath, and going to study medicine.

He told her about helping Spence escape Federal forces in Mossy Creek, and how Spence knew about his grandfather's opium operation.

Widow Perkins raised an eyebrow. "Opium? In Blount County?"

McGlothen was unmoved. "Can you imagine how many other people are involved? The group no doubt sold to both sides during the war."

"Then there was this man in Knoxville who called himself the 'King of Ireland.' Always dressed in black. Strange! Now I wonder if he represents another ring of dealers, or is he associated with McAlpin and his group? Maud, how long have you known Harry?"

"Since he enrolled Spence here in school," she lied. "Six years? But, if I were you, Clint, I would let it be. After all, there are no laws yet on opium. What are you going to do, get up a posse and break it up yourself? I think you would be better off to mind your own business. Stay in town with me and help get the college started again."

"Yes, yes, you're right. We're starting classes this fall. Money is beginning to trickle down from Northern wealth. We may look for more land and more buildings. After all, I can't think of better use of my time and Yankee money, can you?"

"No, Clint, I can't. You always were an idealist and a dreamer."

HEINREICH STORCH BURIED his head on his arms on the table. His eyes were glazed in his flushed face, as he sat almost crying. The bottle of homemade corn whisky sat half empty. Two armies had raped his land, ate the fields bare, taken the lives of two boys, and the embargo had shut off his schnapps supply from Germany.

Moody stared into an empty fireplace.

Willis, the field hand, had stuck by them through the war, and had almost become part of the family. Of course, this was to Willis' advantage, but he covered his tracks well and worked hard. He sat whittling on a cedar stick, letting the shavings fall to the floor.

"Willis, pick up those shavings right now," Gerta yelled. She entered carrying a small plate of venison. "You know I hate sloppiness in my house."

"Gerta, let Willis alone," Storch said. "We've got more to worry about than some god-cursed cedar shavings."

"Yah, yah, I know, but you forget, the Rebels paid you well for your guano," Gerta yelled.

"I know. Glad I made 'em pay me in gold. Even that worries me. If those reconstruction people or even some carpetbagger found out about that, we could be tried for treason."

"No we wouldn't," Gerta said. President Johnson would pardon us. You forget he is from East Tennessee and stands

up for the common man. Besides, I think the North is ready
to forgive and forget, and go on to something else, like building more industry and making more money."

Storch raised up and began to eat. "I hope our first corn
crop is good, but I hope even more that Chamons can find us
more opium. Then, we would make it. It would be like the
old days except without Virgil and J.D. God! I miss them!"

THE ROB ROY paddled toward the bluffs of Memphis before it
took an abrupt left turn at the tip of President's Island and
crawled the last hundred yards up the mouth of the Wolf
River. It inched sideways into the public landing area and
docked. Men threw ropes. Blacks scurried about securing
lines and carrying duffels. Others waited for a carry and a tip
from those off loading.

Spence walked off the gangplank onto Tennessee soil for
the first time in over a year. He looked up and saw hacks
carrying people and walkers on the public promenade, ser-
pentine to the riverbank.

He didn't go ten paces before he heard music from a harmonica. He saw a barefoot black boy sitting on cotton bales,
playing and grinning.

The Negro took a look at Spence, jumped down and
wrestled his bag from him.

"Here, boss! Let me help you with that grip."

"Naw, thanks! I'm strong enough to handle it myself. Go
help one of the ladies," Spence said.

The boy jumped in front of him. "Boss, my name is Pickle,
and for a nickel, I'll tell you how the Yankees came, and besides, I'll carry your grip up the hill."

"Well, Mr. Pickle, what can I say? You're persistent. So
take it!" Spence dropped his duffel to the ground. The boy

had all thirty-two teeth in perfect alignment and white as snow. His grin showed every one of them.

They trudged up the corduroy surface toward the top of the bluff.

"See, boss, the city voted $59,000 for defense in '62, but after Shiloh and Corinth, there wasn't nobody in Memphis left to fight the Yanks. The *Appeal* paper packed up and headed to Grenada, then somebody set fire to all the cotton on Howard's Row so the Yankees couldn't get it and sell it. The next day, thousands of folks lined the bluff to see Mr. Lincoln's boats get put down at the bottom of big Muddy. That was wishful thinking."

Both Spence and Pickle were winded from trudging up the hill, but it didn't keep Pickle from telling his story.

"Now stop for a minute, boss. Turn around. Look around the bend as far as you can see—over the tops of those trees on the island. That's where big clouds of dark smoke told the folk on the bluff that the fleet of Yanks were done firing their boilers. They had armored gunboats, rams, and mortar boats carrying lots of guns."

"So how many did we ha—I mean how many did the Rebs send out?" Spence asked, winded. They neared the top of the hill.

"Ah! The Rebs, they had eight boats with plenty of guts and no hope. No hope at all. The *General Lovell* was the first to go. They rammed her and she sank. Then, the *General Beauregard* and the *General Price* thought they had one of the Yankee rams trapped. Only thing was, the ram slipped away and them two Rebel boats collided and put each other out. Two minutes later a shell got to *Beauregard's* boiler and killed seven of her crew."

"We're at the top of the hill, Pickle. You had better finish your story because somebody is suppose to be meeting me here. Go ahead while I catch my breath."

"I know you got to go, Captain, but the *Little Rebel* and the *Jeff Thompson* were hit so badly that they ran into the Arkansas bank and blew up. The *General Bragg* got rammed, and the old *Earl Van Dorn* took off down river to Vicksburg. Man, it was over in an hour. Do you know what the surrender note said from the *Benton*?"

"No, what?"

"It said: 'Sir, I have respectfully to request that you will surrender the City of Memphis to the authority of the United States which I have the honor to represent. Signed: I am, Mr. Mayor, with high respect, your most obedient servant, C. H. Davis, Flag Officer.'

"Can you beat that Captain? Here he just got through blowing they ass out of the water, and he comes along and says he is the mayor's obedient servant. Don't you think that's funny?"

Spence craned his neck and looked over the crowd at the top of the bluff. Surely somebody would be approaching him soon.

"So what did the Memphis mayor say, Pickle?"

"Ha! He said: 'Sir! Your note of this date is received and contents noted. In reply, I have only to say: That as the civil authorities have no means of defense by the force of circumstances, the city is in your power. Respectfully, John Park, Mayor.'

"I mean, what could he say? The Confederates were captured, the gunboats gone, and the city was just prime for the plucking."

A wagon came driving straight toward the two men. Dust was flying and the driver, an army corporal smoking a cigar, had an air of authority and impatience about him.

"Excuse me," he yelled. "Might you be Dr. McAlpin from Cincinnati?"

"That's right. I'm your man," Spence yelled back.

"Well, I'm here to take you to Fort Pickering."

"I'll help get your bags up," Pickle said.

Spence climbed on the wagon. "Thanks for the story, Pickle. Do you stay around here most of the day?"

"Oh, yeah. I'm always down here looking for odd jobs. If you get bored and want to watch the water go by and calm your nerves, come on down someday. Good luck, boss."

Spence tipped his hat to the boy and gave him a coin. The corporal turned the wagon and headed south on Front Street for the drive to the fort, built after the army's 1862 victory. It occupied the highest part of the bluff. It had two miles of zigzag brick walls with frequent intervals of cannon, as big as 32 pounders. This was to be Spence's headquarters.

THE INITIAL EXCITEMENT of his new challenge soon withered. He split his days in the dispensary at the fort and with the Freedman's Bureau on Pontotoc Avenue. Spence encountered things such as goiters, gangrene, pellagra, cholera, and of course, the ever-hovering specter of the dreaded yellow fever.

He recoiled at the popular therapy of the time. The thoughts of opening the skull to relieve pressure. The bleedings and the flooding the patient's gastric system with mercury, hardly seemed correct to him. The trouble was that he didn't know any other way to try to help. He frequently consulted older medical practitioners in the city for advice, but gained little headway. Patients lived or died whether he treated them or not. This frustrated him immensely.

One autumn afternoon, he walked down Second Street, turned left at Winchester, and headed for the river. He remembered his friend, Pickle, who said he would always be down at the docks. He thought he might bump into him. He could use a little levity, right now.

Chapter Thirty

Sᴘᴇɴᴄᴇ ʟᴀʏ ᴏɴ ᴛʜᴇ grass for an hour with a dandelion between his teeth. Propped on his elbows, he watched the river flow toward Helena, Natchez, Vicksburg, and New Orleans. I wonder if I'll make it down to those places? Maybe some day, he thought.

The magnificence and solitude of the big river had an effect of serenity. It was a mile wide here. He could see the flat fields of Arkansas. His mind drifted.

The rest of my life? God only knows. I may never see Aberdour again, or the family. Bretta and Johanna are you happy? Lochsley, what are you doing? Polly and Mayhew? Am I guilty for killing Virgil and J.D.? Will I go to hell for it? God help me. He lay down on the grass and dreamed to escape his thoughts.

"Well, as I live and breathe! Is this the doctor man who done come down to the river to see old Pickle?"

Opening one eye, Spence looked up.

"Pickle, you mean you remember me after all these weeks, and your other customers?" Spence asked.

"Oh yeah, boss, I remember. Can't reckon why, other than there was something 'bout you, like you was gonna do something good in this town."

"Well, thanks, but today I'm tired . . . and low."

"What's the matter, Captain? Is all that work getting you down?"

"Yeah, in fact, I don't feel like I'm doing much good here, and those lines of patients stretch forever. I'm worked from dawn to dark, and I don't know what to do for half of them, especially over at the Freedman's Bureau—your people."

"They have so many problems," Pickle said. He looked across the river.

"But you're right, Pickle, I have a purpose, but right here is as far as it's taken me. I feel helpless and probably homesick. There must be more out there."

"Captain, you fought in the rebellion, didn't you?" Pickle narrowed his eyes; looked straight at Spence. "You were a Reb?"

There was silence. Spence pulled at his collar.

"How did you know?"

"From your accent I reckin."

More silence. "Pickle, you're mighty smart. Where're you from?"

"Oh, my daddy and all of us were slaves down in the Delta. We got freed after the war. They wanted me to stay around and sharecrop the cotton, but I had to get away. 'Course Memphis is the capital of the Mississippi River, so I drifted up here. Learned to read on my own, so you see, Captain, I've got a purpose too."

"And what's that?"

"I want to have a band someday—to play the music I grew up hearing. A man can't stay on the docks forever, you know."

"True. But how are you going to get up any money? The banks aren't lending except for agriculture, no matter what color you are."

"Yeah, Captain, but I know where there's money—lots of it. Tell you what. You meet me down on Front and Beale Street and I'll show you. There's a long row of buildings for the cotton dealers. They bet on the price of cotton. Some hit it big—some don't. You interested?"

Spence thought back to Big Pa's stories about his days on the docks in Edinborough, speculating on West Indian sugar—back in the '40s.

"Now that might liven things a little. Day after tomorrow—noon?"

"Ha! You got it, boss!" With that he turned and danced away toward the river singing, "Hello, my name is Pickle, and for a nickel, I'll tell you where the money be made . . ."

THE NEXT AFTERNOON the telegraph came while Spence was making rounds at the Fort. What could be wrong at home? He ripped open the envelope. "Will be in Memphis on business Thursday—bringing Becky—dinner at Gayoso Hotel? F. L. Chamons."

What is he coming over here for? As he tended to his patients, Spence tried to piece together the puzzle. After an hour, he thought he knew the answer.

PICKLE WAS WAITING under one of the gas lights on Front Street. They greeted and turned toward the large double doors of the cotton dealer's building along Howard's Row.

"Pickle, before we go in, you must tell me something."

"And what's that, Captain."

"How do you know so much about this place? And can anybody . . . I mean, it's all right for somebody who is not a dealer to go in?"

"You mean, is it all right for coloreds to go in?"

"I didn't ask that?"

"Captain, I don't work the dock all the time. I'm in here a lot when the packets aren't landing. I'm a runner for some of those rich white men. You first." Pickle pushed open the door.

The room was large and busy. Hundreds of 500-pound bales of cotton were stacked awaiting assignment to ports along the eastern seaboard. At the end of the great hall were two large blackboards. Before each board stood a man wearing a white shirt and tie with little black garters around each arm to keep his sleeves from getting soiled by the chalk.

"One board," advised Pickle, "keeps a graph of the daily price fluctuations; the other board keeps the weekly prices. Since the man keeping the weekly board has less to do, he has additional duties—printing monthly prices and passing these out to the fifty or more traders."

To the side was a thin, wiry man sitting behind a table abutting a safe where the money was kept. Beside him a man stood with a revolver.

The yelling and the sign signals from the crowd excited Spence. Men constantly walked to the desk to put down cash. "That's margin money," Pickle said, "used to buy or sell contracts calling for delivery of 25,000 pounds of cotton, or fifty bales, during a certain month in the future."

Pickle pointed out two younger men circulating around the crowd, specialists who barked the current prices, often goading the speculators for more action.

Spence and Pickle watched for two hours. Nobody in the room paid them the slightest bit of attention.

Spence said he had to go back to work, so they walked out into the warm, October sun.

"So, what did you think about that, boss man? Some powerful big money can be made if you know what you're doing."

"For God's sake, Pickle, stop calling me 'boss man.' I'm not your boss. Right now, nobody is. You're free, young, and eager, so you don't have to answer to anybody. If you like, you can call me Captain since I was a captain at one time, or you can call me Doc, or even Spence, but stop that 'boss man' stuff. You'll be a slave in your attitudes all your life if you keep it up."

"All right, I understand, Captain. Now what do you think?"

"Pretty bloody exciting."

"Pickle, tell me about cotton."

"Well, Cap, most of the South's landowners were small. If a man had 200 acres on a river, with good soil that wouldn't wash away, he could get one or two bales per acre.

"You needed six good hands in the field and two in the house. The big boss had to have a 'factor' in a big city to help him get his advance money to plant, and then later to help him get his cotton to good markets."

"When do you plant and when do you reap?"

"We plant it in the April, and hope it don't rain; it better not be too cold, or else it won't sprout. June through August it grows. Needs a lot of sun, a little rain, and some night dew. Come September and October, pick it and hope for dry weather."

"What about the big plantations? I mean the aristocrats who were so much in favor of secession," Spence asked.

"Well, they had more of everything I done told you about. They always had the best land and got most of their income from sending the stuff across the waters."

"How was it . . . being a slave and all? We didn't have them where I'm from. I mean . . . you would never go back, would you?"

"My daddy cost the boss $15 per year. We got strength from hoecakes, fried pork, and molasses. The men folks got two shirts per year, a pair of woolen pants, and a jacket in the fall. We got two more cotton shirts and pants in the spring. Papa got a new blanket every third year. We Negroes had to appear weekly in clean clothes for inspection by the overseer," Pickle said. "And no, I would never go back. What you think I'm doing up here in the big city foolin' around with a white man for? I don't never want to go back behind that plow."

"I guess not."

"Now Captain, I got a heart like anybody else. And I ain't bitter. I heard talk about the slave ships and all, but what you don't hear is that it was the Dutch and Portuguese who done started it and they got off free when it comes to hate. See, everybody done forgot about them. And look at it this way, if my ancestors hadn't been brought over here, I'd be over in Africa somewhere chasing down some animal, looking for my next meal.

"So, I ask you, who got it worse? Me or my brothers back in Africa? Don't get me wrong, I'm glad we done got freed up, but that just makes me want to work harder to make something of myself. Bet you didn't expect that answer."

"No, Pickle, I didn't. You're perceptive. I'm glad we met."

"As for reconstruction, it be too early to tell. If Lincoln had lived, it would have gone good for everybody down South. As for Andrew Johnson, I just don't know . . . He don't like Negroes too much and he hates the old masters—thinks they ought to be strung up for treason.

"The freed slaves will have to go back on the plantations, which I might add, are breaking into many smaller plots. They can be 'croppers' until they save enough money to buy their land. That's the only way they'll be able to do better for themselves.

"They can help send the next generation to school and who knows? To college. Then someday you'll see colored doctors, merchants, lawyers, and teachers living like they're suppose to. OK, Captain! Here's where we split up. Let me know when you want to go back to the exchange. Bye now."

Pickle walked off down the dusty street.

Spence went to the Gayoso House, Memphis' best hotel, and left a note in Chamon's box that he would meet them for dinner at eight.

THAT AFTERNOON, F. L. Chamons took Harry's Conestoga wagon to a small pharmacy facing the corner of Monroe and Third. He drove through an alley and parked in the rear. Inside, he met a man in a blue suit and wide-brimmed hat.

"Afternoon, Mr. Chamons, I'm Flynn Bouguereau. Pleased to be of service." The two men exchanged handshakes, eyeing each other and searching for the other's identity.

Then Chamons said, "I understand Grant's headquarters was at the Hunt-Phelan Home on Beale Street," the prearranged code.

"Ah yes," Bouguereau said. "I believe you're from East Tennessee. We have some business to conduct."

"Yes, it's been a long drive, and we need supplies back home."

The men loaded numerous catties of opium sacks into the false bottom of Harry's wagon; the count was made, and United States greenbacks were exchanged.

"Now that was easy," Flynn said. "I'd be pleased if you and your daughter would have dinner with me tonight to celebrate future business."

"That would be nice, but I wired ahead and have made arrangements to dine with a young doctor from our valley. Another time, perhaps."

Flynn's eyes widened. "Oh, I see. Yes, some other time, perhaps. Mr. Chamons, that boy—might his name be . . . starts with an S . . . Spencer?"

"Why yes, how did you know?"

"We were on the same boat out of Cincinnati when he came here. Didn't talk much, but I was impressed with him. Small world, isn't it? May I ask what relationship he has with you?"

"No blood kin, but he grew up near my tavern. That wagon out there is his grandfather's. He and my two daughters were friends, so I've watched him grow up. Comes from good stock."

"All right, Mr. Chamons, y'all enjoy yourselves, and I hope to see you again. Good doing business with you."

Chamons left and checked the wagon with the livery boy at the Gayoso House. He read Spence's message, went upstairs to his room to wash and to prod Becky into getting ready for dinner.

❖　❖　❖

It was a grand reunion that evening. Spence couldn't get over how pretty Becky had become. She was quick to tell Spence about Jeremiah's visit to the tavern. She giggled like young girls do when they've met a man who makes them weak-kneed.

"Mother wrote and said Jeremiah had visited and spent a night. Nice of him to ride over those mountains just to see me. But I guess it was more important that he saw you, Becky." He threw back his head and laughed, but checked Chamon's reaction from the corner of his eye.

"Well, that sounds nice, but nobody asked me if seeing Becky was important. I say the man is too bloody old for my little daughter," Chamons said.

"Hell, Spence! I was hoping you and Polly would hit it off, and she ups and runs off with the preacher. Then I thought I could still save sweet, young Becky for you. Now she thinks she's fallen for this old bachelor from the other side of the mountains."

"Daddy! Don't say that. Spence has been like a brother and . . . well, he understands, don't you Spence?"

"Of course I understand, Becky. I didn't trust Jeremiah at first—and when he was my first cavalry leader, I hated his guts. But in time I came to respect his wisdom. As the war went on, he let me in on some of his life—provided me with some important . . . What's the matter Becky? You look pale."

Becky weakly asked to be excused.

As she ran to the powder room, Spence and Chamons looked at each other. She returned shortly, but her face was beet-red.

"Excuse me, Daddy. I don't feel so good. May I go to the room?"

"Of course, Sugar. Excuse me, Spence," Chamons said and helped Becky climb the stairs.

"Take her on up and get her on the bed. Loosen her dress and rub her down with a wet towel. I'll send for my kit," said Spence.

Spence summoned a waiter and instructed him to go to Pickle's house and have him bring the doctoring bag.

Thirty minutes later, Pickle knocked on the door of room 402.

Spence was studying the symptoms. There was high fever, protruding eyes; her tongue was red and "furred." Becky complained of pains in her neck, back, and legs. Her pulse was ninety beats per minute. She was confused and irritable.

"Something she ate, Spence?" Chamons asked.

"Hardly. She's got the fever. Yellow fever. Happens here sometimes. I heard back in '56, they had an outbreak and it scared the wits out of the whole town. Hope this is an isolated case—I especially hope it's mild."

Later, Spence gave her morphia for the head pains, and laudanum for the stomach distress.

"Spence, honey," Becky said, slurring her words, "do you still have that stone you used to wear around your neck? The one that girl gave you a long time ago?"

"Yes, Becky, it's around my neck." He reached and put it in her hand.

"Maybe it'll bring me good luck. Polly and I used to be so jealous about that stone and the pretty gold backing. To think a girl would give it to you . . ."

She drifted off to sleep. Spence gently took the stone out of her hand and handed it to Pickle, who laid it on the dresser beside the water bowl.

Later, as Pickle took the towel to the bowl to replenish the water soakings, the corner of the towel dragged the stone from the table onto the floor. It hit with a thud, the stone and the gold back flying apart.

"Damnit, Pickle, now look what you've done," Spence yelled. He left Becky's bedside and picked up the two pieces.

"Captain, I didn't mean to, believe me. I'm sorry. I can get somebody to fix it, I promise."

"So here, take it. I've got to take care of this girl. She could die right here, tonight, if we don't keep her fever down. She may die anyway."

"Oh, my God," Chamons said. He poured a glass of whisky and slumped in the chair. "Why did I even bring her down here to this mudhole. I didn't have to. She wanted to come and see the big city, and to see you, Spence . . ."

"Forget it. She's here and she's sick. Let's try to keep her cool and maybe she'll make it. If she goes into jaundice and starts the 'black vomiting,' then it's all over.

"We may all get it," Spence continued. "That would take the cake, wouldn't it?" he asked no one in particular. "Fight battles—bullets and cannonballs flying, and then end up dying with the bloody, sodden yellow fever."

There was silence, until Pickle spoke.

"Captain, have you ever had the back of this thing off before?"

"No, never."

"Then you've never seen these lines? These lines etched in the back of the rock?"

Spence leaned over and briefly looked as Pickle showed him the stone. He couldn't think of anything now, except keeping Becky alive.

THE MORNING SUN cast its rays through the open windows of room 402. More medicine was given, but the patient suffered from prostration and restlessness.

"Pickle, go to Fort Pickering and get all the alcohol you can find. Bring it here so we can swab the room. And for God's sake, don't tell anybody what's happened! There'll be wholesale panic and we can't stand that. Sneak out the back way if you have to, but hurry."

Spence had to go to his office for the morning, but he returned in the late afternoon to Becky's room. Her fever was still high, and her pulse had slowed to fifty per minute. He recognized Faget's sign. So far, there was neither mucosal bleeding from her mouth, nor bruising from her skin. Twenty-four hours later, he confirmed the attack was about over, and Becky could travel in another day or two. She was extremly lucky.

"SPENCE, MY BOY, I can't tell you how much I appreciate all you've done for us," Chamons said. They were loading the wagon.

"You're welcome, sir. After all that's what I was sent North to learn to do."

"Spence, one more thing. Your grandfather is getting on in years; he's strong enough, but he's probably made his last business trip. Write him when you can. He and Fletcher are getting along about as well as one could expect. Your daddy isn't too well either. He says his amputation hurts and he feels like he still has his leg. What do you call that?"

"Phantom limb syndrome."

"Yeah, that's it. I hope you can come up soon."

"One more thing, Mr. Chamons. Actually, two more things. You may know that I'm aware of your opium business and I'm aware there are other partners involved. Don't you think I should know who they are?"

"Oh, do you now?" Chamons said, surprised. "Son, I can only tell you that Storch is involved, but I can't tell you the other person."

"All right, that's fine. That brings up the other question, and it involves Storch and Big Pa. How is Storch doing?"

"You want to know what I think? I think he's crazy as a loon. The war took two of his boys; armies trampled his fields and made off with everything edible or not nailed down. The worse thing is the bandits knew exactly when he was to make an opium run. So they drained, or stole that is, any of his profits from the last couple of years. Financially, he's barely hanging on.

"Oh, yes. 'Course he hasn't had many runs because powder has been mighty scarce, but I would say his runs have been successful."

"Then somebody is still spying on Storch, right?" Spence asked

"Why yes. I guess that's true, now that I think about it. Storch is spent—an angry man. I just hope he doesn't try to do something to your grandfather. Well, I must go now. Stay in touch." Chamons waved and drove his double mule team out the Poplar Pike.

Spence waved. Becky waved weakly and blew a kiss at Spence.

Spence then thought of the stone. He sat on the front steps of the Gayoso, reached down into his bag and brought it out and cupped it in his hand so no passerby could see it.

Pickle was right. There were strange markings etched on it. A line went upward from the bottom left at around 100 degrees, turned down, went up again, turned down, then went up to the top of the stone, then took one last short turn down.

It looked a little like those price charts on the blackboard down at the cotton market. But how could it be? It had been in Lochsley's family for a hundred years, probably more.

In her wild imagination, Lochsley speculated it may have come from Portugal, a possible source of her ancestry. The date is a mystery. Surely, it couldn't have anything to do with the prices of American cotton. But his imagination was now piqued.

He went to his office and wrote a letter to Professor McGlothen. He carefully measured the lengths of the lines and traced the angles they made. Maybe the professor could figure it out, Spence thought.

LOCHSLEY COLLINS MOVED to Knoxville in the summer of 1865 and took a position with the Farmer's Bank as a teller.

It was on the second Tuesday in November 1865 that a man dressed in black approached her window to make a $500 deposit. He was cordial, but she was unsettled by the sinister look in his eyes. The next Tuesday he was back to deposit $200. He drew $25 in cash from his vest pocket and slid it under the bars and told Lochsley to buy herself something nice because she had been so pleasant to him. She first refused, but the man was persistent.

The bank opened at nine o'clock, Tuesday morning, November 28.

"Mr. Deberry, could I speak with you for a minute," Lochsley asked. Deberry was the chief operating officer who had hired her.

"Sir, there is a man who has been coming in here depositing sizable amounts of money. He's always dressed in black and looks mean to me."

"Lochsley, my dear, what is so unusual about that? Many men fit that description. They don't all scare you, do they? Just give him his deposit slip and carry on," Deberry said.

"Mr. Deberry, I've remembered that it was told to me during the war that a man of this person's description deals in opium and could be a murderer. I want you to know that I took a $25 bribe from him. I think it will lead to bigger things which could affect our bank."

"Now, now, my child, I'm glad you told me, but . . . good Lord, you could be discharged for doing that. Strictly against bank rules, civil rules, and—"

"Mr. Deberry, would I be telling you all this if I wanted that bribe money?"

"Well no, I don't guess you would. What do you have in mind?"

"I'm not sure yet. He'll offer me more, and I'll play along. I need your authority. Who knows, we may solve this."

"Very well. You've been a good and honest teller so far. While this is highly unusual, I'll go along. But you must give me the money for escrow. Is that acceptable?"

"It is, sir."

SPENCE GOT THE letter from Professor McGlothen. It read:

Dear Spence,

I took the liberty to take your request to a colleague of mine at Yale. The ratio of the lines, that is, if one divided the length of a line by the length of the shorter one, would be 1.618. If the smaller one is divided by the larger one, the ratio is .618. My scholar friend found the riddle easy. He said this is known as the golden ratio. He thinks those scratch marks resemble similar markings that go back two thousand years or more. He pointed out that these marks are found in the writings from the ancient Moors and Arabians, who were both excellent mathematicians. These writings indicate that emotions, seasons, empires, prices, have a surge forward and a fall backward, that results in a design like the one you have described to me. I think this finding is remarkable. Hope this is helpful. Keep in touch.

Truly,

McGlothen

Spence looked at the stone. Could this apply to the cotton markets? Do our emotions run in this cyclical fashion? He and Pickle had been going to Howard's Row at least three times per week. He had saved money in case he wanted to go active and buy a contract. First, he wanted to take his new information and watch the boards to see if the theory had validity.

It took two weeks to realize that it did—not every time because the graphs would stall in a sideways pattern and not go anywhere for days at a time. But once buyers outnumbered sellers, the prices would shoot upward, retrace about two-thirds of the initial up wave, then head upward again.

He bought his first cotton contract the Monday after Thanksgiving, requiring $45 margin money. It was a December contract, the first of the new crop year, and if held until expiration, required the buyer to accept fifty bales of cotton at the price contracted for when the contract was bought. He knew that only thread and garment companies who needed cotton actually took delivery of the bales—less than three percent of all contracts bought. His task, along with the other ninety-seven percent of the speculators, was to predict price movements accurately so they could roll over the contract for a profit before the due date of delivery.

Spence's December contract was called the nearby contract, whose price movement time was only three weeks away, had much activity, volume, or open interest. He and Pickle figured there had been two up waves so far, with its intervening correction wave, when the price dropped for three straight days.

Pickle found out about a flatboat hidden down on Wolf Creek that by itself would not have caused any concern, except he found out it was French owned and their agents were at the cotton market actually selling off contracts that caused prices to plummet. The boat was waiting there so the owners could take delivery of many bales of cotton at a very low price.

Pickle made sure the other fellow traders knew of this little scheme of the French, and they would pass along the news until, if for none other than spite, buyers would suddenly multiply, causing the price to soar, completing the final or fifth impulse wave. Afterwards, the price movement would head down, running out of energy.

Now was the time. Spence bought at forty-six cents per pound. In ten days, the price had gone to fifty-five cents. He sold for eleven cents profit, making him $550—more than his whole year's salary as a doctor. He gave Pickle $100 and took the rest to the bank.

He watched the charts for the movements that faked the ratio and made it invalid. This occupied his every waking moment.

Chapter Thirty-one

AT THANKSGIVING BLUE JOHN fixed a large turkey dinner at Aberdour. "Let's eat it quickly, while it's hot," said Harry.

"Not before we pray over it," Mary Clay said.

They held hands and prayed. Harry took the first bite.

"And thank God the blasted war is behind us, even though the Almighty is punishing us for it," Harry mumbled.

"And to thank the war for Spence's chair being empty, and my husband being an amputee, and all of us getting older . . . ," Mary Clay stated, shocked at her own bitterness.

"Now, now, Miss Mary Clay, God ain't doing that to us," said Blue John.

"The hell He isn't," Fletcher said. "It's His way of laying a curse on our foul 'recent unpleasantness' as you're so quick to call it—and I had to sneak off to Kentucky—crawl like a dog in the dark of night to help put down your treason . . . I did it," he screamed, "I paid the price with my body and my soul . . . now look at me. Gaze upon me . . ."

"Fletcher! Hush, hush. Is your leg bothering you?" Mary Clay asked, tilting her head.

"I need a drink. Blue John would you?" Fletcher asked.

CHRISTMAS AND NEW Year's came and went. Spence was lonely. He could remember the big fires in the fireplace, the hot brandy, the gifts, and the happiness during his growing-up days at Aberdour. The emptiness and blandness of holidays away from home bothered him.

He had been through so much in the war that his loneliness did not devastate him, but he did enjoy viewing the water flowing south along the Mississippi River.

"PICKLE, I CAN'T hear a thing—too many people—" Spence yelled, shoving his way through the loud crowd at the cotton exchange.

"It's awful, Captain, look over there at that specialist. Henry, Henry!"

The exchange official looked at Pickle.

"Wait on the man here," Pickle yelled, nodding at Spence.

"What's your bid?" the man yelled.

"Buy two contracts at forty-eight cents," Spence said.

"Got 'em," Henry said, turning and walking toward the board.

This was four days after New Year's and the crowd was frenzied with the March '66 contract. Spence figured he could make a few cents going up, then he would buck the crowd, sell short, and let the third downward wave make him a bundle as it went.

One week later, Spence's calculations came true, to the chagrin of the spiritless few who were left on the floor of the exchange. His bank account was nearing $50,000.

JANUARY IN MEMPHIS was cold and bleak. Trees were bare, the river foreboding, and there were two deep snows. Spence worked at his doctoring job and made money at the cotton markets; other than that, his life was dull and boring.

Spence read in the *Appeal*: "A large number of strumpets of the city, with their gallants, were arrested by police at a masked ball in the Beale Hotel." Yes, there were wild women galore and other distractions in the river city, but Spence never took the opportunity to meet any local girls.

To the rank and file citizens of Memphis, he was only another Northerner down here with the rest of the carpetbaggers, telling them how to run their lives; Spence was hardly cast in the midst of the social whirl by the city's dwellers. This irked him, but he understood.

I'll put in my year's contract, invest money made from the markets and then leave. But where?

SPENCE ARRANGED FOR Pickle to assist him at the medical department at Fort Pickering. They sat together on the riverbank taking a break.

"Cap', I tell you, there are big ears in this town, and eyes that watch closely in the night. I think it's time for us to carry a billy club, or even a pistol."

"You think that's necessary?"

"Sho' do. Especially when you carry your winnings to the bank. It's the Irish I'm afraid of. They're jealous of Negroes getting the jobs and benefits that they might get. If'n they see you and me together, it won't go over too good and we could be in for a nasty time of it, so yasuh! we ought to carry something."

The sounds of steps approaching interrupted their thoughts.

"You Spence McAlpin?" the man asked, irritated.

"I've been all over this fort looking for you. Here's your telegram."

Spence handed him a dime and thanked him for his troubles.

It read:

Your daddy gravely ill. Asks for you. Ride to Aberdour as quickly as possible. Mother. Maryville, Tennessee.

Spence knew that Chamons lost his telegraph capacity when the reconstruction people came into Tuckaleechee Cove after the war. They saw no reason for any one man to have his own telegraph, so Spence knew if the telegram was legitimate, it must come from Maryville.

But he had a suspicion that his mother didn't drive that distance to send it. Yes, his daddy was sick, but still . . .

"Pickle, I have to go, no matter what; I'm not sure I believe it, and I can't say why . . ."

"You ain't riding the length of the state, are you?"

"'Course not. I'm riding the train, taking pocket money and my carbine; I'll buy a horse in Maryville. Tell the corporal to arrange a few days of leave for me."

"That I'll do, but I have a funny feeling. Jus' be careful, hear?"

"I will, but watch those contracts we've got shorted. They know you well enough to let you cash 'em in. I'll wire you when I get there."

Spence got a driver to take him to the station and then he was gone with the night.

❖   ❖   ❖

At the kitchen table, Storch drank his whisky and looked across at Willis.

"I assume you got off that telegram to Memphis?"

"Oh, yes sir. Most likely he'll take the train and be in Maryville by noon tomorrow."

Willis smiled. No one knew he rode to Knoxville last night to tell the King of Ireland about Storch's murder plot. He even told him the exact place Storch would be waiting for Harry. Fletcher sure was a help to tell me his daddy's routine.

Yes, Willis thought, the plot curdles. Now two parties will be waiting to kill Harry. With luck, we can kill Spence, too. I can foresee the end of both the Storch and McAlpin families. Of course, Ireland will take care of this stupid German sitting across the table—maybe a bullet through that fat gut of his?

WHEN THE FARMER'S Bank opened on Wednesday, January 21, 1866, Ireland was in front of Lochsley's window. He shoved a $100 bill under the bars.

"Young lady, you have been so nice to me. Would you help me with one more item? Is it too much to ask to give me the balance in the accounts of Mr. Harry McAlpin and Mr. Heinreich Storch. It'll never get past these ears."

"Mr. Ireland, that's strictly against bank rules. That's divulging private information—"

"Now, Miss Collins, surely that large bill in your hand is enough to allow you to obtain that little bit of information."

"You're a very persuasive man. Give me a moment; maybe I can look it up. You promise not to tell where you got this?"

"To be sure. It's our little secret."

In a few minutes, Lochsley returned to the window.

"Let's see, Mr. McAlpin's total—is $62,482 and Mr. Storch's is $42,987. Seems he lost a lot during the war."

"That's sufficient, young lady," Ireland said. He wrote the totals on a piece of paper. "You wouldn't happen to have access to the widow Maud Perkin's account, would you?"

Lochsley was back shortly.

"Miss Perkins' total is $264,076. Anything else?"

"No, my dear. Actually, I have a little trip to make. You've been a great help. See you next week."

Ireland was hardly out of the bank before Lochsley went to the office in the rear of the bank.

"Mr. Deberry. Now, I need your horse. I'll tell you every-thing later."

"I hope you know what you're doing, young lady."

"I hope I do too."

She took her rifle from under the counter and headed for the door. As she mounted Deberry's horse, she thought of the possible folly on which she was embarking. It might appear strange for a lady with a rifle to be riding through town, not unheard of, but it might turn some heads. Then she saw Ireland join two other armed men on horseback. Her suspicions were confirmed, so she slowly followed the trio. She was careful to linger at a safe distance behind.

The men reached Maryville before noon and headed east toward the Smoky Mountains. By 1:30 P.M. they were going through the cut in the Chillhowie Mountains. By 2:00 P.M. they entered the cove.

"Mr. Ireland, what time did you say McAlpin goes to the well?" one of the men asked.

"Well, his son said his daddy always drew well water at 3:30 P.M., no matter what the weather.

"My man, Willis, promised to have Storch hiding near by. If that McAlpin grandson falls for the telegram, then he'll ride up about the same time. We could have a three-way killing. You boys get the job done and you'll be paid handsomely."

❖   ❖   ❖

SPENCE GOT OFF the eastbound train. He rented a horse at the livery stable and rode toward Tuckaleechee. His stomach churned. He expected the unexpected. His carbine was strapped around his shoulder.

He felt something was going to happen at Aberdour and it wasn't good. The time was just after 3:00 P.M. When he rode through the cut in the mountains, he couldn't see the man hidden behind rocks, nor could he see him flick a mirror signal to Ireland's other man a mile away.

STORCH, MOODY, AND Willis rode through the thicket and climbed by foot to the woods behind Aberdour's big house. They loaded their rifles and hid behind large oak trees.

Lochsley was about a mile ahead of Spence. She could see the men across several pastures. They disappeared into the woods.

When Lochsley reached Aberdour, she went past the barn and hid behind a watering trough. As she crouched, a door slammed and she heard Harry's loud voice sing an old hymn, "Bless Be the Tie That Binds."

She saw movement at the edge of the woods. Ireland's two men walked their horses toward the well.

"Good evening, kind sir," the older man said to Harry.

"Evening," Harry said, startled. He watched the men dismount. They smelled as if they hadn't bathed in months. They wore hats with drooping brims, dirty heavy coats, and scuffed boots. "On your way into the mountains? What can I do for you?"

"We'd be mighty obliged if we could have a drink of water from your well, sir."

"Why, you're welcome to it. I'll let this bucket down and draw up some for you. If you want, you can take the horses down to the barn and they can drink their fill."

"Thanks, very much . . . ," the man said as he glanced at the other man.

As Harry turned the crank, both men reached into their coats. The afternoon sun reflected off the steel of knives—daggers flying from out of nowhere. One cut into Harry's chest; the other pierced his back. He fell instantly. The bucket clanged as it fell back down into the well. Two pools of blood began to grow in the cold dust beside Harry's body.

Seeing this from his hiding place, Storch was dumbfounded. "Somebody beat me to McAlpin," he screamed in German and sprang from behind the tree wildly firing his pistol at the strangers.

One ball killed the younger man instantly. The other man jumped for cover behind the well.

Storch ran toward the well, his shots bounced off the bricks. He didn't see the man in black take aim. Storch felt the sudden fiery mass in his stomach for an instant before he died. He had no way of knowing he fell on top of Harry.

Lochsley had moved to the corner of the henhouse where she could see the action. She raised her rifle, took aim, and fired at Ireland. She saw him grab his shoulder, heard him scream, and watched him desperately cling to his saddle.

Hurt and confused, Ireland couldn't locate the source of the bullet that got him.

Lochsley fired again, knocking Ireland's hat off. He rode at top speed down the hill to escape further harm, cursing loudly.

Spence heard the shots and rode madly toward Aberdour. Ireland approached him on the road and fired twice. Spence jumped from the horse and into a ditch.

Ireland cut his losses and fled toward the west.

The other hired gunman ran from the cover of the well to his horse, mounted and took the same route as did Ireland.

Lochsley turned and ran down the hill through the orchard. She saw Spence and yelled, "Get that man, Spence, he killed . . ."

The man rode around the fence and onto the river road.

Spence's aim was sure. The man fell dead on the ground as a sack of flour would fall—with a soft thud and lifeless.

Spence rode toward Lochsley, jumped off his horse—they hugged.

"What on earth are you doing here?"

"No time for that now, we have more to flush out. Follow me up the hill. Stay low."

Spence saw Harry lying on the ground. Blue John was bent over him crying. Spence dropped to his knees beside Harry.

"Big Pa . . . try . . . try . . ."

"I'm gone, Spence . . . go to your cave . . ." Harry coughed up blood. ". . .the box . . . sand . . . moss."

Harry was dead. Spence bowed his head.

Moody Storch knelt beside his papa, sobbing, making no attempt to fire at anybody.

Nobody but Lochsley saw the movement in the woods.

She yelled, "He's part of them, Spence, don't let him get away."

Spence unloaded his carbine into Willis' back. The man fell hard into the brown winter leaves.

Spence looked at Blue John and Harry, then over at Moody.

"Moody, I want to see you and your mother within twenty-four hours. I'll be at your house in the morning. Blue John and I will help dig the graves, if no one else will."

"You . . . would do that for us?" Moody asked.

"Yes! But now, we need to strap these two over their horses, so you can take 'em home. I'll take my dear grandfather to his resting place."

"Spence," Lochsley said, "I think I can reach Reverend Mayhew in Knoxville to preach the funeral. I must get back over there tonight."

"Did the man in black see you?"

"No, but he's the reason I must be at the bank tomorrow as if nothing had happened. You don't know it, but I'm working at the Farmer's Bank. I'll fill you in on the details later.

Plan to have the burial in mid-afternoon. I'll bring Mayhew and we can talk then. But I'm afraid Ireland will pay a visit to the bank in the morning and—"

"You've been seeing him at your bank?"

"Yes, always in the morning and insists on seeing me. I must go." She ran down the hill toward her horse.

"Lochsley. Thank you," Spence yelled.

"Actually, I didn't do anything," Lochsley said. "Didn't keep anybody from dying. I'm sorry as I can be, Spence."

"Saved my life," he yelled back.

Spence looked to the log house where he grew up. His mother was on the porch hugging a post. Spence walked to her and kissed her.

"Don't go up there, Mama. It's not pretty. Blue John and I will take care of what we can tonight. I'll get Chamons to help.

"Is Daddy inside?"

Mary Clay didn't answer. She looked old, beyond her years.

Spence walked in the house. His daddy sat staring at a fire in the grate, drinking.

"Big Pa is dead, isn't he?" Fletcher said without turning his head to view a son he hadn't seen in five years.

"Yes, along with Storch, and a couple of hired thugs from Knoxville, and that Willis person, Storch's foreman."

"I felt it coming. Like a nightmare."

"Yeah, Daddy, it was part of a dark scheme, a conspiracy. Haven't figured it all out yet. You stay right here. Blue John and I have work to do."

When he turned to leave, he thought he heard his daddy say something, but his words were slurred and incoherent.

❖   ❖   ❖

News of the deaths traveled fast in the cove. Someone rang the church bell at Big Pistol. Everyone living within earshot of the bells knew someone had died. The bell rang sixty-eight times indicating the age of the deceased.

In Cades Cove, Mr. Cable had already begun to make a walnut casket. The wake began at the big house. Blue John dressed Harry in a suit and put him in bed in the downstairs guestroom. Neighbors brought food and mingled, as always, during a wake.

Aberdour was cleared of visitors before midnight. Blue John sat with his departed friend until 3:00 A.M., then he trudged to bed. He whispered to himself as he got under the covers, "Lord, take Mr. Harry under Your loving wings and sweep him into Your eternal rest and peace. Good night."

BY EARLY AFTERNOON the next day, Reverend Mayhew, Polly, and Lochsley rode into Big Pistol in a wagon. Mayhew, firm and stiff as ever, preached a remarkably short sermon.

Mayhew had mellowed in the years since Spence saw him last in the cave. Polly was still pretty and had kept her figure, and he could tell she had molded well into a preacher's wife.

The casket was closed and loaded into a wagon and driven to Aberdour. The pallbearers began the arduous trek up the hill behind the big house to the family cemetery. Men neighbors had dug the grave.

Mayhew said a few words, and the casket was let down. Spence picked up a handful of fresh dirt and threw it onto the top of the casket. He straightened and looked over the bleak, February landscape.

The crowd drifted down the hill. Maud Perkins and Professor McGlothen came over to him to pay their condolences.

"Mrs. Perkins, I would like you to stay at the house while Mayhew and I go to Storch's to give him a proper Christian burial. I've paid Mayhew to deliver it and we won't be long."

"Why, Spence, I guess we could." She looked at McGlothen.

"Sure, Maud, why not?" the professor whispered. "Any comfort we can give will be our pleasure."

Yes, Spence thought, it will also be my pleasure. Stay here and enjoy the drinks and the dainties. I would like to have a moment with you alone, later.

Maude and the professor went into the dining room, had a cup of coffee and some finger food.

Spence went outside to be with his mother to greet and thank the neighbors for all their help and support.

Fletcher limped down to the log house to sit by the fire and drink. He wasn't strong, and the cold air wasn't helping him; the stump of his leg hurt. He knew the diabetes was taking its toll. The thought that he had told Willis about his father and the well water episode neither bothered him nor made him glad. He took a gulp of laudanum from the bottle.

Fletcher poured his drink and he pictured his father lying up on that hillside in the cold ground beside his mother, Kate. He didn't know how much longer before he would be up there, too. He added more bourbon to his glass.

Chapter Thirty-two

SPENCE ENTERED THE BIG house to meet with Widow Perkins and the professor. Spence knew they were tired from the emotions of the day.

"The hour is late and we've all had a long day, so I'll get to the point," Spence said. "Mrs. Perkins, I've known for some time of the opium operation. I haven't known all the owners. Chamons admitted to me about Storch, Big Pa, and him, but he wouldn't tell me the silent partner. Now, I know it is you."

Widow Perkins glanced at McGlothen.

"Never mind, Mrs. Perkins. You haven't done anything wrong in my way of thinking. You've been a good citizen, a fine teacher, and supported me and cared about my welfare. But before Big Pa died, he directed me to a box hidden in a cave. It contained his stock certificates, shareholder's names, and the original contract drawn up by Mr. Forbes. I know you will be applying for the life insurance, so there's nothing more to hide."

"Spence," Maud said, her voice uneven, "yes, that is all true, but I'm only complying with the terms of the contract. Mr.

Forbes doesn't care about any more money. He retired the bonds and the debt obligation long ago. Truth is, I don't need more money, but the insurance needs to be filed for someone, agreed?"

"Oh yes, by all means."

"Well, this did take me by surprise." She looked again over at McGlothen. "Now that we are talking openly and now that my dear Professor McGlothen knows our business, what are we going to do about it?" Maude asked.

Spence said, "Now, let me assure you that you will be all right. But I'm buying out the contract. I'm returning home to Aberdour!"

Maude and Clint sat back in their chairs, speechless. McGlothen arose and poured two brandies.

"I know where I legally stand, now that the principles of the business have changed. I want to reorganize the operation, even disband it if advisable. Much depends on what Britain's Parliament and our Congress do. I believe we need drug laws to protect people. We need to distribute opium for medical use in a different way than your contract did. Opium is a good painkiller, but too much of it destroys lives. We doctors need to educate the public. I want to educate the Congress about the need to set up medicine houses for our doctors to get the medicine," declared Spence.

"Mrs. Perkins, you must quickly file for the insurance claims in your name for the time being, then follow my plan closely. All this destruction in our families was caused by a predator who is in Knoxville and I think I know how to rouse him out."

❖ ❖ ❖

THE NEXT MORNING Mayhew took Polly and Lochsley to Knoxville. Lochsley barely made it to work on time, but with a splash of water to her face, and a cup of coffee, she was fresh enough to greet customers at the bank.

True to Lochsley's expectations, the King of Ireland came into the bank wanting to withdraw $100. He looked tired, drained, and approached the window slowly.

"Good morning, Mr. Ireland," Lochsley said. I expected you in yesterday morning. Hope you had a good trip. You look tired. Are you all right?"

"Why yes, young lady. Had a good trip; actually my horse stepped in a hole and I was thrown. Think my shoulder is sprained. I'm going to the doctor later on. Have you done anything exciting?"

"Oh no, sir," she answered. "I stayed at home last night. Had to catch up on my sleep. I'll see you next time."

Ireland turned and stepped aside to let the next customer get to the window.

SPENCE CAUGHT THE next train back to Memphis. He learned that one of the contracts lost a little, but the other two were winning big. Spence cashed in the winners. He held the loser two weeks, watched it turn around and make a nice profit. He was now aware of the folly of greed and invincibility, so he went about his investing more carefully than ever.

Spence knew his army contract was up at the end of the month. His fortune had expanded to over $400,000 that he split among three banks.

Then the fateful telegram came—the one he had been waiting for.

"Music lessons doing well—sheet music has arrived. Maud."

That evening, Spence went to the telegraph office and sent his wire.

"Make arrangements to disperse sheet music and have other students watch concert. Spence McAlpin."

When Maud received the telegram the next day, she summoned McGlothen. They rode to Aberdour to see Blue John.

They returned to Maryville and waited. Two days later, Blue John arrived with his new friend, Jeremiah Stewart; they boarded at McGlothen's house.

Widow Perkins wired the Farmer's bank in Knoxville.

"Miss Lochsley Collins: Will be making withdrawal day after tomorrow at the instant at your bank. Hope you and friends are well and in place. Maud Perkins."

The next day, the King of Ireland came to the bank.

"Good morning, Miss Lochsley, I would like to make a small deposit."

He gave her $200 and then shoved $100 to one side indicating it was Lochsley's to keep.

"Do you have any news for me this fine day?" he asked.

"You promise you won't tell," Lochsley whispered.

"On my word of honor," Ireland said.

"You know the other day?—when you asked about Widow Perkins from Maryville? Well, the strangest thing has happened."

"Yes, yes, go on, young lady. What has happened?" Ireland drummed his fingers on the counter.

"She sent a telegram here saying she was to make a large withdrawal. To my way of thinking, some big money is to come into the bank."

Be careful, Lochsley. Draw him in as a black widow spider would, she thought.

"You don't say?" Ireland looked around to see if anyone was in line behind him. There wasn't. "Of course, Miss Lochsley, it's no business of mine. But did she say when she was coming for it?"

"The telegram said late tomorrow morning. I can't wait to see how much it will be. But you, Mr. Ireland, must not utter a word of it. Bank business, you know."

"Oh, my dear. Bank business. Nothing will come from my lips."

"Good day, Mr. Ireland." She smiled.

Widow Perkins parked her wagon the next day in the alley behind the bank and walked in to Lochsley's window.

After greeting her customer, Lochsley counted $300,000 and placed it into a brown envelope.

Maud thanked her and walked out to her wagon. As she climbed up into her seat, Ireland came out of nowhere with a pistol and a kerchief over his face.

"G'day, ma'am. I'll take the envelope from you and nobody will get hurt. Quickly now!"

"Why, I can't believe my eyes. You can't rob me in broad daylight!" she protested as she slowly handed him the money.

"That's right, lady. Do as I say and the only thing you will lose are your assets."

Blue John, Jeremiah, and the Federal marshal jumped from their hiding spot behind bushes.

Ireland made an attempt to run, but Jeremiah fired three rounds into the dirt near Ireland's feet.

"Drop the envelope and your pistol and turn around," Blue John shouted.

Ireland did as he was told. The marshal walked to the man and yanked the kerchief from his face.

"Mr. Ireland, I believe our jail has a nice, cozy cell for you while you await your trial for armed robbery, and I believe, murder."

Ireland was escorted by gunpoint to the jail.

That evening the telegram reached Memphis. "Spence. Concert played to standing ovation. Critics will evaluate May 3, 1866. Maud Perkins."

❖   ❖   ❖

SPENCE LEFT MEMPHIS on the train with his money hidden in soft valises. He kept his hand on his pistol for the whole trip. The trip was tiring, but uneventful. He arrived in Knoxville and went straight to Lochsley's window at the Farmer's Bank to deposit his money. Their eyes met with excitement.

On May 3, 1866, with undeniable evidence presented against him, Ireland confessed to the murder of Heinreich Storch. The final piece of the puzzle was revealed during cross-examination. The title, King of Ireland, was only the figment of a warped imagination. Walter O'Conroy was his real name and he was a sailor by trade. In the barroom brawl in 1844 between Storch and Harry, it was O'Conroy's brother who was stabbed in the heart.

From that day on, O'Conroy had vowed to track down the German and Scot, and avenge his brother's death. He nearly succeeded. The trial was straightforward with little defense. The sentence was death by hanging at noon two days hence.

As Spence and Lochsley walked out of the courtroom, they were silent. It was hot, so they walked to a grassy spot overlooking the Tennessee River for the cool breeze.

"Spence, I hate trials. I was nervous the whole time," Lochsley said.

Spence chucked a pebble into the river.

"What are you thinking, Spence?" Lochsley asked.

"Will you marry me?" Spence asked, in a monotone.

The cool wind ruffled their hair, blowing in from the river.

Lochsley put her hands around his arm and looked into his eyes.

"Lochsley? Will you?" Spence repeated.

"I'd love to," she whispered. They kissed there in broad daylight. Neither cared who saw them.

HARPER'S ARRIVED AT Aberdour. The front page told of the "Tragic Race Riots in Memphis."

Spence read that a group of Negroes tried to prevent six Irish policemen from arresting two of their comrades. From there, the "rest of the force, the firemen, the politicians, and the rabble, all rushed to the scene . . . and over the next three days the mob blazed away at Negroes and burned buildings indiscriminately." The toll was forty-six dead—of whom only two were white—seventy-five wounded, five Negroes raped, ten 'maltreated,' and 100 robbed. The mob burned ninety-one Negro homes, four churches, and twelve schools, an estimated $130,000 in property damage.

Pickle mailed Spence a clipping from the *Memphis Appeal.*

The local newspapers deplored the rioting and took great pains to point out that none—or almost none—of the 2,000 paroled Confederates had any part of the action.

But this had little impact, as far as *Harper's* and most of the remainder of the national press were concerned. The media pictured the rioting as brutal retaliation upon the Negroes by former Rebels.

Spence lay down the paper and thought about how correct Pickle had been and how lucky he was to have gotten home safely.

Rocking on the front porch, he thought of how he had bought Storch's estate and sent Mrs. Storch and Moody to Argentina on a steamer. They were eager for a new start in a new place.

Chamons and Maud Perkins agreed to help Spence form the new business. They would now set up reputable drug concerns, using Bouguereau in Memphis, and Thick Neck in Cincinnati, as procurement agents for the selling of medicines.

Ironically, their most fervent new customer was the Eli Lilly Drug Company in Indianapolis, Indiana. Captain Eli Lilly commanded the artillery position that prevented Spence's Confederates from overrunning Federal headquarters at Mossy Creek during the war.

Spence and Lochsley planned to move into the big house after the wedding. Spence spent three days riding from house to house in Cades and Tuckaleechee Coves, informing people that he would deliver their babies and take care of their ills for no fee until another doctor could be brought into the community. This appeased even the staunchest Union sympathizers who might otherwise have tried to hang him.

Spence walked down to the log house to check on his daddy. They had made peace with each other. Due to his son's generosity, Fletcher's bank account was substantial. No longer would his parents need to feel that they had been denied the fruits of Aberdour. There were crops to be planted, and livestock to be fed, so life was to go on.

Spence also made a large donation to Maryville College for the purchase of sixty-five acres of land on which to build a new campus.

As he walked, he smelled the crisp, cool mountain air and thought about the prophecy. God's ways are higher than man's ways. He was thankful to those who had lived, toiled, and gone before him. He was grateful for his heritage of the mountains and his family.

❖   ❖   ❖

MARY CLAY FOUND Fletcher in front of the cold fireplace when she came down to fix breakfast. He was slumped in the rocking chair. The bourbon bottle lay by his feet. She put her hands to her head and yelled, "Spence!"

The church bells in the cove rang at noon. By mid-afternoon, six men carried the casket up the side of Rich Mountain to the family burial grounds. The procession stopped as the casket was placed in front of the grave site. A verse of "Amazing Grace" was sung, lead by Reverend Mayhew.

"Dearly beloved . . . we gather here to pay tribute to the recently departed . . . as for man, his days are as grass; the grass withereth, and the flower fadeth, for the wind passeth over it, and it is gone. All are of the dust, and all turn to dust again . . ."

The pallbearers lowered Fletcher's coffin in the ground. Mary Clay watched Spencer throw in the first shovel full of dirt. A light rain softly splattered the fresh soil.

The crowd sang one verse of "Lily of the Valley," turned, and quietly walked down the mountain.

THE BIG PISTOL church was overflowing. The area outside was crammed with parked buggies and wagons. It was June 10, 1866.

In front of the preacher stood: Becky Chamons and Jeremiah Stewart; Professor Clint McGlothen and Maud Perkins; Spence McAlpin and Lochsley Collins, and Blue John Nelson.

The summer sun shone through the window making Spence close one eye. He remembered that same sun shining that same way during the hundreds of Sundays of his growing-up days. He studied Mary Clay playing the organ. Some things never change. He turned his head and found Polly in the congregation as cute as she was that first Sunday long ago. Mrs. Polly Mayhew winked at him.

The most Reverend Finas Mayhew conducted the litany of holy matrimony and discussed marriage as an institution. He proudly announced that this was the first triple ceremony ever in Blount County.

"And now, my flock, Blue John Nelson, best man for the three grooms, asked me to announce him as a 'former sugar cane hacker' from Antigua, Mr. Nelson, do you have the rings?"

Vows were exchanged and rings were placed. "I now pronounce these three couples husband and wife. Men, you may kiss your bride."

Spence and Lochsley walked down the steps outside the church to meet with their guests. Lochsley giggled and asked softly, "Spence, does this mean I'll get back the stone?"

Glossary

Andrew Jackson—U.S. soldier and statesman from Tennessee. Seventh president of the United States.

Andrew Johnson—former U.S. senator and governor of Tennessee. Spokesman for the eastern Tennessee mountaineers and small farmers. Staunch Unionist. Abraham Lincoln's vice-president. Became seventeenth president of the United States.

Carthage—famous city-state of antiquity founded on north coast of Africa by the Phoenicians of Tyre in 814 B.C. Ruled the Iberian area (future Spain and Portugal) before giving way to Rome.

Catties—Malay-Chinese weight equal to 1.3 pounds. One-hundredth of a picul.

Cumshaw—the tip given to smugglers.

Demurrage—the Chinese emperor's charge when a ship exceeds the allotted free time to be unloaded.

Dinner—Southern term for the midday meal; lunch.

Dry as a chip—as dry as thin, flat pieces of wood.

Draw, up a draw—a natural drainage way, more shallow and open than a gorge or ravine.

Doric columns—from ancient Greek architecture; boldness, strength. Fluted columns with no base.

Forward contact—an old term for a futures contract, which occurs when a processor of a product, or commodity, agrees to sell a quantity of the commodity at a specified price for future delivery. Risk speculation.

Golden section, golden mean—the division of a length such that the smaller part is to the greater as the greater is to the whole. Example, height of the human body divided at the navel—the navel to floor height divided into the total height will be .618—the same as the navel to the head divided into the navel to the feet. Discovered by the Greeks, the principle was applied to buildings, art, and even to prices and the rise and fall of cultures.

Laudanum—an alcohol tincture of opium.

Moors—Muslims of mixed Arab, Berber, and Spanish origins, who ruled much of Spain before being gradually pushed out between the eleventh and seventeenth centuries.

Main—the cockfight arena.

Nubian—ancient region from the Nile Valley in Egypt, east to the Red Sea and west to the Libyan desert.

Picul—Chinese weight equal to 133.3 pounds.

Pillars of Hercules—seven hills on the north coast of Morocco, Africa, which face across the Straits of Gibraltar into Spain. Where the Mediterranean Sea meets the Atlantic Ocean.

Punic Wars—Virgil's Aeneid tells of Princess Dido of Tyre who fled from her brother Pygmalion, king of Tyre. Dido founded Phoenician culture along the North Africa coast. The inhabitants of these outposts and Carthage itself were known to the Romans as Phoenikes (Phoenicians), whence the adjective Punic is derived. Thus, the struggles by Rome to rule over Carthage.

Phoenicians—an ancient land corresponding to modern Lebanon, parts of Syria, and Israel. Listed in the Old Testament and poems of Homer as Tyrians, or Sidonians. Phoenicians were merchants, architects, textile workers, and they excelled at navigation and seafaring. Their culture extended along the African coast and later into Portugal.

Portugee—term used by the Melungeons in the mountains of East Tennessee to describe their source of ancestry. Portugal had been an independent country since the twelfth century. Portuguese people easily could have descended from the peoples of Carthage and earlier Phoenicians. Much traffic and trade existed between Carthage and the Portugal/Spain area.

Secesh—short slang form of secessionist; rebel, confederate.

Tuckaleechee—one of many coves in the Great Smoky Mountains of East Tennessee. Old Indian word.